From HELL to Breakfast

BLUE FEATHER BOOKS, LTD.

For Mable Johnson Watkins,
Who's not to blame for a word of this.

From HELL to Breakfast

A BLUE FEATHER BOOK

by
Joan Opyr

This is a work of fiction. All characters, locales and events are either products of the author's imagination or are used fictitiously.

FROM HELL TO BREAKFAST

Cover design by Mari SanGiovanni
Cover layout by Ann Phillips
Cover painting by Patricia Koch

A Blue Feather Book
Published by Blue Feather Books, Ltd.

www.bluefeatherbooks.com

ISBN: 978-0-9794120-7-3

First edition: January, 2009

Printed in the United States of America and in the United Kingdom.

Acknowledgements

This was an easy book to write and a difficult book to edit. I like to think that made it a better book, but that's for the reader to decide. I'll just stick my fingers in my ears and sing la, la, la, la. You may think this juvenile, but I'm in good company. Leonard Woolf used to go through the newspapers and clip out bad reviews so that his wife, Virginia, wouldn't see them. Good old Leonard. Not every writer is destined to take a long walk off a short pier, but no one likes a rotten tomato.

But of course a bad review is not the same as an honest critique, and I owe a great deal to the many readers, editors, and advisors who read draft after draft of this book and offered sincere encouragement and honest assessment. So many people read the book in its various incarnations that I scarcely know where to begin and, as always, I am afraid that I'll inadvertently, carelessly, or just plain absentmindedly leave someone out. If your name should be here and it isn't, I apologize. You're memorable, really you are; I'm just damned if I can remember. Here is my best effort:

Thank you to Therese Harris for a complete and thorough edit of the first draft. You restored my faith and my confidence, and my debt to you is immense. Thank you to Saundra Lund, Lynne Pierce, Peg Mercer, and Debi Robinson-Smith—great friends and critical readers. My sincere gratitude to TM Stoker for reading multiple drafts of the novel, long past what must have been the point of "For God's sake, not again," and for offering fresh insights and encouragement each and every time.

Thanks to Fran Fuller at the Seattle Mystery Bookshop and my undying love to her for insisting that she can sell as many copies as my publisher can print. And speaking of publishers, no one has been more patient, more professional, more enthusiastic, or more completely on board with this project than Emily Reed and Caitlin d'Aguiar of Blue Feather Books. What a pleasure it has been to work with these women and this company.

My love and thanks to Mari SanGiovanni for designing a beautiful cover and to Patricia Koch for allowing me to use her wonderful painting of the Palouse, the same painting that also graced the cover of my first book, *Idaho Code*.

My love and gratitude to my family, Polly Opyr, Micheal and Johnny Pender, Kathleen Pender, and Nicole Opyr and Christopher Hutton. I'd also like to thank my kids, Sofie and Harry, the best kids in the world. I'd like to thank them for all the peace and quiet while Mummy was writing and editing, but my kids are very smart. They know a snow job when they see one.

Finally, I would never have finished this book without my dear friend and ass-kicking editor, Andi Marquette, and my wonderful wife and ass-kicking provocateur, Melynda Huskey. Andi, I love you in a totally platonic and non-creepy way. Melynda, I love you and it's not platonic. We'll talk about creepy later.

"If it's worth doing well, it's worth half-assing, especially in the corners."
—Debi Robinson-Smith

Chapter 1

Just say no.

I should never have succumbed to the temptation to numb the pain of Sam's death by smoking his stash. I should have burned it or flushed it or tossed it away. I should never have held onto it. I should never have hidden it beneath the ceramic planter that holds the enormous rubber tree in our living room.

I won't lie. Smoking pot is fun. A couple of puffs leave you loose and mellow and happy with the world. Bill "I didn't inhale" Clinton knows this. Nancy Reagan knows this. Everyone knows this, but no politician has the guts to admit it because Grandma and Grandpa Voter don't approve. Pot is déclassé, unlike martinis, wine, and Valium. Also unlike alcohol, pot doesn't bring you down, give you cirrhosis of the liver, or make you mean, and there's every reason to believe that smoking marijuana has real, measurable medical benefits. I know it helped my brother Sam with his appetite, his nausea, and most important of all, his mood. He was better for having toked up, and that's God's honest truth.

But smoking pot will make you stupid. It will make you incredibly dumb. I know I should not have given in and smoked his stash. But I did. And that's how I ended up with the world's dumbest tattoo and a very unhappy girlfriend.

Sylvie and her mother have dinner together at least once a week. I'm always invited to come along, and sometimes I go. Other times, I leave them to it. Sylvie's an only child, and she and Kate are very close. They need their together space. Me? I'm one of five kids from a loud, boisterous family. I appreciate an evening alone with a good book and some Dinah Washington on the stereo.

My mistake was in believing that there's no such thing as too much of a good thing. As soon as Sylvie left, I opened up the windows, retrieved Sam's stash from its hiding place, and popped Dinah into the compact disc player. She sang, "Cry Me a River," "I Don't Hurt Anymore," and "Since I Fell for You." By the time I got to "Willow Weep for Me," I was wreathed in sickly sweet smoke, crying, and singing along. I wanted my brother to be alive. I wanted my girlfriend to be at home. A few songs—a few puffs—later, and I was finally tired of wallowing in self-pity. My throat was sore and I wanted... what did I want? I thought about it for a moment. I wanted a bag of potato chips and a liter of Pepsi. I wanted a lot of something made out of marshmallow, chocolate, and sugar. I switched off the stereo, tucked my wallet into my back pocket, and made my unsteady way to the Jones Street Market.

I had junk food on the brain. Twinkies, pink coconut Snowballs, chocolate Swiss rolls and Moon Pies. I was still miserable, and I was still lonely. Most of all, though, I was hungry. I had no intention whatsoever of stopping at Cow City Tattoo. I didn't mean to look at the art on offer, to go inside and ask a few questions about pain and prices, and no one could have been more surprised than I was to find myself lying face down on a table while a man with a dragon on one arm and a tiger on the other buzzed these magic words onto the small of my back:

Property of Sylvie Wood. If found, please return to 521 South Main Street, Cowslip, Idaho.

Nothing itches like a fresh tattoo. The artist covered mine in antibiotic ointment and placed a sheet of cling film over it. I'd spent all of my potato chip money and then some. I thanked him for his work and headed back home, stomach growling. Sylvie was still out—a good thing, as the apartment reeked of pot smoke. I set up a box fan in the living room window facing out and turned it on high. I also went a bit wild with the air freshener. By the time I was done, the place smelled like Woodstock if it had been held in my grandmother's bathroom. It was the best I could do. Because of the itching, I took my T-shirt off. I turned the stereo back on, flopped face down on the sofa, and let Dinah sing me to sleep.

* * *

It was close to midnight when Sylvie came home. Every light in the apartment was on, Dinah was still singing, and I was still groggy.

"Hello, baby," I mumbled, not bothering to look up. "Did you have a nice dinner?"

"Yes," she said. "We went to that new Italian place, Buca di Maggiano. Did you get something to eat?"

"No."

"Bil, you can't go on like this. No food, no sleep. You have to—"

She stopped just in front of the sofa. I stared at her golden brown legs, so shapely beneath her linen shorts. In ten seconds flat, I was stone cold sober. I imagined spending the rest of my life never again smoothing those thighs beneath my hands. I imagined moving back in with my parents. I tried to guess what laser tattoo removal might cost. Sylvie reached out and lifted the plastic wrap. It was only a moment or two before she put it back.

"Sylvie," I began. "I don't know what came over me. I'm, uh, sorry?"

It was some time before she spoke. She just stood there, hands resting lightly on her hips while I stared forlornly at her knees.

When at last she spoke, she said, "What I want to know is what you're going to do if we move."

* * *

"I want you to see a grief counselor," Sylvie said.

I politely chewed my sugar-frosted cornflakes and swallowed before answering. "It's only been two weeks since Sam's funeral."

"I know that. I still think you should go."

"This is about the tattoo, isn't it?"

"Yes."

I'd expected her to deny it, and I had an answer all ready: I was sorry I'd smoked the pot and I wouldn't do it again. Now I was obliged to think through my hangover and come up with another excuse. I took a big bite of cereal and then spoke with my mouth full. "I hate counselors."

"Bil," Sylvie said reasonably, "you're studying to be a counselor."

"I know," I snapped, "and that's why I don't want one. I know what's the matter with me. My brother is dead. I can't bring him back. Without pain, Sylvie, there is no living, or at least no living fully. I'm sure it would be easier if I were able to shut down emotionally or put this in a box, but I don't have an off switch. You know that. I just have to work through this as best I can."

She recoiled slightly, but after two years together, she was getting as used to my bluff as I was to her quiet calm—a quiet calm that masked an iron will.

"As best you can," she mused. "With the aid of marijuana and a tattoo artist? What next? Hash and a piercing?" Before I could plunge the spoon into my cereal again, Sylvie reached across the table and stopped my hand. "Sweetie, I don't want to come home and find you higher than a kite and covered in chain mail."

"I hadn't thought of that." I tried to picture what all I might have pierced. My nose? My eyebrows? My navel? Sylvie would probably cope, but it was hard to imagine what my mother would do. Have a fit and fall in it? It might be worth the pain of the piercing just for that.

"Bil," Sylvie said, taking my hand and forcing me to look her in the eye. "I love you. Nothing will ever change that. If you want to cover yourself with cubist paintings or get a pair of nipple rings, that's your business. But I don't want you doing things that you'll come to regret, and you can't smoke away your grief. What are you going to do when Sam's stash runs out? Call his old dealer and buy more?"

I thought about Sam's dealer, Jake the Snake. If he'd ever bathed, it was beyond living memory. He lived in a shack in the middle of nowhere, a weird recluse with a high fluting voice and an ethereal giggle. No, once Sam's stash was gone, it was gone.

I closed my eyes and shook my head. "I am all pot-smoked out," I said. "The tattoo has cured me. It itches like hell, you know."

"I don't know," she said. "Maybe I'll get one myself and find out."

My eyes snapped open.

"Don't look at me like that," Sylvie said. "I was just checking to see if you were paying attention. You really need to talk to someone—a professional someone—about how horrible and sad you feel. I don't want to push you, Bil, but…"

"You're pushing me."

"Yes," she agreed. "I am."

"You have a plan," I said flatly.

Of course my girlfriend had a plan. I knew this with complete certainty, the way I knew that night followed day, that I'd never win the lottery, and that, when it came right down to the wire, the Seattle Mariners would find some way to fuck it up in the playoffs. Sylvie planned. She executed. She got things done.

"You have an appointment," Sylvie said. "Tomorrow at two. Her name is Sally Hernandez, and she's in practice with my therapist."

"And she's gay-friendly?"

To her credit, Sylvie did not roll her eyes or dismiss me as a moron. "Of course," she said. "Sally's a lesbian. Her partner is an artist—the one who sells those Venus of Willendorf pots at the farmer's market. Bil, I'm only asking that you go once and give her an honest chance. I think you'll like her, and I think it will help."

"Only once?"

"Only once."

"And if it doesn't help and I hate her guts?"

"Then I might ask you to try someone else," Sylvie admitted. "And I'll tell you some*thing* else—if I find your brother's stash, it's history."

We finished our breakfast in silence. It wasn't until we were in the living room sipping coffee that we spoke again.

"I really am sorry about the tattoo," I said.

Sylvie laughed. "I'll bet you are. Did it hurt much?"

"I have no idea."

She shook her head. "I don't know what I'm going to do with you. But I'll let you in on a secret. I'm not sorry about the tattoo. In fact, I think I'm flattered. It's not my name in a big red heart, but it is kind of sweet."

"Is it?"

She put her coffee cup down and moved along the sofa until we were side by side. She put her arm around me and held me close.

"Yes," she said. "I think you must want to be stuck with me. What other woman will want you now that you have my name written on your ass?"

"The small of my back," I corrected.

"That's what you think." She reached behind me, pushing me forward with one hand, and tugging at the waistband of my boxer shorts with the other. "The 'y' on the word 'property' drops all the way down."

Chapter 2

I hated the grief counselor on sight. She had short gray hair and a tanned, healthy, pleasantly wrinkled face, the kind you get by spending your life outdoors skiing, rafting, bicycling, and being an all-around sports dyke. I would have known she was a lesbian even if Sylvie hadn't told me. The pink triangle earrings, the peasant skirt, the Birkenstock sandals—she was a lesbian of the Meg Christian era, attractive in a comfortable-with-herself, no-neuroses sort of way that made me want to slap her.

"I'm Sally Hernandez." Her voice was deep and pleasant. I hated her more.

She held out her hand. Five silver rings on her fingers. I shook her hand firmly and made eye contact. "Wilhelmina Hardy, but everyone calls me Bil."

"Bil," she said. "Would you like to have a seat?"

"Not especially, but I don't suppose I can stand for fifty minutes."

"You don't want to be here?"

I didn't answer. Instead, I looked around the room. The walls were sponge-painted a pale orange over light tan. There were weavings hanging everywhere, as well as a couple of Mexican masks, some painted wooden flutes, and a lot of healthy plants hanging from hooks in the ceiling. On a bookshelf next to the analyst's couch, Sally Hernandez had the largest African violet I'd ever seen. I was amazed in spite of myself.

"What do you feed that thing?" I asked. "The blood of virgins?"

Sally laughed. "This is a college town, Bil. Virgins are pretty thin on the ground. I just talk to it a lot and give it the occasional pinch of encouragement."

"A pinch of encouragement? Does that mean you sprinkle something on it?"

She shook her head. "No, I mean I pinch it. Like this." She reached out and plucked off a couple of velvet leaves. "It likes to be pinched. I think it keeps it wondering, makes it try harder."

"You have an existential plant," I said. "I hope you know that's weird as fuck."

She laughed again, and I sat down on her plush sofa. She took the chair opposite me, a blue twill thing that screamed IKEA. She held a yellow legal pad in one hand and a fountain pen in the other.

"Are you going to take notes?" I asked.

"Not if you don't want me to."

"I don't care."

She shrugged. "Do you mind if I doodle?"

"Be my guest, but at ninety bucks an hour, I'll expect you to give me the pictures at the end of our session. Perhaps it'll be something I can frame?"

"That depends," she said, "on whether or not you like abstract art. And Bil, do you think you might be overdoing the whole hostile thing? I know you don't want to be here. This is grief counseling. Why would you?"

I had no answer for that, or, rather, I did have an answer, but it was one that I didn't like. When I said nothing, Sally continued, "I should tell you that I already know quite a bit about you. I know that you're getting a master's degree in clinical psychology at Cowslip University. I know that you're a gifted student. Don't be surprised—I have friends in the department. I've heard your name quite a lot."

"Gifted?"

She smiled. It was getting harder by the minute to dislike her. Her eyes were a warm brown and the laugh lines between mouth and nose softened her features. "Yes, gifted. But not driven."

It was my turn to laugh. "I'm a younger child," I said. "The fourth of five. I leave driven to my older sisters."

"Tell me about your family," she said.

I leaned back. "How much time do we have left?"

She looked at her watch. "Forty-five minutes."

"That's not enough. Here's the shorthand version. I have three older sisters: Ruth, a doctor; Naomi, a lawyer; and Sarah, a librarian. I'm the fourth. My brother, Sam, was the youngest, but only by six months. Sarah, Sam, and I were adopted. Sarah and Sam are black. I might be white, but then again, I might not. Does this bother me? Not really. I was born in Louisiana, so I think the correct technical term for me is 'mulatto.' If that's what I am, then I'm just pale enough to qualify as 'passing.' Is it easy growing up in an interracial family in northern Idaho? No, of course not. What's my father like? Quiet, reasonable, and often in hiding. What's my mother like? Jumping Jesus, just stop me if you've heard it. Do you know about Emma Hardy?"

Sally Hernandez nodded.

"Everyone does. My mother is infamous. She's a cross between hell on wheels and a barrel of monkeys. She has more energy than an atomic bomb and she's capable of doing at least as much damage. I love her, I hate her, and I don't know what I'd do without her. She's bossy, manipulative, nosy, supportive, politically active, and brilliant. She's always up in your face and she's a complete asshole. No one ever feels neutral about my mother. She's either feared and loathed or adored and admired. She's like Eva Peron only without Argentina. And, just for the record, she'd object to that analogy because she's not a fascist. She's a socialist except at tax time, when she temporarily becomes a libertarian. This happens every year. It lasts about two weeks, from the middle of April to the beginning of May, and then we're back to normal, or what passes for normal in my family."

"You're close to your mother," she said.

"Let me think about the word 'close,'" I said. "I don't know. Sometimes, it's more like there's no getting away from her."

"Do you want to get away?"

"Yes. No. Maybe."

"Tell me about Sam."

"My brother died as he'd lived—with criminal charges pending."

"Is that all you want to say?"

"For the time being."

"Okay."

"Okay?" I repeated.

"Yes," she said. "I'm not here to beat information out of you, Bil."

"Then you really are a therapist and not my mother."

Sally put down her notepad. I saw that she'd doodled what looked like a caricature of Groucho Marx—a big nose with a mustache, glasses, and bushy eyebrows.

"What do you want from me?" she asked. "I mean, what do you hope to accomplish here?"

I thought about this for a moment. "I want to feel better."

"Better about what?"

"About everything. About me, about Sam, about his dying."

"Do you want to talk about that?"

"No," I said honestly. "I want you to guess."

"Fine," said Sally. "I don't usually do this, but it's your dime and you know a thing or two about how therapy works—enough for me to treat you as I would a fellow therapist. What I think is that the subject of your brother's death is too painful to talk about. He died young. You have issues with him that will never be resolved. You feel guilty and conflicted. You loved him and you miss him, but you're angry—angry with him and angry with the world. How am I doing?"

"So far, so good."

"Okay," she continued. "Here's my analysis. You're smart, Bil, and you're good at deflecting. You feel things deeply. Perhaps I might be able to help if you were willing to work with me, but I don't think you are. You're here against your will. I'm in the business of listening to what people want to tell me, and helping people who want to be helped. I can't do anything for you if you don't want me to."

We had a staring contest and Sally won. I blinked, sniffed, and examined my tennis shoes. She said nothing. I waited.

"You're right," I said at last. "I don't want to be here."

"You're free to go."

I shook my head. "No, I'm not. I can't sleep. I don't eat properly. I've stopped exercising and I've taken up smoking pot. I've got a tattoo on my ass that says something really stupid. I love my girlfriend more than anything in the world, but I'm afraid she'll leave me if I don't sort myself out. I'm afraid she'll leave me no matter what. I'm afraid she'll die, or I'll die, or we'll both die because, in the end, we're all going to die."

I looked up. Sally smiled and patted me on the hand. "Are Thursday mornings a good time for you?"

"Yes."

"Next week, then," she said. "Nine o'clock. Our time today is up."

"Just one more thing," I said.

"Yes?"

"Can I have that picture of Groucho Marx?"

"Very good." She laughed and tore the page from her notebook. "Are you a Marx Brothers fan?"

"Yeah. *Duck Soup*, *A Night at the Opera*. Funny stuff."

"It is indeed."

"I'll tell you what," I said. "I didn't want to come here today, and I'm sure I won't want to be here next week, but I'm glad you don't think that I'm Chico or Harpo. I can work with a woman who recognizes my inner Groucho."

"Ah, Bil, you're onto me. You're going to be a tricky client."

I quoted Groucho. "Anyone who says he can see through women is missing a lot."

"Don't look now," Sally quoted back. "There's one too many in this room, and I think it's you."

Chapter 3

It was Sally's bright idea that I begin keeping a journal. It was my bright idea to backdate it. If I wanted to come to terms with my grief, then I needed to revisit the causes. The only question was where to begin. With Sam's diagnosis? He'd lived with non-Hodgkin lymphoma for nearly six years, from the age of seventeen until his death. Or did the story begin with his first chemotherapy and radiation treatments? He was different after that, weaker physically but stronger willed.

Or maybe it all started much earlier, with his first unhappy brushes with the law. He'd been in and out of trouble since puberty—pot-smoking, petty theft, trampy girlfriends. I thought about all of these things, but what I kept coming back to was Sam's last criminal act, a spectacular and spectacularly stupid attack on the sewer pipes of Cowslip.

I thought back to July 5, just a few months ago. Sam and his friends had run out of firecrackers. They'd set off all of the screamers, fireballs, grenades, and bottle rockets they'd bought down at Half-a-Hand Fireworks on the Nez Perce reservation—more than four hundred dollars' worth, the whole of Sam's disability check. They'd tried making Molotov cocktails, but a plastic Mountain Dew bottle doesn't break when you fill it with gas and torch the wick. It just melts. At some point, they got the bright idea of mooching around for some dynamite. In the middle of nowhere, Idaho, explosives are not hard to find. Farmers, loggers, hunters, and miners—all of them love things that go boom. Look in the right barn or beneath the bench seat of the right pickup truck, and you'll find a stash that the Unabomber would envy.

Sam and his friends hit pay dirt at the rock quarry across the road from my parents' house, where they found—and stole—a pack of blasting caps. They dropped one or more of these down an open manhole at the corner of Jackson and Third. The resulting explosion cracked a sewer main and backed up toilets across five city blocks, including the one in my apartment. It also scared the hell out of a City of Cowslip sewer inspector who had gone down the manhole to check for leaks. The poor man got his eyebrows singed off but was otherwise uninjured.

The sewer incident was vintage Sam: bad company, bad judgment, bad outcome. His excuses were vintage as well. He didn't deny having done it. He said that he didn't know anyone was down the manhole. In order to believe that, you'd have to believe that Sam had missed all of the Day-Glo orange cones and the large "Man at Work" sign. Second, my brother claimed that he didn't know that sewer gas was explosive. As Sam was infamous for having once given himself second-degree burns during a fart-lighting competition, no one was buying that, either. Finally, Sam claimed he hadn't stolen the blasting caps. He'd gotten them from "some guy."

Some Guy was a standing joke at our house. He was a magical creature, a cross between the Tooth Fairy and the Dollar Store. Some Guy appeared at times and places Sam could never seem to remember, and it was always Some Guy who cleverly filed the names and serial numbers off all of those bargains and freebies and once-in-a-lifetime offers that fell happily, accidentally, and, of course, honestly into Sam's possession.

At the Lewis County Jail, Sam went into Lee Harvey Oswald mode. He insisted that he'd acted alone. No one was with him when he'd acquired the blasting caps, and no one was with him when he'd blown the sewer main. The cops knew better. Emma knew better. Worst of all, I knew better and, if I'd wanted to, I could have named names. In retrospect, perhaps I should have. What I thought at the time was that if Sam wasn't going to snitch, neither was I. It was none of my business anyway. I'd spent the last two years doing my damnedest to draw some clear boundaries with my brother, and not getting involved in his petty criminality was my line in the sand. No matter what, I was not mopping up after him. My brother had gotten himself into this mess; he could get himself out.

Except, of course, that he couldn't.

* * *

I'd been in the bathtub with my head underwater when I'd felt the boom from Sam's sewer bomb. I stood up, wrapped myself in a towel, and climbed out of the tub to make certain that the rest of the apartment was still in one piece. I'd gotten as far as the hallway when the phone began to ring. I reached for it just as a two-foot geyser shot up from the toilet. I stopped and let the answering machine pick up.

It was Emma, wanting to know if I'd seen Sam. She said he'd gone off with Calvin Knox and some other young tearaways. She was sure he was up to no good. She'd been to all of his usual haunts, she couldn't find him, and so could I please...

The water shut off behind the toilet was so rusty I couldn't move it. Our apartment was ancient, and the plumbing dated back to the roaring twenties. The geyser kept spraying. I tried to stop it by taking my towel off and shoving it down the bowl, but after a minute or so, it gurgled up, swirled out, and flopped onto the floor. I backed out and shut the door. Retrieving another towel from the linen closet, I pushed it firmly into the gap between the bathroom tile and the shiny polished wood of the hallway. While Emma rattled on, filling up the tape on my answering machine, I dressed quickly and went across the hall. I knocked on Donny and Suzy's door. They weren't home, but I could hear the sound of running water in their apartment, too.

I went downstairs to bang on the door of the building's manager-in-residence, Mrs. Olafsson. No answer. Just the sound of more running water. My mother was still talking to the answering machine when I trudged back upstairs. How anyone who smoked two packs a day could expend that much breath boggled the mind. I collected my car keys and changed the fully-soaked bath towel for a larger beach towel. I used my cell phone to call Suzy at the hospital, Donny at the sheriff's department, and Mrs. Olafsson's emergency line. In each case, I got voice mail. I thought for a moment. A plunger? I'd loaned it to Donny and Suzy. I needed to make a quick trip to the hardware store.

Emma was still talking as I closed the front door. What a gasbag. What an annoyance! I'd told her a dozen times that I was bowing out of the Sam and Emma Show. I had a life, a good life, and I wanted to keep it. Sylvie came first—first, last, and always. Emma had tried to pull some bullshit about Sylvie having married into the family and therefore she'd assumed the family's responsibilities, but if my mother had hoped to co-opt Sylvie into Sam's assorted dramas, I soon disabused her of that fantasy. The first and only time Sam had borrowed money from my girlfriend, I'd hunted him down at the Jones Street Market and read him the riot act.

I'd assumed the boom I'd heard was localized. Our building had been rocked six months earlier when the old gas boiler blew, and less than a week after we'd moved in, a Russian graduate student on the floor below us had flushed a fish head down the toilet. It had gotten stuck in the pipes and created a similar geyser effect. Our apartment was an Art Deco beauty, but sometimes it felt like a death trap. Windows were painted shut, the plumbing groaned, and the appliances would have looked old to Wilma Flintstone. I was wondering what could possibly have gone wrong this time as I crossed the parking lot to my pickup truck.

A normal woman from a normal family would have been surprised to find Sam crouching behind her Toyota, but I'm not a normal woman, and I don't have a normal family. What I have is a sixth sense for idiocy. The boom, the gushing water, suddenly it all made sense. I opened my mouth to say "what the fuck have you done?" But then I thought, why bother? I closed my mouth and waited for the lie.

"Oh, hi," Sam said casually. "Are you going somewhere?"

"I'm going to buy a plunger," I replied. "My toilet's exploded."

Sam kept his face expressionless. Three other boys materialized from the other side of the truck. I recognized one of them as Calvin Knox, the son of Preacher George Knox.

"Did you hear me?" I said. "My toilet has exploded. Water is gushing everywhere."

No response. I changed tacks. "Mom is looking for you."

"I know," Sam said. "Can you give us a lift?"

"No. I've only got room for two, and I'm only going to the hardware store. I need a plunger."

Sam shook his head. "Forget the plunger. It won't help. The city is switching off the water at the main line. Can you take us as far as Jim's Burgers? Steve and Joe can ride in the back." Sam gestured at two crabby-looking teenagers, one a short, heavily-freckled redhead, the other a tall, skinny kid with a big nose and long, blond dreadlocks. The redhead was holding a leash at the end of which was an awkward, skinny, frightened puppy—so scared he was shaking.

I could handle exploding toilets and lying brothers, but the sight of that terrified dog pushed me over the edge. "What have you done, Sam?"

My brother looked at the dog. "He'll be fine. He doesn't like loud noises."

"You're a fucker," I said. "A spoiled-rotten, no good fucker. You know that, don't you?"

Sam shrugged. "Are you going to give us a ride, or what?"

I ought to have refused. I ought to have asked Sam some pointed questions or sent him upstairs to my waterlogged apartment and made him call Emma. But I didn't. He gave me a shifty grin, his lips sliding up over teeth that were still bright white despite his bad health and his perpetual pot-smoking. When he tried, my brother could look about ten years old. He was by any reasonable standards a bad guy, but he wasn't malicious, or at least that's how I felt when he smiled at me in that slippery we-both-know-I'm-shitting-you way.

Against what was left of my better judgment, I said, "Fine. I'll give you a ride, but Steve and Joe will have to crawl under the tarp and keep very still. I don't want to get a ticket. As for the dog, I want him up front, sitting in your lap. The poor thing is a nervous wreck. You want to tell me how you know the city is switching off the water at the main?"

"No."

Calvin climbed into the truck first, crossing quickly to the middle. This allowed Sam, who walked with a cane, to sit by the door. Steve handed Sam the puppy, climbed into the back with Joe, and we were off.

I cast a sideways glance at Calvin, who was awkwardly negotiating the lumpy middle of the bench seat, his crotch balanced precariously over the stick shift. I was surprised that Calvin would be considerate of Sam's disability. The Knox family was not known for its sensitivity. Daddy George was the belligerent, sexist, and homophobic pastor of a belligerent, sexist, and homophobic church, and Mama Mary Sue looked as if she were made out of old rubber bands—everything about her was stretched too tight.

The Knoxes—or, as my mother called them, the Knoxious—had come to Idaho from some mud hole in Mississippi as part of a campus Christian group called Green Tree Ministries. George Knox was a big, bluff man with a beard like a carpet and a violently unnatural, puffed-up brown hairdo. It might have been a wig. It might have been a beaver. Whatever it was—animal, vegetable, or mineral—it was as fake as Knox's love the sinner, hate the sin bonhomie. What Knox said to your face and what he wrote were two separate things. In public, he was all smiles and blandishments, a fat and friendly preacher. In print, he called for a return to Old

Testament law, complete with public stonings for gays, adulterers, and disobedient children.

By Cowslip standards, the Knoxious were newcomers. They'd only been around for about ten years. I'd gone to high school with two of the Knox daughters, Rahab and Moira. There was a younger one too, Fiona, but like Calvin, she'd been home-schooled. The Knox ministry had grown beyond campus and was spreading through Cowslip like a virus. Using Green Tree as a springboard, Knox had founded The Church of the True Vine and begun importing members from other states. The man was nothing if not ambitious. He was an ex-Marine, and he made a big deal about having served in Vietnam. He'd written a book called *Finding Jesus on the Ho Chi Minh Trail*.

What I knew of Knox's military career was largely filtered through Captain Schwartz, my best friend Tipper's mother. There were rumors that Knox had left the Marine Corps under some kind of cloud, but no one seemed to know the details. Captain Schwartz was also a Vietnam veteran, but she rarely spoke about her experience. Still, when Knox published his book, the Captain went ballistic.

"I've never heard such a load of shit," she said. "You can bet your bottom dollar that George Knox wasn't anywhere near the Ho Chi Minh Trail. Sitting on the gear in the rear, more like. Those are the ones who want to brag about their time in country."

Knox had a column in the *Cowslip Herald-Examiner* called "Perfect World." It had been running in the paper for nearly a year to raves from his flock and hisses and boos from the rest of us. Knox had aired his views on everything from pre-millennialism to his dreams of a Christian theocracy. There was no subject on which he was not a self-appointed expert. Childrearing, the manly joys of swilling brandy and smoking cigars, the proper Christian division of labor—women were not fit to change a flat tire or balance a checkbook, and men should never do the dishes or cook, though they could and should grill steaks on special occasions.

To date, the worst thing Knox had written was a piece about women's suffrage. He was in favor of repealing the 19th Amendment. God made man the head of woman, and that meant God wanted men to make all of the really important decisions. He cited a lot of hooey about the gender gap and wept bitter tears over the fact that many women must be going into the voting booth and canceling out the Godly decisions of their husbands.

In liberal, hippie, feminist Cowslip, the "Suffering Suffrage" column had caused a near-riot. There was a flurry of letters to the editor, and the Coalition of Women Students had marched on the Green Tree Ministries office. Knox being Knox, he ate up the publicity with a spoon. His next column was a whining piece about the intolerance of Democrats and other assorted lefties and, in fact, the negative reaction to his column was proof that Christians were a persecuted minority. Thanks to *Roe vs. Wade*, flag-burning, school prayer, and the Gay Agenda, the Jesus-loving white man just couldn't get a break. More letters to the editor, more marching, and George Knox got his dream come true—a full five minutes on CNN. He was in seventh heaven.

I looked at kid sitting next to me. Unlike his father, Calvin Knox was handsome. Like his mother, he was very thin and very blond, but the resemblance ended there. When Mary Sue Knox smiled, her face cracked open like an egg. Calvin smiled easily, and his laugh seemed genuine. Many people found him charming. I couldn't stand him. I'd been around him just enough to know that beneath the smile was an ego as fat and dangerous as his father's. I'd seen flashes of his inflated sense of self-worth in the way he tossed around big words like "incarceration" to kids who couldn't spell busted. I wasn't certain when Calvin had hooked up with Sam, and I didn't know why. Preacher's son gone wild, I suspected.

As I climbed into the driver's seat of the truck, I began to wish that I'd made the dog ride under the tarp with Steve and Joe. He smelled like a pungent mix of urine, chicken soup, and a hint of— what? Was it bananas? Whatever it was, it was awful. I tried breathing through my mouth.

"Watch your... um... knees," I told Calvin, my hand hovering between his crotch and the stick shift.

"Oh, right." He glanced around at the truck's interior, which was packed to overflowing with coffee cups, gum wrappers, and books and papers from school.

"Yeah, it's a mess," I said. "Sorry."

Calvin smiled. "No problem. Thanks for the lift."

The smell was getting worse. "The air-conditioning's broken," I lied, "so we'll have to roll the windows down. Sam, you and that wretched mutt are sitting on my leather jacket. Just put it on the floor—neatly!"

Calvin giggled, a high-pitched squeak that made him sound even younger than he looked, and he looked about fourteen.

"Calvin," I asked abruptly, "how old are you?"

"Jesus," Sam grunted. "You're as bad as Emma."

"Shut up, Sam. How old?"

"Twenty-one." Catching my look of disbelief, Calvin smiled. "If you like, I'll show you my driver's license. I take after my dad. He doesn't show his age, either."

"Your dad—" I began, but then I reconsidered. Best not to go there. I'd tangled with George Knox a few years back over an anti-gay ballot proposition. Why should I bother to point out that Calvin's father wore an awful wig that didn't make him look younger, it just made it harder to stamp him with an accurate sell-by date.

I changed tack. "How're tricks over at the concrete octopus?"

Calvin laughed. "So that's what you infidels call it."

"Among other things."

"The Church of the True Vine is the fastest-growing church in Cowslip," he said, "and Green Tree Ministries has more than doubled in the past three years."

"That's a nice sound bite, Calvin. I believe it's the same one your dad used on CNN. I heard that Green Tree opened a branch office at Washington State University. Is that what you mean by doubled?"

"There are lies, damned lies, and statistics," Calvin replied.

"Very nice again," I said. "You know your Disraeli." I glanced at Sam and then back at Calvin. "Tell me something. Do your parents approve of the company you keep?"

"No," Calvin said easily. "But like I say, I'm twenty-one. Do you mind if I turn on the radio?"

"Be my guest."

He scanned up and down the dial before settling on Cowslip University's alternative station. I wanted to ask him a few more questions, but Sam was right. I was acting like my mother. Why should I care if he hung out with Calvin Knox? Why should I care about Calvin Knox, period?

Because I was nosy, that was why. The Church of the True Vine had recently finished building an enormous structure on the edge of town. Long bunker-like wings shot off from an enormous octagonal center that housed the actual church. The assorted wings held a kindergarten through grade twelve primary school, a seminary, a dormitory for the seminary students, the off-campus office of Green Tree Ministries, and George Knox's own personal publishing house, The Root of Jesse Press. The church claimed six hundred members, but that was an exaggeration. There were about two hundred adult members. All the rest were children. The Church of the True Vine opposed all forms of birth control, and it wasn't uncommon for Knox's parishioners to have a dozen kids.

Despite their fecundity, Knox and his crew were small potatoes compared to the Catholics and Mormons. Since the battle over anti-gay Proposition One, however, The Church of the True Vine had taken an unappetizing interest in local politics and, as a voting bloc, they were often able to punch above their weight. In the last election, they'd managed to get two of their parishioners onto the six-seat city council. Aided and abetted by a couple of old boy Republicans, they'd shoved local politics sharply to the right.

The first act of the new city council was to ban any public display of the female breast. No topless dancing—as if we had any to start with—no running around town in a jogging bra, no low-cut blouses, and no public breast-feeding. In hippie-dippy Cowslip, the latter was tantamount to a declaration of war. Sylvie, Sarah, and my mother had helped organize a group called Justice for Us Girls or JUGS.

I had a thesis to write, so all I did was sign their petition. Just for fun, I'd also offered to organize a topless march down Main Street, but I was roundly and soundly rebuffed.

At Jim's Burgers, Calvin Knox thanked me politely for the lift.

"Yeah," Sam added. "Thanks, Bil."

Shocked by this display of good manners, I said they were welcome. My faith in the sullen rudeness of youth wasn't restored until I held up the edge of the tarp so Steve and Joe could slither out.

"Man, that sucked," Steve said. Joe grunted his agreement.

"I'm sorry, boys," I said. "The limo's in the shop." They looked at me, grim-faced and glum. I turned to Sam. "Wait—you don't have to tell me what you did, but you do have to call Emma."

"I'll call her when I feel like it," he snapped. "Quit minding my business."

"When she asks if I've seen you," I told him, "I'm not going to lie."

He shrugged. "Whatever. Can I borrow ten bucks?"

I opened my mouth to ask what for, but then I caught Calvin's ironic smirk. Fuck him. I opened my wallet and handed Sam the money. Sam, in turn, handed me a small bag of pot.

"Oh, no," I said. "I'm not holding this for you."

"Please," he said. "If I get picked up with this on me..."

"You'll go to prison, where you belong," I finished. He gave me that stupid slippery grin. I shoved the bag down deep into my jeans pocket. Then, to hide my shame, I bent over to pet the dog. He'd stopped shaking and was taking an interest in something on the ground that smelled even worse than he did.

I stood up, wiping my hand on my jeans. "Whatever you're up to, Sam, I don't want to know. And you can take my jacket off and put it back in the truck. It was a gift from Sylvie. I don't want you walking off with it."

Sam gave a fake shiver. "But I'm cold, Sis. I won't lose it. I promise. See you 'round."

"Sam—"

"I'm going to be out late tonight, and you know I can't go home and get my own jacket. Emma will be there."

"You mean the cops will be there."

"Yeah, I know." He paused and then said, looking away, "Thanks, Ratty."

That was a low blow, a throwback to our childhood and happier times. When Sam and I were small, *The Wind in the Willows* was our favorite book. Emma read it to us over and over again. We imagined that we were Badger and Rat, and our house was Toad Hall. Emma, with all of her plans and schemes, was the Amazing Toad, the Glorious Toad. Later, it was a sick joke when Badger found himself in trouble and in jail while Toad and I sat in Toad Hall, trying to think up ways to bust Badger out.

Sam's friends giggled. We ignored them. In some distant, parallel universe, I was still Rat, Sam was still Badger, and our mother was the amazing, crazy, irrepressible Toad.

"Just remember, Badger," I said as firmly as I could. "You owe me." In response to his slight nod, I added, "About my exploding toilet—what did you do, drop a stick of dynamite down a sewer main?"

I was pleased to see that Steve, Joe, and even Calvin looked shocked. Sam, on the other hand, just laughed. "Close," he said, "but no cigar. I'll call you, Bil."

"Yeah," I replied. "And it'll be collect from the county jail. You'll be asking for bail money."

It was the last conversation we ever had.

Chapter 4

On the tenth of August, I woke up happy. Summer school was over and fall classes wouldn't start for another three weeks. No teaching, no grading, no office hours. I might have improved the shining hours by working on my thesis, but there was plenty of time for that. I had until December 15 to finish. No worries.

I was sorry to admit that grief counseling had already helped. In the weeks since Sam's funeral, I'd woken up miserable and I'd woken up indifferent, but I hadn't woken up happy. Happy was new. I glanced at the clock on the bedside table. It was just after ten, and the apartment was warm but not yet hot. I was in bed alone, which meant that Sylvie, who slept on the side next to the wall, had somehow managed to crawl over me without waking me up. So, I'd slept soundly for a change as well. I cupped my hand, breathed into it, and sniffed. I could smell spearmint toothpaste working hard to cover the odor of garlic. Hell's bells. I had indeed slipped out sometime after midnight for a bowl of late-night *pho*. That wasn't a dream.

About a year ago, a Vietnamese restaurant had opened only a block from Sylvie's and my apartment, and I'd been eating there almost every night since Sam's death. I was hooked on *pho*, and I loved Vivian Nguyen-DiRisio, the woman who ran the place. When I couldn't sleep, I crept out of bed and walked down to Pho From Home, where I ate enormous bowls of noodles with beef flank, brisket, or tendon. The idea of eating tendon was gross, but in practice, I didn't care. It all tasted good. I listened to Vivian talk, and I relaxed into the food and the patter.

Vivian had been born and raised in a village just outside of Saigon. She might have been in her late fifties or early sixties. I wasn't sure, and I wasn't about to ask. She looked young but she said that she was ancient—old and wise. Vivian was married to the new math professor at Cowslip University. He was a good twenty-five years her junior and looked and talked like Joe Pesci. He'd gotten his Ph.D. at Columbia, and they'd moved to Idaho from New York.

Vivian liked having a young husband. "Men are like dogs," she'd say with a laugh. "If you get when they're puppies, you can teach them not to piss on floor."

I pulled on a T-shirt and a pair of shorts and slipped into the bathroom so I could brush my teeth thoroughly and gargle with mouthwash. Satisfied that my breath was now completely minty-fresh, I drifted into the living room. The windows were open and the smells of harvest wafted in. We grow soft wheat in the Palouse region of northern Idaho, the kind used to make ramen noodles rather than the hard kind used to make bread. The smell is sweet without being cloying, like freshly mown hay.

I took a deep breath and looked out over the low rooftops. In the distance, the colors of late summer seemed impossibly vivid. Smooth hills of yellow-gold rolled on for hundreds of miles beneath an endless blue sky, a landscape as amazing in its way as a tropical paradise. It was no wonder that old hippies like my parents loved the place. We had all of the advantages of rural living with very few of the detractions.

Cowslip was home to an expensive liberal arts college and, consequently, to all of the socialists, radicals, and liberal Democrats who either taught or attended classes there. We were an anomaly in conservative Republican Idaho, a progressive island in a sea of right-wing goofiness. Not that the left can't also be a little odd—our population of twenty-five thousand managed to support a witchcraft supply store, three tattoo and piercing parlors, and a shop that sold nothing but clothes made from thick, itchy hemp.

My mother was a Cowslip native. My dad was born in Oregon. They met at Cowslip College, recently rechristened Cowslip University. After they married, they traveled from coast to coast while Hugh collected graduate degrees and Emma collected children. They adopted me in Louisiana when my dad was at Tulane. They got Sam in California and Sarah in Virginia. Their biological children, Ruth and Naomi, were conceived, respectively, in my father's Cowslip College dorm room and a Ford Econoline van. When Hugh was offered a tenure track position at his old alma mater, my parents jumped at the chance, thinking in their typically blinkered way that Cowslip would be a great place to raise an interracial family. And, in some ways, it was. The only problem was that it was located in Idaho.

I basked in the sunshine. I didn't just feel happy. I felt good. Apart from the trip to Vivian's, my sleep the night before had been unaided. No alcohol, no sleeping pills, and no sneaky hit from Sam's nickel bag. A good thing, too, as I couldn't afford another tattoo. The one I had still itched like a mother.

Sylvie was in the kitchen grinding coffee beans. I leaned against the windowsill and closed my eyes. Perhaps I was cured. With that in mind, I retrieved what was left of the stash from beneath the ceramic planter in the living room and weighed it in my hand. It was half-empty. I should flush it down the toilet. I should do something to restore my moral rectitude. Instead, I put the bag back under the planter. I knew my pot-smoking was driving Sylvie crazy. How could it not? It was entirely out of character for me, and besides, nothing whiffed quite like Sam's cheap bud. Still, I was seeing a grief counselor. Maybe soon I'd be ready to let the weed go.

Donny Smith, a Lewis County sheriff's deputy, lived across the hall from us. Every time I lit up, there was a chance that he might catch the smell as it wafted through the two-inch gap beneath our front door. It was a slim chance. Donny's partner, Suzy, said that Donny had adenoid trouble and couldn't smell a thing. Lucky me. Suzy also said that Donny snored like a buzz saw. Lucky Suzy.

There was nothing wrong with my nose. I followed its lead down the hall and into the kitchen. Mingling with the smell of wheat and coffee was the unmistakable aroma of sizzling bacon.

Sylvie stood at the stove with her back to me. I paused in the doorway for a moment to admire the view. Long tan legs stretched beneath a loose blue T-shirt, white bikini underwear just visible beneath the hem. I was a lucky woman. I slipped up behind her and wrapped my arms around her waist. She smelled like chamomile shampoo and Ivory soap. I kissed her on the neck.

"Mmm," she said. "You slept well last night."

"I did."

"You got up and left the apartment, but that was only for *pho*, right?"

"Right."

There was a long pause before she said carefully, "So maybe you don't need the pot anymore."

"No, I probably don't need it. I just—"

I just what? I just can't get rid of anything that belonged to Sam, not even his weed? I wanted to say it, but I felt foolish. I wasn't saving his nickel bag. I was smoking it. It wasn't like I'd put it in a safe marked "Sacred Stash: Do Not Touch."

Sylvie said nothing, just leaned back in my arms. I decided to change the subject. "So, what's the bacon in aid of?"

"It's in aid of breakfast," she said, laughing.

"I don't suppose…"

She pointed at a mixing bowl on the counter. "Pancake batter, ready for the griddle, and there's fresh coffee in the pot. I hope you know how spoiled you are."

"I do, and I like it." I kissed a spot higher up on her neck, and then another just beneath her left ear. I reached up automatically to brush aside her ponytail, forgetting for a moment that it was no longer there. She'd had her hair cut into a short bob. I still wasn't quite used to it, and I'd made the mistake of looking more shocked than pleasantly surprised when she'd come home from the salon.

Hoping she hadn't noticed my hesitation, I tickled the nape of her neck with my fingertips. Her skin was smooth and soft, and her new haircut emphasized the long, graceful line from her ear to her shoulder. I decided, at last, that I liked it.

"What are you doing?" she said, smoothly turning around in my arms and reaching up to clasp her hands behind my head.

"Admiring your new haircut."

She lifted one perfectly arched eyebrow. "You're a week late."

"No, I'm not. I liked it from the start."

"Oh? I believe what you said was, 'Good grief.'"

"No, I didn't."

"Yes, you did." Sylvie's gaze was piercing. Her eyes were a bright sparkling green with flecks of gold surrounding the pupils. Wolf eyes. I pressed my forehead against hers and looked down, trying to think of something clever—and appeasing—to say.

"You're not wearing any shoes."

She laughed. "That's a non sequitur. What does my being barefoot have to do with whether or not you like my new haircut?"

"It doesn't have anything to do with it. It's just, well, you know that I have a thing for your shapely feet."

She wiggled her toes. "You're barefoot, too, but go on. I want to hear more."

"As I've told you before," I said, covering her feet with my own, "if you wish to remain unmolested by my amorous attentions, you must remember to wear shoes and socks. In fact, you must wear big thick wooly socks and heavy leather hiking boots. Even in the bathtub."

"Sounds uncomfortable. What about loafers?"

I shook my head. "You always wear loafers without socks, and my imagination runs wild." I reached behind her to turn off the burner. "I've heard that bacon can be reheated in the microwave."

Sylvie laughed again, a low, full sound that seemed to well up from deep within her. We looked at each other, and she dropped a light kiss on my lips. "Okay."

"You know what I like about you?" I said.

"What?"

"You're open to suggestion."

I kissed her slowly and deeply, welcoming the rush of desire that moved like hot liquid from my mouth to my abdomen. Reaching under her T-shirt, I traced a line up from her stomach to the soft full curves of her breasts. In response, she buried her hands in my hair and pulled me close.

"Thank God," I whispered. "I was beginning to worry."

"I wasn't," she whispered back. "I knew it was just a matter of time."

"You've been very patient with me."

"No, I haven't," she said seriously. "I love you."

Even before Sam's death, when I could see that his health was failing, I'd lost interest in sex. I'd lost interest in everything. I'd taught one session of summer school, treating my freshman composition students to an excellent impersonation of a zombie at the chalkboard. I'd gotten their papers back to them far too late, and, because I felt guilty for not giving them my full attention, I'd handed out As and Bs like candy. No one flunked, and no one complained, but I'd cheated them. I'd been a crappy teacher.

I'd cheated Sylvie, too. I'd rebuffed her advances. I'd explained that I was tired, and I was tired, but that wasn't the whole truth. I was miserable. When she asked me if I wanted to talk about it, I always said no. After a while, she stopped asking.

I knew I needed to trust her. I needed to believe that she wouldn't leave me if I showed her how awful I really felt. Instead, on the really bad nights, I waited until she fell asleep. Then I'd hit Sam's stash or pay a visit to Vivian and her big bowls of *pho*.

Today, I felt different. I didn't know why. No pot, no *pho*, just a beautiful, desirable woman in my arms for whom I felt not only love but pure, blissful, overwhelming lust. I really was happy. I hoped it would last.

I took a deep breath and pulled Sylvie close. "It's been three months," I said. "I might be a little rusty. Do you think it's like riding a bicycle?"

She gave me a look that could have fused glass. "It's nothing like riding a bicycle. Come on." She took my hand. "I'll show you."

The phone rang.

"Don't answer that," she said.

"I wasn't planning to," I murmured.

We did a quick waltz from the kitchen to the hallway, tripping over one another in our haste. The phone rang twice more before the answering machine picked it up. As soon as I heard the voice, I tried to kick the bedroom door shut, but Sylvie pulled me down onto the bed and kissed me.

"Bil," Emma trilled. "Are you there?"

"We'll call her back," Sylvie said.

We sat up long enough to pull our T-shirts over our heads and toss them onto the floor by the dresser. Then we fell back together. Though the voice on the answering machine grew increasingly shrill, I concentrated my attention on the soft hollow at the base of Sylvie's throat. She ran her fingers through my hair and pressed her palms against my ears. It was no good—I could still hear my mother.

"I hope you're not screening your calls, Bil, because you know what I think of that."

I tossed a pillow at the door, missing it by a mile.

"I don't care if everyone else does it. You are not everyone else. It's rude to just sit there, pretending you're not at home."

"Christ almighty," I muttered. "The black telephone's off at the root, Ma. The voices just can't worm through."

Sylvie pushed up against my shoulders, forcing me to lift my head. "What did you just say?"

"The black telephone's off at the root," I repeated. "It's from a poem by Sylvia Plath."

My own Sylvia looked bemused. I kissed her again, slowly working my way down from her mouth to the swell of her breasts. The voice on the phone grew distant.

"What are you talking about, Hugh? Of course she's at home. She's probably still in bed. How do I know? Because she lives like a fucking vampire, that's how. Awake all night, asleep all day."

Sylvie tugged at my hair. "You were quoting from 'Daddy,' weren't you?"

"I'm not bothering her," my mother went on. "I'm worried about her."

I sat up abruptly. "How long is that fucking answering machine tape?"

"Too long," Sylvie agreed. "Go find out what she wants and then unplug the phone." She pushed her underwear down over her hips and tossed them onto the floor next to our T-shirts. I felt like weeping, but she just smiled and ran a long finger down my arm. "Go on. I'll wait."

My mother was now singing. "Bil, you're a pill, you should answer your phone, if you pick up then I'll leave you alone."

I snatched the phone out of its cradle. "Jesus H. Christ, Emma. Was all of that really necessary?"

"You *were* screening your calls," she accused.

"I was busy. What do you want?"

"Is that any way to talk to your mother? I just want to hear your dulcet voice. When was the last time you came out here for a visit?"

I thought for a moment. "Four days ago, Tuesday. We had dinner. You burned the spaghetti."

"Ha! That didn't slow you down. You ate two plates."

"We didn't eat until nine o'clock. I was starving. Now what do you want?"

"I want you to come out for a visit. And please bring Sylvie."

I sighed heavily. "When?"

"Now," she said. The "of course" was implied.

"I can't come right now. How about this afternoon?"

It was her turn to sigh. "When?"

I did some quick math. "How about three o'clock?"

"Three o'clock? What are you going to be doing for the next five hours?"

I thought about lying. I thought about saying it was none of her business. I thought about hanging up. Instead I said, "I'm going to be having sex, Ma. Excellent, mind-numbing, house-shaking sex. What with one thing and another, I haven't really felt like it lately, but today I intend to make up for lost time. It might take five hours. It might take ten. It might be that I'll give you a call sometime next week—that is if I've got enough energy left to make it all the way down the hallway to the telephone."

In the silence that followed, I heard the unmistakable creak of bedsprings. Sylvie was either getting up to put her clothes back on, or she was off to lock herself in the bathroom until the men in the white suits came to get me.

"Well," said my mother. "I guess I called you at a bad time."

"You did."

"Three o'clock?"

"Yeah, I suppose so."

"Listen," she said. "Please drive your truck."

"Why?"

"Because," she paused for effect, "I hate to think of you trying to ride Sylvie's motorcycle after the day you've planned. Good-bye!"

Chapter 5

"Do you suppose they had to reconsecrate the church after Sam's funeral?" I traced the outline of Sylvie's ribs with my index finger.

She yawned luxuriously. "Why? Because of the music? You played all of his air guitar favorites."

"Actually, I was thinking more about my eulogy."

"Your eulogy was wonderful, Bil."

I stopped tracing and rolled onto my back. "I used the phrase, 'Up shit creek without a paddle.' How often do you hear that in church?"

"Rarely," she agreed. "You also said, 'Freedom's just another word for a sister who's willing to make bail.' It was a good eulogy. It was honest." She turned onto her side to face me and smoothed her hand over my right breast. "My turn now."

"Careful, you know I'm ticklish." I put my hands behind my head and stared at the ceiling. "I made reference to his taste for young bimbos, his criminal career, and his pathological loyalty to his pot suppliers. I talked about the shower of shit that rained down on Third Street as a result of his final escapade. We played "Freebird," "Stairway to Heaven," and "Piece of My Heart." Granny nearly choked to death. I saw her. She started gasping and Ruth had to slap her on the back."

Sylvie's hand moved lower. I shifted position to accommodate her. "I can't think of anything in the hymnal that would have been as appropriate. You also talked about Sam's generosity, his kind heart, and his love for his family. You talked about your childhood and your nicknames, Ratty and Badger. As for your grandmother, she was a little surprised, but she'll get over it." She grinned wickedly. "Besides, she's a high church Episcopalian. You said 'shit' in the Unitarian Church. That might be a point in your favor."

"I said 'shit' twice in the Unitarian Church, but you're probably right." I gave an involuntary groan. "There, that's the spot.

Yes. You know," I tried to continue my original thought, "the Unitarians are probably used to it. They probably have a special fucking and blinding service every third Sunday."

Sylvie paused in her ministrations. "For someone who doesn't go to church, you're a terrible religious snob."

"Please, don't stop. I'll shut up in a minute, I swear. Thank you." I sighed contentedly. "Look, I just think that if you're going to go to church, then why not go to a real church? The Unitarians take the summers off. No church. What's that about?"

"It's about you promising to be quiet and concentrate."

"I'm just saying that it seems too easy. If you're going to do the God thing, then why not get a fire and brimstone lecture on sin and eternal damnation? Why not have some fun? Tremble with fear at the wrath of the Almighty. Sing some really great hymns—no, don't laugh. Did you check out the Unitarians' hymnal? It was awful—a bunch of guitar odes from the Kumbaya sixties about peace, love, and understanding. I could borrow some of my mother's Summer of Love albums and get the same effect."

I ignored Sylvie's exasperated snort. "Okay, okay. I'll stop talking now, I promise. Hey, you know why you shouldn't piss off a Unitarian?"

"No," she said.

"Because they might burn a question mark in your yard."

"Ha-ha," she said. "Very funny. Now why don't you just shut up and kiss me?"

"That's your solution to everything. Sex. I try to have a serious theological conversation with you—"

I was happily silenced by the firm press of her lips. It was well past three, but I didn't care. For the first time in months, I felt solid and connected, like a person who had a future. Sylvie loved me, and I loved her. Some day, I might be able to think about Sam without feeling guilty and falling to bits. In the meantime, this was peace of a sort. Who knew how long it would last? I might wake up in a cold sweat in the middle of the night, craving Sam's crappy bud and Vivian's exotic vermicelli, but right now, at this moment, neither Sylvie nor I had any responsibilities. The fall semester didn't begin until the first of September. Twenty free, relaxing, sunny days stretched out before us.

I was caught in the embrace of Sylvie's warm, knowing hand. In for a penny, in for a pound. My mother could wait.

* * *

I dozed in Sylvie's arms then lay awake for a while, staring at the ceiling, thinking about Sam. He never made it to his arraignment. He had a heart attack in jail. Technically, that killed him, but Sam being Sam, he actually managed to die twice. The emergency room doctors resuscitated him, but too much time had passed, and he was brain dead. He was only twenty-four.

In the Intensive Care Unit, the vigil began, and if any part of Sam retained any awareness, I know he loved it. We were all gathered at his bedside: me, Sylvie, my family. Even Granny was there, and so was Kate. There was also a motley assortment of juvenile delinquents and slutty, under-aged bimbos. Sam's friends. I didn't know if my mother was too distraught to run them off or too tired to care, but in a strange way, I was glad to see them. They lent the proceedings a certain morbid levity. The boys all wore dirty T-shirts and stared at their feet, and the girls wept great pools of black mascara. I found the raccoon-eyed excess of their grief comforting. They were doing what I wanted and needed to do—weeping uncontrollably and howling at the unfairness of it all.

My brother was no angel. Jail was his second home, but he'd spent his teens and early twenties staring death in the face. So he'd chosen to live his short life to its crazy, criminal fullest. Who was I to judge him? To some extent, I even understood. I also thought it was fortunate that, for the most part, Sam had taken out his anger on things and not people. He was hell to live with but he was never intentionally mean.

Amidst all the weeping, my mother acted the stoic prairie woman. It was her favorite role and she played it well. Public displays of anything except anger were unacceptable to her. Emma stood at the head of the bed, stroking Sam's hair. She didn't cry. Her face remained hard and expressionless, her jaw set. In her eyes, Sam was not a petty thief and a small-time troublemaker. He was a sturdy pioneer, and she intended to behave as if he'd dropped dead on the Oregon Trail. Not in jail. Not in a hospital. Not surrounded by gypsies, tramps, and thieves.

Inside what passed for Emma's psyche, she was a miserable mess. I was certain of that. On the surface, however, she showed nothing. My sisters cried quietly. My father and Granny bawled out loud. It was up to me to keep Emma company in her stone-faced misery, not that I was any good at it. I can't do stoic. My face has always been an open book. Sylvie says I don't wear my heart on my sleeve. I wear it like an opera cape, clasped around my neck and flapping out behind me.

By standing with Emma, I wondered if I was betraying Sam. There was nothing my brother loved more than a maudlin scene— the death of Old Yeller, the boy shooting his pet deer in *The Yearling*. The Indian practice of suttee would not have struck Sam as over the top. If we'd built a giant bonfire and climbed on it to mourn his passing, he would have considered it his just desserts, a flaming cherries jubilee at the end of his tragic, comic life.

In the end, there's nothing especially dramatic about switching off life support. In Sam's case, we weren't letting him die; we were letting him go. A few shallow, rattling breaths, and then he was still. For three days, all that had stood between my brother and eternity were a few strangely cheap-looking machines.

* * *

Sylvie bagged out of going with me to see Emma. I left her reluctantly, curled up on the bed with a bag of pretzels and a cheap paperback.

"Where are the keys to Helen?"

"Front left pocket of my brown jacket," she said. "Are you looking for trouble? You know your mother hates it when you ride the motorcycle."

"My mother needs to get a grip." I leaned down to kiss her goodbye. "This shouldn't take long. Expect me back around eight. Oh, and if I were you, I wouldn't bother getting dressed. It'll save time."

"I'll see you when I see you," she said with a laugh, waving me out the door.

I climbed onto the Honda and stroked the gas tank affectionately. Sylvie had often accused me of dating her to get to Helen. I loved this motorcycle. Nothing could beat the thrill of riding—the sounds, the smells, and the wind on my face and in my hair. I looked up at the sky. Not a cloud in sight. Smiling happily to myself, I turned the key and pressed the start button. The engine roared to life and commenced a rhythmic throbbing between my knees. I'd just turned around with the intention of stuffing my helmet into one of the saddlebags when my girlfriend, wrapped in the bed sheet, stuck her head out of our living room window. I switched the engine off.

"Put that helmet on," she shouted, glaring down at me.

An old woman walking a Chihuahua, a teenager on a skateboard, and two men working on the electrical lines in front of our apartment building stopped to stare at me.

"I was planning to. I was just warming up the engine first."

"I have three words for you," Sylvie yelled. "Persistent vegetative state."

"Okay, okay." I pulled the helmet out of the saddlebag. "I'm putting it on, see?"

She shook her head and slammed the window shut. I snapped the chinstrap, waved to the electrical workers, the skateboarder, and the woman with the dog, and slid the bike carefully out of the parking lot, remembering to look both ways and use my turn signal.

It was a quarter past six when I pulled into my parents' driveway. Emma was waiting for me on the front steps, a cigarette in her mouth and a pile of butts on the ground by her feet. Her scowl swept first over me and then over the motorcycle. Finally, it came to rest on the dial of her watch. I switched off the engine and went to meet my doom.

She was wearing one of her sweet old lady getups, a pair of pale pink stretch pants and a navy blue sweatshirt with a yellow duck embossed on the chest. It occurred to me, not for the first time, that she ought to be arrested for fraud. There was nothing sweet about my mother. She'd started wearing these ridiculous I'm-a-nice-Mormon-grandmother outfits when my brother started getting arrested. She claimed that they disarmed the cops and gave her an edge in dealing with them. There was a certain logic to that—she didn't fare nearly as well when she wore her Angela Davis T-shirt—but what really gave her an edge was her terrifying, irrational temper. The dough-faced recruits at the Lewis County sheriff's department didn't know what to do with a chubby middle-aged woman whose favorite word was "fuck." When the streams of invective began to fly from my mother's mouth, the cops couldn't take cover fast enough.

I noticed that the duck running across Emma's ample chest was chasing through a field of poppies after a wayward red balloon.

"Very cute," I said, pointing at him. "He'll never catch the balloon, but he's got a good chance at that streak of catsup. And what's that yellow stuff? Mustard?"

My mother glanced down. For a moment, I was afraid that she might peel some off and taste it. "Probably. I had a hamburger at the Toot and Tell It."

"When was the last time you did laundry, Ma?"

She shrugged. "It was clean when I put it on this morning." Fixing me once again with her paint-stripper stare, she said, "Never mind my clothes. Do you know what time it is?"

I glanced at my naked wrist. I never wore a watch. "Half past a freckle?"

"I hate it when you ride that motorcycle. You dawdle. How long can you stay?"

"I don't know. I promised to grout the bathtub tonight."

"So that's what you people call it." She laughed like a gurgling drain and took a final drag on her cigarette. When the glowing ember reached the filter, she tossed the butt down to join its friends.

"How long have you been sitting out here?" I asked, gazing pointedly at the pile of butts.

"Half an hour. Maybe longer," she lied.

"You're going to wind up in an iron lung."

"Yeah, yeah, so enough about me." She stood up. "Where's Sylvie?"

"She stayed home to watch a documentary on PBS."

"You lie like a rug. You humiliated her with all of your naughty sex talk. I'm sure she's embarrassed to death. She'll never want to come out here again."

"Right. Where's Dad?"

My mother stopped smirking and her face took on a strange expression, something between wounded and chagrined. "Bil," she said portentously, "I have something to tell you."

For just a second, my heart plunged into the icy depths of my stomach. Had my father actually left her? Emma was hard to live with, and Sam had been nearly impossible. Had Hugh finally snapped? I'd read that the loss of a child sometimes led to divorce. True, Sam was no longer a child, and they'd had seven years to prepare themselves, but death affected people in unpredictable ways. For God's sake, if Hugh divorced Emma, I'd become a weed-smoking insomniac permanently.

These painful meanderings came to an end when I recognized the look on Emma's face. It wasn't chagrined; it was shifty. In fact, it was nearly identical to Sam's toothy grin. The resemblance was a triumph of nurture over nature.

"What?" I asked suspiciously.

Emma took a deep breath. "This," she began heavily, "is your childhood home. I know how you feel about it. Your father and I had hoped that you and Sylvie might move out here someday to raise your own family. Lots of gay and lesbian couples are having children. There's no reason you two can't—"

I held up a hand. "Stop. Are you nuts?"

My mother changed gears. "You know the old Kornmeyer place?" she asked. I shook my head no. "Yes, you do. Two hundred acres, just over the ridge." She gestured toward the hillside behind our house. "It's been on the market for years."

"So?"

"Your father and I have bought it."

I heard the words, but they didn't make sense. "You what? Why?"

"Because we're tired of living across the road from those anhydrous ammonia tanks. It was fine when it was just a gravel pit over there. The dust was terrible, and the stink of diesel fumes from all those rumbling trucks, but it was only in operation for four months out of the year. Everything changed when they began renting to that fucking Ag Chemical business. Look at that eyesore, Bil."

I looked. The gravel pit across the road had been in operation for twenty years, cutting a deep, dark scar into the basalt flow of the hillside. Though my father had planted a five-foot hedge in front of our house, it wasn't tall enough to obscure the blue and white chemical tanks of Robertson's Agricultural Supply. They loomed above the lilacs like metal giants.

"Your father and I have had it," my mother said quietly. "We went to the title company on Friday and closed the deal with Kornmeyer. We're moving."

I sat down on the ruins of a hanging porch swing. One of the chain hooks had pulled out of the boards above making the back left corner list sharply. I tried to remember how long it had been that way. Five years? Ten?

"I don't understand this, Emma. You've lived across from those tanks for five ages. You've spent so much time and energy petitioning the county, calling the EPA, harassing their delivery trucks... are you giving up?"

"I'm tired of losing," she replied. "And I need a change. Not a dramatic change. I'm not packing up and moving to the Mojave Desert. I just want some peace and quiet. I don't feel like fighting any more."

"Then it's time to call the embalmers," I said without thinking. "Oh, God, Ma. I'm sorry."

My mother laughed. "Don't look so crushed. It's all right. Ours is not a tactful family. We can't stop ourselves from talking about rope in a house where there's been a hanging." She lit another cigarette, and we sat in silence until she'd finished it.

"Thanks for not telling me over the phone," I said.

"You're welcome."

"I suppose you want my help telling Sarah and the others."

The shifty look reappeared. "Um, no," she said.

I stood up. "Damn it! Did you tell them first?" She opened her mouth to speak, but I shook a warning finger at her. "How long? And if you say, 'how long what,' I'll kill you and make it look like an accident. How long have I been out of the loop?"

"Naomi was with us at the closing," she admitted, adding defensively, "She is the family attorney."

"And?"

"And… We might have taken Sarah and Ruth out to lunch afterwards. But we weren't trying to leave you out. We just knew that you'd feel this more keenly than the others. They were older when we moved here. Ruth was sixteen. You were only six."

"Stop," I said disgustedly. "I'm going home."

She shrugged. "Suit yourself. I was kind of hoping you'd go with me to check out the new property."

"Why?" I demanded, towering above her in a way that I hoped was menacing. "Why would I want to go anywhere with you?"

"There's an old shack on the Kornmeyer place," she said. "No running water, no electricity. We were planning to knock it down and build something new, but..."

"But what? Martha Stewart won't give you planning permission?"

"But," she continued, "the shack is not abandoned. It's rented. Some fool has been paying Dick Kornmeyer eighty dollars a month to live in it."

"Ha! And you want me to help you deliver an eviction notice?"

"No," she answered calmly. "I want you to help me make sure that our tenant isn't dead. Kornmeyer says that the rent's three months overdue, and there's a funny smell coming from inside."

"Funny smell? Mother, you have pulled some shit on me, but if you think I'm going on a corpse-sniffing hunt with you, you are ten times crazier than I thought."

Emma cackled with glee. She ran her fingers up my arm in a creepy tickle. "Bugs. Worms. Maggots. Don't be such a pussy, Bil!

If the place even whiffs of putrefaction, we'll leave immediately and call the heat."

"The who?"

"The County Mounties, the PoPo, Johnny Law."

I shook my head. "I don't speak your language, oh stranger from another land."

Emma laughed. "The cops. The fuzz. Your friend, Donny."

"I'm still not going."

"Listen," she said. "It makes perfect sense. I own that property. It's mine. If there's a deadbeat tenant up there stinking out the place, I want to be the first to know. It's not like he's going to bite us, is it? We go, we look, we come back." My mother snapped her fingers in my face. "Easy!"

And just like that, I was swept away. I knew there must be good arguments against what she was saying, but I couldn't think of any.

"Jesus God," I said bitterly. "Sometimes, I feel like a Labrador retriever. I only dream that I'm thinking, but then you whip out the tennis ball, and the illusion is shattered."

"It's not that bad," my mother said soothingly. "You're much more like a border collie. A lot of shedding, but not so much drool."

Chapter 6

"Speak of the devil," Emma said as a long blue Buick pulled into the driveway. The car was vintage 1970s, as was its driver, a fat bald man in a dirty pair of Carhartt overalls.

"The devil who?" I asked.

"Dick Kornmeyer," she whispered as he walked toward us. "He's the richest man in Lewis County, and one of the most powerful. County commissioner."

"He dresses like a fucking bumpkin."

"Shut up," she hissed. "Hello, Dick. What can I do for you?"

"Not much," Kornmeyer bellowed. "I stopped by to talk to you about this year's CRP payment."

"The what?" my mother said.

"CRP," he repeated, even louder. "Conservation Reserve Program. I haven't cropped that land of yours in four years. Government pays me not to."

"How much?" Emma asked.

She lit up a cigarette and directed the smoke at Kornmeyer. He coughed a bit and reached behind his left ear. The resulting squeal told me that he'd turned on his hearing aid. Too cheap to do that much, I gathered. Didn't want to run down the batteries on the damn thing.

"Fifteen hundred," he said. "I thought we should prorate it. When CRP pays you for the full year, you pay me for January through July."

"You want seven months' worth of my CRP money," my mother said.

Kornmeyer reached behind his right ear and turned his other hearing aid on.

"Only fair," he said.

"You want me to give you eight hundred and seventy-five dollars."

"Only fair," he repeated.

38

"No," said my mother.

Kornmeyer adjusted both of his hearing aids. Now the squeal was horrendous. I stuck my fingers in my ears and shook my head.

"When will your husband be home?" Kornmeyer asked.

My mother's eyes narrowed. She stubbed out her cigarette in the driveway and took a step toward Kornmeyer. He moved back. The man was filthy from head to foot. His overalls were ancient, as was the dirt ground into the waist and knees, and his logger boots had the look of many a resole. This was the richest man in Lewis County? To judge by the stubble on his jowls, he was saving on razor blades too.

"You can come back when my husband is here," Emma said, "but don't think you'll get a different answer. We paid you a fair price for that land—more than fair, according to our attorney. We were stupid. We were in a hurry. We should have had the place appraised—by our own appraiser. You charged us an extra two hundred an acre."

Kornmeyer ignored this. He switched off the right hearing aid and asked my mother again when Hugh would be home.

"Tonight," she said. "About six. But don't bother to come out here. You can just call."

"I prefer to deal in person," Kornmeyer said.

"Fuck off," my mother replied.

"What?" Kornmeyer reached behind his ear but my mother's raised voice stopped him in mid-squealing adjustment.

"Save your batteries, you cheap bastard," she said. "Fuck. Off. Did you catch that?"

Kornmeyer caught that. He stomped off back to his car, hefted his bulk into the driver's seat, and drove off. Visible through the rear window, resting on the package shelf, was a collection of Beanie Babies—all kinds. A horse, a pig, a unicorn.

"What the fuck was that?" I asked my mother.

"A walking, talking agricultural subsidy," she said. "And the cheapest man alive."

* * *

"Let's go," Emma said, pushing past me. "I'm afraid we'll have to take that crotch rocket of yours. The house is at the top of a steep hill, and the driveway is overgrown with weeds. I don't think the Queen Mary will make it."

I glanced at my mother's old station wagon, which sat rusting in the driveway under a cottonwood tree. A small pool of oil glistened beneath the engine. The Queen Mary was ready for the boneyard. My mother shouldn't be driving it to town, much less up any insane Palouse hills.

"Wait," I said. "Why don't you just call the sheriff's department?"

Emma shook her head. "Your brother has been dead for less than a month and already you've forgotten. The cops, Bil Hardy, are not your friends."

"For God's sake, Emma. Donny Smith is my friend."

She stopped and stared at me. "We'll talk about that later. There are two reasons I don't want to call the fuzz. The first is that as of noon on Friday, Kornmeyer no longer owned that shack. It became the legal responsibility of your father and me. The second—and this is directly related to the first—is that the tenant is Jake Peterson."

"Jake Peterson," I repeated, recognition slowly dawning. "Not Jake the Snake? Sam's dealer? Oh God, Emma, there's no telling what he's got in that shack. Pot plants, a meth lab..."

"Exactly."

"But what if he's in there? What if he's not dead? What if he shoots us?"

Jake was a Vietnam vet, a Marine. He was also an old Moscow boy. He'd spent six years in Fort Leavenworth for selling dope. His brain was pickled, and I'd never seen him in anything but a pot-induced stupor, but Sam said that he had a bad temper. Jake also had a Swedish sniper rifle, a souvenir from the war. Sam had seen it and been mightily impressed. When I'd asked if Jake had let him fire it, he'd looked at me as if he were the Pope and I'd asked if he'd groped the Virgin Mary.

My mother laughed merrily. "Oh, for God's sake. I'm not afraid of Jake the Snake. I used to babysit the little bastard when I was a teenager. He was only three or four, a sweet little thing with a face like a flower petal. Who knew he'd grow up to be so fucking worthless? If he's in there—and if he's still breathing—I'm going to give him thirty days' notice and a chance to clear out whatever he's doing."

"If he's still breathing," I repeated.

"Yes," she agreed.

"And if he's not?"

"We'll remove and destroy any illegal substances, and then we'll call *your friend* Donny Smith."

"You don't need to sound quite so venomous. Donny's a good guy."

"And he's dating Suzy," she said. "Yes, I know. The fact that he's openly gay speaks well of him. However," she said and thumped me on the chest with a stubby finger, "he was your brother's jailer. He's also a great big Mormon from a great big Mormon family. His grandfather owns a massive cattle ranch down south of Riggins. The Smith family is richer than Croesus. Donny Smith is 'the man,' and don't you forget it."

"'The man'?" I asked, incredulous. "What are you, a Black Panther? I don't care if Donny's grandfather is First President of the Mormon Church. Suzy Parker-Smith is the most terrifying drag queen in the known universe, and Donny lives with her out in the great wide open. He takes her to sheriff's department picnics. Suzy went to the last one wearing a red and white polka-dot *I Love Lucy* dress."

"And so?"

"And so?" Now I was hopping mad. "Listen, you old, white, privileged bat. You're more 'the man' than Donny Smith. You're Mrs. I-Own-Two-Hundred-Acres. You're Mrs. Slum Landlord. We're on our way to evict your eighty-dollar-a-month Vietnam vet tenant. Unless, of course, he's dead."

"Hmm," she said calmly. "There is that. God, I hope he's not dead. I don't suppose we could call Donny. You'd be bound to blab, wouldn't you?"

My jaw fell open. "Blab?"

"Still," she went on. "As cops go, Donny's the only one I even remotely trust. Because of Suzy, of course."

"You've just... you can't..." I stammered. "You're not human. Who are you and what have you done with my mother?"

"Don't be silly," she carried on. "You know I like Suzy. Did you know that I'm teaching him how to sew?"

"Teaching him how to sew what? G-strings?"

"Quilts, actually. He's got quite an eye for color, and he can stitch fourteen to the inch. Must be his medical training. He was a Navy corpsman back in the eighties. Became a nurse when he got out."

All the wind went out of my sails. Being angry with my mother was like being angry with a tornado or a volcano or some other force of nature. It was also like being angry with a mental patient.

My father often said that my mother's thoughts were like streetcars—there was another one along every five minutes.

"Jesus, Ma. Tell me, did Kornmeyer know Jake the Snake was a dealer?"

"Kornmeyer." She scoffed. "That cheap farmer bastard. Do you know he tried to get your father to pay him Jake's overdue rent? Kornmeyer owns property around here worth millions, and yet he's willing to charge eighty bucks a month for a shack that ought to be pushed into the ground. No, I don't know if Kornmeyer knew or not. If he did, I'm sure he didn't care. Everyone's money is green."

"I don't like this, Emma. Hang on a second—what do you think you're doing?"

My mother had climbed onto the motorcycle and sat down. In the driver's seat.

"Here," she tossed me the helmet. "Do you have a spare?"

"No, I left the other helmet at home. You can't—"

"You forget," she interrupted. "I grew up riding these things. I know how they work. Now, hop on."

Typical. She hated me riding a bike, but she was a damned expert. With a mixture of aggravation and dread, I climbed on the back. Emma rocked the bike off the kickstand and leaned over, searching in the vicinity of her right leg.

"It has an electric start," I said, pointing at the button.

"Pussy bike," she muttered.

Engine noise drowned out my response. My mother spun the bike around in the driveway, spraying a rooster tail of gravel behind her, and we were off. Up the road two miles, around a ninety-degree turn—which my mother took at a terrifying clip—we screeched to a halt at the foot of a long slope and pulled onto the shoulder. I looked up. At the top of the hill stood a small, crooked house. A few flecks of white paint clung desperately to the clapboard siding which barely clung to the house. Several boards near the top had sprung loose and were curling out into the open air. As for the roof, it was a memory of shingles covered in places with rusty red tin.

I tapped my mother on the shoulder. "I don't see a driveway," I yelled.

She pointed to the ditch in front of us where someone had planted a four-foot metal stake with a broken orange reflector on top. If I looked closely, I could just make out the beginnings of two deep, dry ruts. The grass that grew around them was at least waist-high. I tapped her again.

"No way. We're not riding up that."

She revved the engine and plunged forward, bouncing me off the back of the bike and into the grass. She stopped and switched the engine off.

"Break anything?"

"Only my ass," I replied tersely. "It's got a crack in it."

Cackling with glee, she climbed off the bike and offered me a hand up. I waved her away. "Forget it. I don't want your help."

"Suit yourself."

My mother on a mission was a sight to behold. Despite the fact that she was short, fat, and smoked like a chimney, she climbed up the hill like a mountain goat. I followed along in her wake, stopping halfway to pant for breath. I'd already twisted my ankle by stepping in a gopher hole, but I got my revenge when Emma fell ass-over-teacup into a patch of Scotch thistle. She stood up and brushed herself off.

"Stop laughing," she said. "Can you feel that?"

"If you mean ticks, yeah. They're probably crawling all over us."

She shook her head. "No. Feels like something buzzing or humming."

There was a noise like the sound made by high-tension power lines, but there were no power lines in sight. "You're right," I said. "What is that?"

"I don't know. Something's not right here. Look at this grass—no one's driven up here for a while." She pointed back down the hill. "Jake must park at the bottom and walk up."

"Wouldn't you?" I asked, rubbing my sore backside. "This would be hell on your shock absorbers. I don't think you could drive it at all in the winter."

We continued up the hill. On closer inspection, the house looked even worse than from a distance. All of the windows were boarded up, and some had pieces of roofing tin nailed over them. The front window was covered with the gold boomeranged drop leaf from a fifties Formica table. Though it hadn't rained since April, the front porch looked waterlogged. It sagged away from the house as if it were hoping to slide down to the road and hitchhike to Georgia.

Emma and I looked at the porch and then at one another.

I said, "'Last night, I dreamt I went to Manderley again.'"

My mother laughed. "Very nice," she said and continued the quotation. "'It seemed to me I stood by the iron gate leading to the drive, and for a while I could not enter, for the way was barred to me.' Then something about spirit possession."

"I forget," I said. "I used to know the whole first paragraph by heart."

"An excellent book. I love the movie, too. I think the woman who played the housekeeper, Mrs. Danvers, was in your club."

"Was she?" I asked, still contemplating the rotting porch. "Dame Judith Anderson. Given a choice, I think I'd rather have Joan Fontaine."

"You do have Joan Fontaine," my mother said. "Sylvie looks quite a lot like her. You keep your eyes on that prize, Bil Hardy. You are very, very lucky. I'd be sorry if you two broke up. And, of course, I'd miss you."

"Yeah, yeah," I said. "You know, sometimes you're a little too supportive. You're kind of a PFlag Hag."

"Ungrateful child. So," she asked facetiously, "who weighs less, you or me?"

"I'm a hundred and fifty pounds, not counting my boots."

"Well, unless your boots weigh another thirty, you're the lightest. Up you go."

I reluctantly mounted the rickety steps and stepped across the groaning porch boards. The front door was padlocked. I knocked loudly, a couple of times. I hollered, "Hey, anybody home?" I felt like an idiot. Finally, I tried the handle. It didn't turn, probably because it was rusted in place. I examined the padlock. It was new, or at least it wasn't as rusty as the hasp it was attached to. Several pairs of old tennis shoes were lined up next to the door, along with a five-gallon glass carboy, a bicycle frame, and a coffee can full of surprisingly shiny nails.

I pounded on the door again, just in case. It was in the pause afterward that I heard the music. I held very still.

"What is it?" Emma whispered.

"It's Frank Sinatra, 'I'll be seeing you,'" I said.

Emma put her foot on the bottom step. It screamed in protest. "See if you can pull a board off one of those windows."

"With what, my bare hands?"

"Oh, out of my way."

Though I feared for my life, the porch held us both. Emma examined the windows on either side of the door and, picking the one covered by the drop leaf, wedged her fingers under the edge and gave it a mighty yank. It didn't budge. "Damn it," she said. "Would you look at that?"

She'd driven a long splinter into the pad of her index finger.

"It'll probably turn septic," I observed. "When was the last time you had a tetanus shot?"

"I'll soak it in peroxide when I get home." She sniffed the air. "Can you smell that? Kornmeyer was right. Something definitely stinks."

I tried to place the odor. "A cat?" I suggested.

"Cats," she corrected. "Multiple. Twenty-seven of them, all using the same dirty litter box."

"Ah, shit," I said. "I told you Jake was probably running a meth lab. This place reeks of ammonia." I sniffed again, and after a moment's consideration, I said reluctantly, "I think there's something else as well."

"Sickly sweet and pungent? Kind of nauseating?" When I nodded, my mother said, "Put your shoulder to that door, Bil."

"I can't, Ma. It's illegal."

"I own this opium den," she replied. "We're going in."

It was no use arguing. I did as she asked, giving the door a tentative push. It moved a little. I shoved harder and then harder again. The next thing I knew, the door and the door frame were lying on the floor of the shack, and I was lying on top of them. A cloud of dust and rotten wood billowed up around me, and a rusty old wheelbarrow dropped onto my back. I coughed until I was blue in the face.

My mother stepped through the hole, over me, and over the door. She lifted the wheelbarrow and shoved it aside.

"Who keeps a wheelbarrow in the house?" I demanded.

"A meth-making bum," said Emma. "Upsa-daisy!"

She took my hand and pulled me up hard.

"Wait," I said. I think I'm caught on the handle of that—" a loud ripping sound followed by a rush of air told me that I'd lost the ass of my jeans. "Fucking wheelbarrow. Goddamn it!"

Emma laughed. "Here, bend over so I can brush the spiders out of your hair. Don't panic—I'm just kidding. Don't worry about your pants. Your father will have something you can borrow."

My father was only a little bit taller than my mother and just as round. "I'll take a pair of Sam's, thanks."

"Not possible, I'm afraid. I gave his clothes to the Cowslip Food and Clothing Bank." Catching my look, she went on defensively, "And what I couldn't donate, I sold to Johnson Pawn. Close your mouth. I gave the money to the food bank as well. It's what your brother would have wanted. He was always volunteering there."

"Volunteering? That's a stretch. He was sentenced to community service."

We waited for the dust to settle and peered into the gloom. For a shack, the small living room was surprisingly homey. There was a plaid loveseat, a coffee table, and a wooden magazine rack filled with copies of *National Geographic*. An end table sat next to the sofa, and on top of that was a half-filled cup of coffee. A perfectly round patch of green mold covered the surface like wall-to-wall carpet. It glowed in the gloom, illuminated by a halogen floor lamp plugged into an orange extension cord.

"I thought this place didn't have running water or electricity."

"That's what Kornmeyer told us."

I followed the extension cord. It ran along the left side of the room and through a hole cut into the wall. "There's another door here, but it's padlocked. This is where the music is coming from. The urine smell, too." I sniffed the air and then had to stifle my gag reflex.

"Something is definitely dead in there," my mother declared. "Can you force the door?"

"No," I said firmly. "I can't. I bruised my ass, ripped my pants, and did something awful to my shoulder. You can knock it down yourself if you want to, but I'm not doing it."

"Christ on a cracker, Bil. What if he's hung himself?"

"Come on," I said. "Let's go around back. Maybe there's another way into the house."

I fought my way through four-foot-tall weeds to a plywood lean-to that had been tacked onto what I assumed was the kitchen. Piled in front of and around the door were old pots and pans, dirty rags, stacks of newspapers, an old mattress, and about half a cord of firewood. I pulled the rubbish and loose wood aside, getting a few splinters in the process, and yanked on the warped back door. I didn't find the kitchen entrance, but I did find the source of the buzzing noise.

"Jesus Christ," I said, immediately slamming the door. "That's the biggest wasps' nest I've ever seen. Ouch!" I slapped a wasp on my arm just as another one stung my right cheek. "Fucking hell!"

"Get out of there, you idiot," my mother said.

I scrambled up over the newspapers and mattresses and scratched at a third sting on the back of my hand. "Goddamn it,

Emma! I cannot wait for the day when I get to pick your nursing home."

"Ha," she said. "You won't get the chance. I'll shoot myself first." She swatted at a couple of wasps that were buzzing around my head. "Come on," she said. "You're attracting the things. Look around here on the other side. See? There's a nice path, a little covered storage area, and—oh yes, a gas-powered generator."

"And the fucking back door," I remarked bitterly.

"I'll get that, shall I?" asked Emma.

My mother, who was often as lucky as she was dreadful, tried the handle. The door opened smoothly. The hinges didn't even squeak. "I found the source of the music," my mother said. She sailed through the open door as if she were delivering a gift basket. She soon came back out with her hand over her nose.

"Good God," she said. "Dead coyote."

I lifted the neckband of my T-shirt up over my nose. This served the dual purpose of hiding my smirk and filtering out the dead animal smell. I stepped past Emma and into the room. It was a dead coyote, all right. It had a bullet hole in its head, and someone had nailed it up on the closed door leading into the living room. I couldn't tell how long it had been rotting in the August heat. The skin had pulled away from the jaws, exposing the teeth in a horrible grimace. As I stepped closer to take a look, the corpse twitched.

"Holy fuck!"

I jumped back, knocking over a Formica table stacked with Mason jars. A small transistor radio crashed down with the glass and began to hiss.

"What's the matter?" Emma yelled. "Are you okay?"

"No!" I yelled back, rubbing my hip where I'd banged it on the table. "You and your bright ideas. Remind me never to answer my phone again."

"Just get on with it," my mother said. "The sooner in, the sooner out."

The Formica table was clearly the source of the drop leaf nailed over the front window. Carefully, I picked up the radio and gave it a shake. It crackled back to life. Frank Sinatra had finished crooning and Peggy Lee was now singing "Why Don't You Do Right?"

The coyote was definitely moving. Its stomach was hugely distended, and gas was escaping from mouth and backside in low, horrible, intermittent rumbles. I tried breathing through my mouth, but I could still smell it. The mix of death, gas, and urine was overwhelming.

"It stinks like a meth lab," I said over my shoulder. "And a coyote mausoleum, and a public toilet. I don't see any evidence that he's been cooking meth here, though. No hotplates, no flasks, no empty Sudafed boxes."

"What about all of that broken glass?"

"Jars," I said. "Canning jars."

"Uh-huh. And the urine stench?"

"I don't know. Maybe he pees in here. Maybe he pees in jars." I shut the door behind me and pulled my T-shirt back into place. "Man, that was nasty. Who would do that to a coyote?"

"Jake Peterson," my mother replied. "Coyotes are vermin. It's always open season on them. Or perhaps it was a disgruntled customer." She lit a cigarette. "I'm going back out front to look around a bit more. Are you coming?"

"No, thanks. I've had enough. I'll wait for you down the hill."

In the ten minutes or so it took Emma to complete her snoop, I took stock of my injuries. The wasp stings had begun to swell. The ones on my cheek and the back of my hand burned like mad, and I seemed to have acquired one on my scalp. There was blood on the right sleeve of my T-shirt and I lifted it up to find a three-inch scrape. My jeans were unsalvageable. I tucked the torn flap into the waistband of my boxer shorts. No way it would hold on a motorcycle ride back to town. Given the state of my backside in general, I'd have to leave the bike at my parents' house and get Emma to give me a lift home in the Queen Mary. What had begun as a lovely day—sexual gratification followed by bacon and pancakes, followed by more sexual gratification—had turned into a wretched afternoon of physical pain and breaking and entering. It was as if Sam had never left us.

I moved into the shade of a nearby birch tree and gingerly sat down. Though it was only a few degrees cooler, it felt nice. A blackbird sang in the branches above my head, and I felt my jaw relax. Up until that point, I hadn't realized I was tensing it.

Emma sauntered down the hill, smoking pensively. "I don't think Jake pees in a jar. I think he pees in a bucket," she said. "I found a white plastic container in a corner of the living room. That would account for the urine smell."

"How rustic. Was the bucket full?"

"I didn't look in it," she said. "I also don't look into the tissue when I blow my nose."

"You're a real lady. Listen, Ma, I think I'll wait here. You ride the bike home and then come back and pick me up in the car."

Chapter 7

"'Everyone that passeth by her shall hiss and wag his hand,'" said Suzy.

"Go away. I'm not in the mood." It was after eight o'clock. Emma had dropped me off with a cheery good bye, and I'd hobbled my way up the stairs wanting nothing more than a few bushels of Sylvie's sympathetic attention and a good night's sleep.

"'Awake, ye drunkards, and weep; and howl, all ye drinkers of wine.'"

"I am not drunk," I said, rounding on him. "And you can stop spouting the Bible at me. What's gotten into you, anyway? The holy parakeet?"

"That's Paraclete," Suzy corrected. "Oh wait, you were making a joke. Ha, ha. A learned joke, I must admit. There's hope for you yet. If we could just clean you up and hand you off to The Church of the True Vine, I'm sure they could cure you of your unnatural desires."

"What do you want, Suzy? Apart from a pearl necklace to complete your very fetching ensemble."

Suzy swished obligingly, showing off his neat shirtwaist dress, complete with flouncing skirt and shiny black pumps. He looked like Donna Reed with an Adam's apple.

"Thank you for noticing," he said. "You, on the other hand, look a little the worse for wear. And you seem to be wearing Danny DeVito's pants. What have you done to yourself?" He took my chin in his hand and subjected me to an intense nurse's scrutiny. "What's this on your face? And your arm? Calamine lotion?"

"They're wasp stings," I said. "So yes, it's Calamine. Now, if you'll excuse me, Sylvie is waiting."

"No, she isn't. She's gone out with her mother. She left you a note."

"How do you…"

"Well," he drawled, "I'm psychic. Also, I saw Kate come up, and then I heard Sylvie say, 'I'll just leave Bil a note.' Now, why don't you come over to my place and we'll wash off this ridiculous Calamine? It's for chicken pox, not wasp stings. I'll put some Benadryl cream on them, and then you can help me with a little problem."

I allowed myself to be led into Suzy's den of iniquity. It was truly tasteless, from the darkly paneled walls to the tartan plaid sofa. A flock of wooden geese with brass wings flew above the fireplace, an ornate cuckoo clock chimed the half-hour, and a bearskin rug, complete with head and claws, rested on the floor.

"Sit down," he said, shoving me onto the sofa, "and let Nurse Parker-Smith do her thing."

He disappeared into the bathroom and emerged a minute later with an enormous tackle box. This he opened to reveal three trays of gauze, alcohol swabs, and ointments galore, as well as a wide selection of prescription pill bottles. I picked one of these up.

"Tetracycline, five hundred milligrams. Got any Valium?"

"Yes. Five milligrams. But don't ask, you're not having any." He wiped off the Calamine with a wet washcloth and daubed on some white cream. "Now, let's have a look at that shoulder. No, don't think you can hide from me. I *am* an emergency room nurse."

"Yes, I know. But you're off duty. Ow, that burns!"

"It ought to. It's alcohol. Heavens above, what have you done to yourself?"

"I've been visiting my mother."

He tsked mildly. "That dreadful Emma. If you weren't so old, I'd call Child Protective Services. There, a little Neosporin and a Band-Aid. Any place else you'd like me to kiss and make better?"

"Yeah, my sore ass."

It was a joke I soon regretted. Suzy took hold of the back of my trousers and flipped me over face down on the sofa. As my pants were only held up by a belt and a prayer, he had them halfway to my knees in five seconds flat.

"You've done this before, haven't you?" I said.

"Oh my Aunt Fanny!" he hollered. "Property of Sylvie Wood? When did this happen? My God, does she know?"

"Of course she knows," I snapped. "We don't get undressed in the dark."

"Too much information," he announced. He swept a practiced hand over my ass, slapped me lightly, and yanked my pants back up. "You'll live. Some nasty scratches, a few ugly contusions, and a ridiculous tattoo. My diagnosis? The scratches will heal, and the bruises will fade. As far as that tattoo is concerned, you're fucked. I recommend that you avoid bicycle riding, miniskirts, and mooning."

I sat down gingerly. "I want a Valium, Suzy, and I want it now. Why do you have all those drugs, anyway? I'll report you to my sister Ruth."

"She'll laugh in your face," he replied. "Every nurse on earth has a tackle box just like that one. Now, don't you want to know why I dragged you in here?"

"You mean apart from the insults and the vicious first aid? No. Can I have a beer? Hugh only had one left in the fridge and my mother wouldn't give it to me."

"Oh please," Suzy said. "I live with a Mormon. Do you think I'm allowed to keep beer in the fridge? What if the angel Moroni stopped by and went looking for a glass of milk? I keep a bottle of medicinal vodka under the bathroom sink. It's behind the spare rolls of toilet paper."

"Fine. I like mine with three cubes of ice and a twist of lemon."

Suzy glanced at the cuckoo clock. "Donny's on night shift," he said. "He won't be home until after three. I think I'll join you."

As he crashed around in the kitchen, banging the ice cube tray on the counter and singing to himself, I conducted an inventory of his drug supply. Amoxicillin, Etodolac, Lomotil—if I ever had a sinus infection, arthritis, or diarrhea, I knew where to come.

I closed the tackle box. According to Ruth, Suzy was an excellent nurse. He had years of experience working trauma in Seattle, so he was a dab hand when it came to car wrecks, kids with the flu, and hunting accidents—the stuff that made up the bulk of Cowslip's hospital emergencies. Suzy and I had met two years previously when he'd come to town with a group of political activists to help organize opposition to Proposition One. It was then that he hooked up with Donny Smith, a closeted Mormon cop. Suzy fell madly in lust. Violins played, worlds collided, and he never went back to Seattle. They seemed very happy together. Donny was big, beefy, and earnest. Suzy was so fey he probably had to weight his shoes to keep from floating off the ground. Theirs was a definite case of opposites attracting.

Under Suzy's spell, Donny had come roaring out of the closet. He seemed to be dealing pretty well with his colleagues' homophobia and his family's shock. Two of his four sisters were still speaking to him, and one of his five brothers had just sent him a birthday card. He still had some trouble with his own internalized homophobia, though. He had pretty rigid ideas about gender. If I asked to borrow a wrench, Donny would instead come over and fix what was broken. Letting him clear a nasty hair clog out of our bathroom drain seemed to have cured him of that, at least temporarily.

Donny was macho in a soft and squishy sort of way and, strangely enough, I think it helped that Suzy was a drag queen. Although to be frank, Suzy wasn't much of a drag queen. He looked more like a transvestite who didn't give a damn. When Suzy got a job in the emergency room at Cowslip Memorial, I was disappointed to discover that he wore green scrubs and tennis shoes. I'd half expected him to head off to work dressed like Corporal Klinger from *M*A*S*H*.

Suzy came out of the kitchen bearing two vodka tonics in Burger King glasses.

"What," I said, laughing. "No silver tray?"

"Shut up and drink," he said. "Listen, I want you to look over a little e-mail for me. Do a bit of editing."

"Why?"

"Because you've got a Master's in English and a tongue like a machete." He picked up his drink and led the way to a computer desk in the front bedroom. While we waited for his modem to connect, he said, "I've joined the Slip-Fifty listserv. You know it, don't you?"

I shook my head. "I don't do chat groups."

"Honey, you should. Once you get started, they're like crack cocaine. Slip-Fifty is a community chat group, a bunch of local citizens trying to imagine what Cowslip will be like in the year 2050. That was the original idea, anyway. Now, it's just a place for the hippies to argue with the fundamentalists. It was your mother who got me onto it. She's been fighting an online war with Old Man Knox for about three months now, and she's called upon me for some Biblical reinforcement. I've been lurking for a while, but this is my maiden voyage, so to speak. My very first post."

Suzy was the son of a Pentecostal minister. That my atheist mother would ask him for Bible help didn't surprise me. Neither did the fact that she and Suzy had joined forces to fight the predations of religious fundamentalism. What did surprise me was that my mother was using e-mail.

"Emma can't set her own alarm clock," I said. "She's practically a Luddite. How did she get onto the Internet? Does she actually have an account? Shit! She's not using my dad's university account, is she?"

Suzy laughed. "No, she's not using your dad's account. Do you think he'd be stupid enough to give Emma his password?"

I relaxed. "Explain, if you would, how all this got started. My mother doesn't know how to use an ATM card. What the hell is she doing on the computer?"

"I taught her," Suzy said proudly. "In exchange for sewing lessons. About six months ago, when your brother was in the ICU with bacterial pneumonia, I used to stop by and check on Emma. Just to make sure she was eating, keep her company, that sort of thing. It was always late at night after the rest of you had gone— those awful hours between three and five in the morning. One night we were talking and I said that I wished I could sew. She said she'd teach me. I asked what I could teach her in return, and she said I could teach her how to use e-mail. She said your father had just bought a new computer that he claimed was for both of them, but clearly that was bullshit. She didn't know how to log on, and she wasn't about to ask him. I guess they'd had some sort of fight about word processing back in the dark ages, and she didn't want to revisit that. Do you know that she's been typing all of her college papers on some old Smith Corona?"

Well, yeah, I did know. When we were kids, Sam and I asked our parents for a computer. We wanted to play games—really sophisticated stuff like King's Quest. My mother, Sarah, and Naomi all wanted a new typewriter. Sarah was in high school and Naomi was in college. Hugh sided with Sam and me while Emma sided with Naomi and Sarah. Ruth broke the deadlock. Hugh bought our first computer, and Emma bought a typewriter. Long past common sense and ordinary reason, the stubborn ox had refused to learn word processing.

I pulled an ice cube out of my glass and ran it over the stings on my arm. "What I don't understand, Suzy, is why my mother didn't ask me. When I was an undergrad, I worked in the English Department's computer lab. It was my job to teach people like Emma how to use e-mail. I would have taught her anything she wanted to know."

"Oh," Suzy lied. "It's embarrassing to ask your kids to teach you things." When I let this pass, he went on quickly, "I have to say, she took to it like a duck to water. In no time at all, she was surfing the web, researching things, finding out information. Then she got hooked up on this Slip-Fifty listserv. It's addictive—all of the town gossip appears there first. Emma told me about it and I logged right on. Until your mother came along, The Church of the True Vine were holding forth unchallenged on matters of feminism, theology, and politics. Your mother let 'em have it."

"Does this list have an archive?"

"Sure. Do you want to see?"

I held up my empty glass. "Another one of these first, I think."

* * *

My mother wasn't just a frequent poster to Slip-Fifty. She was a terrible list hog. Four, five, six posts a day, most of them sent between ten p.m. and two a.m., and almost all addressing the various goings-on at The Church of the True Vine. Emma had dug up some astounding dirt. George Knox had been drummed out of the Army in the early seventies, dishonorably discharged. Green Tree Ministries was not his first pastoral appointment. He'd led some evangelical church in Mississippi until he'd been caught with his hand in the collection box. Finally, he was self-taught and self-ordained. My mother took great glee in pointing out that the only credential Knox had was an associate's degree in electronics from some half-assed technical college.

Emma seemed to have read most of The Root of Jesse Press publications, and she quoted from them freely. George Knox maintained that it took the word of two women to counter the testimony of one man. He argued that wives and daughters weren't just subject to their husbands. They *belonged* to them. Any woman who didn't belong to one man belonged to all men. He compared single women who lived outside the care of their fathers to public toilets—and public toilets were the dirtiest, weren't they?

It was unbelievable stuff. Knox argued that slavery was Biblically appropriate and, as it had served to Christianize the African heathens, on the whole it had been a good thing. George Knox envisioned Cowslip, Idaho as the New Jerusalem. What was worse was that he pictured himself as the new Solomon and The Church of the True Vine as the third temple.

I read through Emma's posts and Knox's responses. My mother was right. George Knox was insane, and his followers were either lockstep toadies or deeply delusional, but Emma often looked like a loony herself. She relied heavily on personal attacks:

"Nice photo of you on the church web-site, Georgie-Porgy. Are you smuggling Bibles under that sweater, or are you just happy to see Jesus?"

She described Knox as a bloated, lard-assed, beached whale. She didn't bother to check her spelling or her punctuation, she hopped from non sequitur to non sequitur, and she cracked appalling jokes about the missionary position and onanism. She took a story Knox told about being anointed with oil and suggested he take a vat of it, fry up some doughnuts, roll them down Main Street and take a flying fuck at them.

Suzy refilled my glass twice. By vodka and tonic number three, I felt ready to help him with his post. George Knox was a complete shit-for-brains. He'd mistaken his dick for a flagpole, and when he whipped it out, he expected the whole world to salute. Reading him made me tired and angry, but Knox was not my mother. He was free to make an ass of himself, and good luck to him. Reading Emma made me want to edit every typo and correct every misspelling. I wanted to take the many kernels of good argument and polish them up like a military boot—a boot my mother could shove so far up George Knox's insidious, pompous ass that he'd taste Shinola for the rest of his life.

I turned reluctantly to the task of editing Suzy's post. I'd never read his writing, and I was afraid I might hurt his feelings. Fortunately, it was a pleasant surprise. Suzy was measured and thoughtful. He stuck to his point—that Biblical literalists were either obliged to believe many contradictory things, or that they had to pick and choose what to believe, just as they accused moral relativists of doing—and he cited reams of text from the King James version in support of his arguments.

The post took no time at all to edit, and when I was finished, Suzy handed me yet another drink. I said, "This is good work, Suzy, but why do you bother? People like George Knox never listen. They were born with their minds already made up."

Suzy looked thoughtful, or as thoughtful as could be expected of a drunken Donna Reed. "I don't know," he said. "I guess I don't like them thinking they own the Bible." He held up his drink and sloshed it for emphasis. "I can play sword drill with the best of them."

I shook my head and blinked in surprise. I'd become bleary-eyed. I held very still and waited for Suzy's face to come back into focus. "Sword drill? What's that?"

"It's when the Sunday school teacher calls out a chapter and verse, and the first one to find it in the Bible gets a point. It's called sword drill because 'the word of God is quick, and powerful, and sharper than any two-edged sword.' It's easy stuff for the preacher's kid, but... here." He picked a Bible up off his desk. "I'll go you one better. I'll turn my back. You pick out a chapter and verse at random, and I'll tell you what they are."

"Like what?" I asked. "In the beginning, God created—"

"No!" he shouted over his shoulder. "Flip through at random, put your finger on a verse, and read it to me."

"Okay. Um, how about, 'And the three hundred blew the trumpets, and the Lord set every man's sword against his fellow, even throughout to all the host.'"

"It's about Gideon," he said. "Judges. Chapter seven?"

"Wow."

He laughed. "Oh, don't be impressed. Once upon a time, I could have recited the rest of the verse as well. Now, I'd have to check."

"Don't give me that," I said. "You're amazing."

Suzy looked pleased. He sipped his drink.

"Do you ever miss it?" I asked. "You know, attending church and stuff."

He nodded. "All the time. I don't miss what my father preached—I don't miss that at all—but I do miss the fellowship, and I miss the emotion. A Pentecostal church is a passionate place. You get a good preacher, and the congregation is on fire. I miss the music, too."

If he hadn't looked so sad, I might not have done what I did next—or rather, if he hadn't looked sad and I hadn't been so drunk. I said, "Tell you what, Suzy. I'm going to perform an old party trick. Sit down on the bed and close your eyes, okay?"

I waited until he'd done as I asked. Then I paused, took a deep breath, and sang the first verse of "Farther Along."

"My God," he said, his eyes snapping open. "You're a soprano! Spinto or dramatic, unless I miss my guess. What's your range? Do you know?"

"Three octaves plus a bit," I replied. "I can sing A3 to C6 in full voice. Once I'm warmed up, I can hit low D."

"Two below middle C?" he asked excitedly.

"Yes. Is that what you mean by spinto?"

"Forget spinto. With that range, you're a dramatic. Don't you know the technical terms?" I shook my head. He explained, "A spinto soprano is fine and dandy, but a dramatic gets to sing all the best stuff. The final aria from *Madame Butterfly* or the role of Siegelinde in *Die Walküre*."

"You're losing me," I said. "I'm a fag hag, not an opera queen."

"We'll soon fix that," Suzy said. "You know your range. You must have had some formal training?"

"Not really. I know what the Cowslip High School music teacher told me and I know my way around a keyboard. Sam and I had a year's worth of piano lessons before Mrs. Anderson got frustrated and gave us the boot. After listening to my hallway rendition of the Bugs Bunny version of *Carmen*, the music teacher asked me to join the Glee Club. I thought she'd lost her mind. Me and glee?"

"Me and thee and glee," Suzy said, laughing. "Do you know any other hymns?"

"Of course. I'm a closet holy roller." I finished my drink and refused a refill. "Actually, when I was first coming out to myself, I got worried. My parents don't believe in God, but my grandmother is religious, and I wondered in a vague sort of way if there really was a hell. My first girlfriend was kind of a nut."

"Geraldine Hamish." Suzy nodded knowingly. "Big Presbyterian, big old dyke."

"Does everyone in this town know my business?"

"Oh, sweetie." He patted me on the knee. "That is ancient history. You survived, and she seems to have gotten over whatever hang-ups she might have had."

"No shit," I said. "It would be quicker to list the women in this town Hamish hasn't slept with than the ones she has. I think there are only two, unless Sylvie has a secret she hasn't shared with me. Anyhow, back when I knew Geraldine, it was grope and then pray. That got me worried, and so I used to sit up late at night watching Jim and Tammy Faye Bakker. In the end, I decided they were idiots, and I wasn't damned. The unfortunate side effect is that I came out with a secret love for gospel music, especially the Appalachian hillbilly kind."

Suzy clapped his hands with delight. "We used to sing 'Farther Along.' It's one of my favorites. Can you sing something else?"

"Sure. Make a request."

"Wait. Can you read music?"

"Yes."

"Excellent." He took my hand and led me back into the living room. On the wall opposite the fireplace was an upright piano. Suzy rooted around in the bench and pulled out a book of sheet music called *All-Time Greatest Hymns*. "Right," he said, flipping to a page near the back. "Can you sing that?"

"No problem."

Smiling happily, Suzy banged out the chords of "How Great Thou Art."

We played until the cuckoo chimed eleven and Mrs. Olafsson pounded on the ceiling with a broomstick.

"Let her call the cops," said Suzy. "My husband's the law."

"And Mrs. Olafsson is our landlady. Best not to piss her off. Besides, I'm getting hoarse."

"Okay," he agreed. "Besides, your honey's probably home by now. Although if she were, I would have thought she'd come over. She's bound to have heard us." Something in my expression must have given me away because he asked, "She does know about your hymn singing, doesn't she?"

I shrugged. "Sort of. I don't sing very often, and no one knows I sing hymns. I've only ever sung them to myself."

"That's a shame," he said seriously, "because you surely missed your calling. You could have been a soloist at my father's church, and that's not something we take lightly. You ought to treat Sylvie to an a capella concert."

"That might be a little difficult," I demurred.

"The religion thing make her nervous?"

"No, it's not the religion thing. It's the singing. And it's not her, it's me. Sometimes, when I hum along with the radio or just croon quietly to myself, Sylvie sings along, too, and..."

"And what?"

"Sylvie is a beautiful woman, Suzy. I love her to pieces. There's not a thing in the world that I wouldn't do for her."

"Except listen to her sing?"

I nodded. "She can't carry a tune in a bucket."

Suzy nodded sagely. "'Many waters cannot quench love, neither can the floods drown it.' Or so says the Song of Solomon. Don't you worry about that bucket. One of these days, you'll be old and deaf."

"Thanks for the cold comfort," I replied. "And the vodka." I stopped in the hallway and turned around. "She is perfect, you know."

"I know," he said. "So go home to her!"

Chapter 8

I crept back to my apartment, trying my best to look sober. I needn't have bothered because Sylvie wasn't home. She didn't come back until after midnight.

I'm ashamed to say that when I heard her key in the lock, I sat bolt upright on the sofa, where I'd been lying nearly comatose, and snapped, "Where have you been? Do you know what time it is?"

"Bil," she said, as if she were surprised to see me. "I've been out to dinner."

I blinked at her owlishly. My contact lenses were sticking to my eyelids, and I was having trouble focusing. Sylvie had a piece of rope in her hand, and tied to the end of it was what looked like a half-starved coyote. It sat patiently on the floor next to her and stared back at me.

I closed my eyes a few times, trying to clear my vision.

"What's that?" I asked stupidly.

"That," Sylvie said, "is a dog. I found it tied to the front doorknob."

"When?"

"Just now. How much have you had to drink?"

"Not much," I said. "Three vodka and tonics."

"Suzy?" she guessed.

"Suzy."

"Then it's more like six. He does a long pour. Bil, we can't keep this dog."

"No," I agreed. "But why would we?"

"Because this note was taped to the door." She handed me a dirty envelope on which was written:

This is your bother Sam's dog. We can't keep him no more. He needs some shots. He eats a lot. He has tapworms.

"My bother Sam," I said. "They got that part right. What is that thing? A dingo?"

"No," Sylvie said. She sat down next to me on the sofa. The dog sniffed at my feet and then curled up on the braided rug in front of me. "He's a German Shepherd, and he's four months old."

"What? A real German Shepherd? Not some misbegotten mutt?"

"Open the envelope," Sylvie said.

"Good gravy." It was a form for the American Kennel Club. I looked closely at the paperwork. "For a small fortune, I can register this creature. He's got a certificate of pedigree. His sire is Herr Siegfried von Crapenfuss, and his dam is... no."

"Yes," Sylvie replied. "His dam is Devouring Fire's Brunhilde. This animal," she said, patting the pup on the head, "is one of George Knox's dogs."

I read aloud. "Dog was born on March 25. Ownership transferred to Samuel Hardy by Calvin Knox on July 5." I looked up. "Sam was arrested on July 7 and his funeral was on the thirteenth. He couldn't have had this dog for longer than what? Two days?"

"Long enough to name him," Sylvie said. "Keep reading."

I read, and then I closed my eyes. "Jesus Christ. He named the dog Jesus Christ. My brother was such an idiot."

"His sense of humor was not subtle," Sylvie observed diplomatically.

I reached down and scratched the dog between the ears. He flinched at the touch of my hand. "Jesus Christ. Poor bastard. Who do you suppose left him here?"

"Calvin?" Sylvie suggested.

"No way. This dog has been washed." I leaned down and sniffed the top of Jesus's head. "Johnson's Baby Shampoo, I think. He hasn't had his shots, and he was tied to our doorknob with an old piece of what looks like clothesline. Besides, Calvin Knox can spell. Remember, his daddy runs a classical Christian school. Very snotty."

"Then I don't know," Sylvie said. "Perhaps it was a choir of angels."

"Ha ha. It was more likely some of Sam's old friends. Francie Stokes, maybe, or those two skanks he was hanging around with just before he died, Steve and Joe. They—wait! Sylvie, I know this dog!"

"You know Jesus Christ?"

"Yes. The last day I saw Sam, the day he blew up the sewer main—"

"And ruined our bathroom tile and the floorboards in the hallway."

"That day. Sam had this dog with him. He was with Calvin, Steve, and Joe, and I gave them all a lift to the hardware store. The dog sat on Sam's lap. He smelled awful, or Calvin smelled awful—someone or something stank. I rolled down the windows but it didn't help. You wound up having the truck detailed."

"So," Sylvie said to the dog. "You're the one who cost me two hundred dollars. No, don't suck up. Pay up." Jesus had begun washing Sylvie's fingers with his big sloppy tongue.

"Stop that," I told him. "That's my job. Good grief, what's this? A tick?" I plucked at a lump behind the dog's left ear. "No. Just some indefinable uck. Oh, man, it feels like dried liver."

"Here." Sylvie handed me a tissue. "Wipe it on this and go wash your hands. And when you come back, would you please bring the air freshener? Jesus may be freshly washed, but underneath the perfume, he still smells a bit like nasty dead thing. Probably rolled around on a dead squirrel."

"Typical Sam," I said. "He couldn't have saddled us with a nice Siamese cat, could he?"

When I came back from the bathroom, Sylvie was serving Jesus a late night snack in the kitchen. After he'd slurped up two mixing bowls full of water and devoured an entire package of hotdogs, he trotted contentedly into the living room and resumed his place on the rug in front of the sofa.

"Bil..." Sylvie said.

"I know. We can't keep him. He has tapworms."

"No, that's not it," she said. "We'll worry about Jesus later." Her forehead furrowed into a deep frown. "I had dinner with my mother tonight. She wanted to tell me that she's seeing someone, and that it's serious."

"Oh?" I tried to concentrate on what she was saying, but I was thinking about Calvin, my brother, and Jesus Christ, who was licking his front paws as if they were covered in beef gravy. The sound was disgusting, like a six-year old with a Slurpee. "Who's she seeing?"

"Captain Schwartz," Sylvie said.

I looked up. "Jesus Christ! No way!"

The dog barked.

* * *

We talked for half an hour, or, rather, Sylvie talked and I listened. I tried to listen sympathetically, but it was late. I was tired, half-drunk, and wasp-stung. I was also at a loss. I knew and loved Captain Schwartz, and I knew and loved Kate, Sylvie's mother. Sure, they were an improbable couple, but not impossible, or so I thought.

I said, "Your mom is dating Captain Schwartz, and she says she's happy. That's a good thing, isn't it?"

Sylvie's eyes lost their dazed look. With an almost audible snap, she focused on my disheveled appearance—the strange clothes, the red welts on my arm, the fact that I'd fallen asleep on the sofa with one shoe on. Then she spotted the note she'd left for me, the one I'd missed when I'd stumbled in. It was still taped to the lampshade. She plucked it off and handed it to me. I folded it in half without reading it and tucked it between the sofa cushions.

"When I came in, did you ask me where I'd been?" She spoke in a calm, even tone, but I wasn't fooled. Unless I answered very carefully, fur would fly, dishes would break, and shit would hit the fan.

"I know what you think," I said, affronted, "but I did not come in here falling down drunk. Yes, I had a couple of drinks with Suzy. I was injured before that. My mother bounced me off the back of the motorcycle. I was attacked by wasps, obliged to knock a door down with my shoulder, and... Are you laughing at me?"

"No," she lied, making a poor effort at controlling herself. She schooled her features into something that vaguely resembled sympathy. "Why don't you tell me what happened? I can see that Suzy has treated your wounds."

"How can you tell?"

She lifted the sleeve of my T-shirt. "Your shoulder is clean and bandaged and there's ointment on your wasp stings. You were over there hitting the vodka pretty hard, though, weren't you?"

"I told you, I only had three. When you hear my story, you'll see that I earned them." I gave her a brief summary of events, ending with, "And then Suzy caught me at the front door. He invited me in to do some editing. You weren't home and I lost track of time. I'm sorry. I hadn't planned on drinking the night away."

"It's all right," she said. "I shouldn't take it out on you. It's just... I need to fight with someone, and I can't fight with my mother."

"Why not?"

"Because we're not like you and Emma."

"Of course not." I put my arm around her shoulders. She leaned against me, and I smoothed her hair. "You and your mother are sweet, reasonable people who never go around breaking and entering."

She laughed. "That's not what I meant. I mean my mother and I don't communicate that way. We're not good at clearing the air. I love her, but we've never been very open with each other. She came and picked me up tonight, we had a lovely dinner, and then she said she had something to tell me and she hoped I'd be happy because she was happy. That's when she told me she was seeing Rebecca Schwartz."

"But you're not happy."

"No."

We sat in silence for several minutes. I was glad Emma wasn't a lesbian. My father would have made a damned ugly woman. Apart from that, it might have been nice to have some company in the family. Someone who really understood. Sylvie was a lesbian, and her mother was a lesbian. That seemed like a good thing to me.

The effects of the vodka were beginning to wear off and I felt tired and sore. I yawned. "So. Your mom and the Captain. It was kind of inevitable, don't you think?"

Sylvie sat up and glared at me. "What do you mean?"

"Nothing!" I held up my hands in mock surrender. "It's just that your mom came out two years ago. Since then, she's gone to a few dances, attended a few support groups, but she hasn't dated anyone. She's quite attractive—she looks like an older version of you—and here's her nearest neighbor, a woman who just happens to run a lesbian separatist women's collective and is also about the biggest dyke in Cowslip. The Captain and your mother are nearly the same age. They see a lot of each other in the ordinary course of events. Didn't it ever cross your mind that they might someday get together?"

"No," she said firmly. "It didn't. Rebecca Schwartz is... well, she's exactly what you said. She's the biggest dyke in Cowslip. More than that, she's like the poster lesbian for the Pacific Northwest." She stood up and began pacing. "Radical, separatist, promiscuous..."

"That's not fair," I interrupted. Unwisely.

"I know you admire her," she said. "What is it you're always saying—that she's your role model?"

"When I say that, I don't mean... I'm not suggesting..."

"That you'd like to sleep with every woman in the tri-state area?" she continued. "Change partners as often as you change your socks?"

"No! No, I don't want to do that, and Captain Schwartz doesn't... okay, she does, but she's fundamentally decent. She hasn't settled down, so to speak, but it's not like she's a nomad or something. She's lived in the same place for twenty years. So she's had a bit of spice in her life. Not everyone is cut out for monogamy."

"Spice? As in variety? If she had any more spice she'd be a curry."

I had to bite my lip to keep from laughing. "Sylvie, honey, why is this upsetting you so much?"

"I don't know, I don't know, I don't know." Suddenly, she looked as tired as I felt. She sat back down. "Why are you defending Captain Schwartz?"

"Force of habit," I assured her. I slid down the sofa and put my arm around her again. "Not because I want to be a curry, too. I don't want anyone but you. You know that. I'm a Lutheran potluck tuna noodle casserole—no spice at all. Just a little pepper."

Sylvie leaned back. Jesus got up and put his head in her lap. She sighed and scratched behind his ears.

"Stupid dog," she said. "Those pants are ridiculous, Bil. Is your dad really that short?"

"His legs are. Let me ask you something—and this is just a hypothetical question—how would you feel if your mother were dating someone other than Captain Schwartz?"

"Like who?"

I tried to think of the most upstanding lesbian I knew. No one local seemed to qualify, so I had to go national. "Susan Sarandon. I know, she's not a lesbian, but how would you feel if your mother were dating her?"

Jesus closed his eyes. One paw had crept up to join his head. It was only a matter of time before he wormed his way onto Sylvie's lap. I shoved him off.

"Come on." I encouraged her. "How would you feel?"

"Jealous," she said at last. "Susan Sarandon is hot."

"Off my arm, you hussy." We wrestled good-naturedly and Sylvie fell on top of me. "Careful of my injuries," I warned. She wriggled around for a bit, just to be annoying, before settling comfortably against me, her forehead resting on my cheek.

"I suppose you're right," she sighed. "My mother is fifty-one. She probably knows what she's doing."

"Probably." I let my hand, which had been resting on the small of her back, wander down to the lovely curve of her buttocks. "Do you know what I'm doing?"

"Striking out?" she suggested.

"Really?" I asked, aghast.

"No, not really." She stood up, pulling me with her. "Come on. I'd do anything to get you out of those trousers."

* * *

Just after two a.m., Jesus announced that he needed to go out. He whined and pawed at the bedroom door. Sylvie shifted in my arms and murmured, "I suppose we should be glad he's house-trained."

"It would be better," I whispered into her hair, "if he were potty-trained."

More whining and pawing.

"Bil."

"Hmm?"

"He's your bother's dog."

I gave up and swung my legs out of bed. "I'm not ready to put my contact lenses back in. Where are my glasses?"

Sylvie yawned and stretched. "Top of the bedside table. Left to your own devices, you'd toss them on the floor or in the laundry basket and never find them."

I leaned over and kissed her. "You're such a tidy soul."

"I'm a tired soul," she said. "Put your pants on, darling, and take Jesus Christ for a whiz. If he pees on Mrs. Olafsson's hardwood floors, she's going to kill us."

"Ha!" I said. "They're already ruined. Remember?"

With Jesus tied to his rope once again, I found myself walking the familiar path from my apartment to Pho From Home. The restaurant was officially open from noon until one a.m., but Vivian never knew when to quit. She was scrubbing the counter when I tapped on the glass of the front door. She motioned for me to come in, but I pointed at Jesus, who was sniffing the air with more than a passing interest. Vivian bustled around the counter and opened the door.

"What's that?" she asked, pointing at the dog.

"What does it look like?"

"Tomorrow's lunch special," she replied. "Ha! I got you! You're making stupid white face. You shock too easy, *ô-môi*. Come in, come in, and bring lunch special with you. If cops come by, we tell them you're blind. You want some *pho*?"

I did want some *pho*, but I shook my head. "No, thanks. I'm just taking Jesus Christ here for a walk."

"You name that dog Jesus Christ? You are *dien cai dau, ô-môi*. What's-his-name from the concrete octopus will come and get you for blasphemy."

Ignoring my half-hearted protests, Vivian put an enormous bowl of *pho* with sliced beef flank in front of me. Jesus got a bowl as well, only without the broth. He ate it like he'd never seen food.

"You starve him?" Vivian asked.

"No," I said between bites. "Someone else did. He's a stray and just arrived on my doorstep tonight. And I am not dinky-dow. That means insane, right?"

Vivian cocked her head to one side. "Good guess. It's more like crazy."

"Okay, I'm not crazy. And I should tell you that I looked up *ô-môi*. It's some weird kind of fruit. You have to break it open and suck out the juice. Apparently, it's an acquired taste. The thing I read said it had a peculiar smell."

Vivian crossed her legs. "Oh Bil, I am going to pee laughing," she said, gasping for breath. "*Ô-môi* is fruit—it's special fruit, just like you."

I paused with the chopsticks halfway to my mouth. "Do you mean gay?"

"Yes! Women are *ô-môi*. Men we call *bay-day*."

"Is *ô-môi* insulting?"

Vivian came around the counter and hugged me so hard that I dripped *pho* down the front of my T-shirt. "No! Gay women call themselves *ô-môi*. We have lots of women like you in Vietnam. You think you invent gay?" She stopped embracing me and slapped me hard on the back. "White people—you think you invent the wheel. You think you invent the noodle. You don't! We invent fireworks. We invent everything. You steal it and then you forget. Very convenient."

Jesus had long since finished his *pho* and was looking hopeful. Vivian took his bowl away and shook a finger at him. "Greedy guts," she said. "No more for dogs. Too much will make you sick."

I finished my own bowl. "Do you have any *ô-môi*?" I asked.

"Apart from you? No. It smells awful, like... uh..."

"If you say crotch, I'm leaving."

Vivian crossed her legs again. "I love you," she said, giggling like mad. "You make me laugh. If I didn't have a sexy young husband, I might take you away from your cute little blondie." She winked outrageously. "How is she? Does she know you sneak here to see me every night?"

"It's not every night," I said.

"No," Vivian agreed. "I'm closed on Sunday. Tell me about this dog. You get him tonight? Why?"

"He belonged to my brother. I don't know where he's been since Sam died. Someone left him tied to my front door with this bit of clothesline."

"What will you do with him? Keep him?"

I shrugged. "I don't know. Sylvie doesn't want a dog, and we live in a third-floor apartment. I'll probably try to find him a home."

Vivian shook her head. Her hair was short and dark with only a few strands of gray. Even when she wasn't hooting with laughter, and that wasn't often, she still looked amused. It was her eyes. They were a rich, dark, dancing brown, and the skin at the corners was perpetually crinkled. Vivian was short, but she was by no means small. She was as round and solid as a butterball and as sexy as hell. She projected complete self-confidence and total awareness and she had a talent for seeming completely absorbed in whatever it was she was doing: cooking, cleaning, talking, or listening. She was intense without making you feel uncomfortable.

She looked at me and then down at Jesus. "No, you won't find him a home. He has a home. He was your brother's dog. You will keep him."

"I don't see how."

"I do," she said. "You are stubborn, like me."

Chapter 9

The next morning, Sylvie half-dozed on one end of the sofa while I sat on the other end, reading the Cowslip police log. Our local rag, the *Cowslip Herald-Examiner*, printed the police log twice a week. Reading it was one of the great entertainments offered by our tiny metropolis.

Sylvie yawned. "Anything exciting? A stabbing? A riot?"

"Yeah, listen to this. It's under the heading Welfare Check," I said. "560 North Madison, Sunday, 7:35 p.m. Concerned reporting party requested that officers check on friend who had not been seen for several days. Officers complied and found subject was fine but suffering from a chest cold."

Sylvie planted her feet firmly in my lap and wiggled her toes provocatively.

"How much money does Donny make?"

"Thirty-six thousand plus benefits." I stopped petting Jesus and began stroking the sole of Sylvie's left foot. The dog gave a plaintive sigh and dropped his head onto his paws. "Six thousand more than he made as a sheriff's deputy working out in the county."

Sylvie said, "Clearly being a Cowslip cop is far more dangerous. Someone with a chest cold might cough on you. Tickle the other foot?"

"Of course. Coughing is not the only hazard, my sweet. Listen to this: we have here one, two... a grand total of five animal problem complaints. And here's another welfare check, one traffic hazard, and, oh, here's a good one," I said. "Monday, 11:15 p.m. A moose was reported wandering aimlessly through the Jackson Avenue housing development. Moose was pursued but eluded authorities. It was not apprehended." I looked at Sylvie. "Who would try to apprehend a moose?"

"Boris and Natasha?"

"Very funny. We also have a report of a headless black cat. Its owner seems to have put a black sock over its head and let it outdoors to frighten the neighbors. Here's a noise complaint—reporting party claimed it sounded as if upstairs neighbors were tap-dancing in bathtub. And then there's… Jesus Christ!"

"No," I said to the dog, "not you. Lie down. Here's one across the road from my parents."

I read aloud. "Tuesday, 4:00 a.m. Reporting party said vehicle with no headlights on entered gravel pit on Bryce Canyon Road and parked by anhydrous ammonia tanks at Robertson's Agricultural Supply. Vehicle was left running. Reporting party said she suspected vehicle's occupants were stealing product for manufacture of methamphetamine. She—" I stopped short. "That'll be Emma. What was my mother doing up last night at four o'clock in the morning?"

Sylvie, who'd worked her right foot up under my T-shirt, gave me a poke in the ribs with her toes. "You were up last night at four o'clock in the morning."

I glanced at her out of the corner of my eye. "So were you, but we weren't spying on a gravel pit. I never should have said I thought Jake Peterson might be running a meth lab. Now my mother's gone vigilante."

"Well…" Sylvie yawned again. "Since he wasn't home when you broke into his shack yesterday afternoon, I'm guessing that it wasn't him in the gravel pit. How are your various injuries this morning?"

I lifted the newspaper above my head and rotated my shoulder. "That's all right, and"—I wiggled back and forth in my seat—"my ass is sore but improving. How about you? Are you feeling any better?"

She stopped laughing and sighed. "I guess. I don't know, Bil. It doesn't really matter what I think, does it? My mother and Captain Schwartz are dating, and I'll just have to get used to it."

"Maybe not," I said thoughtlessly. "It might not last."

In the pregnant pause that followed, I had time to wonder whether the injury to my ass had caused permanent brain damage. I didn't want to try and save myself. I wanted to fold the police log into a paper airplane and fly myself out the window.

I said, "What I mean is, your mother might decide that Captain Schwartz isn't her type after all."

Sylvie drew her feet back and tucked them up neatly beneath her. A full retreat. I stood up.

"Why don't I make some coffee?" I suggested. "I can either poison my own or turn my back discreetly while you do it."

"I'm not angry," she said. "Not with you, anyway." She ran a hand through her hair and looked at me. "It's just... that's exactly why I don't want my mother going out with Captain Schwartz. It's not the dating I'm worried about. It's the after. If my mother takes the Captain seriously, if she thinks this might be permanent..."

"Do you know that she does?"

Sylvie shook her head. "She didn't say and I didn't ask. We had dinner. She asked how you were doing, I told her, and then she said she'd been seeing Rebecca. I actually said, 'Rebecca who?' My mother laughed and said, 'Rebecca Schwartz. The Captain.' I don't know what I said after that. Probably nothing. I was speechless. My mother talked about being happy and hoping that I'd be happy for her. We didn't talk about their relationship in any detail. We turned on the television, we watched the end of *All About Eve*, and she drove me back home. But Bil, she was positively glowing. She looked like... Bil! Don't make that face!"

"What face?"

"That speculative face. I know what you're thinking."

"Well, I... um... I expect they probably have... don't you?"

"I haven't given it any thought," she snapped.

"Okay!" I said. "It wasn't like I was giving it a lot of thought. She's your *mother*. I'm not a complete pervert. And are you going to yell at me every time we talk about this?"

"I wasn't yelling."

"No," I said. "You were doing that thing you do instead of yelling. That thing where your body goes all stiff, you glare at me, and your voice gets really loud."

The corners of her mouth twitched. Taking a chance on the hope that it was mild amusement and not an attempt to bare fangs, I stepped over the dog and stood next to her. "Honey, this is the second day of our summer vacation. My mother ruined day one. Is there anything we can do to keep *your* mother from wrecking day two?"

"There is." She took my hand and let me pull her to her feet. "You can take me to Wawawai."

"And Jesus?"

"I suppose he'll have to come, too. Bil?"

"Yes?"

"Do you think we could change his name? Call him Fido or something?"

"Are we keeping him, then?"

We both looked at the dog, who was gazing up at us expectantly. He was housebroken. He didn't bark. He was adorable—all legs and head and soulful brown eyes.

Sylvie tugged at my hand. "You're smitten with him, aren't you?"

I nodded. Silly tears were stinging my eyes and my nose had begun to itch.

"It's okay," she said. "I'll have a word with Mrs. Olafsson. She loves dogs. When I moved in, she had a horrible stinky poodle named Snuggles. It smelled like a dormitory urinal. If we put down a pet deposit and change his name, I think we'll be fine. Mrs. Olafsson is a liberal Lutheran, but a dog named Jesus Christ... she'd have a fit."

I felt wildly happy. I held her tight and kissed her thoroughly.

"Are you sure?" I asked. "He is sort of a child substitute."

Sylvie looked taken aback. "Do you want a child?"

I thought for a moment. "I don't know. Do you?"

"I don't know."

We both looked at Jesus again. He was smiling at us, his long tongue lolling out of the side of his mouth. "He looks like Boo Radley," I observed.

"Well, we can't call him Boo," Sylvie said. "Me and you and a dog named Boo? I hate that song. Why don't we call him JC?"

"JC," I repeated happily. "I like that."

"Good. Now kiss me again, and I'll go pack a picnic. In the meantime, you can take JC down to Animal Fair and buy him a proper collar and leash. Rolled leather is the best," she advised. "That's what my mother buys for her dogs."

Sylvie's mother was a millionaire a few times over, but I refrained from making this less than politic observation. "Any other commands, your majesty?"

"Yes," she replied. "Fifty pounds of good quality puppy food. No junk. Some dog biscuits, several chew toys, a bed, shampoo, nail clippers, and two large stainless steel bowls, one for food and one for water. Oh, and ask if they have any pills for 'tapworms.' Also roundworms, hookworms, and any other intestinal parasites JC might have acquired during his wandering in the wilderness. While you're gone, I'll make an appointment with the vet my mother uses for her dogs. S-H-O-T-S," she spelled.

I did a quick mental calculation. "There goes my half of this month's rent."

"I know," she said. "Just imagine how much a baby would cost."

Chapter 10

Wawawai, Washington, is a park on the Snake River about twenty-five miles from Cowslip. We often went there to climb the rocks, have picnics, and jump off the small cliffs into the ice-cold water. Along with the isolated top of Hayman's Butte, the sidewalk table farthest from the door at the Cowslip Café, and a particular tree in an old cedar grove called Traveler's Rest, Sylvie and I considered Wawawai to be one of "our" spots.

Halfway there, I began singing "Why Wawawai?" to the tune of "Why do fools fall in love?" This earned me a slap on the arm.

"Ouch," I said. "Remember my wasp stings."

"You're tough," she replied.

"And you're cruel." I leaned over and kissed her anyway, though first I had to shove JC out of the way.

"Watch the road," she advised, kissing me back.

"Tease."

"Horn dog."

"Good lord." I laughed. "Where did you learn that one?"

"From your best friend, Tipper," she said. "He warned me about you. He said you were insatiable."

"And?"

She wiggled her eyebrows lasciviously. "So far, so good."

The parking lot at Wawawai was mercifully not crowded. There were only three other vehicles besides ours. I didn't pay any particular attention to them, though in retrospect I should have. We made our way to one of the more secluded spots only to find my sister, Sarah, sunning herself on a beach towel.

"Jesus Christ," I said. The dog barked.

Sylvie laughed. "All we need is a cat named 'Fuck' and you'll be cured of your swearing."

I said, "Is there nowhere we can go to escape from my family?"

"I love you, too," Sarah smiled up at us. "It's nice to see you, Sylvie. How have you been? I wouldn't know because Bil never calls me unless she wants something."

"Ha!" I pointed an accusing finger at her. "Don't talk to me about calling. Why didn't you call me last Friday?"

She looked puzzled. "What about last Friday?"

"Who did you have lunch with and why?"

"Oh," Sarah said, realization clearly dawning. "That."

"Yes, that." I took Sylvie's hand and gave JC's leash a yank. "Come on, honey. Let's go somewhere less crowded."

"Where?" Sylvie asked.

"Anywhere," I snapped. "Away from this traitor."

Sarah laughed ruefully. "I'm sorry, Bil. Really. I didn't know anything about this property business until Emma called me at work and said that she and Dad wanted to take me out to lunch. As you know, I'll do anything for free food, so I went. You should have been there with us. I told Emma she was being stupid. She said she wanted to get you on your own to tell you, but you know how she is. When she gets an idea in her head, she can't be moved. I do think it's a good thing, though, don't you? Emma needs a project. Building herself a new house might be just the ticket."

"She's got a house," I pointed out. "What's she planning to do with that?"

This was something I should have asked Emma. Between the wasps, the attempted break-in, and the dead coyote, I'd somehow forgotten to find out what she and my father planned to do with my childhood home. The stricken look on Sarah's face told me all I needed to know. I was grateful for Sylvie's hand in mine.

"Where did you get the dog?" Sarah evaded.

"From our late brother," I replied. "A posthumous gift."

"His name is Jesus Christ," Sylvie said. "We've decided to call him JC."

"Wisely," Sarah observed. "Can you keep a dog in your apartment?"

I shrugged. "We'll find out. Tell me, Sarah, what is Emma going to do with the house?"

"Bil, I'm sorry..."

Whatever Sarah had been going to say was interrupted by the appearance of a tall, dark man with the thickest mustache I'd ever seen.

"Buck," Sarah said. Her voice was soft and honeyed. She stood up and kissed him lightly on the cheek. "This is my sister, Bil, and her partner, Sylvie Wood. Girls, this is Buck DeWitt."

Buck held out an enormous meaty paw. "Pleased to meet you, Bil," he said, smiling and shaking my hand vigorously. "And you, Sylvie. And who's this fine fella?" He reached down and patted JC so vigorously that the dog's head bobbed up and down like a car toy.

"This is the Son of God," I replied. Sylvie gave me the pointy elbow, but I didn't care. She was an only child and didn't understand the finer points of vetting your sister's boyfriends. "Jesus Christ. We call him JC for short."

"Good name. We had a pup called Sweet Jumping Judas. Must be a western thing." Buck squinted up at the sun. "Could it get much hotter? I feel like an earthworm on an electric fence."

I glanced over at Sarah. My sister was drop-dead gorgeous. Six feet tall in her stocking feet with dark brown skin, prominent cheekbones, and a rich, expressive mouth, she looked like a runway model. She might have been advertising lipstick in *Vogue*, something ridiculously expensive made out of crushed diamonds, mink oil, and the ashes of Grace Kelly. But she wasn't a model. She was a reference librarian at Cowslip University and she dressed like a Guatemalan bag lady. She was especially fond of the hemp clothing store, embellishing their thick green offerings with shoes, scarves, and enormous handbags in assorted neon colors.

Buck DeWitt was a good four inches taller than Sarah. It might have been six if his legs hadn't bowed. He was dressed like the Marlboro Man. Everything about him screamed Montana ranch hand. Despite the fact that it was late summer and he was visiting a swimming hole, he wore a long-sleeved plaid shirt, tight Wrangler jeans, and brown pointy-toed cowboy boots. I looked at my sister, hoping for some explanation of exactly who and what Buck DeWitt was, but she continued to gaze stupidly up at him.

"I'm sorry I'm late," he said. "I had a mare with a prolapsed uterus. Took forever to get the damned thing back in."

Sarah brought herself back down to planet Earth. "Buck is a veterinarian," she explained. "He specializes in horses."

"Oh, good," I said. "He's not an amateur gynecologist."

Buck laughed. Sarah giggled. I caught Sylvie's eye and we enjoyed a psychic moment. "Whoa, Nelly," we said telepathically.

"I've heard a lot about you, Bil," Buck said politely. "Sarah talks quite a bit about her family. So far, you're the first member of the Hardy clan that I've met."

"She's saving the best for last," I assured him. "You just wait until you meet our mother. How would you describe her, Sylvie?"

My girlfriend smiled. "Emma is wonderful. Smart, funny, politically active..."

"Loud, over-bearing, insanely nosy," I added. "You know how curiosity killed the cat? In Emma's book it doesn't matter because the cat died satisfied."

"She sounds like a hoot," Buck said.

"That's one way of putting it. I have to say that it's really nice to meet you, Buck. We rarely get to meet any of Sarah's friends. She's very secretive about... some things."

"Bil," Sarah warned. "Enough. I told you she was a joker, Buck. Still, she does yeoman's work with our mother, so I suppose I owe her."

"Speaking of," I continued, "what were you going to say about the house? Whatever it is, I'm not going to like it, am I?"

Sarah frowned. "No, you're not. They've already sold the house. To Robertson's Chemicals."

I waited, hoping she might be cracking some kind of cruel joke. Robertson's had offered to buy my parents out half a dozen times, usually after Emma had filed yet another petition against them with the county. Each time they made an offer, my mother would come up with some graphic directive about what they could do with their dirty money.

"Emma sold to the enemy?" I asked, incredulous. "When?"

"About a week after Sam died," Sarah said. "Robertson's offered them the appraised value of the property plus ten percent. That was how they could afford to buy the Kornmeyer place. They paid cash for it. They'll use the equity to take out a construction loan to pay for a new house."

"And in the meantime?"

"In the meantime..." she hesitated. "Emma should have told you this, Bil. In the meantime, they're renting our old house from Robertson's."

I took a deep breath. "Let me get this straight. Our parents are paying those evil, polluting, soul-destroying bastards for the privilege of living in their own house?"

"Not technically. The house belongs to Robertson's now. I'm sorry."

I shut my eyes. If I concentrated on my anger, with any luck, I wouldn't cry. "Sarah, how could she? We grew up there. Sam grew up... that was our home."

I opened my eyes. My sister and I looked at each other for a long moment, letting the loss of Sam float in the air between us. Buck shifted his weight uncomfortably from foot to foot. Sylvie moved her hand to the small of my back. It was no use. I was going to cry, and Sarah was, too. Lucky Sylvie. Lucky Buck.

The tension was broken by a ringing telephone. Sarah looked around absently and Buck patted his pockets.

Sylvie said, "I think it's coming from your handbag, Sarah."

"Of course." My sister reached down, rooted around in a monster of orange straw and pulled out a cell phone. "Hello? Hello. Emma, I should have known. Your ears must be burning. What? Why, yes, as a matter of fact, I do happen to know where she is. Would you like to speak to her?"

Sarah handed me the telephone.

"Hello, mother," I said sadly.

"Where are you?"

"Wawawai."

"How quickly do you think you can get here?"

"It depends on when I leave. Or," my voice grew harsh, "if I leave. I don't want to see you right now. I don't know if I'll want to see you next week. You're a sneaky, back-stabbing old..."

"It's about an hour from Wawawai to here," Emma interrupted. "Listen, make up some excuse for Sarah. Tell her I've accidentally set fire to the kitchen again, and that I need your help to replace the cupboard doors before your father gets home."

"As if. Look, Ma. I am more pissed at you right now than I have ever been. Sarah told me about you selling our house to Robertson's. How could you keep that from me?"

"Never mind all that," my mother said dismissively. I was about to argue but she cut in, "Your friend Donny Smith just stopped by. They found Jake Peterson."

"Where?"

"In the shack."

"In the shack? But what..." I stopped, suddenly aware that there were four pairs of ears listening to my conversation. Even JC had his head tilted to one side, a short, hairy eavesdropper. "Shit. What was he doing?"

"Nothing," Emma said. "He was dead."

I put my hand over the phone and spoke to the waiting crowd. "I have to go home. A little domestic disaster."

"Emma's set fire to the kitchen again," Sarah explained to Buck. "It happens about once a month."

I turned my back to them and asked quietly, "Are you sure he's... you know?"

Emma gave a short laugh. "Of course I'm sure. Donny Smith is in our bathroom right now, barfing his guts out. Someone has blown Jake Peterson's brains from hell to breakfast."

Chapter 11

We were halfway to Cowslip before Sylvie spoke.

"You were lying about the kitchen fire. What's really going on?"

I kept my eyes on the road and paid scrupulous attention to the speedometer. "Jake Peterson is dead. He seems to have been shot."

"Oh." She adjusted the air conditioning vents, put her foot on the dash to retie her shoe, and played with the lever that adjusted the side-view mirror. Finally, she said, "I'm sorry this man is dead, but why exactly are we rushing off to your mother's house? I heard you ask if Donny was there. Is there some problem I don't know about?"

The highway was narrow, and the shoulder on the right dropped twenty feet down to a small, rocky creek. The people of eastern Washington don't believe in guardrails. It was survival of the fittest. A semitruck passed us doing at least twenty miles over the limit, the wind of his wake giving my Toyota a good buffeting. I gave him the finger.

"Bil?"

"I'm listening," I said. "I just don't know how to answer. Jake the Snake was found in the shack on my parents' new property. He must have come back sometime after Emma and I broke in. The problem is..."

"Go on."

"The problem is that he was shot. Someone blew his brains out."

"Oh," she said again. There was a long pause. "Could have been suicide."

"Yes," I agreed. "But that's not what Emma seems to think."

"Hmm."

I looked at Sylvie. She was staring disapprovingly at one of her fingernails.

"This is just a wild guess," she said, her tone splitting the difference between apprehension and aggravation, "but I'd be willing to bet that the sheriff's department isn't happy that you and Emma broke in there yesterday."

Though I was feeling more than a little apprehensive myself, I couldn't help laughing. "Oh, baby, if you think Emma told them about that, then you don't know my mother. She'll have peppered them with God only knows what lies. Be prepared to think on your feet."

"Why?"

"Because if we don't back her up in whatever story she's concocted, yours truly is going to jail."

* * *

I was relieved when we turned into the driveway and there were no patrol cars waiting for us. Instead, there was just Emma sitting in her usual spot, puffing away like a nicotine dragon. She sprang off the porch as we drove up and charged the driver's side door.

"You took long enough," she huffed. "Where have you... what's that?" She poked a chubby finger at JC.

"It's a toaster," I said. "Do you have a problem with it?"

"No," she said. "Is it housebroken?"

"Yes, it is. And it has a name, too. Jesus Christ. Want to know where I got him?"

"No," she said. "Not at the moment, anyway. We don't have time. Into the house," she commanded, "before your father gets home."

We trailed along behind her. Sylvie moved reluctantly. I followed in habitual obedience. My mother ushered us into the house and closed the front door behind her. She leaned against it and, with breathless drama, said, "Who, besides the two of you, knows that we broke into Jake's house?"

"No one," I assured her. "Wait. Except for Suzy."

My mother's eyes narrowed. "Get me the phone." There ensued a ten-minute conversation in which Emma extracted a solemn promise from Suzy not to mention our perfidy to Donny. In return, Emma promised to relate all the details to Suzy as soon as she knew them—Suzy knew no greater love than the love of gossip.

"Yes," Emma went on. "A favor?" She listened intently. "Of course. Consider it done. Signed, sealed, and delivered with my personal guarantee. What? Let me think. If I were you, I'd try the Community Theatre. They're bound to have someone there who can do it, or they'll know someone. Sure." She glanced up at me and laughed. "Oh, I assure you, I wouldn't miss it for the world. Thanks, Suzy. And don't worry about Donny. No harm will come to him. I'll fill you in just as soon as I can, I promise." She hung up.

"What was that about a favor?" I asked.

Emma ignored me. "Right," she said. "Piece of cake. Quickly, let me fill you in on the details before Hugh gets home."

"Just a moment." Sylvie spoke tentatively, "I don't know quite how to put this. I like Suzy a lot, but he's..."

"A pair of loose lips with hairy legs and a mini-skirt?" Emma suggested. "I know, and he's married to Barney Fife. But we don't need to worry. He'll keep his word. What *we* have to do is plan our next move."

This was too much for me. I'd felt almost torpid since the phone call at Wawawai, but now I awoke with a start. "Plan *our* next move? What's going on here? I know you lied to Donny, Emma. You wouldn't tell a cop the simple truth if your life depended on it. My question is, what kind of bullshit story did you spin?"

My mother gave me a martyred look. Speaking as if she were the epitome of truth and sagacity, she said, "I did not spin a story. I told the truth. What I didn't do was offer to do their job for them."

"Meaning?"

"Meaning what they didn't ask, I didn't tell."

"Oh, my God." I fell back onto the sofa. "There is such a thing as lying by omission, you know."

"I haven't done that, either," she said. "You know that bastard, Sid Castle?"

"You mean Detective Sid Castle, Donny's boss?"

"Yes. He's in charge of the investigation. After Donny found Peterson, he called Castle, and let me tell you, that fucker couldn't get out here fast enough. He was wetting his pants at the thrill of investigating an actual murder."

"Wait," I said. "How do you know that it's murder?"

"I was just getting to that. Here's what happened. Donny dropped by here about noon to follow up on a complaint I made last night."

"The anhydrous ammonia tanks," Sylvie said. I was pleased to see that my mother was nonplussed.

"It was in this morning's police log," I said. "Go on."

"Oh. Okay. Well, I heard those little shitbirds over there. They thought they were being sneaky, sitting in the car with their headlights off. Ha! I got your father's flashlight out and shone it right on them."

My father's "flashlight" was a two million candlepower spotlight. He also had a pair of night vision binoculars—his latest toys. For years, Hugh had been convinced that amazing wildlife moved across our hillside in the dark of night, and to prove his point, he'd equipped himself with a load of KGB surplus from some ridiculous military supply catalog. Unfortunately, he was incapable of staying up past nine o'clock, so Emma was the only one who got any use out of the Wild Kingdom setup.

"Did you see who it was?"

My mother hesitated. "Yes and no. I couldn't pick them out of a lineup because they were fifty yards away. There were two of them, and this is just a guess—don't look at me like that, Bil, I'd bet money on it—I think they were your late brother's friends, Steve and Joe. Those worthless, dumb-assed, shit-for-brains—"

I stopped her. "Did you see the vehicle?"

"Sort of. It was parked behind the ammonia tank. I got part of a license number. Two, two, three, something."

"And you gave that to Donny?"

"Of course! He's got enough information to drag their asses in and question them. It's not my fault if..."

I waited.

"Fine," she snapped. "I dropped the fucking flashlight, didn't I? I was trying to call the cops on the cordless phone and keep the light on Steve and Joe at the same time. The thing just slipped out of my hand, and now there's a big fat crack in the lens."

"Oh, Jesus Christ," I said. The dog barked. My mother looked down at him.

"Is that a German Shepherd?" she asked suspiciously.

"It's an Alsatian," I hedged.

Her eyes narrowed. "Sophistry. That is a Nazi police dog. Why, Bil Hardy, do you have a Nazi police dog?"

JC wagged his tail. I smiled.

"I have an Alsatian because my brother Sam left one to me. Sylvie found this poor thing tied to our doorknob last night. Sam got him from young Calvin Knox. I believe you're a cyber-pal of his father's?" I continued, relishing Emma's open-mouthed stare. "Oh, yeah, Suzy showed me last night what you've been getting up to online. You're the new flame queen of the Slip-Fifty listserv. Funny how you have time to send four e-mails a day to George Knox, but you can't call or drop me a line to say that you've sold my childhood home to those Ag Chemical bastards across the road."

My mother was at a loss for words. I savored the moment. "So, where have you hidden Dad's flashlight?"

Emma snapped back into focus. "I have not hidden it. It's in your brother's room."

"In his closet or under his bed?"

"Shut up," she said.

"Why don't you just tell Dad? He can buy another one."

"And admit I dropped it? Never."

"Please," Sylvie interrupted. "I think we're losing the thread. You called the sheriff's department last night. They came out to investigate. Did you talk to them?"

"You bet I talked to them," Emma said. "It was Donny and some other young punk. I marched over there and told those bozos that, as usual, they were a day late and a dollar short. If you want to catch crackheads stealing anhydrous ammonia, you can't show up an hour after you've been called..."

"Crank-heads," I corrected. "Methamphetamine is called crank."

"No, it isn't. That's heroin."

"No, heroin is smack."

"It's horse," Sylvie interrupted, giving me a look that could have frozen Niagara Falls. "About the anhydrous ammonia. You told Donny that you suspected they were a couple of meth heads. Why? Was it clear they were stealing chemicals? Did you smell ammonia?"

My mother put a cigarette in her mouth but didn't light it. "No more than usual," she said. "Thanks to Robertson's, this place always reeks of ammonia. But that makes no never mind. It doesn't take a genius to work out why two kids in a car would be over there in the middle of the night with their headlights off. It's simple, isn't it? Bil put me onto the idea yesterday."

"I what?"

"Meth," Emma said. "You got me thinking about meth. Robertson's is supposed to lock their gate. It's part of their conditional use permit from the county—they're required to secure the premises. But do they? Do they, hell! There's enough unsecured fertilizer and diesel fuel over there to make an atom bomb."

"I think you'll find that an atom bomb requires uranium," I said. "So, you spoke with Donny. Did you mention that you thought it was Steve and Joe?"

"Of course," she said.

"Did he ask why you thought that?"

"No."

"Right. So Donny just nodded politely, marked you down as a nosy nut-job, and left. Then what?"

"And then nothing. I went to bed." She gave me her shifty look.

"This is what I mean when I say lying by omission. Why were you up so late in the first place, Emma? You and Hugh go to bed at nine. And don't tell me you heard the car because your bedroom is at the back of the house."

She took the cigarette out of her mouth. "I couldn't sleep."

"Lying by omission!" I shouted. "You couldn't sleep. And therefore?"

"And therefore I got in my car and drove over to the Kornmeyer place. Are you satisfied? I took the flashlight and I walked up the hill. It was just the same as when we left it. The door was still lying in the middle of the floor, so I propped it back up on its hinges. Then I came back home. End of story. I went outside for a quick smoke, and that's when I heard the car. The lights were off, but they'd left the engine running."

Sylvie sat down on the sofa. I sighed heavily and joined her. Might as well make ourselves comfortable while we squeezed the whole truth out of my mother.

"When were you in that shack? I mean, at what time?"

"I don't know. Two o'clock, maybe three. I poked around for a few minutes. I tripped over that fucking wheelbarrow." She stopped to glare at me, as if this were my fault. "I saw nothing I hadn't seen already, and then I left."

"You didn't see a corpse?"

"Of course not!"

I tried to think about what this meant. "When did Donny find Jake Peterson?"

Emma looked at her watch. Then she shook it. "This thing is broken," she said. "Donny must have found him sometime after noon. He was back here and barfing in my toilet by a quarter to one. I know that because the clock chimed."

"What made him go up there?" Sylvie asked.

"I did." Emma snorted in disgust. "He stopped by to ask me a few more questions about last night. Instead, I asked him a few questions about Jake the Snake."

"For mercy's sake, why?"

She shrugged. "He was here. Jake Peterson was missing. I wondered if Donny knew anything. Don't look at me like that, Bil. Donny is nearly as big a gossip as Suzy. How was I supposed to know that he'd leave here and go straight to the Kornmeyer place?"

I would have known, and what's more, my mother knew. She sent Donny there, I was sure of it. Emma could never let anything rest.

"Did something at the Kornmeyer place bother you last night? Why did you go up there? What was it?"

"Just a feeling," she said.

"What kind of feeling? Because unless the ghost of Jake Peterson reached out and felt your ass, I don't see any reason why you would have been boneheaded enough to send Donny up there. After our break-in and that mess we made..."

"Oh, belt up," she said. "I sent Donny up there because of something someone posted to the Slip-Fifty listserv."

"This is like pulling teeth," I complained. "What was it?"

"A message." Emma lit a fresh cigarette and took a deep drag. "Or more like a warning. I was advised to mind my own business, to quit concerning myself with George Knox and The Church of the True Vine, and to confine my nosiness to my own problems out here at Toad Hall."

It took some effort to control the tremor in my voice. "Who wrote that, Ma? How could they know?"

"I don't know," she said. "He—or she—used a pseudonym."

"What name?"

"Badger."

"No," I said slowly. "That's... That's not..."

"It was cruel," Sylvie said. I was grateful for the comfort of her hand resting on my thigh. "Cruel and gratuitous. Someone who knew Sam well?"

"Must have been," Emma said. "Or someone who was at his funeral. Bil read from *The Wind in the Willows* and called Sam Badger during the eulogy. Do you remember?"

I nodded. "Good-bye, Badger."

"It's all right," Sylvie whispered. "You'll see Sally again on Thursday."

"Who's Sally?" my mother asked.

"No one," I said. "A counselor. Okay?"

"Okay," she said. "I'm sorry I asked. I didn't mean to pry."

"Yes, you did, but it doesn't matter. I've been seeing a grief counselor."

"Is it helping?"

"Yes."

"Good," Emma said. Her voice became brisk. "I have no evidence to back me up, but I think it was George Knox himself who posted it. Your brother knew Calvin, and that little shit was at the funeral."

"I thought he was estranged from his father," Sylvie said.

Emma laughed bitterly. "Why? Because he was hanging out with Sam? No. He might like a walk on the wild side, but he's still in the fold. He's the old man's heir apparent. George Knox talks about that boy like he's the second coming. Calvin is so smart. We see in Calvin the product of a classical Christian education. Calvin is a chip off the old block."

"That scrawny little weasel?" I said. "I don't believe it."

"Believe it," Emma said. "Either his father doesn't know what Calvin gets up to on his days off, or he doesn't care. They believe in predestination at The Church of the True Vine, and the Knox family is among the elect. They're going to heaven no matter what they do here on earth." Reading my look, she added, "Get Suzy to explain it to you. I tried to raise you free of that superstitious claptrap. You know what I think of religion."

"Yes, Karl Marx. I know. Please spare us the lecture."

"Jesus went out for a pack of cigarettes two thousand years ago," she continued, "and he never came back. Don't wait up for Daddy! The idea that we should be governed by George Knox or any other asshole's interpretation of the Bible..."

"Stop!" I insisted. "You are offensive on this subject, and you always have been. There are people in this very room—people who are not fools or deluded or idiots—who happen to believe in Jesus."

"Oh." My mother stopped short. "Sylvie? I'm sorry. I didn't mean—"

"Not just Sylvie. I believe in God, Emma. I don't know about Jesus. I think the jury is still out."

That had her bouncing backwards. I rarely talked to my mother about my religious beliefs because she never took them seriously.

As long as she was at a disadvantage, I decided to press home another point. "Right. Let's get back on topic here. Some jerk on your little listserv decided to push your buttons and now, as a consequence, we've got a dead body on our hands. Donny knows that there was a break-in, and he probably thinks that it had something to do with Jake's murder. That's not good. You'd better hope they don't fingerprint us, Ma."

"What would it matter?" my mother asked. Her tone was annoyingly reasonable. "My fingerprints ought to be up there. I own that fucking shack."

"I don't own it. Why are my fingerprints there?"

"Because I took you up to have a look around, as is my right. You're my daughter. That shack was my property. We're in the clear."

"No, we're not. You still haven't explained why you think Jake was murdered. Couldn't he have shot himself?"

"Maybe," she said. "But he couldn't have moved himself. Donny reckoned he'd been dead for about two days."

"Two days?" I shook my head. "I don't understand."

"I think I do," Sylvie said. She looked at my mother, who motioned for her to continue. "You and Bil were in the shack yesterday afternoon. You went back between two and three last night. Jake Peterson wasn't there, alive or dead. But when Donny went up at noon today, there he was."

"Exactly," said my mother. "Sitting on the sofa with his brains splattered all over the wall behind him. Do you understand now, Bil?"

I understood. Our sheriff's department was not high tech. They couldn't trace a criminal based on a dropped hair or a footprint in the mud. During the twenty years I'd lived in Cowslip, we'd had ten homicides and maybe four or five missing persons. The only crime the sheriff's department had actually solved was the murder of an old lady, and that was only because they'd pulled her son over for speeding and found her body in the trunk.

"Oh, no," I said. "You have to tell them, Emma. The cops need to know that Jake wasn't killed in that shack."

"They already know," she said. "I heard them talking. The shotgun blast was inflicted post mortem. Jake Peterson's brains were all over the wall but not his blood. Well, there was some blood, just not enough."

Sylvie made a small gulping noise. I squeezed her hand.

"Without going into gory detail, Ma, did they say anything about why someone might want to shoot a dead body?"

"To obscure his identity, I suppose. Judging from the damage, they think he took one straight to the face. They're over there right now, you know. We could hop in the car and..."

The near-retching at my side, coupled with my own squeamishness, made me say quickly, "I don't think they'd appreciate that, Emma. Besides, didn't you say you were expecting Dad home at any minute?"

"Damn! Was that a car door?"

"You'd better talk fast," I advised. "Why didn't you tell them we'd been in there? I know you hate the cops, but that's no reason to lie to them, especially about something like this."

"I didn't tell them because of what else they found. Yesterday, we assumed that the locked door in the living room led to that back area where the radio was, but we were wrong. There's a room in between those two. That's where the urine smell was coming from, not from that bucket in the corner. Jake had quite a meth lab set up in that middle room: ammonia, a cooker, and enough Sudafed to clear King Kong's sinuses. I decided that ignorance was our best defense. If the cops don't know that we broke in, then we don't know that Jake was cooking meth."

I didn't get a chance to point out the flaws in her logic. My dad came into the house, effectively ending our conversation. He looked unruffled and incurious, which was how he always looked. It didn't matter what was going on. Fire, flood, or plague of locusts, my mother supplied all of the movement in their relationship. She pitched the fits and felt the outrage. Hugh's great purpose was to serve as an anchor—a hopeless task, as the poor man had clearly chosen to moor the Titanic.

"Hello Bil, hello Sylvie." Hugh turned to my mother, smiling grimly. "So, Emma, Donny Smith tells me we need to find ourselves a new tenant."

Chapter 12

Sylvie decided to ride her motorcycle home. I handed the keys to her reluctantly.

"We could just leave it here for another day," I said.

"I'd rather take it home now."

"Meaning you don't want to have to make another trip out here anytime soon." She nodded. I leaned in and kissed her. "That makes two of us. Here's your helmet. Ride carefully, honey."

"Meet you back at the apartment?" she asked.

"Yeah. I thought JC and I might stop by the store first. We're out of Twinkies and potato chips."

"Sorry," she said. "They weren't on the grocery list."

"I'll forgive you for that oversight."

She didn't put her helmet on or make any move to start the bike.

"You look worried," I said.

"I am worried," she said. "But not unduly. What's the worst that could happen? You broke in and your mother lied about it. She owns the place, though, so I don't see that as being too serious. Jake was a drug dealer, and someone killed him. It worries me that the body was moved and that it was maimed."

"Yeah," I agreed. "If it's any comfort, my mother doesn't own a shotgun. Do you think I'm an accessory to anything?"

"No," Sylvie assured me. "Not to anything truly criminal. I think..."

"Go ahead."

"I think you should spend less time with your mother. Just for a while." She bit her lower lip. "I'm sorry, Bil. It's your family. It's not for me to say..."

"Stop," I said quickly. "It is for you to say, and what's more, you're right. I'll tell you what I think—I think we should stop thinking about this. Let's spend the rest of the day eating junk food and watching Bugs Bunny. What do you say?"

Sylvie surprised me by putting her hand on the back of my neck, pulling me to her, and kissing me hard. When she stopped, I had to lean against the bike to catch my breath.

"I say we skip the Bugs Bunny," she said, "and rent *Desert Hearts* instead. Are you up for that?"

"I am. I am very up for that."

She gave me a searing look, put her helmet on, and started the bike. I watched her roar out of the driveway. JC barely nodded. He was lying placidly beneath the cottonwood tree, chewing on a stick.

"Nice show," Emma called from the front porch. "I hope the guys over at the gravel pit enjoyed it."

I chanted my favorite mantra: "I am not to blame for my mother."

* * *

The best video selection in town was at the Cowslip Foodway. The store's owner, Chip Ferguson, had a taste for foreign films and what he called "exotic" titles. The very exotic he kept in a small room behind the beer cooler. This had included gay and lesbian movies until Chip's mother, Hulda, died. That was when Chip, who was nearing fifty and as camp as a wet tent, had come roaring out of the closet and the gay and lesbian films had come out with him. They now had their own lavender shelf behind the customer service counter.

Chip was leaning on the counter now and smiling broadly. I wanted to like Chip. I felt sorry for him. After his mother's death, he'd gone from closet queen to Queer Nation as soon as the casket lid was closed. All the years of secrecy and silence had unhinged his brain and worse, his tongue. Now there was nothing he wouldn't talk about at the top of his lungs. From tea bagging to butt plugs, if he was thinking about it, he said it. Try as I might to be broad-minded, there were some things I really didn't want to know. Chip's blond wig was nearly the same color as his tobacco-stained teeth. He wore brightly colored polo shirts—often with an argyle vest—perfectly pressed khaki pants and deck shoes with no socks. I was happy to make pleasant conversation with Chip about the weather or the Mariners, but I didn't want to hear about how he was making up for lost time with assorted members of the Rotary Club, the Moose Lodge, the Masons, and the Kiwanis.

"Hi Bil," he beamed. "How's it hanging?"

I knew from past experience that the answer Chip wanted was "big and hairy and hard to carry." What I said was, "I'm fine, Chip. Sylvie and I were thinking we'd pop some corn and watch a movie tonight." I cleared my throat. "Do you have *Desert Hearts*?"

Chip winked at me. "Sorry," he said. "You're five minutes too late. I just rented it out. How about *The Incredibly True Adventures of Two Girls in Love*? Or..." He leaned forward conspiratorially. "You might want to pay a visit to the room behind the beer cooler. There's a new one in there about two young women and a garden hose."

I ignored this. "I'm not really in the mood for teenage angst," I said, "so I'll skip the *True Adventures*. How about *The Hunger*?"

"Susan Sarandon and Catherine Deneuve?" The wink was rapidly becoming a tic. "That one I have. Don't you just love the cello and the gauze? And that sex scene—it's nearly enough to turn me. Magnifique! We're running a special. Three films, three nights, three dollars. Is there anything else you'd like to see?"

Yes, I thought. I'd like to see a film clerk with his own hair, a quiet voice, and a sense of discretion. What I said was, "How about *The Hunger*, *Aliens*, and *Personal Best*?"

Chip grinned. "A natural trilogy. If I were you," he said with another wink, "I'd watch *Aliens* first."

I tossed the videotapes into the cart and quickly headed for the snack food aisle. Rather than risk leaving JC in the car, even with the windows down, I'd fastened his leash to the bicycle rack under the shade of the front awning. I could see him through the front windows—he was licking something off the concrete. I needed to get a move on. Barbecue-flavored potato chips, Twinkies, cold beer, and a bouquet of roses, and then I'd be on my way. I twirled the cart around and was preparing to make a run for it when another cart rounded the corner and knocked me flat on my ass.

"I'm sorry," said a booming voice. "Didn't see you there... Bil!"

Captain Schwartz abandoned her cart and bore down upon me, pulling me up from the floor and wrapping her muscular arms tightly around my shoulders. Unable to hug her back, and also unable to breathe, I choked out a greeting. "Hi, Captain. How've you been?"

"Good," she said. "Very good. And you?"

"Fine."

"Glad to hear it. Heard anything from that worthless son of mine?"

"Not for a couple of weeks," I said. "He's busy with his corporate pimping job."

"Tell me about it," she said proudly. "The money they pay him is obscene."

Tipper Schwartz, the Captain's son, had been my best friend since junior high. Fresh out of college, he'd taken a job in the sales department at Microsoft and risen like a rocket. With his annual bonus, he was able to put a down payment on a condominium and buy a ridiculous red sports car that he called "The Penile Enhancement."

"It's depressing to think that Tipper and I are the same age," I said.

Captain Schwartz smiled kindly. She was a big woman, as tall as Sarah but built like a tank. Though I was fairly muscular and broad-shouldered myself, she made me look like the runt in the before picture in a Charles Atlas ad.

"You're in graduate school, aren't you?" she asked.

"Yeah. I'm getting double masters' degrees in English and Psychology. Sylvie's working on her Ph.D."

"You'll get there, Bil."

"But I won't get to Microsoft. Not unless Bill Gates goes bonkers and needs a shrink with a big vocabulary."

The Captain laughed, a loud, raucous sound that seemed to bounce off the cans of soda behind us and echo around the store.

"You haven't been out to Fort Sister lately."

Theoretically, Fort Sister was a women's retreat and artists' colony. Its real name was Blood Moon Women's Haven, but no one called it that. Although women came from around to the country to write, paint, hold conferences, and worship Mother Nature, Fort Sister wasn't so much a collective as it was a lesbian separatist boot camp. Captain Schwartz liked guns, and she was planning a left-wing queer response to a right-wing evangelical Armageddon.

"You're still playing softball, aren't you?" she asked.

"No. I've been too busy with school." I pinched my stomach to demonstrate that I could grab more than an inch. "I'm afraid I'm getting flabby. I need to do something. Rejoin the team or go back to the gym." Or stop eating *pho* at one o'clock in the morning, I added silently.

The Captain slapped the flat of her hand against my abdomen. "Nonsense, Bil. You're as fit as a fiddle. But maybe it's not softball you need at the moment," she said sagely. "Your brother's death— that was very hard. Perhaps some Tai Chi? I'm doing a little yoga myself these days, and it feels pretty good. I seem to be getting back a bit of my old flexibility."

"I'll say," said a woman's voice behind me. "You can bend over to tie your shoes now without your knees making that awful creaking sound. Hi, Bil."

The hug Kate gave me wasn't as exuberant as the one I'd gotten from Captain Schwartz but it was no less warm and sincere. Sylvie's mother and I enjoyed a friendly relationship though I was always a little nervous around her, in part because she looked so much like her daughter, with the same intense green eyes, the same blonde hair. Kate's hair had begun to turn gray above her ears. When I looked at her, I sometimes felt as if I were looking at one of those computer-generated age projections: this will be your girlfriend in twenty-six years. It was unnerving, especially as Kate was still very attractive. Although I wasn't biologically related to Emma, I was terrified by the thought that I might somehow turn into her.

"I'm sorry you couldn't come to dinner last night," Kate said. "Sylvie told me you were visiting your mother. How is she?"

"Same as ever. Ornery as hell and in and out of trouble." Figuring they'd read about it in the police log anyway, I briefly described the situation with Jake Peterson, leaving out the story of our break-in. "Jake seems to have been running a meth lab up there. Emma is fit to be tied. She's afraid the Feds are going to swoop down and seize her property."

"I don't think it works that way," said Captain Schwartz. "One of your sisters is an attorney, isn't she?"

"Naomi. She's a public defender. In the case of Emma, I expect she'd recuse herself. Even if they weren't related, she'd have to be a fool to represent our mother."

The Captain laughed. "I don't think it'll get that far. I was thinking more along the lines that she might be familiar with the drug laws."

"Of course."

In the silence that followed, I tried to think of something to say that would indicate that I knew they were dating. I also wanted to let them know that if they were happy, I was happy. At the same time, however, I didn't want to seem too overjoyed about something that was making Sylvie miserable. Seeking inspiration, I looked into the Captain's shopping cart. She had three cans of whipped cream, a flat of fresh strawberries, and a bottle of champagne. She also had *Desert Hearts*.

"So that's where that movie got to," I said. "Sylvie and I are having to make do with potato chips and *The Hunger*."

It was a shame that I was, as the Captain had noted, as fit as a fiddle. There was absolutely no chance that I could feign a heart attack with any degree of conviction. I couldn't faint, I couldn't hide, and I couldn't fall down dead. Instead, I had to stand there and tough it out as the two of them looked first at me, then at each other, and then began laughing.

"Good night, Bil," said Kate, leaning forward and kissing me on the cheek.

"Yes, good night, Bil," said the Captain, winking extravagantly. "I'd put those chips back if I were you. The strawberries are on sale."

I watched them as they walked down the aisle, heads close together, shoulders touching, as pleased as punch with each other. Poor Sylvie. If Kate and the Captain could get through three cans of whipped cream and six pints of strawberries, they were better women than we were. Perhaps I'd take that yoga class after all.

* * *

Sylvie put the remains of her Twinkie down on the coffee table. "I don't like this at all, Bil."

"Here," I offered. "Have a Ding Dong."

"You know what I mean." She took the Ding Dong anyway. "This is..."

"Stupid? Unnecessary? Illegal? I know, but I don't know what to do about it. Now that my mother's lied to the police, we're stuck. I can't go into the station and say, 'Here's what really happened, please don't prosecute her.' Why would they listen to me anyway? The Hardy family does not have a stellar reputation with law enforcement."

"What about Suzy?"

I nodded. "The weak link. I'll talk to him."

"He doesn't go on duty at the hospital for another two hours."

"Shall I invite him over for tea and Twinkies?"

"Please do."

* * *

Suzy perched on the rocking chair in his scrubs and clunky white nurse shoes. Without his wig and mascara, he looked like

Richard Gephardt. His hair was thin and reddish, and his eyelashes were so pale as to be almost invisible. He'd eschewed our offer of junk food in favor of a rice cake, which he was now chewing thoughtfully.

"The way I see it," he said, "it's none of my business why your mother swore me to secrecy. I gave her my word, and my word is my bond."

"You're a strange bird, Suzy," I said. "I don't like dragging you into this, and I don't like my mother asking you to keep secrets from Donny."

He laughed. "Honey, you don't know the half of it. I *have* to keep secrets from Donny. If he knew the complete and unexpurgated story of my life, his little Mormon head would burst wide open. Drinking, smoking, fornicating... I have violated all of the Words of Wisdom and lost every Pearl of Great Price in my necklace. Now, your mother promised to fill me in. Why don't you do that instead?"

I looked at Sylvie, who nodded her approval.

When I'd finished, Suzy said, "Quite right not to tell that Sid Castle anything. He'd get it ass-backwards and wind up clapping your mother in irons. Better to just let that hang."

"But they'll think the break-in is related to Jake Peterson's murder," Sylvie said.

"So what?" said Suzy. "Bil did someone a favor by knocking that door down. It stands to reason that whoever fired that shotgun put Jake's body in the shack. They might not have knocked the door down—I suppose they could have used his key—but they didn't have his explicit permission to go in. He was already dead."

"Good God," I said. "You're as amoral as my mother."

"I prefer the term 'differently moraled,'" Suzy said. "I don't think the ends justify the means, but the ends do sometimes justify themselves."

I picked up another Twinkie. "And on that happy note... wait." I put the Twinkie down again. "If Jake was shot in the face to obscure his features, how did the police know it was him?"

"I can answer that," said Suzy. "He had a big tattoo on his bicep that said 'Jake.' Donny said Sid was mincing around like Miss Marple on crack when he found that. He had Donny take half a dozen photos of the thing. Do you know that Sid was fired from the Bozeman Police Department for incompetence? Imagine. He wasn't smart enough for Montana."

"Good lord. What does that say for Cowslip, Idaho?"

"That we're desperate."

Sylvie looked thoughtful. "If he wasn't shot to obscure his features, then why?"

"I've been giving that some thought," Suzy said. "It reminds me of a patient who came into the ER in Seattle—a woman with a gunshot wound to the head, dead on arrival. The coroner ruled it a suicide. It wasn't until the woman's brother requested an autopsy that they realized she'd been suffocated. Her husband's now serving twenty-five to life in Walla Walla."

"How could that happen?" Sylvie asked.

"Heavens above," said Suzy. "It happens every day. The coroner is busy, the case looks straightforward, and he makes a bad call. That won't happen here, of course. The coroner is Bil's sister."

"What?" This was news to me.

Suzy explained. "When old Lindquist died last month, Ruth volunteered to take over. She's been appointed by the county on an interim basis until the next election. There are so few cases that it doesn't interfere with her work in the ER, and it saves the county the cost of organizing a special ballot. I think they pay her some ridiculous pittance, maybe a hundred dollars a month."

"Holy shit. This really is turning into a family affair. If only Jake Peterson were Sarah's long-lost father, we could all be involved."

Suzy reached out and pinched my cheek. "That, my little butch, is one of the many joys of small-town living. There are no degrees of separation. Anyhow, if my theory is correct, Jake Peterson might have been shot to hide the fact that he died of something other than being shot."

"Like what?"

"Who knows? Suffocation, like that poor woman in Seattle. Poison, overdose, snake bite, a red hot poker up the ass—something that was inconvenient to someone, somewhere."

We sat and pondered this. I reached out for a Hostess cupcake, but Sylvie slapped my hand. "You're going to put yourself in a diabetic coma," she said.

"Fine. Can I have a potato chip?" She nodded. I risked the wrath and took an enormous handful. "So, Suzy, in exchange for your silence, my mother offered to do you a favor. What was it? Is she going to sew you a chintz miniskirt or quilt you a G-string?"

Suzy hesitated. We made brief eye contact, and he glanced at Sylvie. She looked up.

"What?" Sylvie said.

"Come on, Suzy. Out with it."

He sighed. "Emma told me that you'd help out with a little group I'm putting together."

"What kind of group?" I asked suspiciously.

"A singing group," he replied. "The Mighty Queer Gospel Quartet. We're singing two weeks from now at the JUGS benefit. I'm a tenor, Donny is a bass, and, if I can talk her into it, I know a wonderful contralto. All we needed was a piano player and a dramatic soprano."

"A dramatic soprano?" Sylvie sounded bemused.

I closed my eyes. I could kill Suzy and my mother and then bury them both in the same hole. It wouldn't need to be particularly deep. I could cover them up with the shreds of my dignity.

"Bil is a dramatic soprano," Suzy enthused. "I'm sure you've heard her warbling in the shower." Suzy patted me on the arm. "You wouldn't know it to look at her, but she sings like a nightingale—a big butch diesel dyke nightingale."

I avoided Sylvie's gaze. "I don't think..."

"Don't worry," Suzy said. "You won't have to wear a dress. A tuxedo will do. I'll rent one for you. And probably another for our contralto."

"Who's your contralto?" Sylvie asked.

Suzy spoke quickly. "Rebecca Schwartz," he said. "Our first practice is Friday at her house, 7 p.m. Don't look so stunned, you two. The Captain grew up in North Carolina singing in a Baptist choir. No," he said, wagging his finger at us, "she is not Jewish. Schwartz is her ex-husband's name. Before that, she was Rebecca Hiney."

"Hiney?" I asked.

"Ex-husband?" said Sylvie.

I looked at my girlfriend. Sylvie was staring at Suzy in puzzled consternation. She didn't look displeased, exactly. Just amazed. A terrible thought struck me. My mother had advised Suzy to call the Community Theatre for a piano player. There were several possibilities, but my run of bad luck suggested only one.

"Who's the piano player, Suzy?"

He beamed. "Your grandmother! Isn't that nice? She plays the piano from time to time for the Episcopal Church. I thought we'd do three songs and then an encore. We don't have much time to get ourselves ready, and we're not the only act."

"I'm not doing it," I said firmly.

"You must."

"Suzy, I can't. I've never sung in a choir."

Suzy thumped himself proudly on the chest. "Not a problem. I have whipped many a rank amateur into shape. Quite apart from that, I'll pick the songs very carefully. As the soprano, you'll be singing lead. All the rest of us will be doing the harmonies. You've got the easy part."

"I am not a public performer, Suzy. I've never sung for an audience."

"You can do this," Suzy insisted. "And it's for a good cause. We're going to use the proceeds to fund a petition drive. We need twenty-five hundred signatures to get a citywide referendum on the ballot to overturn the topless ordinance. You'll be fighting for your rights to T and A."

Suzy left shortly thereafter. I wanted to strangle him, and yet I was sorry to see him go. I closed the door behind him and turned to face Sylvie. Oddly enough, she was smiling.

"Let's take a shower," she said. "I'll wash your back and you can sing me the final aria from *Madame Butterfly*."

Chapter 13

I woke up the next morning to the sound of dresser drawers opening and closing. I opened my eyes and squinted. Sylvie was up and dressed and packing my clothes into a small suitcase.

"So, that's it then," I said. "You've had it with me."

She zipped the top of the suitcase closed and sat down on the edge of the bed. "Far from it," she said, leaning over to kiss me. "I don't get nearly enough of you—I mean just you, without any entanglements."

"I'm sorry," I began. "I know my mother runs amok, and I let her—"

"Stop." Sylvie kissed me thoroughly. When we came up for air, she said, "We're not going to talk about your mother, not today, anyway. I think we need a change of scenery. I've booked us a suite at the Coeur d'Alene Resort."

I sat up. "Really? But it's the height of the tourist season."

"They had a vacancy. I took it."

"Sylvie, that must have..." I was about to say "cost a fortune." The look on her face told me to let it go. We argued occasionally about money, mostly about the fact that she had a ton and I had none. Sylvie was an only child. Kate Wood had inherited a mother lode of property and cash, she'd invested wisely, and she was able to see to it that her daughter wasn't obliged to live like most graduate students—in a rat-infested flophouse eating macaroni and cheese. That seemed fair enough to me. Why live like a dog if you don't have to? But Sylvie felt guilty about it, especially as I insisted on benefiting as little as possible from her mother's largesse.

Tipper had told me many times that I was a fool. I'd married money, and I ought to try thinking of myself as one of those Kennedy wives.

"Yeah," I'd said, "anorexic, pinched, and alcoholic."

The temptation to kick back and enjoy Sylvie's frequent offers of elegant dinners, trips to San Francisco, and help paying my share of the electric bill was certainly there, but the danger as I saw it was that I was already inclined to indolence. I'd taken a year off between high school and college to bum around Seattle, working just enough odd jobs to keep from starving. Then I'd enrolled for two years at the University of Washington, where I failed to distinguish myself academically. Finally, in my junior year, I'd transferred to Cowslip College, losing countless credits in the process. Only now was I beginning to show any initiative. I'd been a worthless undergraduate, but I was at the top of my graduate classes in both English and Psychology. Double MAs in single time—that was my goal. While I wasn't certain that poverty engendered discipline, it seemed like my last, best hope.

"How long are we staying?" I asked.

"Two nights. We'll come back Friday morning."

I had a choice to make. Should I offer to pay half and skip buying groceries for the rest of the month or should I smile and accept? Was it really so leech-like to just shut up and be gracious? Sylvie waited.

"What about grief counseling?"

"I thought you could postpone."

"Thank you," I said at last, wrapping my arms around her waist and kissing her. "Does our suite have a Jacuzzi?"

She smiled. "Absolutely, plus a fridge and a mini-bar. For the next forty-eight hours, we can lock out the world. Just you and me, champagne on ice, and a deep, hot tub with a lot of bubbles."

"Sounds wonderful." I started to pull her into a firmer embrace and then stopped. "Um, as much as I hate to be the snake in Eden, what if there's some emergency here and someone—I won't say who—tries to get in touch with us? You know she won't hesitate to call out the National Guard."

Sylvie smiled confidently. "I've left a note for Suzy. On pain of death, he has permission to give out our location if, and only if, something truly urgent comes up. Accident, illness, or fire, and I don't mean a kitchen fire. Your mother's house has to burn down completely. I think we can trust Suzy to make the right judgment call."

"What about incarceration?"

"That's not an emergency," she replied firmly.

"You're right," I agreed. "It's just an everyday aggravation. My sisters have more bail money than I do, anyway. Would you hand me my contact lens case?"

"Oops. I think I packed it." She rooted around in the suitcase. "Here you go."

I put the lenses in my eyes and blinked. Sylvie came sharply into focus. "What about JC?"

"Suzy's taking care of him, too."

"Good. Maybe I'll forgive him for this singing business. Does the Coeur d'Alene Resort have cable?"

"Yes," she said laughing, "but I was hoping we'd make our own entertainment."

"Of course. Did you pack my tap shoes?"

"No way. I've seen you dance." I gave her a good-natured shove. "Okay, okay. Listen," she said seriously, "at some point I do expect to hear you sing—I mean really sing. You got out of it last night by using some clever diversionary tactics."

"Come on," I argued. "When two women get into the shower together, it is not so one of them can sing. Besides, I thought you liked my diversionary tactics."

"I love them. Now tell me, what exactly is your vocal range? Suzy went on about it like you were Jessye Norman. Can you really sing opera? I've heard you humming pop and country. What else do you sing?"

"I sing hymns," I said, resignedly. "Very old, very Baptist, holy roller hymns."

"Bil," she said, ruffling my hair. "You have got to stop lying."

* * *

If Lake Coeur d'Alene were any more beautiful it would be part of Canada. Idaho certainly doesn't deserve it. The southern part of the state is high desert—dry, hot, and sandy red. Lake Coeur d'Alene looks like a Scottish loch—mysterious, cold, and deep. Green hills rise on either side, and the water runs for several miles through a deep gash cut into the landscape by a receding glacier at the end of the last ice age. It has always been one of my favorite spots on earth.

Unfortunately, for several years the nearby bedroom community of Hayden Lake had been home to Aryan Nations, a very small group of skinheads who nevertheless managed to get more than their fair share of media coverage. Once a year, they marched through downtown Coeur d'Alene, angering the local shopkeepers and always, somehow, managing to make it onto the national news.

"If we got rid of Aryan Nations," I mused, "do you think it would be possible to annex the whole of northern Idaho to Alberta?"

"There are probably easier ways of becoming a Canadian." Sylvie pulled into the parking lot next to the resort. "We're here," she said. "Why don't you get the suitcase out of the back and... is anything the matter?"

I stared at the hotel. It was enormous, an impressive stucco building, several stories tall, and right on the edge of the lake.

"I have performance anxiety."

"Really," Sylvie said, sliding across the seat and nuzzling my ear. "That's a new one. Are you sure you don't have expensive hotel anxiety?"

"No." I let myself be nibbled on for another minute or two. "I'm sorry that I haven't sung for you. I mean apart from crooning in the shower and stuff."

"If I were cruel," she said, "I'd ask you why. Instead, I'll be kind and tell you. It's because you can't stand to hear *me* sing."

"Oh, honey, that's not..."

"Yes it is," she interrupted. "I know you have a lovely voice. I didn't realize that it might be extraordinary until last night. You've been holding out on me. I've heard you singing to yourself from time to time, but you always stop when you realize I'm listening."

I could feel my face flushing. "I don't mean to," I muttered.

"I know you don't," she said. "Bil, I know I can't sing. I am entirely tone deaf. And"—she put a finger on my lips—"it makes you cringe when I try."

I couldn't deny it. It was the truth. "Sylvie, you must think I'm a monster."

"On the contrary," she said softly. "I think you're very sweet. You didn't want to hurt my feelings."

Some time later, I pulled away and said, "If it's any consolation, I can't appreciate Bob Dylan or Neil Young, either."

"Are you suggesting that I'm really an off-key musical genius?"

I pretended to give this serious thought. "No."

She laughed and kissed me again. Finally I said, "I think we'd better check into our room. Coeur d'Alene is pretty, but it's still Idaho. And look, this place is crawling with potbellied guys with brush cuts." I peered out the window. "And they all seem to be wearing POW-MIA T-shirts. Must be some sort of military convention. Are you sure this is a good idea?"

"Yes," Sylvie said firmly. "I'm sure. Forget about the middle-aged jarheads and come back here."

"How you exhaust me with your sexual demands." I laughed. I wasn't laughing for long. I removed her roving hands from beneath my T-shirt. "I mean it this time. We'd better get to our room. I don't want to get arrested. Or suffocate. This truck is hot in more ways than one."

She rested her beautiful, silky blonde head on my shoulder. "No more performance anxiety?"

I smiled broadly. "None whatsoever. I am ready to give you the best forty-eight hours of your natural life."

"Excellent," Sylvie said. "But we're not getting out the truck just yet." She turned the key in the ignition and switched the air conditioner on high. "I mean it, Bil—I am not waiting another minute. Sing to me, damn it!"

I took a deep breath and pushed the notes up with my diaphragm. "My bologna has a first name, it's… ow!"

* * *

Over the noise of the Jacuzzi jets, I treated my love to several examples of my motley and peculiar repertoire: "Abide with Me", "Precious Memories", and "Angel Band". When I reached the soaring chorus of "How Great Thou Art", she burst into spontaneous applause.

Sylvie crossed her heart with a soapy hand. "As God is my witness, I will never so much as hum in your presence ever again. If you sat up late at night watching the Metropolitan Opera, do you think you could teach yourself to sing *Lakmé* or *Carmen*?"

"I very much doubt it. But here, how's this?" I dropped my voice a couple of octaves and sang the first lines of the "Largo al factotum" from *The Barber of Seville*.

Sylvie laughed. "Don't tell me you learned to do that watching *The PTL Club*."

"Nope. Bugs Bunny."

She splashed me.

"No, really. You have no idea how much time Sam and I spent watching cartoons. He could do the voices—Elmer Fudd, Daffy Duck. I did the music, and I always got to be Bugs. Sam gave me the best lines."

I felt myself tearing up. "Shit. I know he was a pain in the ass. He was always doing something stupid and dragging me into it, but Sylvie, I miss him—I miss him every day. Before he got sick, Sam wasn't... his personality changed. He turned into someone I hardly knew, someone I didn't like. It was the illness. It was..."

I slapped at the water, sending a great arc of it over the edge of the tub and onto the floor. "Oh, who am I kidding? Sam was always a jackass. He never knew how to pick his friends, but he was loyal to them. My God, the falls he took for those worthless idiots. He started shoplifting in junior high, hanging out with juvenile delinquents, and smoking weed. When we were little, though, he was sweet—the best little brother in the world."

Sylvie eased across the tub and pulled me into her arms.

"For God's sake," I cried against her shoulder. "Why am I still doing this?"

"It's all right," she said, stroking my hair. "This is how you feel."

I wiped my eyes with a wet hand. "Damn. Some butch lesbian *I* am." I extricated myself from her embrace and stood up. "This water is too hot. I feel like a boiled lobster."

I dripped across the room and fell face forward onto the bed. Sylvie followed after me with a towel and patted me dry. I rolled over onto my back. "I'm sorry. I don't know where that came from."

Sylvie dropped down beside me, propping herself up on one elbow. "The steam has made your hair curl."

"It was curly to begin with. I'm surprised it hasn't turned gray."

She twisted a piece around her finger and gave it a tug. "As black as ever. And your eyes are just as blue." She kissed me. "Would you rather be comforted or distracted?"

"Distracted."

"Right." She pursed her lips, thinking. "We could go to dinner or maybe a movie. There might be something on cable..."

"I thought you meant distracted," I said, feeling a bit more like my old self.

"What did you have mind?"

I traced an intricate pattern on her breast with my fingertip, enjoying the way she caught her breath. "I know a nifty trick with an ice cube."

"That's... intriguing," she said slowly. Her breathing had become shallow, and I liked the sound she made as my hand slipped lower. "I think there's an ice machine just down the hall. Why don't I put a robe on and pop out for a minute?"

"Sounds like a plan."

She was gone longer than I expected, and when she came back, the expectant, seductive look was gone. Instead, she looked disconcerted.

"What, no ice?"

"No, no, I found the ice." She rattled the bucket to demonstrate. "I also found your sister, Naomi. She's staying just down the hall."

I sat up. "God damn it! She doesn't know what room we're in, does she?"

Sylvie shook her head. "She didn't ask. Bil, she had someone with her."

I raised my eyebrows. "Really? A man?" Sylvie nodded. "Oh, ho, Naomi. Out of the office at last. What did he look like?"

"He looked like Sarah's boyfriend, Buck DeWitt."

Chapter 14

We let the ice melt in the bucket and went out to dinner.

"Buck DeWitt is two-timing Sarah with Naomi?" I chewed vigorously on a piece of underdone pasta. We'd picked our restaurant for convenience, not reputation. Big mistake. "What is it about my sisters and that bow-legged cowboy? He's hideous."

"I wouldn't go that far," Sylvie said. She'd wisely ordered a salad. I made a mental note that even in dodgy restaurants, it's hard to fuck up lettuce. "I suppose he has a certain rugged appeal."

"Please. He looks like he's been riding the range with the James boys. And that disgusting mustache—wait, I take it back—he doesn't look like one of the James boys. He looks like one of the Village People."

Sylvie laughed, covering her mouth with her hand.

"He does," she agreed. "You don't suppose...?"

"What, that he's gay and dating *both* of my sisters to cover it up? That seems like beard overkill. No, I think the sheep have more to fear from him than the manly men of Cowslip. Did he recognize you?"

"I don't think so. He didn't say anything."

"Yeah, well, he wouldn't, would he? If he admitted he knew you, then he'd have to say where you met, and the jig would be up. What did Naomi say?"

"A very curt hello."

"Rude bitch."

"No," Sylvie said. "I think she was surprised to see me. Surprised and embarrassed. You don't think your sisters have any idea they're dating the same guy?"

"Absolutely not," I said adamantly. "As kids, they refused to share Barbie dolls. Share a boyfriend? Never. No, Buck DeWitt is two-timing them. My question is where did he meet them? Naomi and Sarah don't move in the same circles. Naomi lives at the office, and Sarah meets most of her dates on campus, usually trolling around the stacks in the library. I keep telling her to quit picking up men who read Louis L'Amour."

Sylvie pushed her plate away. "That's the worst salad I've ever had," she said. "How can you fuck up lettuce?"

I laughed. "Either you're psychic or we've already been together too long. Maybe they got our orders mixed up. They cooked your greens and forgot to boil my pasta. Buck said he was a veterinarian, didn't he?"

"Large animal," Sylvie said. "And Sarah said he worked with horses."

"Well," I shrugged. "Neither of my sisters can ride. Sarah has Sasquatch, but I don't think a really fat cat qualifies as a large animal. Naomi doesn't have a pet. She's not home enough to keep a goldfish alive. I suppose it's possible that Buck came into the library at some point, and Sarah met him there. But Naomi..."

"Is defending him on criminal charges?" Sylvie suggested.

"Having to do with large animals," I said.

We both shuddered.

Sylvie asked, "Are you going to tell Sarah and Naomi that he's dating both of them?"

"You're joking, right? Do you want to be a widow?"

"No." Sylvie shook her head. "Do you really think they'd take it out on you?"

"Not intentionally. I'm just afraid of the collateral damage. When that cowboy gets caught—and he will—my sisters will blow him up like Sam did that sewer main. I don't want to get caught in the flying shrapnel. Picture it—belt buckles, mustache combs, cans of Skoal, pearl snaps..."

"I see your point," she said.

Rather than take a chance on dessert, we walked arm in arm to the candy store just up the street from the hotel. I was filling a bag with saltwater taffy and root beer barrels when I noticed a young man standing next to a bin of Mary Janes and talking urgently on his cell phone. It was Calvin Knox. I gestured to Sylvie and we moved close enough to eavesdrop.

"Don't be stupid," he was saying. "I'll be back tonight. We'll take care of it then... No, you fucking idiot, that's not possible. Dead people stay dead. That's only a movie, you dick. I'm telling you, just leave it. Walk away. Go back to the shop and wait for me there."

"Enough of this," I whispered to Sylvie. "I'm beginning to feel like my mother." I walked up behind him and said loudly, "Calvin Knox! Fancy meeting you here."

He switched his cell phone off and turned on a dime. He stared at me for a moment before recognition dawned. "Oh, uh, hi, Wilhelmina. How have you been?"

"No one calls me Wilhelmina," I growled. "That's my grandmother's name."

He flinched. "Sorry. Um, Sam sometimes..."

"Yeah, I know he did." I relented and gave him a slight smile. "I'm sorry. Wilhelmina is one of the many tortures inflicted upon me by my mother. Sam used it to get under my skin."

He nodded. "I'm sorry. And I'm sorry that, you know..."

"That he died? I'm sorry, too. Thank you."

Sylvie came up and stood beside me. I caught Calvin giving her an appreciative glance and treated him to my standard back-off glare. I did it from force of habit rather than genuine annoyance. Sylvie was the object of a good deal of speculative attention. She was extraordinarily good-looking, and men and women alike found her attractive. She was, by and large, oblivious to all of them, and men were of absolutely no interest to her—a fact that some of them found hard to reconcile with her appearance. In the early days of our relationship, I was sorely tempted to clock quite a few with a beer bottle.

I didn't need a blunt instrument to bludgeon Calvin. My glare must have been harsher than I'd intended. He flinched again and looked down at his shoes.

I smiled at Sylvie. "What did you get?"

"Licorice all-sorts," she said. "Don't grimace like that. I won't make you eat them."

"Calvin, this is my partner, Sylvie Wood. Sylvie, Calvin Knox."

Sylvie gave him a distant, appraising look. "Pleased to meet you," she said after a second or two.

He opened his mouth to reply, and then his face fell. "Excuse me," he said quickly. He brushed past us and walked briskly to the front door, where a fat man wearing a blue suit and a VFW hat stood impatiently. I'd have known that Hershey's Kiss hair anywhere: it was Daddy Knox. They had a brief conversation, Calvin paid for his candy, and they left together.

"That was weird," I said.

"Which part?"

"All of it. Calvin seems to be having some trouble with the spirit world. The dead stay dead? That's not good evangelical theology."

"No," Sylvie agreed. "But are Calvinists evangelicals? They believe in predestination, so what would be the point in trying to convert souls? We're all damned or saved from the beginning of time. There's nothing we can do about it."

"Good point."

We paid for our candy and left the shop. Outside, Calvin and George Knox were standing about ten feet away, talking to a third man, who must have been some sort of big military muckety-muck. He was in service uniform, a short-sleeved khaki shirt, dark green trousers, and a hat that the Captain called a piss-cutter. The left side of his shirt was covered in ribbons, and he had metal oak leaves on his hat and collar. I knew that bronze oak leaves were for majors and silver were for lieutenant colonels, but I wasn't close enough to make out the color. The man was very tall and very fit, almost wiry in build, and his hair was clipped Marine Corps short. In fact, even if he'd been out of uniform, everything about him screamed Marine. He stood bolt upright, as if he had a steel rod instead of a spine.

Calvin stared at his shoes as the man talked, and George Knox looked uncharacteristically cowed. I thought, "Career Marine officer meets ex-Marine gone to seed," and wished we were standing closer.

"Wait," I said to Sylvie. "Let's eavesdrop some more."

"I thought you were tired of acting like your mother," she whispered.

"Never mind that," I replied. "Look over there. The man in uniform looks really familiar. I can't place him, but I'm sure I know him."

Sylvie looked. "I see what you mean," she said. "I'm sure I don't know him, but maybe we've seen him on television?"

"Could be," I mused. "I was thinking I'd seen him closer to home."

"Can you hear what he's saying, big ears?" she asked.

"Shh, I'm trying." I could only catch the odd word, blown to me on the mild breeze. "Something about 1972, their unit, and a reunion—a battalion reunion? And Fox News. The guy in uniform just said Fox News. Maybe that's where we've seen him."

"I wouldn't be at all surprised," said Sylvie. "Come on, Bil. You've listened enough. Besides, Calvin is giving me the eye."

"Oh, is he?" I took her arm possessively. "Would you like me to go over there and thump him?"

"My hero," she said, fluttering her eyelashes. "Of course not. In case you haven't noticed, I can take care of myself. I just want to get away from George Knox." We began walking back toward our hotel. Sylvie popped a licorice into her mouth. "What a creep. Knox came to speak at the Episcopal Church once, back in the days when I still attended. It was horrible."

"I'm sure," I said, talking around my candy root beer barrel. "Why did the piss-cops invite him? I wouldn't have thought he was their type at all."

Sylvie shrugged. "Some of the old ladies wanted to hear what he had to say on the subject of women priests. That's when they were trying to decide whether or not to offer the minister's position to Leslie Adams."

"By old ladies, you mean my grandmother, don't you? She hates women priests. Emma says she's going to insist that Leslie do Granny's funeral—or, if she doesn't feel up to it, then maybe the chief crone of the Cowslip Wiccans."

"That would be harsh," Sylvie said. "Your grandmother was the ringleader. She gave it her all, but Leslie got the job, anyway. She's great. Attendance has nearly doubled. I'd go back to the Episcopal Church, but it never really felt like home to me."

"No?"

"No." She gave me a sideways glance. "I prefer the Unitarians."

I laughed. "Don't mind me. I'm a religious snob, remember?"

As we wandered up the street Sylvie said, "You're frowning. What are you thinking?"

"I'm not frowning. I'm sucking on this root beer barrel." I crunched up the remains and swallowed. "Actually, I'm wondering why Calvin is up here with Big Daddy. He's not a Marine. Do you suppose his father is hoping he'll join the service?"

"Could be," Sylvie said. "Or maybe he wanted him to meet some of his old Vietnam buddies."

"Uh-huh. You know my mother has been doing some of her research, meaning she's been nosing around in George Knox's life. If she's right—and there's no guarantee that she is—then Knox left the Marines under some kind of cloud. Why would he want to come up here and meet any of them?"

"I don't know," Sylvie said. "Your mother could have her facts wrong. There seem to be a lot of ex-military guys in his church."

"True. Maybe he's up here recruiting."

Sylvie nodded. "And Calvin, as the heir-apparent, is learning the ropes."

"Hmm," I said. "That boy sails pretty close to the wind. He was running around with Sam's crowd, playing the wild preacher's son. Now here he is with daddy, greeting the troops. He's got a cell phone, like a big fat drug dealer..."

"Bil," Sylvie laughed. "It's 1996. Not everyone who has a cell phone is a drug dealer. Your mother has a cell phone. My mother has one. Your sisters all have them. I'm thinking we might make the leap and get one ourselves—or maybe two."

"I can't afford a cell phone, Sylvie."

"Bil..." she began.

"And you cannot pay for all my treats and gadgets," I said firmly.

She didn't answer. We'd reached the hotel. It really was an impressive structure. Our room had a lakefront view and a fireplace. We walked through the revolving doors, stepped into the elevator, and I pushed the button for our floor. Sylvie moved next to me and put her arms around my waist.

"Stop glaring," she said. "I won't buy you a cell phone if you don't want one."

"I do want one," I said. "I just can't afford one."

"And you'll be angry if I get one for you, even if there's some sort of special deal that makes it cheaper to buy two?"

"You're making this hard," I said.

"Bil," Sylvie said, putting her mouth very close to my ear. "Why don't we have this conversation later? We pass by the ice machine on the way to our room. Do you still want to show me that trick you were talking about earlier?"

"What do you think?" I asked, turning to kiss her.

"I think," she said, "that we've reached our floor. Race you!"

Chapter 15

I could hear the phone ringing in our apartment from the bottom of the front stairs. I ran up all three flights and rescued my answering machine from a torrent of swearing.

"Hello, Tipper."

"Woman, where have you been?"

"In Coeur d'Alene," I replied. "Hiding from my family. How are you?"

"I am interesting," he said. "Very interesting."

It had been nearly a month since I'd heard from him—a long time between phone calls from Tipper, who sometimes rang twice a night.

"You are that," I said. "No question. So what's his name, where did you meet, and what's his sign? Is he Mr. Right or Mr. Right Now?"

"His name," Tipper said, "is Thomas P. Schwartz. We've never met, I think he's a Pisces, and he's Mr. All Wrong. There's no love lost between us."

"Hold on a second. Your name is Thomas P. Schwartz. I forget what the 'P' stands for."

"At the moment, perturbed," said Tipper. "And my name is actually Thomas P. Schwartz, Junior."

It took me a few moments to process this information, and another few to recover enough to speak. Sylvie had just come in the front door, carrying the suitcase I'd dropped on the landing in my rush to the telephone. It occurred to me that a discussion of Captain Schwartz's ex-husband might not put her in the best of moods.

"Your father?" I asked quietly.

"Yes," Tipper said. "My father. As much as my mother would like people to believe that I sprang fully formed from her Athenian forehead, I am, in fact, the product of sperm and egg. Two days ago, out of the blue, the other half of my reproductive equation called me. He says he wants to meet me. In Cowslip."

"But... but..." I stuttered.

"That's what I said. I thought it was a joke at first. Imagine— we've never laid eyes on one another. He and my mother parted company just after she got pregnant. By mutual consent."

I sat down on the floor in the hallway. "This is interesting news, Tipper."

Sylvie stepped over my legs. "I'm going to take a shower," she said. "Tell Tipper I said hello."

"Tipper, Sylvie says..."

"I heard her," he replied. "Tell her I said 'hello' back. How's she doing with this affair d'amour between my mother and Kate?"

"Oh, that's a tough one," I hemmed, waiting for Sylvie to go into the bathroom and turn on the water. "As well as might be expected."

Tipper laughed. "That's what I thought. I certainly don't blame her. My mother is notorious. It's my hope that she's serious this time."

"Has she said anything?"

"Plenty. Whenever we talk, it's all Kate, Kate, Kate. Your gorgeous mother-in-law is apparently a cross between Aphrodite and Saint Joan. How long this euphoria will last, I don't know."

"Could I at least be cautiously optimistic?"

"Absolutely," he said. "But just to be safe on the safe side, you might pick a nice deity and pray to her as well."

Though the bathroom door was ajar, I was fairly certain Sylvie couldn't hear me over the noise of the water.

"Okay," I said. "The coast is clear. Spill the beans about daddy dearest. Until Suzy set me straight a few nights ago, I thought Schwartz was your mother's maiden name."

"My mother's maiden name was Hiney," he said. "Rebecca Hiney. All the kids at school called her Betcha Hiney. That alone was reason enough to get married."

I tried and failed to picture Captain Schwartz married to a man. Any man. She'd spent several years in the Women's Army Corps and served in Vietnam. Tough didn't begin to describe her. Even macho seemed a bit weak. Who was Thomas P. Schwartz, Senior? Was he even more strapping than the Captain, or was he one of those weedy little guys you sometimes see clinging hopelessly to a large woman, like the small male spider who mates once and then becomes the female's post-coital snack?

"Wow... um... wow," I said. "So what did he say? How did he find you?"

"That," said Tipper, his faint North Carolina accent growing more pronounced, "is a tale. He found me in *The Advocate*. You remember when I performed at Seattle Pride as Snatches Mississippi?"

"How could I forget?"

"Well, *The Advocate* did a little piece on the politics of performance art and interviewed me and another couple of drag acts, Cherries Jubilee, Eartha Slit, and a drag king called Harry Pye. They also identified us by our real names. My father found the article and looked me up in the phone book."

"Your father reads *The Advocate*?"

Tipper sighed heavily. "I can't believe you ever worked in a computer lab. He got on the Internet and ran a search on my name. God knows how many hits he got, but that article came up first."

"Jesus Christ, Tipper. Why was he looking for you? Did he say what he wants?"

"Yes and no."

In the pause that followed, I did what I always do when I'm nervous—I pulled a book of matches out of my pocket, lit one, and burned down the loose strings on my cut-off jeans. "Ouch," I said, when the flaming remnants of a string fell on my bare leg.

"Put those goddamn matches away," Tipper said, showing off his encyclopedic knowledge of my bad habits. "I'll bet Sylvie doesn't like you playing with fire."

"She likes me just as I am," I lied.

Tipper was right, of course. Sylvie hated my string burning. I put the matches back in my pocket and waved my hand to dissipate the smoke.

"Go on," I said. "Carry on with your story."

"I don't know how to explain it," Tipper said. "Our conversation was really weird, sort of like a version of old home week from *The Twilight Zone*. He talked about how he met my mother and why they got married."

"And?"

"And I already knew most of it. My mother was on her second tour of duty in Vietnam. Like every other woman over there, she volunteered. Mama looked like the butch version of General Westmoreland, and even then, she liked girls in a big way. Maybe she acted on that, maybe she didn't. Anyhow, she got clocked. The brass was on to her, and she was running scared when my father appeared on the scene. They married in haste and repented at leisure. He didn't talk about his motivations, but he was well aware of hers."

"He knew she was a lesbian?"

"No. He knew she was under suspicion for being a lesbian, but he liked her. She seems to have liked him, too. They got married to save her career. It didn't work, and neither did the marriage."

"What happened?"

"Mama got pregnant. She's always said that she really wanted a baby, but I wonder if she didn't just get carried away and decide to give heterosexuality the old college try. My parents were together for a grand total of two weeks, just long enough for Mama to get a bun in the oven. So much for the marriage save. She got drummed out of the WACs anyway, which is what they did to pregnant women in those days. My father stayed in. He retired a few months ago after thirty years in the Marine Corps."

"The Marines!" I croaked.

"Oh, for heaven's sake, Bil. What other kind of man would have the cojones to schtupp my mother?"

That answered my earlier spider question. "Jesus Christ!" From across the hall, I heard JC barking in Suzy's apartment. Using my quiet voice, I said, "Fucking hell, Tipper."

"I know," he agreed. "I did learn a few things I didn't know. My parents met in Tokyo. My father was a first lieutenant. Mama was already a captain. They were each on R and R, and they met over a bowl of rice noodles or some such. It was not romantic. It was quick and dirty. My mother drank him under the table, and he apparently liked that in a woman. They were married, they made me, and he went back to the front. She went back to the 95th Evac in Da Nang. The rest of their contact was by mail or telephone."

I stopped him. "You're speaking a foreign language to me, Tipper. The 95th Evac?"

"Bil," he said testily. "What do you think my mother did during the war? She wasn't Rambo. She was an Army nurse."

"But she's not a nurse now," I said stupidly.

"No," he replied. "She's not. And she hasn't been a nurse since she left the service. You're damned lucky if she'll help you put on a Band-Aid. My mother does not talk about Vietnam. You know that. The most she's ever said to me is that she will never nurse again as long as she lives. Too many young men died in her care. She loved the Army, but she hated that."

"I'm sorry," I said.

"It's all right," Tipper replied. "My mother loves her firearms, and she's a terrible uniform queen, but she hates war. Post-traumatic stress disorder. She has nightmares, you know—really terrible ones. What she needs is a fucking good therapist. Instead, she has processing circles. She's demented."

"I'm sorry," I said again. "I didn't know."

"It doesn't matter," he said more kindly. "Now you do. I don't think I'm giving away state secrets. My mother loves you. She might have told you all of this herself if you'd asked. At any rate, she won't be bothered, that you know. Mama doesn't like talking about her feelings, and that's what Vietnam is all about—feelings, and a deep and abiding sadness. I wish she'd let it all out a bit more, but I'm glad she's not like that fucking George Knox."

Now I was really confused. "That fucking George Knox? What does he have to do with anything?"

Tipper laughed bitterly. "Guess how my father found out that my mother lived in Cowslip? He met up with George Knox at a company reunion in Coeur d'Alene. Echo Company, Second Battalion, Fifth Marines. Do you know that that's all I know about my father? I have his name, I know where he served, and I know his company and his battalion."

"I'm sorry," I said. "Tipper, there's something..."

"It's okay," he interrupted. I waited. There was a long pause before he continued, and I had a hard time keeping my fingers away from the matches.

Finally he said, "I don't know how the subject of my mother came up, but it did. The Major said that he'd been planning to drive all the way to Seattle to meet me, but he thought it might be better if we met in Cowslip."

"Tipper," I said, changing the subject slightly. "I told you that Sylvie and I were in Coeur d'Alene. I think we may have seen your father. We saw a man in uniform talking to George Knox. Oak leaves on his collar."

"Bronze or silver?"

"I wasn't close enough to see."

Tipper sighed. "If the leaves were bronze, that could have been my father. He retired as a major. What was Knox wearing?"

"A piss-cutter hat and his blue preacher's suit."

"Not allowed," Tipper said. "You either wear all of the uniform or none of it. This is the Marine Corps, woman! That was probably a VFW hat. I suppose we're lucky Knox wasn't wearing his Vietnam utilities."

"What's up with you and Knox?"

"Don't you read Slip-Fifty?" Tipper asked. "I've been getting into it with that fat bastard over whether or not women should be allowed to serve in the military. Never mind gays—Knox hasn't gotten it through his thick skull that the fairer sex has been holding its own on the battlefield for centuries. Apparently, the man has never heard of the Amazons or Boudica. Anyhow, he named my mother particularly. Suzy forwarded the e-mail and I joined the list to defend the Captain's honor."

"Why didn't Suzy call the Captain?" I asked.

"Three reasons," Tipper said. "One, my mother is not on Slip-Fifty, and I don't want her on there. It would be bad for her blood pressure. Second, George Knox is trumpeting his service in Vietnam. You and I both know that my mother will not answer him in kind. Finally, the Captain doesn't always speak with her mouth. I don't want to have to bail her out of jail when she knocks that asshole's teeth down his throat and invites him to chew his own ass out."

I had nothing to say to this. I'd never known the Captain to be violent. She liked her guns, but she didn't use them on anything except a paper target. Still, the thought of Knox belittling her service made me want to hit him.

Tipper was in mid-sentence when I began actively listening again. "... not that Knox could wear his utilities. I doubt the fat bastard could fit into anything he wore in 1971. Besides, it was so damp in Vietnam that your clothes rotted and fell off after a couple of months, beginning with your underwear."

"Thanks for that image," I said. "George Knox, going commando. Please, Tipper, about your mother's marriage..."

He sighed. "I know. Mama hated being married, even if it was only for five minutes and only for convenience. She wasn't meant to be anyone's wife, especially not a career Marine's. My father seems pretty clear on that point. He also says that he wasn't cut out for parenthood. They worked out some sort of arrangement that was satisfactory to them both and went their separate ways. It's always been just me and Mama—after Mimi died, anyway."

Mimi was Tipper's grandmother, a formidable old woman who'd farmed tobacco for a living. I knew Tipper had spent much of his childhood with her. When Mimi died, the Captain sold the farm, left North Carolina, and used the money to move to Idaho. She'd bought a hundred acres just outside of Cowslip and founded the Blood Moon Women's Haven, AKA Fort Sister. She told me once that she'd always dreamed of living in a women's collective. In the sixties, the WAC was as close as she could get.

"What are you going to do?" I asked. "Are you going to meet him?"

"That's why I'm calling you," Tipper replied. "Could you pick me up at the airport tomorrow night?"

"Cowslip or Spokane?"

"Spokane." He made a shuddering noise. "I have no intention of flying into Cowflop International. The only planes that land there are powered by rubber bands and hamsters on little treadmills."

"It's not that bad. I took the Seattle Shuttle once."

"So did I. It was like being shot from a cannon. My flight gets in at nine-thirty, gate A15. I'm sorry it's so late. It was the best I could do on short notice."

"No problem," I said.

"Bil," he said soberly. "I am coming to Cowflop because my father has some unfinished business to transact with Mama. He wouldn't say over the phone what it was—and, yes, I did ask. Mama doesn't know he's coming. I'm going to meet him on Sunday afternoon. On Sunday night, I'll break the news to her that he's resurfaced."

There was a pause, during which I imagined first the Captain's reaction, then Kate's, and then Sylvie's. The image of a shopping cart filled with whipped cream and strawberries swam before my eyes.

"Holy Mary, Mother of God."

"Don't get Catholic on me," he said. "I'm counting on you to help me keep the peace. Also, I want you to come with me to meet the Major."

My slow-moving brain ticked over and a cog clicked into place.

"Wait. Major? Your father outranks your mother?" This piece of information was, for some reason, more difficult to process than anything else Tipper had told me.

"I'm sure that'll be a sore point," he said, "and by sore point I mean a festering wound. My mother was ambitious. She wanted to be a general. She's never blamed me personally for having been drummed out of the Army. She blames the brass, and she blames my father. I think she also blames a faulty condom, but we won't go there."

I could hear JC across the hall in Suzy's apartment, barking his head off. I had Suzy's keys. I needed to get the dog before he tore the door down.

I said, "Of course I'll come to the airport, Tipper, but Sylvie is..."

"I know," he said. "Look, don't say anything to her right now. Bring her with you and I'll see what I can do to soften the blow."

"There isn't room. My truck is too small."

"Then call your mother and borrow the Queen Mary. Otherwise, we'll just have to bunch up and let our feet hang out the windows. Bring her, Bil," Tipper ordered. "I'm much better than you are at coping with angry females."

I didn't disagree.

Chapter 16

I had expected choir practice at Fort Sister to be a tense affair. Although Sylvie decided to come with me and make a good faith effort with the Captain, my hopes were not high. I felt guilty for giving her an edited version of my conversion with Tipper—for only telling her that we were picking him up at the airport and that he'd specifically asked that she come.

"That was sweet," she said. "I've always liked Tipper."

"You used to like his mother," I reminded her.

"So I did," she agreed. "Come on. We don't want to be late."

Kate was there when we arrived, apparently because she was almost always there. Her dogs, Elvis and Priscilla, had taken up semi-permanent residence in the Captain's kitchen. Their monogrammed dog beds rested next to the wall between the stove and the pantry. Sylvie shot me a baleful look when she noticed this but said nothing.

The Captain and Kate met us at the door, and we all greeted one another in friendly fashion. Elvis, a black Lab, and Priscilla, a Samoyed, swarmed Sylvie. We'd taken JC with us, and after some preliminary sniffing and growling, Elvis and Priscilla decided that he was acceptable. Once they'd all stopped running around, Sylvie and I each got a kiss from Kate. The Captain gave me her usual bear hug. Sylvie, on the other hand, got a smile and a kind pat on the shoulder. Wise, I thought. Sylvie and the Captain were not yet on hugging terms.

After chatting for a minute or two, Sylvie, Kate, and the Captain wandered into the living room where Suzy and Donny were waiting. I went back outside to keep an eye out for my grandmother's car.

Exactly fifteen minutes late, Wilhelmina Aldershot, the mistress of melodrama, made her grand entrance. She roared up the long driveway in her lethal Buick and screeched to a dusty halt, narrowly missing the bottom step where I was standing.

"Hi, Granny," I said, stepping carefully around her front bumper.

"Bil!" she cried. With surprising agility, she leapt out of the car and squeezed me mercilessly. "Why are you here?"

I looked down at her. Granny looked like my mother, only shorter, grayer, and fatter. She viewed the world with a sort of shrewd amazement, though, and like Emma, she was a megalomaniac. She assumed that all right-thinking people believed as she did. Those who didn't she wrote off as either inconsequential or mentally ill.

"I'm here because I'm singing," I said.

"Oh? With whom?"

Granny was undeniably ditzy. According to my mother, it was all an act. She played senile because she wanted to move in with my parents and torment Emma until one or the other of them shuffled off this mortal coil. I doubted that. Granny made no bones about what she thought of my parents' house. She referred to it variously as a tip or a midden. How this might change when they built their new house—or if they built their new house, barring the Feds seizing it because of Jake Peterson's meth lab—I didn't know. Personally, I suspected that Granny played ditzy because she thought it was cute. She wanted people to mistake her for one of those hilarious old ladies on television.

"I'm singing with *you*, Granny," I said. "And Suzy, and Donny, and Captain Schwartz. You're playing the piano."

"Oh, I know. Won't it be fun?"

"Hang on a second." I took her arm to keep her from going into the house. "You do know that you're playing for a JUGS benefit, don't you? Suzy told you that, right?"

"Jigs," she said. "Irish dancing. Isn't that Suzy a lovely girl?"

"JUGS," I corrected. "Not jigs. JUGS stands for Justice for Us Girls. It's the group that's working to overturn the new breast ordinance. No Irish dancing. And listen, Suzy isn't..." I thought better of this and stopped. "Never mind about Suzy. The point is that we are raising money for a petition drive. We intend to repeal the breast ordinance. Do you understand?"

She waved a hand and pooh-poohed me. "Oh, I know all about that. Sarah brought me something to sign. Such a silly ordinance— I've never seen a bare breast in Cowslip, and I've lived here forever. I saw plenty when I went with the Women's Auxiliary to Las Vegas. We went to one show that was nothing but topless girls. I told Millicent Rutherford it looked like fried eggs dancing on a plate."

On that happy note, Granny pranced up the steps and into the kitchen. Once inside, however, she stopped as if she'd been shot. "Which way?" she whispered.

"This way," I said, leading her to the only other door in the room.

"I've never been out here before," she whispered. "This place has... a reputation. No one's going to be naked, are they?"

"No," I whispered back. "You won't find any fried eggs here."

The usual assortment of artists, poets, astrologers and softball players were milling around the Captain's enormous living room. I recognized Cedar Tree, née Beatrice Johnson, a painter who seemed to have unlimited financial resources. She'd arrived at Fort Sister sometime in 1993. Captain Schwartz operated her women's retreat on a sliding scale, but Tipper told me that she'd gotten so tired of Cedar Tree, she'd taken to doubling her monthly fee. And still Cedar stayed. She was crouched now in front of the cold stone fireplace, wrapped in a gauzy shawl and muttering to herself over something that looked suspiciously like dungeons and dragons gaming dice.

Granny shook hands with the Captain and Kate and kissed Sylvie on the cheek. "You get prettier every day," she said before turning to greet Donny and Suzy.

"The old hypocrite," I whispered to Sylvie. "She's told half the town that we're going to hell."

"I know," Sylvie whispered back. "But I think she's sucking up to my mother."

"You mean she's sucking up to your mother's bank account. She probably wants a donation for the Community Theatre."

"Pay attention, you two," Suzy commanded. "I now call this choir to order. Singers over here. Mrs. Aldershot, please take your seat at the pianoforte. The rest of you, disport yourselves as you see fit."

Sylvie sat next to her mother on the sofa. The rest of us gathered around the Captain's baby grand.

"I thought we'd start with a quick scale to get some idea of the tone and pitch of each of our voices. Just a simple do-re-mi."

I cleared my throat. "Um, I'm not really ready to sing in front of an audience."

Suzy turned to the Captain, who nodded, stepped into the middle of the room, and clapped her hands. "Attention all nonessential personnel. Make yourselves scarce. Except for Sylvie and Kate, that is."

Kate laughed. Sylvie's face assumed an expression of patient loathing that I hoped neither her mother nor the Captain noticed. The room cleared and Suzy invited Granny to play middle C on the piano.

"My pleasure," said Granny, banging the note with unnecessary force.

"Yes," Suzy said, shaking his head. "Thank you, Mrs. Aldershot."

"Call me Wilhelmina," she shrieked.

Suzy sang his do-re-mi first, followed by Donny and then the Captain. They sounded great. Donny had a sweet, accomplished baritone. I complimented him on it, and he blushed profusely.

"You know how Mormons are," he said. "We're a singing church."

"I thought the Lutherans were the singing church," Granny said.

"The Lutherans are too uptight to do any hymn justice," Suzy declared. "They sing without passion. Damned anal-retentive Germans."

"You got that from Emma," I said, pointing my finger at him. "She's got a bug up her butt about the Germans."

"I don't know why," Granny said. "Such an interesting people. So disciplined."

"This quartet," Suzy continued firmly, "will be disciplined but not German. Your turn, Bil. Do-re-mi."

I closed my eyes and took several deep breaths.

"Do-re-mi," I sang. "Fa-so-la-tee-do."

I held the last note longer than was strictly necessary because I'd caught Granny gazing at me skeptically. That'll show the old bat, I thought. Sure enough, when I opened my eyes, I found that her gaze had become speculative.

"Cowslip Community Theatre is doing *The Pajama Game* this fall," she said. "Why don't you try out?"

"Thanks," I said with a laugh, "but no thanks." Granny was forever trying to get one up on her archrival, Millicent Rutherford, whose granddaughter had starred in the spring revival of *Oklahoma!* "In fact, I'd rather be dead."

"Poor Jud is dead." Granny tsked. "But that's a different musical."

The Captain interrupted whatever Granny was going to say next. "I hope you've picked a lot of songs for soprano," she told Suzy. "Bil is wonderful."

"That was my plan," Suzy replied. "Nuh-uh. No objections, Bil Hardy. It has to be this way. You have the strongest voice and the least experience. The rest of us know how to harmonize. Now, here's what I thought: we'll sing 'Blessed Assurance,' 'In the Sweet By and By,' 'Bringing in the Sheaves,' and 'When the Roll is Called Up Yonder.' That's two weepy creepy and two happy clappy. Do you know them, Bil?"

"I know them," I admitted.

"And I can play them backwards," Granny declared. She beat out the opening chords of "Blessed Assurance." The Captain and Donny winced, and Suzy looked as if he thought we might be better off with a karaoke box. Granny played merrily on, hitting notes that could only have been reached with the aid of a third hand.

"We'll have to work on the tempo," Suzy said. "And the chords."

Granny stopped suddenly. "What will you do for an encore?"

I laughed. "What encore?"

Suzy, however, was regarding me seriously. "That's a good question. What about 'Jesus Wants Me for a Sunbeam?'"

"You must be kidding."

"Or 'What a Friend We Have in Jesus,'" the Captain suggested.

"'I'd Rather Have Jesus,'" Donny cracked, displaying his rare sense of humor. "I'd like to hear Bil sing that."

"Me, too," Suzy and the Captain chorused.

"Oh, yeah? 'Tell it to Jesus.'" I replied.

"Tell it to the Marines," Suzy said.

They rolled around laughing. I stole a glance at Sylvie and Kate. They had their heads together and seemed to be chatting amiably. Tell it to the Marines, indeed. I hoped Tipper was as good with angry women as he claimed to be. Otherwise, come Sunday, we'd need to call in a battalion or two to deal with the bloodshed.

* * *

After Granny left, the rest of us sat out on the front porch, drinking beer. All except for Donny, that is, who had a cup of caffeine-free herbal tea. He sat a little way apart from the group and stared out at the starry night. I picked up my beer and moved my chair next to his.

"How's your investigation?" I asked in as casual a tone as I could muster.

"Hmm? You mean the Peterson case?"

I nodded.

"I don't know," he said with a shrug. "Sid's in charge of that."

"That's a shame," I said. "Suzy and Emma both think he's an idiot. Any hot leads?"

"Sid thinks he might have one on the shotgun."

"I thought shotguns were untraceable."

"Generally," he agreed. "But Sid thinks he might be able to identify this one. The shooter fired at close range with a 20-gauge. The coroner, your sister, picked a bunch of pellets out of Peterson's brain and... I'm sorry, is this making you sick?"

"No," I said, noticing too late that it was Donny who looked a little green around the gills. "Well, maybe just a little."

He took a gulp of his tea. "It's okay. We can talk about something else."

"No," I said quickly. "I mean, I don't mind talking about Peterson. Let's just skip the gory parts. Any idea how long he'd been dead before you found him?"

"Two or three days. The coroner—sorry, I keep doing that—your sister thinks he might have died late Saturday night or early Sunday morning, but it was so hot those two days. The heat makes determining the exact time of death tricky. Bodies decompose and bloat and... and stuff like that." He gulped more tea.

As usual, my mother's eavesdropping was infallible.

"Yuck," I said. "No need to go any further. I've seen dead deer at the side of the road. Bloated and... explosive."

"Exactly," Donny said quickly. "I was out at your mom's place this morning."

"Why?"

"Following up on my own..." He stopped and looked embarrassed.

"Yes?"

"I was following up on my own lead," he went on. "It's really Sid's case, but I've got some ideas. The night before we found Jake Peterson, someone broke into Robertson's Chemicals. Your mom phoned in the complaint."

"You think the two things might be related?"

He nodded. "I do. Sid doesn't. He says the timing's all wrong. If the guys who broke into Robertson's were involved, it would mean that they got the ammonia first and then dumped both it and the body at the Kornmeyer place. If they had the body with them, and your mom was shining a light on them and everything, then why didn't they shoot her, too?"

"Because they didn't have a silver bullet?" I suggested.

Donny laughed. I didn't care what my mother thought, I'd long since decided I liked him. It was hard to tell if moving in with Suzy had done wonders for Donny's personality, or if he'd been a funny guy all along and coming out of the closet had brought him out of his shell.

"There is that," Donny said. "The problem is that I'm just a deputy. Sid's the detective. I can make suggestions, but he makes all the decisions."

I swigged my beer and he sipped his tea.

"Darn," he said suddenly. "This isn't public knowledge, Bil. I'm afraid I got carried away. If you wouldn't mind, please don't mention it to anyone, especially not, well... you know."

"You mean my mother?"

He shook his head. "No. Your mother knows everything. She always does. It's your sister Ruth I'm worried about. I don't want her to think that I can't keep my big mouth shut. Even if I can't." He smiled ruefully. "Suzy is right. Cops are terrible gossips."

"It's okay," I said. "I understand. The coroner's report is still confidential. Don't worry. I'm not likely to see Ruth, and if I do, I'll keep what you've said in confidence."

"Thanks." He set his teacup down on the porch railing. "You have a lovely voice. I can't believe you've never sung in a choir. Does your church not have one?"

Poor guy. He had such an open, honest face. I felt like I was about to break the news to him that there wasn't a Santa Claus.

"I don't have a church," I said. "My mother was raised Episcopalian but she turned atheist long before she adopted me. I've been a few times with friends, I go to weddings and funerals, and as a kid I occasionally went to mass with my grandmother. That's the sum total of my religious experience."

"Then where did you learn how to sing all those hymns?"

"I guess I'm kind of an idiot savant. You know, like *Rain Man*? I learned by listening to religious broadcasting. *The PTL Club* and crap like that."

"Wow. Really?" He hesitated. "Bil, would you...?"

"Would I what?"

"You delivered the eulogy at your brother's funeral. I don't know if you saw me. I was on duty and so I had to come in uniform. I sat in the back so I wouldn't disturb anyone."

"That was kind of you," I said, thinking both of Donny attending Sam's funeral and of my mother's reaction if she'd seen him in his cop gear.

"I had a brother who died young," Donny said. "His name was Daniel. At his funeral, the choir sang 'Danny Boy.' That's not a choir song. It's a song for a soloist. It's a song for someone like you. I was wondering..."

"Now?" I asked.

He nodded. I was on my third beer, and I'd already sung in front of everyone on the porch.

"Okay, Donny."

I began quietly. As everyone stopped talking to listen, I raised my voice. Forget delivering a eulogy. I should have sung at Sam's funeral. "Danny Boy" was perfect. I sang without pyrotechnics, without vocal gymnastics—just the right notes at the right pitch and sung with the right emotion. The song soared and I soared with it.

When I finished, there was a long silence. Donny was crying softly on Suzy's shoulder. Suzy stroked his dark curly hair and shushed him. I reached out and gave Donny an awkward pat on the knee. Then I looked around at the stricken faces, Captain Schwartz's included.

"You should warn a body before you do that," she said.

"It's the song," I said. "It's a killer."

"It's not the song," the Captain said. "It's the singer. Joe Feeney on *The Lawrence Welk Show* never had that effect."

Kate broke the tension by laughing. "Honey, Bil and Sylvie are too young to remember Lawrence Welk."

Suzy said, "Not to mention *The Carol Burnett Show, Hee-Haw, Sonny and Cher, Donny and Marie...*"

Donny lifted his head from Suzy's shoulder. "Surely everyone remembers *Donny and Marie!*"

We all laughed. Sylvie said. "I remember most of those shows, especially *Donny and Marie.* That incredibly camp, bitchy Paul Lynde was on their show. I wonder if the Mormons knew then what an old queen he was?"

"How could they have missed it?" Suzy asked. "The man couldn't open his mouth without bursting into flames."

"No, they missed it," Donny assured us. "We can be pretty clueless about non-Mormons, Suzy. We live in our own little world."

"Utah," Suzy said. "Fair enough. The Catholics have Rome."

"And Italy, and Ireland, and Poland," I added.

"And Spain," said Suzy. "And Latin America, and the Philippines. The Catholics have got an eighteen-hundred-year head start on you, Donny."

"We're catching up," Donny said. "And we've got gymnasiums and swimming pools."

This was a side of Donny I'd never seen. I liked it.

"Bil," Donny turned to me. "Would it be too personal to ask if you believe in God?"

I thought for a moment. "No, it's not too personal. Yes, I guess I do believe in God. I don't believe in organized religion, and I don't necessarily believe in everything I'm singing. I don't think Jesus wants anyone for a sunbeam, me included, and I prefer the really morbid hymns, the ones where life is a series of Job-like trials and the only thing you have to look forward to is death. Appalachian hymns."

"You're an untutored Methodist," Suzy said.

"Are you sure I'm not a Pentecostal? Or a Baptist?"

"Nope. Pentecostals have an absolute belief in their own sinfulness. For us, hell is a constant, present danger. Baptists, on the other hand, have an absolute belief in other people's sinfulness. They worry about themselves from time to time, but mostly they're focused on damning you."

"It's true," the Captain agreed. She, Kate and Sylvie had moved their chairs over to where Donny and I sat. "Baptists always skip over that part about judging not lest ye be judged. We go straight to separating the sheep from the goats."

"Interesting," Kate said. "What about Episcopalians?"

"Whiskey-palians," Suzy said. "If you're high church, you're not worried about hell. You're worried about who God is going to allow into heaven. Will they be the right sort of people, or will heaven be divided into sections? On this side, Nieman Marcus and on that side, Wal-Mart."

Kate laughed. "Very good!"

"What about The Church of the True Vine?" I asked. "The men drink and smoke and generally do whatever they like, but the church is anti-fornication and anti-birth control. The women have to be subservient, and men essentially own their wives and children."

"True Vine is a hybrid," Suzy explained. "A gathering of the worst elements of Presbyterianism, Puritanism, Calvinism, and plain old sexism. Some fundamentalists believe in the doctrine of perfectibility. The True Vines believe in the doctrine of election."

"What's that?"

"Do you know what a Free Will Baptist is?" the Captain asked. I shook my head. "Free Will Baptists believe God created us with free will. We have the power to choose between right and wrong. God knows what we're going to do, but it's our own actions that determine our ultimate destiny. Heaven or hell."

"At Church of the True Vine," said Suzy, "they believe that God has already decided who's going to heaven and who's going to hell. It doesn't matter what you do. Your fate is predetermined. Even if you wanted to be saved, you couldn't be. God picked his souls for time and eternity before you were ever born."

"Sounds rotten to me," Sylvie said. "You can be faithful and still go to hell?"

"Yes," Suzy said. "Faith alone is not enough, and works don't even come into it. But that's not the worst part—just as God deliberately created some souls for salvation, he created others to be damned. That's the Doctrine of Election. The True Vines believe they're pre-destined to go to heaven. They are the elect."

"That's worse than rotten," I objected. "Where's the incentive to be nice? Where's the incentive to be a decent human being?"

"Exactly," Suzy said. "They can be as nasty as they like in this life. Now, they might want to be good as a sign that they're going to heaven—sort of like driving a Cadillac so that everyone will know you're rich—but nothing can change the mind of God. He deliberately created some people for heaven and others for hell. No amount of evangelizing can open the ears of someone God has predestined for eternal damnation."

I turned to Sylvie. "At last I see the attractions of Unitarianism. The music is crap but the doctrine is good."

"Thank you," she laughed. "Come with me this Sunday. We'll probably sing 'Kumbaya.'"

"Where do the Mormons stand on all of this?" I asked Donny.

Before he could answer, Suzy spoke up. "They've got the best deal of all, don't they, honey? When Donny dies, he gets to be the god of another planet. I'm plumping for Mars. You girls can have Venus."

"Try telling that to my granny," I said. "She thinks that *you're* a girl."

Suzy wiped an imaginary tear from his eye. "That's so sweet," he said.

"Hmm," Donny mused. "If Mrs. Aldershot thinks you're a girl, Suzy, I guess she's already living on her own planet."

Chapter 17

Sylvie and I were debating the relative merits of playing strip Scrabble or strip poker when Emma called. I looked at the clock. It was five past eleven.

"Where have you been?" my mother asked without preamble. "I've been trying to reach you for two days."

"Coeur d'Alene," I replied. "I left a number with Suzy. Why didn't you leave a message on the answering machine?"

"Telling Suzy is not the same as telling me," she said. "You could have been kidnapped or dead. And I didn't leave a message on that damned answering machine because you never call me back."

"I suppose if I'd been kidnapped, someone would have sent you a ransom note. If I were dead, you'd have gotten a visit from the police. And I always call you back, Ma, just not as quickly as you'd like."

I could hear my mother breathing heavily. I counted to ten and waited for the storm cloud to blow over. A nasty sucking sound told me that she'd lit a cigarette.

I said, "I hope you're out on the porch with the cordless phone. Whenever you smoke in the house, you drop ashes all over the sofa cushions."

"My cushions are my ashtray," she said. "Do you want to know why I called?"

"Other than to ream me out for having a life?"

"Other than that. I got a visit from Dick Corn-holer today."

I couldn't help it. I laughed. "Dick who?"

"You heard me," she said. "The cheap bastard farmer who sold me two hundred acres of misery. He stopped by to show me what he got in the mail this afternoon."

"Which was?" I prompted.

"A letter and a check. From Jake Peterson."

I stopped laughing. "You're joking. How could that be?"

133

"It's quite simple," she said. "The letter was an apology for paying the rent late. The check was for the money owed plus the next three months. That's why Kornmeyer stopped by—the future rent belongs to us. I don't know why he didn't pocket the whole thing. We'd never have known."

"Slow down," I said. "Peterson's check—when was it dated?"

"Friday, August 7."

"And the envelope—when was it postmarked?"

"Monday, August 10."

"Then Peterson couldn't have mailed it himself."

"No," she agreed.

"Does Kornmeyer know that Peterson is dead?"

There was a long pause while Emma huffed in a lungful of nicotine. "Yes. I told him. That's why he went straight to the bank and cashed the check."

"Jesus wept."

"Indeed. Do you want to see the letter?"

My heart dropped to the floor and bounced back up like a yo-yo. "You haven't given it to the police?"

"Not yet," she said. "I want to go to Kinko's first and make a photocopy."

"Are you insane?" I bellowed. "Go away, you mental case! Stop calling me!"

"Sorry," she said matter-of-factly. "I'm afraid I can't oblige you. The Queen Mary won't start, and I need a ride to town."

* * *

"I have a father and three sisters, and they all have cars. Why me?"

The moon was shining through the windshield, illuminating the letter on my mother's lap. Though Emma had tried to hand it to me, I'd refused to touch it. Curiosity might have made me agree to drive her to town, but it didn't extend to handling misappropriated evidence. That, and I felt a vaguely superstitious fear about playing around with a letter from a dead man.

"Could you speed up?" Emma said. "I'm afraid your father will wake up and notice I'm gone."

I put my foot down and watched impassively as the speedometer shot past seventy. With any luck, the cops would pull me over and I could say, "Here she is. Take her."

"Hugh wouldn't wake up if you set his hair on fire," I pointed out. "Why didn't you drive yourself to town in his car?"

"There's something wrong with the clutch," she said. "You have to push it in twice to get it to go into reverse, and then it makes an awful grinding noise."

"He needs a new car," I said viciously. "And so do you. But instead of buying something you actually need, you sell our house to a fucking chemical company and buy a shack full of corpses. Hey! No smoking in my truck!"

Emma tucked the unlit cigarette back in the pack and tucked the pack back in her bra.

"I guess you woke up on the wrong side of the bed," she said. "In Coeur d'Alene."

"Don't start with me. I'm a grown woman."

"Scarcely."

"Listen, Emma, I'm serious. If you keep dragging me into your nonsense, Sylvie is going to divorce me. She's madder than hell that I came out tonight to drive your sorry ass to town. Don't make me pick between you and her because I'll pick her."

"Don't be silly," she said, poking out her bottom lip. "Sylvie knew what she was getting into. You marry one Hardy, you marry all of us."

I remembered Sarah, Naomi, and Buck DeWitt. I stifled a laugh.

"What is it?" Emma asked suspiciously.

"Nothing. Welcome to Kinko's."

The store was brightly lit and empty of customers. Not surprising, really. It was Friday, it was after midnight, and all the people with good sense were safely tucked up in their innocent beds. Cowslip rolled up the sidewalks at nine p.m. The only places open twenty-four hours a day were Kinko's, the hospital, and the House of Pancakes.

"And the police station," a voice whispered in my head. My rage slowly ebbed away, replaced by nervousness. It seemed unlikely that Sid Castle would suddenly appear at Kinko's, but you never knew. In a small town, you ran into unlikely people in unlikely places. No doubt it was also my imagination that the clerk at the register was staring at us through his greasy curtain of brown hair.

My mother fumbled the letter out of its envelope and spread it flat on the copier. She turned it first one way and then another, aligning the right edge with the bottom of the glass.

"That's exactly the opposite of what you need to be doing," I said. "Align the left with the top. You want an eight-and-a-half by eleven copy, right?"

"Good thing I brought an expert with me," Emma snapped. She adjusted the letter, closed the lid, and punched the green copy button. Nothing happened. She punched it again. "This goddamn thing isn't working."

"That's because you need a copy key."

"A what?"

"One of these." I handed her a copy key from the counter. She stared it as if expecting it might suddenly break into a song and dance. "Oh, for God's sake." I took the key back. "You insert it here, where it says 'Insert Copy Key.'"

"You're as cross as two sticks," she observed. "If you act like this at home, no wonder Sylvie's annoyed with you. How many copies should I make?"

"None!" I shouted. The clerk jumped, dropping a ream of colored paper. I lowered my voice. "You should have taken that thing straight to the police. Now it's got your fingerprints all over it."

My mother rolled her eyes. "So what? Kornmeyer brought it to me and I touched it. That's allowed. *He* cashed the check."

"And gave you part of the proceeds."

"No he did not. He offered me part. I said I didn't want any of Peterson's money."

"Oh good for you. You're so noble."

"You don't know the half of it," she sniffed. "I think I'll make two copies of the letter, and two of the envelope. What will that cost?"

I looked up at the price chart. "Twenty-four cents plus tax. Why are you making that sour face? You are such a cheap ass!"

"One of these copies is for you," she said. "I want you to study this letter and tell me what you think. And I am not a cheap ass."

"Oh yeah? I ought to start charging you for gas and mileage."

"Unnatural child."

"Unnatural mother."

She finished her copies and folded the letter back into its envelope. I pulled the copy key out of its slot and handed it to her.

"Give this to the clerk. It tells him how much to bill you."

"I'm sorry," she said suddenly. "It's late and I'm sure you're tired."

I waited for the other shoe to drop. When it didn't, I said, "I am tired. It's been a long day and... I guess I'm sorry, too. I shouldn't have called you a cheap ass."

Emma flashed me a brilliant smile, only slightly marred by the gap from her missing front teeth.

"I don't know about that," she said. "You'll have to pay for the copies. I left my purse at home."

*   *   *

There was nothing remarkable about the letter. Peterson's handwriting was untidy but legible. He apologized for being late with the rent and explained that he'd been visiting his mother in Colorado Springs and had just gotten back. He was paying in advance for the next three months. He hoped that would be all right. He promised to contact Kornmeyer sometime in the future about extending his lease. The envelope was postmarked in Spokane. That wasn't surprising. Letters mailed in Cowslip were always marked in Spokane due to some weirdness in the postal system.

I put the copies on the coffee table and switched off the light. Sylvie was asleep when I got home. She'd been aggravated beyond endurance both by my mother's call and by my willingness, however reluctant, to do Emma's bidding. It wouldn't be fair to say we'd had an argument. I'd apologized, and she'd retreated into stony silence. I'd apologized again, and then I'd left. Not exactly a knock-down, drag-out.

Thanks to many years of psychology classes and a modicum of common sense, I was not without insight into my present situation. My family was enmeshed. We were in and out of each other's pockets all the time. We fought constantly. We treated one another and the world at large to an appalling and generous host of ill-informed opinions on all sorts of subjects, and none of us knew when to quit.

Sylvie had no siblings. She had a nice, if somewhat distant, mother who kept herself to herself and never made any unreasonable demands or asked any rude questions. There was bound to be a certain amount of friction in our relationship. The difference was that I was used to friction. I'd grown up with a shitload of it, and, to be honest, I wasn't sure that I knew how to operate without it. There was some part of me that enjoyed a good, fair fight.

I was in touch with my inner Emma.

I opened the bedroom door. JC got up to greet me but he didn't bark. He wagged his tail, and I patted his head.

"Go lay down," I whispered, and to my surprise, he did.

I stripped my clothes off and folded them into a neat pile. I laid them on top of the dresser. In the stillness, I could hear the muffled chime of Suzy's ridiculous cuckoo clock. I slipped quietly into bed, though not, it would seem, quietly enough.

"Well?" Sylvie asked in the darkness.

"Well what?"

"No *pho*?"

I was taken aback. "Why would I have stopped for *pho*?"

She rolled over to face me. "Why not? As long as you were out, I thought you might make a night of it."

"What?"

"Oh, no," she said. "Don't act like I'm being ridiculous. Your mother calls. You go. It doesn't matter what I want. It doesn't matter if we have plans."

"Look, I'm sorry about that," I said. "You can't imagine I'd rather be out gallivanting with my mother than here with you."

"Can't I?" she asked.

"No! Sylvie, I'm sorry. If you're asking me to choose between you and my mother..."

"I'm not asking that," she said.

"I wish you were," I said, "because I'd choose you. I told Emma that tonight. You are my first priority. Always."

There was a long silence. JC came up to the edge of the bed and nudged my hand. I scratched him behind the ears and told him to go lay down.

"You smell like photocopies," Sylvie accused.

"How can someone smell like photocopies?"

"You smell like toner," she insisted. "Toner has a smell. I have a very sensitive nose."

"I'm sorry," I said. "Would you like me to take a shower?"

"No." She rolled away from me and faced the wall. "Are you angry with me?"

"Oh, baby." I put my arm around her waist and pressed myself firmly against her back. "I'm not angry with you. I can see that you're angry with me."

"I was angry. I'm over it now. What did the letter say?"

"Nothing. It was a complete waste of time." I squeezed her tightly. "I really am sorry."

"I know." The stiffness went out of her body and she relaxed. "So am I."

"My mother thinks that when you married me, you married her."

"I'm beginning to think that, too."

"It's not true, you know. I'd push her over a cliff for you." I put my hand on her hip and gave it a gentle shake. "Go on, test me. Ask me to push Emma over a cliff."

Sylvie giggled and moved my hand from her hip back to her stomach. "I don't want you to push her over a cliff. I just want you to erect a few boundaries."

I sighed heavily. "Believe me, honey, I've tried. I keep sandbagging the levy, but she's like a hundred-year flood. The wall is never high enough."

"I should be more understanding," she said.

I disagreed. "No, you shouldn't. You should push me like you're pushing right now. Emma always goes too far. I need to learn to say no. Okay?"

"Okay."

I gave her hip a shake. "You seemed to be having a good time earlier tonight. I saw you talking with Captain Schwartz."

"Yeah," Sylvie said. "She can be charming when she puts her mind to it."

"She can," I agreed. "What were you talking about?"

"You. She thinks you're pretty terrific. Smart, funny, voice like an angel."

"Stop, you're embarrassing me. And?" The muscles of her stomach rippled beneath my fingertips.

"And nothing. Go to sleep."

"You don't mean that."

"No, damn you, I don't."

She rolled over and kissed me fiercely. When we paused for breath she said, "I hate to think what this says about the state of my psyche. We talk about your mother, my mother, and my mother's girlfriend and now all I want is to..."

She kissed me again and lifted her hips to my hand.

"Mmm," I said. "Perhaps you have an Electra complex."

She pulled my head back down. "Shows what you know," she whispered against my lips. "What I have is an electrical complex. You keep flipping my switch."

Chapter 18

The drive to Spokane was long and hot. I turned the truck's air conditioning on maximum and still the heat rose in waves from the black dashboard. Tipper's flight was due in at nine-thirty, which meant we'd had to leave at seven to be on the safe side. Just in time for the full blast of the setting sun to shine through the window and bake the side of my head.

"JC has an appointment with the veterinarian," Sylvie said. "Day after tomorrow. Shots, worming, and he's being neutered."

"Is he? That's good." I flipped the visor to the left, ducking to keep it from hitting me in the forehead. "I wish I'd thought to roll the windows down this morning. It's like an oven in here."

"Hmm." Sylvie fiddled with the radio. She looked cool and comfortable in her white cotton sundress. "Did Tipper say how long he'd be in town?"

"No. There are some cassettes in the glove box."

"You mean you don't want to listen to Christian radio?"

"No, thanks." I looked at the clock. "No wait! I do. It's time for George Knox's show, The True Vine Tabernacle. Suzy said we should listen in. Today's sermon is about the lack of modesty among today's modern women."

"No," Sylvie said. "I don't think I can bear it."

Despite her protests, she tuned the radio to Knox's broadcast. The sermon was already in progress.

"True feminism is truly feminine," Knox intoned. "It is the Christian duty of the father, the husband, and the brother to preserve and protect the women in their lives. A woman who belongs to no man belongs to every man."

"Not again!" I shook my fist at the radio. "That's just an invitation to rape. Fuck off! Concrete octopus, my ass—we ought to call that compound of his *Jurassic Park*. You do know that Knox is staging a counter-demonstration on the day of the JUGS benefit, don't you?"

"No one will go," Sylvie said confidently.

"What are you talking about? Every right-wing crackpot in Cowslip will be there."

She laughed. "I don't think so. Not when they hear that today's modern women are having a breast ordinance fashion show."

"Please explain." I switched off the radio and enjoyed not hearing the sound of that smug and ponderous voice. "If George Knox were any more self-important, he'd pop wide open."

"Probably," Sylvie agreed. "Have you actually read the breast ordinance?"

"I've read the summaries in the *Herald-Examiner*," I said. "It bars public breast feeding, female cleavage—both breast and butt—and nipples."

"It's a little more specific than that," Sylvie said. "It actually goes to the trouble of defining what's meant by the word 'cleavage.' It's the space between the breasts and/or the space between the buttocks. By being so specific, they've made a big mistake. It's still perfectly legal to show the sides and bottoms of one's breasts, and it's perfectly legal to show the bottoms of one's buttocks. Put a strip of duct tape across the crevices in question and cover your nipples with a couple of pasties and, according to the ordinance, you're legally clothed. We thought we'd stage a fashion show and let everyone know exactly what this ordinance covers... and what it doesn't."

"You're not!"

"No," she laughed. "I'm not. The adhesive on duct tape makes me break out. I'm wearing a wet T-shirt. That's legal, too. Eyes on the road, please!"

I stopped blinking at her and turned as much of my attention as I could back to driving.

"Are you having this fashion show before or after I sing with the Mighty Queer Gospel Quartet?"

"We haven't decided yet."

"Please make it after. I can't possibly sing about Jesus to an audience full of women wearing wet T-shirts and duct tape."

"You could try closing your eyes."

I pretended to give this serious consideration. "No, I don't think so. If this is a burden the Lord has given me to bear..."

She hit me on the arm.

"Ouch. Whose idea was this anyway? Sarah's?"

"In part. It was Naomi who pointed out the loopholes in the law."

"Naomi? That girl has gone plumb wild. She's not going to wear a wet T-shirt, is she?"

"I don't know," Sylvie said. "She might."

I paused to consider this. Naomi was well built. She was short and skinny, but she had larger breasts than Sarah.

"Sylvie, what do you think the odds are that both of my sisters will show up at this thing topless *and* with Buck DeWitt?"

Sylvie shuddered. "I wouldn't lay odds. It could get ugly."

"You're not kidding. And if Emma or Granny turn up in a wet T-shirt, I'll need some of that duct tape to put over my eyes."

* * *

We found Tipper downstairs in the baggage claim area, sitting on the side of a luggage carousel. He looked hot and tired. Nevertheless, he leapt up when he saw us and raced forward to seize us both in a lavish hug.

As soon as I reasonably could, I stood back and cast a critical eye over his outfit. He was wearing a white shirt, khaki pants, and shiny black loafers.

"Look at you in your corporate drag," I said. "Where's the wig? Where's the mini-skirt? Where is Snatches Mississippi?"

"What's the matter?" he asked. "Am I too butch for you? Afraid I'll steal your girl?"

He shoved me to one side, grabbed Sylvie, and kissed her on the lips. "Well?" he asked, lifting his head. "Have I turned you straight?"

"No," she said thoughtfully. "I think I feel twice as gay."

Tipper released her. "Oh, well. I guess clothes don't make the man."

"Yeah, yeah." I put a proprietary arm around my girlfriend. "Just keep your dirty mitts to yourself. You look good, Tipper. Is that a new haircut?"

"It's a new hair color. I had some highlights put in, see?" He turned his head from side to side.

"What do you need highlights for? You're as blond as Sylvie."

They looked at one another and laughed.

"Honey," Sylvie said, "I was naturally blonde until I was twelve. After that, my hair darkened. Now, I give nature a helping hand."

"Render her some little assistance," Tipper added.

I tried unsuccessfully to keep from sounding shocked. "Do you dye it?" I croaked.

Sylvie smiled. "I get my hair highlighted every six weeks. Why do you think my salon appointments are two hours long?"

"I just thought you had a really careful hairdresser."

"She does," Tipper said. "Believe me." He picked up a lavender duffel bag and tossed it to me. "Here, muscles, make yourself useful. So, what's the news from little house on the fucking prairie? Are the sheep in the meadows and the cows in the corn? How's the old gray mare? I hear she ain't what she used to be."

"Shut up," I said fondly, hefting the bag up onto my shoulder. "The truck is this way. Have you eaten?"

"Two packets of pretzels and a Budweiser. It was a wretched flight."

"You want a hamburger?"

"No. I want two double cheeseburgers, a large order of fries and a chocolate milkshake. Just go to the nearest drive-through. It's a long ride home, and I am anxious to plant my poor, cramped butt on your soft, spacious sofa."

I tossed his duffel bag into the back of the truck. "That reminds me," I said. "Are you staying with us or do you want me to drop you off at Fort Sister?"

He raised his eyebrows and inclined his head slightly in Sylvie's direction.

"I was hoping to stay with you," he said.

"Of course," Sylvie answered. "You're always welcome, Tipper."

He smiled and kissed her. "Thank you," he said extravagantly. "Mama has turned my bedroom into a lesbian library. I don't think I could sleep with *Our Bodies, Ourselves* staring at me from the shelf. I might feel an overwhelming urge to get out a hand mirror and look for my cervix."

"You might find it," I said.

"Exactly!"

Over my objections and Sylvie's, Tipper insisted on sitting in the middle. As he was well over six feet tall, this meant I had to reach under his left knee to change gears, and when he ate his mountain of food, I got ketchup and chocolate shake dripped all over me.

"That was lovely," he said, wiping his lips daintily with a paper napkin. "What shall I do with the trash?"

"Stuff it in the bag and sit on it," I suggested.

"I don't think so. These pants are new." He took the bag and shoved it onto my lap. "Your jeans, on the other hand, have seen better days."

He stretched his arms along the back of the seat and closed his eyes.

"Cozy?" I asked, trying to shift the truck into fifth gear.

"Absolutely. Wake me when we get to Colfax."

I didn't need to wake him. He woke himself. It was after eleven and the moon had risen high in the sky.

"Ah, look at that," he said. "Moonlight reflecting off a thirty-foot-wide concrete drainage ditch. Isn't it romantic? It's just like Venice."

"Fuck the moon," I replied. "You know what a speed trap Colfax is. Either move your leg or help me downshift."

"Say the word," he said. "Is that fourth?"

"No, damn it, it's second. Move your knee!"

"She's so irritable," he whispered loudly to Sylvie. "I don't know how you stand her. Is she really worth the bother?"

"I think so," Sylvie said.

"Must be all that kinky sex."

He shrieked loudly when we both hit him.

Tipper cracked a few more jokes about kinky sex and about the sights and sounds of beautiful downtown Colfax. When we reached the other side of town and were able to speed back up to sixty, he said, "Sylvie, I have something to tell you. No, I'm serious, and I want you to promise not to be angry with Bil. I made her swear she wouldn't mention it to you."

Sylvie leaned forward in her seat to look at me. I kept my eyes glued to the road.

"I've got a strange situation on my hands," Tipper continued. "My father called last week. He wants to meet me."

Sylvie stopped glaring at me and looked instead at Tipper. "Your father?"

"I know. You didn't think I had one, did you? Well, same here. The thing is, that's why I've come to Cowslip. He wants to meet me and talk to my mother. I think I'm supposed to act as a kind of facilitator."

"But... why?"

"That's the tricky part," he said gently. "I don't know why, and my mother doesn't know he's coming. I have to meet him first, find out what he wants, and then break the news to her. Whatever it is, she's not going to be happy."

In the long pause that followed, I noticed that my speed had dropped to thirty miles an hour. I reached beneath Tipper's leg and shifted gears.

"Does she hate him that much?" Sylvie asked.

Tipper shook his head. "No. I don't think she hates him at all. I think she's forgotten he ever existed. It'll be like a visit from Bob Marley's ghost."

"That's Jacob Marley," I corrected.

"You don't know my mother." Tipper squeezed Sylvie's shoulder. "Honey, I know you're worried about Kate. Quite frankly, so was I. That's why I called Mama this morning and had a good long talk with her. I asked what her intentions were regarding your mother."

There was a long pause before Sylvie said, "And?"

"And she says that she loves Kate. This," he continued slowly, "is the real deal. My mother swore to me on a stack of bibles that she would never do anything to hurt your mother. I know that in the past constancy has not been the Captain's strong suit, but when she gives her word, she means it. Rebecca Schwartz has fallen like a ton of bricks for Kate Wood. If the feeling is mutual, well... this is not a temporary thing."

We passed the turnoff for Albion, a town even smaller and less exciting than Colfax. Sylvie and Tipper looked contemplative.

I took my chances and ventured a question. "Tipper, are you suggesting what I think you're suggesting?"

"Yes," he said. "I think Sylvie and I are going to be sisters."

Chapter 19

Back at the apartment, Sylvie made polite conversation for exactly half an hour. Then she excused herself and went to bed, taking JC with her. I wondered when JC's dog bed had migrated from the hallway into our room. I knew I hadn't moved it, but I said nothing. Vivian, as usual, had been right. There was no way that Sylvie and I would be finding a new home for our child substitute. JC was ours for keeps.

Tipper and I waited until we heard the sound of the bedroom door clicking shut. Just to be on the safe side, I also switched on the stereo. Tipper wiped imaginary sweat from his brow.

"What do you think?" he whispered. "I tried my best."

"I know," I whispered back. "I think she'll be fine once she gets used to the idea. She only found out they were dating about a week ago."

"Her mother hasn't gone out with anyone else, has she?"

I shook my head. "Not that I know of. I think your mother is the first."

Tipper rolled his eyes and sighed dramatically. "Talk about jumping in at the deep end. I give Kate full marks for bravery. Come to think of it, I suppose I should give my mother full marks, too. It takes an intrepid woman to seduce a fifty-something lesbian virgin."

"Keep your voice down," I said. "We don't know that Kate *was* a lesbian virgin. She was just in the closet. Who knows? She might have had secret lovers all over the Pacific Northwest. It's not like she'd tell us, is it? I hope she did. Her marriage to Sylvie's father was miserable. He's been dead for nearly two decades. I'd hate to think that Kate was faithful to that creep until she came out two years ago."

"You're right." Tipper chewed pensively on his upper lip. "There's a difference between being in the closet and being celibate. Not even priests go twenty years without sex."

146

"Cynic."

"Realist." He kicked off his loafers and propped his bare feet up on the coffee table. "If you're not too tired, sweetie, let's change the subject. Why don't you tell me how you've been? You look a lot better than the last time I saw you."

"You mean at Sam's funeral? I am better."

"Good," he said. "You did a bang-up job on that eulogy. I have no idea how you kept it all together. It must have been a superhuman feat."

"Not really." I shrugged. "I was on autopilot. Nothing much was penetrating."

Tipper treated me to one of his piercing looks. His eyes were a clear green, the color of spring wheat. "It's all starting to get through now, though, isn't it? No sleeping pills, no late-night drinks, no"—he pinched his fingers together and held them to his lips—"little tokes from Sam's stash. Don't look so surprised! Sylvie was worried about you. She called me to ask my advice."

"Did she really?"

"Yes. She said you'd picked up some out-of-character bad habits. You'd stopped exercising, you were hooked on *pho*, and you'd lost all interest in your, uh, other pursuits." He wiggled his eyebrows suggestively.

"She did not," I said, horrified.

"No," he admitted, "she didn't. She was very discreet. That last part was just an educated guess. Ah-ha!" he laughed. "You can blush but you can't hide! I've known you far too long, my darling Bil. You pretend to be all laid-back and easy-going, but you are prey to intense passions. Hidden depths and all that. Anyhow, I told her not to worry. Given world enough and time, you'd get off the Maui Wowie and back onto the treadmill. I told her before she knew it, you'd be chasing her around the kitchen with a rubber spatula and a can of frosting. That's how it is with you lesbians, isn't it? Always licking chocolate off each other?"

I blushed deeper. "You've been watching too many movies."

"Who needs movies? How long did I live at Fort Sister?" He screwed up his face into a disgusted pucker. "Chocolate, honey, whipped cream, strawberries... what? Did I say something? You just blanched."

I told him about meeting Kate and the Captain at Foodway. He laughed.

"Don't tell me," I said. "The Captain's done the strawberries and whipped cream thing before."

"Many times," he said. "But let's not mention that to Sylvie. And let's hope that none of those big mouths at Fort Sister spill the beans or the fruit or anything else. My mother has gotten up to quite a lot these many promiscuous years, but she says that's all in the past. I think it's best if Kate and Sylvie believe that all of my mother's erotic tricks are entirely new and original. Mama and her strawberries." He shook his head. "It really ought to be cherries, don't you think?"

"Don't go there," I said. "You're talking about the Captain and my mother-in-law. My gorgeous, sexy mother-in-law."

"You're a complete pervert!" Tipper said with a laugh. "You need to stick a toothbrush in your ear and clean out that filthy mind."

"It wouldn't help. My fantasies are classically Freudian." We sat in companionable silence for a while, listening to Eva Cassidy's *Live at Blues Alley*.

"Have you heard Eva's version of 'Over the Rainbow?'" I asked.

"That hackneyed monstrosity? No. I don't even listen when Judy sings it."

I got up and changed disks. "Eva Cassidy is not Judy Garland. She's better. You won't believe this—it's amazing. I didn't think it was possible to breathe new life into 'Over the Rainbow.' I've got a friend in Maryland who sent me a bootleg copy. Listen," I said, "and be converted."

Tipper listened. When the song was over, he said, "Play it again." I did, and then I played it a third time and a fourth. Finally Tipper said, "Enough." I wiped my streaming eyes on the bottom of my T-shirt, and Tipper blew his nose into a white linen handkerchief.

"My friend in Maryland says that Eva has metastatic melanoma. It's terminal."

"Goddamn it," Tipper said heartily. "That angel is dying and Cher lives?"

"Shh." I hushed him. "Suzy might hear you. He'll come over here and take your drag queen card away. Tipper?"

"Yes?"

"Thank you."

"For what?"

"For helping Sylvie."

"Fie," he said. "It was nothing. If you hadn't straightened out, I'd have come here and personally dragged you off to rehab or therapy or jail—whatever she thought was best."

"Gee, thanks. I don't know if I should feel flattered or betrayed."

"Sarcastic devil. What you ought to feel is conspired against. All in your best interests, of course. That girl adores you. Don't you ever take her for granted."

"I won't. Just for the record, I adore her, too. Here, take a look."

I turned around and lifted the back of my T-shirt. Tipper grabbed the waistband of my jeans and yanked them down an inch or two.

"Idiot. What if you move?"

"Funny, that's what Sylvie said. And my mother. And Suzy."

Tipper settled himself down into the sofa cushions. I'd only turned on one of the living room lamps, but the room was plenty bright. The moon was shining through the blinds and across the hardwood floor.

"You poor thing," he said. "You're a hopeless romantic, aren't you? You love Sylvie and she loves you. Sometimes, I hate you both. No, shut up. I don't mean it. I'm only saying that I envy you." He leaned forward and seized my knee. "Listen, honey, I'm going to offer you some damned good advice. Do not worship the water that Sylvie walks on. Treat her right, but remember she's not made of sugar. She won't melt. I know it's alien to your nature to look for a happy medium but it's the best course of action. Tell Sylvie when you're upset. Don't just act like a jackass and then apologize and shut her out."

"How do you know I do that?"

He reached over and lightly slapped the back of my head. "How do I know you sneak out in the middle of the night and eat *pho*? How do I know you confide in some woman named Vivian? How do I know anything? Suzy tattles on you constantly!"

I was tired of being serious. I was also tired of talking about my intimate relations. "With me it's all or nothing," I said quietly.

"And that's another thing," Tipper said. "How come Suzy's the first to know about your secret musical talents? I hear Saturday, August 29, the Mighty Queer Gospel Quartet will be the hottest ticket in town."

"Will you come back for the concert?" I asked. "There'll be lots of women wearing wet T-shirts and duct tape."

He grimaced. "That is *not* an incentive. If you'll recall, my gate swings in the other direction. Still, if I can get away from work, I'll be there."

"Are you still a raging success or have they fired you?" I asked hopefully.

"With my bonus this year, I'll pay off the mortgage. But don't despair. It's not too late for you to grow up and join us corporate troglodytes. When do you finish your assorted MAs?"

"One in December, the other next May."

"My goodness. That Sylvie must be a kitten with a whip. No!" He raised his arms to deflect the cushion I'd tossed at him. "I'm just kidding. What do you plan to do then?"

"I don't know. Spend the summer as a greeter at Wal-Mart and then become a Sun Valley ski bum."

He took his feet off the coffee table and stood up. "Forget everything I said. I'm going to wake Sylvie up and tell her to leave you. You're worthless."

I whacked the back of his knees and he fell onto the sofa.

"Not entirely," I said. "I have decided to put my Sam and Emma experience to good use. My psychology master's is in counseling."

He laughed so loudly I had to shush him again. "Sorry. Whatever happened to physician, heal thyself?"

"What's that supposed to mean?"

"Nothing," he said with a feast of eye-rolling. "How's your mother?"

I debated giving him a dismissive answer. My mother was the same. She was insane. We both knew that. My brother's death had blown a hole in Emma's life the size of a truck. Since she was herself the size of the sun, the hole was sometimes hard to see, and yet there it was, a great sucking vacuum, demanding to be filled. The problem was not that I was unable to resist family intrigue; the problem was that I was afraid my mother might collapse on herself like a dying star.

I said, "She and my dad have sold the house. They gave up fighting the Ag Chemical people and accepted a financial settlement. At some point, they're going to build a new house on a new piece of property and shift twenty years worth of books and trash and ratty old furniture to some sterile, white-walled, cracker box of a house."

"Ach," he said, affecting a German accent. "Und how do you feel about zat?"

I laughed. "Damn you, Tipper. I feel like shit."

"I know," he said seriously. "We all hate change."

"You don't. You roll with the punches."

"Don't kid yourself. If you think I was thrilled about this business between my mother and Kate, you've got another think coming. I was unhappy for almost the same reason as Sylvie. If my mother did her usual love 'em and leave 'em, what would happen to the three of us? I'd never be invited to sleep on your lumpy sofa again."

"Lumpy? I thought it was soft and spacious." I yawned. "Besides, Sylvie wouldn't hold it against you."

Tipper yawned back. "I know for a fact that you are not that naïve."

"No," I admitted, "I'm not. You'd still be my best friend, but I'd have to meet you secretly somewhere in the middle of Washington. Maybe at one of those roadside fruit stands." I stood up. "I'm sorry, Tip. It's past my bedtime. I'll get you some sheets and a pillow and then I'll say goodnight. When and where are we meeting your father tomorrow?"

"The Cowslip Café, outside, at noon. Thanks for coming with me. I'm really not looking forward to this."

I reached out and patted his head. "I owe you," I said. "And if he's the guy I saw up in Coeur d'Alene, you can take some comfort in knowing that Major Tom looks pretty normal. Nothing like Gomer Pyle or Oliver North."

Chapter 20

Major Tom was late. By my watch, twelve o'clock had come and gone, and we were heading for half past. Although the Cowslip Café was only two blocks from my apartment, Tipper had insisted on arriving thirty minutes early. He said that when his father showed up, he wanted to be lounging at a table with a cup of coffee in his hand. This, Tipper felt, would give him the psychological advantage. One hour and three double lattés later, he was not lounging. He was jiggling his leg nervously and scanning each new arrival for a jarhead haircut.

I reached under the table and grabbed his leg. He nearly jumped out of his skin.

"What?"

"You have got to relax, Tip. Switch to decaf."

Cowslip on a Sunday morning was a surprisingly lively place. People going to church, drunks making their way home, joggers, dog-walkers, and an assortment of four-wheel-drive pickups roaring up and down the street for no apparent reason made for a constant and entertaining visual display. JC rested peacefully under the table, full of biscotti. I sipped my coffee and gazed idly at the shop windows.

Directly across from the Café were the Goodwill store, Hopkins Pharmacy, and Johnson Pawn. The Goodwill window featured cross-country ski boots, a toboggan, and a headless mannequin in a red sequined dress—hard to know if the seasonal display was left over from last winter or getting a three-month jump on the Thanksgiving rush. Hopkins Pharmacy had gone for some sort of books theme. I squinted but couldn't read the titles. I turned my attention to Johnson Pawn. A small woman stood in front of the store window, blocking my view of the leather jackets and electric guitars. She had on jeans and a white T-shirt, and the back of her head looked strangely familiar.

I stood up and yelled. "Hey, Ruth! Over here!"

My sister crossed the street, dodging the pickup trucks. "You're up early," she said. "Early for you, I mean. Hello, Tipper."

"Hello, Ruth." He stood up and kissed her delicately on the cheek as if she were his maiden aunt. I supposed that's what she was turning into, though at only thirty-two it seemed like kind of a waste.

"Where's Sylvie?" Ruth asked.

"Um," I hemmed.

Tipper came to my rescue. "Sylvie wisely decided to stay home and read a book." He was being tactful. Sylvie had awoken at six a.m. and gone for a two-hour run. When she came home, she took a shower, put on a skirt, and announced she was going to attend service at the Unitarian Church. There were strained good-byes all around.

"Would you care to join us?" I asked. "Tipper might be needing CPR. He's had six shots of espresso."

"Just for a minute," Ruth said, pulling up a chair. "There's less caffeine in espresso than in a regular cup of coffee. He'll probably survive. What brings you two out on a Sunday morning?"

"It's a long story," I said. "How about you?"

"I'm on my way home to sleep. I pulled an all-nighter."

"Ooh, anything gory? A decapitation? A spontaneous combustion?"

"My, what a fertile imagination you have." She gave us a tired smile. "We did have three severed fingers. Some guy got his hand caught in a turbine and brought in the parts in a beer cooler. With the beer. He drank two while Suzy did the intake."

Two tables over, a bleary-eyed drunk pushed away his plate of fried eggs.

Doing my best to sound nonchalant, I said, "I understand you're now the county coroner."

Ruth wasn't fooled. She eyed me suspiciously before helping herself to my last biscotti. Under the table, JC barked.

"*Acting* coroner," she said. "Who's the pup?"

"An inheritance from our late brother. His name is Jesus Christ. You did Jake Peterson's autopsy, didn't you?"

"I did," she said. "But if you're pumping me for information on Emma's behalf, don't bother. I've told her everything she needs to know. You're going to have to wait like everyone else for the police to make it public. Is that dog really named Jesus Christ?"

"Yes," I said. "He really is. Sylvie and I just call him JC. You're no fun, Ruth." I turned to Tipper. "My sister is the coroner, and this is a gossipy little town. I ought to get the advance scoop. Come on, Ruth—is it true that Peterson was dead for two days before someone shot him?"

She squinted at me through her wire-rimmed glasses. Her eyes were a sparkling blue. Ruth and Naomi were both short, cute brunettes, but while Naomi looked like a young Emma, Ruth looked more like our father. I knew absolutely nothing about her private life—not even if she had one. As a doctor, she was all about work. Before that, she'd been all about high school, college, medical school, and her residency.

"Did you get that classified information from Donny?" Ruth asked.

"No," I answered almost honestly. "I got it from Emma. She hung around when the cops came and she eavesdropped on Sid Castle. You know he can't keep his mouth shut. Is it true?"

"You're like a dog with a bone," she said, laughing. "Yes, it's true. More or less."

"More or less? I thought you could tell that sort of thing from rigor mortis."

I could tell I'd scored a bull's eye. Ruth's face assumed an expression of patient condescension and she shifted into lecture mode.

"I am not a forensics expert," she said. "I'm an ordinary physician working with ordinary resources. We're talking about Cowslip, not Quantico. My resources are limited. Rigor is one element in estimating time of death, but it's not the only thing you look for. In this weather, if a body sits in a hot place, like a metal shed or the trunk of a car, the processes of decomposition speed up exponentially. In this case, I wasn't as interested in rigor mortis as I was in livor mortis."

"What the hell is that?"

"The bruising of death," Tipper said. "Sorry, I don't know anything about it. I'm just translating from the Latin."

"You're right," Ruth continued. "Livor mortis is the bruising of death. When your heart stops beating, your blood stops circulating. Your red cells drop down into whatever parts of your body are lowest. After about two hours, these parts turn a bruised color, and if the body isn't moved for some time, the red cells break down and the color fixes."

"So that's how you tell time of death?"

"No. What I'm saying is that you have to look at a variety of factors: rigor, internal temperature, green stains on the abdomen. Of course, in this hot weather, everything gets tricky. Peterson's body lay around somewhere and got good and hot. He was a bloater when the cops found him. Smelled like nothing on earth."

"Really? That's interesting. But you still haven't answered my question. Are you certain about the time of death?"

Ruth laughed. "As certain as I can be. There's a fairly new technique where you take some of the vitreous humor from the eyeball and determine time of death by measuring the percentage of potassium present."

The bleary-eyed drunk pushed his chair back noisily, dropped a twenty-dollar bill on the table and left. It occurred to me that not everyone talked about vitreous humors and dead men's eyeballs at the breakfast table.

"Did you do the eyeball thing?" I asked.

"Nope. I gave the police my best estimate based on the tests I know first-hand how to perform. This isn't the Kennedy assassination, Bil. It's a small-time drug deal gone bad."

"Close enough for government work, eh?"

"Yep," she agreed. "And now you've gotten all the information you're going to get out of me. Time to change the subject."

"So..." I pursed my lips and pretended I was trying to think of another topic. "What's Naomi up to these days? Keeping busy?"

Ruth eyed me suspiciously. "Since when do you care what Naomi does?"

Naomi and I were oil and water. She liked to goad me, and I couldn't resist rising to the bait. For Christmas, she'd given me a copy of *The Seven Habits of Highly Effective People*. I'd given her *The Book of Mormon*.

"I don't care," I said. "I'm just asking to be polite."

"No," Ruth disagreed. "You've got a reason. I can see it in your eyes. Perhaps I should take a sample of your vitreous humor."

"Yuck!" Tipper and I said simultaneously.

"I'll tell you the truth. I don't see much of her. She's out a lot, and lately we haven't... all right, Bil. You know something. Spill it."

"I might," I said. "Does Naomi ever bring anyone home?"

Ruth looked at me as if I'd grown a second head. "Home? To our apartment?"

"Yes. You two haven't taken a vow of celibacy or anything, have you?"

"Of course not. It's just... I work a lot of nights. I suppose Naomi might bring someone back to the apartment." She pondered this for a moment, pulling at her shirt and scratching the left side of her chest. "No. I think I'd know if someone else had been there."

"Little telltale signs?" I suggested. "An extra toothbrush in the bathroom, a mustache mug, a pair of cowboy boots under your breakfast table?"

"You know who you're acting like," Ruth warned.

"No," I said. "I'm nothing like Emma because I really am going to tell you. Our sister, Naomi, was spotted at the Coeur d'Alene Resort in the company of a cowboy."

"A cowboy?"

"A cowboy. You know—bow legs, big hairy lip, shit-kicker boots."

"Must be going around." Ruth took her glasses off and pinched the bridge of her nose. "Sarah was with some dude on Friday night. I ran into her at The Underground. It was country-western happy hour, half-price on boilermakers. He was good-looking in a Garth Brooks sort of way, but he had one of those walrus mustaches, the kind you have to comb all the time or else it gets beer foam in it."

"I think it's the same cowboy, Ruth."

"No!"

"Yes." I told her about meeting Sarah and Buck DeWitt at Wawawai and about Sylvie spotting him with Naomi at the Coeur d'Alene Resort.

"Have you told either of them?" she asked.

"No."

"Good," she said. "You buy yourself a big cowboy hat and keep this under it."

"You don't think they should be warned?" Tipper asked.

Ruth shook her head. "Bil thinks she and Naomi don't get along. She knows nothing. She's eight years younger than I am, and six or so younger than Naomi and Sarah. You had Sam to play with growing up. I had those two. When we were teenagers, Naomi threw a hairbrush at Sarah—it left a welt on her forehead the size of a silver dollar. Sarah waited until Naomi was asleep and took the scissors to her hair. She didn't cut it short. She cut out chunks. Naomi looked like she'd lost a fight with a lawnmower. This is not the first time they've dated the same guy."

"Who?" Tipper and I demanded.

"Trevor Olafsson."

"My landlady's son?"

"That's the one," Ruth said. "He asked them both to the prom. I think he was hedging his bets. He assumed that one or both would turn him down. Instead, they both said yes."

"Why don't I remember this?"

"You and Sam were ten. You lived in your own little world— setting small fires, building hill forts, stealing butter knives from the kitchen and pretending to be pirates. You didn't give a damn what the big girls were doing."

Ruth was right. We didn't. Sam and I were inseparable. We slept in the same bed and wore the same clothes until we were in junior high school. JC rested his chin on my leg. I reached across the table, took a slice of Tipper's bacon, and fed it to the dog.

"What happened?" I asked.

"Emma," Ruth said. "She gave them her stock lecture on family loyalty and insisted that they both call Trevor Olafsson and tell him they could not go. Naomi tried to get around Emma by asking if she could go to the prom stag. Emma said yes and then found out that Naomi had planned to meet Trevor there. Sarah cried a river, and Naomi was grounded until college."

"And Trevor?" I asked.

"Gay as a goose," Tipper said. "Don't ask how I know."

"Ruth," I said speculatively. "Naomi fights with me now. She and Sarah haven't gone at each other like that for years. Do you think our family is regressing? I mean, since Sam's death, Emma and Hugh have sold the house, our sisters are dating a guy who looks like a Fisher-Price toy..."

"And you?" she asked.

"I'm seeing a grief counselor." Before she could ask any further questions, I said, "Let's go back for a minute. You said you saw Sarah and Buck DeWitt at The Underground? That is a cheap, nasty dive frequented by poor graduate students like me, and penny-pinching librarians like Sarah. What in the hell were you doing there?"

"Drinking half-price boilermakers," Ruth said defensively.

I slapped my hand on the table. "I rest my case. You've gone nuts, too."

"I have not! You and Sarah are not the only members of this family who know how to have a good time. I went out with a few friends from work and we all got lit up like Christmas trees. It was great fun." She scratched at her chest again. "I even learned how to line dance. I think."

"I'm sorry," Tipper interrupted. "But you seem to be bleeding."

Ruth looked down at her T-shirt. There was a spot of fresh blood the size of a dime over her left breast. She pulled the collar away from her chest and had a good look down inside.

"Damn," she said. "I was afraid of that. Excuse me. I've got to head back to the ER."

"What the hell have you done to yourself?"

She hesitated and then answered resignedly. "I got my nipples pierced on Friday night. The woman who was teaching me to line dance works at that piercing parlor on Fourth Street. The left one seems to be infected. I knew I should have gotten barbells. These rings catch on everything."

"Mother of God," Tipper whispered.

"Does Emma know?" I asked, half in horror, half in admiration.

Ruth stood up. "Close your mouths, children. I'm glad to know that I still have the power to shock. No, our mother does not know. I am thirty-two years old, nearly thirty-three, and these are my tits. I have not gone nuts."

I waited a beat. "Does Suzy know?"

"No, Suzy doesn't know, either. You are the first person I've told."

I felt scared, nonplussed, and flattered. Ruth, my brainiac sister, had nipple rings. She went drinking with friends at The Underground. She had a wild streak I knew nothing about.

"Somehow, some way, Emma will find out," I warned her, "and she will go ballistic. Would you like me to run interference? Get my tongue pierced or something?"

Ruth smiled. "It's sweet of you to offer," she said. "You're the best hurdler in the family, jumping over Emma in a single bound."

"I am?"

I'd always thought I was our mother's fall guy, her patsy. Day and night, I lived at her elbow, doing her crazy bidding.

"Which of us has carved out a real personal life for herself?" Ruth asked. "Which of us is happily married?" She reached down and patted JC, who stretched luxuriously at her touch. "You even have a baby. A German Shepherd baby. I'll bet Emma doesn't approve."

"No, she doesn't."

"There you go," Ruth said. "A bit of healthy boundary setting. Naomi is always right in the thick of things. Sarah just cuts Emma off. I rarely figure in her schemes and plans because I don't challenge her assumptions." She looked down at her shirt again.

"Damn, that itches. I may have to take the left ring out. A shame. I kind of like how they look."

Ruth patted me on the head, much as she'd patted JC. "Good-bye, Bil. Good-bye, Tipper. Have a nice visit."

Ruth walked to the edge of the sidewalk. She stood on the curb for a moment or two, then turned around and came back.

"Bil," she said. "There's a leather jacket in the window of Johnson Pawn."

"For God's sake. Are you going to buy a Harley to go with your piercings?"

"I wasn't planning to. I think the jacket is yours."

"Mine?" I said stupidly.

"Yes. It's got your name written on it." Ruth spoke carefully, as if she were about to deliver a fatal diagnosis. "Bil, you're my sister. I know that graduate school is expensive. If you need to borrow money, all you have to do is ask. That jacket has got to be worth more than the thirty-five bucks Johnson Pawn is asking."

Chapter 21

Bil Hardy, as large as life, was written on the collar label in black permanent marker. It was my handwriting. Sylvie had given me the jacket for my birthday, and she'd laughed at my insisting on making it as theft-proof as possible. I pointed out that she was laughing because she didn't have siblings.

She didn't have a brother like Sam.

At first I couldn't think how the jacket had gotten to Johnson Pawn. I couldn't remember the last time I'd worn it. Sometime in the spring before the weather turned warm. Then, as I stood there, I saw Sam once again in the hardware store parking lot on the day he blew up the sewer main. He was walking away with my jacket in his hand.

I ignored the 'Closed' sign and tried the handle anyway. When I found it was locked, I kicked the living shit out of the door.

"You sons of bitches!" I yelled. "Goddamn you!"

Tipper took my arm.

"That's my jacket," I said stupidly. "Sam pawned my fucking jacket."

"I know, honey," Tipper said gently. "And I know this is hard. But just for the moment, you have to calm down. As soon as the store opens, we'll go in and sort this out."

"I want my jacket, Tipper." I didn't know why I was on the verge of tears.

"We'll get your jacket," he said. "Later. Right now, we need to go back to the Cowslip Café. I think that man over there might be my father."

Tipper's father was the man Sylvie and I had seen in Coeur d'Alene. Apart from being very tall—taller even than Tipper—he was an ordinary-looking man in his mid- to late fifties. He had a plain face, neither ugly nor handsome, and there was something about him that suggested that he could, if he wanted to, slip into a crowd and disappear without being noticed. In this, he was the polar opposite of Tipper's mother. The Captain couldn't disappear at a butch convention if there were five hundred other dykes dressed just like her.

The initial meeting was stiff. Tipper introduced himself and then he introduced me. Major Schwartz shook my hand and apologized profusely for being late. He said that he was traveling cross country in a motor home and couldn't find anywhere in town to park. He'd settled at Traveler's Rest, a cedar grove at the edge of town, and from there he'd walked to the Café.

Major "Please, call me Tom" Schwartz didn't apologize for or explain his twenty-four-year absence, and Tipper didn't ask any questions. Major Tom chatted amiably about the drive from his home in Washington, D.C., to Cowslip, Idaho, about his plans to amble down the Pacific Coast Highway and visit California and Mexico, and his hopes of eventually getting a job with a defense contractor. He mentioned that he had a little dog named Drudge who could do dozens of clever tricks.

"Drudge is a Shih Tzu," said Major Tom. "Smartest dog you've ever seen. Though that shepherd of yours seems fairly bright. Looks like a well-bred animal, too."

I didn't know about that. JC had sniffed the Major's hand, recoiled quickly, and hidden behind my legs. He was now making small gurgling noises in the back of his throat—not quite a growl, more like an upset stomach. Probably the biscotti.

As Tipper and the Major talked, I tried to pay attention. It wasn't easy. The sight of my leather jacket in the Johnson Pawn window had driven all rational thought from of my head. Had Sam really walked off claiming he just wanted to borrow it temporarily and marched straight into the pawnshop? Did he think so little of me that he'd sell my jacket for beer money? Or did he think he was being funny? Did he do it as a joke? Was he planning to tell me it was there so I could go reclaim it but instead wound up in the hospital, dead before he could deliver the punch line?

I'd loaned Sam twenty bucks that day. Why didn't he borrow more money and leave my jacket alone? Nothing made sense. Why was Sam dead? Why wasn't he alive and well so I could take out my rage once and for all on his worthless, thieving, jacket-pawning hide?

Absorbed in my own thoughts, I didn't notice at first that the tenor of the conversation had changed. Tipper had leaned forward and was listening intently to what his father had to say.

"... I assumed incorrectly that everything was in order. We'd both signed the paperwork, and I was scheduled for a hearing before the judge. Then, my orders changed. I couldn't make the court date, and my attorney couldn't reschedule. That was all right, though. My attorney said he'd contact Becky, and she could attend instead. Well, he didn't call her. He dropped dead of a heart attack while I was flying over Southeast Asia. I didn't find this out until a few weeks ago. Back in 1972, I got some paperwork in the mail, copies of the papers we'd signed, and I just assumed everything was final."

"But it wasn't," Tipper said.

Tom Schwartz shook his head.

"And you want me to tell my mother." Tipper turned his gaze from his father to me, blank despair cascading from his eyes to his chin.

"I'm sorry," I admitted. "I didn't catch that last part. Tell your mother what?"

"That she's still married," said Major Tom. "To me."

* * *

I gave Tipper the keys to my truck. He didn't ask me to come with him, and I didn't volunteer. When sufficiently riled, Tipper's mother, like mine, had the power to suck all of the air out of a room. My responsibility now was triage, and that, alas, began at home. I walked up the steps to my apartment, and, for the first and only time in our two-year relationship, I hoped that my girlfriend would be somewhere else.

If wishes were horses, beggars would ride. Sylvie was not only home, she'd made lunch—a cold crab salad and crusty French bread. She'd also stopped by the bakery to buy dessert. My heart sank. The stereo was on and tuned to the classic country station, always a sure sign that she was in a good mood.

"Wow," I said, my gaze shifting from Sylvie to the cheesecake on the table behind her. It was at least four inches high, with two dozen perfect peaks of whipped cream encircling the pile of raspberries on top. A beautiful woman, a beautiful lunch, and my favorite dessert, and yet, somehow, it still seemed appropriate to hear Dwight Yoakam singing about being cold and dark alone, and wanting his baby to come home.

"Yes, well." She looked embarrassed. "I've had a chance to think, and I think maybe you're right. If my mother is happy, why shouldn't I be happy for her? Life is short."

"And nasty and brutish as well," I agreed. "How was church?"

"It was nice," Sylvie said. "Very nice. I like the minister. She's smart and funny and... where's Tipper?"

"Gone to see his mother."

"Oh." She pulled out a chair and sat down, gesturing for me to join her. "How did it go with his father?"

Cloth napkins, as well. I shook mine out and placed it across my lap. "Okay, I suppose. Major Tom is kind of strange."

"In what way?" she asked, helping me to a generous serving of crab salad.

"I don't know how to describe it," I said. "He's like a space alien, the father from another planet. He got there forty-five minutes late and then rattled on forever about absolutely nothing."

"What did you think he'd talk about?" Sylvie asked. "This is the first time he's met Tipper. Is it the Major who's strange or the situation?"

"Both," I admitted. "Listen, he doesn't have a house. He has a Winnebago. He has no fixed abode, and he likes it that way. He has a Shih Tzu named Drudge, he says he's always wanted to see Mexico, and he likes to play poker. His favorite game is a thing called Texas Hold-'em"

Sylvie paused, the fork halfway to her mouth. "That's what he talked about?"

"Mostly. I wasn't really listening. I ran into Ruth. She's gotten her nipples pierced." I didn't give her time to process this. "Sylvie, that leather jacket you gave me last year for my birthday. It's in the window at Johnson Pawn. Sam took it, and he sold it. Probably for drug money."

Sylvie put the fork down and reached for my hand. "Bil."

"Damn it. I swore a solemn oath to myself that I would not cry."

"Sweetheart," she said. "It's okay."

"It's not okay. The rotten, rotten bastard. He's dead, and I can't... I can't..." I dashed at my streaming eyes with the napkin.

"Are you sure it's your..." Sylvie stopped. "Of course you are. I remember you wrote your name on the label. Bil, I'm so sorry. Sometimes... Sam did things like that. I'm sure it wasn't out of malice."

"And I'm sure it was."

The urge to cry receded and, strangely, so did the rage that had accompanied it. I felt coldly analytical, more like the counselor I wanted to be than the sister I was.

"Over the last few years of his life, Sam turned into someone malicious. He turned spiteful, selfish, angry, and mean. He put other people at risk because he didn't care. I wish I could forget all of that and pretend that he was some kind of saint because then I could justify missing him. As it is, I feel like one of those battered wives who won't prosecute because she claims she still loves her husband."

"He was your brother," she said kindly.

"He was. But he's gone, Sylvie, and if I'm completely honest, I don't know if I really miss him. I don't miss all the insanity. I know I've been crying and falling to bits and saying that I want him back, and sometimes I really do. But then I wonder if I feel bad because I'm supposed to feel bad. Who is it that I really miss? I don't miss the person that Sam was when he died—a worthless, thieving hophead. I miss the little kid who was my best friend, but he disappeared a long time ago. Maybe what I miss is my own childhood."

"'It is the blight man was born for,'" said Sylvie. "'It is Margaret you mourn for.'"

That was it. The ice that had enveloped my heart cracked open.

"Come here," I said, pushing my chair back and pulling her onto my lap. "I knew there was a reason I loved you. You're the only botanist-slash-geographer on earth who can quote Gerard Manley Hopkins."

"So that's why you love me," she said. "I wondered."

We sat quietly for a long time, our salads forgotten, while the radio played a succession of miserable country songs: "I Fall to Pieces," "Where Have You Been," and "Lock, Stock and Teardrops."

"You know what this is, don't you?" I asked. "It's the Cowslip version of the pathetic fallacy. Instead of the weather reflecting my mood, I've got Patsy Cline."

She grimaced. "That's kind of sad, isn't it?"

George Jones crooned the opening verses of "Farewell Party." Sylvie looked at me. "He knows she'll be glad when he's gone?"

"Lyrical genius," I said. "It's the definition of maudlin."

"It's the definition of self-pity."

"Alcoholic self-pity."

"Alcoholic, pill-popping self-pity."

"Alcoholic, pill-popping, my-wife-done-gone-and-left-me self-pity. The best kind."

Sylvie and I started laughing and we couldn't stop. We laughed until we wept and fell off the chair. We wound up on the floor, clinging to one another. Sylvie was the first to regain control. She lifted her head and looked down at me.

"Honey," she gasped. "We'll buy your jacket back as soon as the pawnshop opens tomorrow morning."

"Oh, no." I shook my head. "We're not going to buy it. They're going to give it to me. It was stolen."

"Whatever you want. It's up to you."

I reached up to tuck a stray strand of hair behind her ear. "I love you," I said. "I'm crazy about you. I want very much to make love to you, right this minute. But there's something else I need to tell you. It's about Major Schwartz."

"I love you, too," she said. "More than you know. And I guessed you had something else to say."

"How?"

She smiled down at me. "You've got a very expressive face. You'd better hope the police never question you. You couldn't lie to save your life."

"Don't worry." I winked. "I've got a plan. When they come for my mother, I'll turn state's evidence. I'll sing like a canary."

"That seems reasonable."

Sylvie stood up and reached down to help me to my feet. I dusted myself off and moved to pick up my chair, but Sylvie pulled me into her arms.

"Bil," she said, "don't tell me the rest of the Major Tom story just yet. There's something else I want to do first."

"Darling, anything. I'll fly you to the moon, buy you a kitten, massage every inch of your person with sweet almond oil—you name it. Take me into the bedroom. I'm all yours."

"Later," she said, kissing me. "I'd love all of that except the kitten. But first, before you tell me any more bad news, let's eat this goddamned cheesecake. I have a feeling I'm going to need the energy."

Chapter 22

Sylvie took the news surprisingly well. In fact, she was mildly sympathetic. Because of her mother's terrible marriage, she was inclined to side with the Captain. Major Tom had admitted that he'd dropped the ball. The fault was clear, and it should be easy enough, Sylvie thought, to sort it all out.

"After two years," I said, "you still surprise me."

"Good," Sylvie said. "I'd hate to be boring and predictable."

Five o'clock rolled by and then six. Half a cheesecake disappeared. Sylvie fell asleep on the sofa while I looked through a stack of Agatha Christies, most of which I'd already read. Things were either going very well with Captain Schwartz or very poorly. I could easily picture both scenarios:

Tipper and his mother sitting on the front porch, laughing, drinking, and cracking jokes about the vicissitudes of fate.

The Captain taking after Major Tom with a baseball bat.

I was pondering this latter possibility when I was struck by an awful thought. I eased Sylvie's feet off my lap, went into the hallway, and dialed Ruth and Naomi's number. Naomi answered on the fourth ring.

"Hello?"

"Hello," I said. "Is Idaho a community property state?"

"I'm fine, Bil. Thank you for asking. And yourself?"

Damn her, anyway. "Sorry," I said through gritted teeth. "How are you, Naomi? I hope I'm not calling at a bad time."

"As a matter of fact," she said, "you are. I was in the middle of dinner, and I have guests."

"Guests?" I asked. "As in plural dinner companions?"

"Guest, guests, what business is it of yours?"

Question answered. I could see that a heaping helping of bow-legged cowboy love had done nothing to improve her temperament.

"Sorry," I lied. "Didn't mean to be nosy. Would you please, dear sister, tell me if this is a community property state or not?"

"It is," she answered grudgingly. "Why do you want to know?"

"I'm asking on behalf of a friend. It's not important, but listen: what if you'd been married to someone for twenty-five years but you didn't know you were still married because you thought you were divorced. Would that someone be entitled to half of your property?"

"I don't know," she said. "Perhaps. You'd certainly deserve to lose it because you'd be an idiot. Who thinks they're divorced but doesn't know for sure? Jesus, Bil, the next time you decide to get drunk and play Trivial Pursuit, call someone else. My pasta's getting cold."

"Wait," I said. "Before you go, who in your opinion is the best divorce lawyer in town?"

"James Beam," she said without hesitation. "He might be a drunk and a pussy-hound, but no one can beat him in a court room."

"Not even you?"

"No one," she repeated.

She hung up without saying goodbye. While it was true that I liked to goad her, Naomi was also innately provoking. If she were a coin, both sides would be tails. When she and Sarah found out they were dating the same man, God help Sarah. She was sweet and pleasant and gorgeous and a man would be crazy not to pick her. Naomi was just plain ruthless. In hand-to-hand combat, my money was on the short one. If Naomi wanted Ragtime Cowboy Joe, she'd have him—whether he liked it or not.

I didn't like my sister very much, and the feeling was mutual. Still, it was too bad that she had chosen to specialize in criminal defense work. There was no one I'd rather have on my side in a courtroom. My sister lost from time to time, but she always played to win. I had a feeling that Captain Schwartz might well find herself in need of a good lawyer.

I went back to the living room.

"What was that all about?" Sylvie asked.

"Community property," I said. "I think we need to make a trip to Fort Sister."

"Now? But Tipper has the truck."

"We'll have to take the motorcycle," I said. "Sylvie, there's a chance that Major Tom might have a legitimate claim to half the Captain's assets."

"Fort Sister?"

"Yes, Fort Sister. There is a distinct possibility that Drudge, the Major's Shih Tzu, might be joining Elvis and Priscilla in the Captain's kitchen."

"I'll get my jacket," said Sylvie.

* * *

We found Tipper talking with the Captain and Kate in the large living room. They were sitting by the grand piano, and though they enjoyed some privacy thanks to the angle and arrangement of the furniture, they were not alone. Cedar Tree was in a far corner, listening to Celtic music, and painting a picture of a half-clothed woman that looked, depending on the angle, like either Stevie Nicks or Mount St. Helens. Four other women, Leaf, Willow, Rain, and Margaret T. Birnbaum, were sitting in a group in front of the fireplace, knitting.

Leaf, Willow, and Rain had been at Fort Sister nearly as long as Cedar Tree. They were in their forties and were, respectively, a painter, a poet, and a sculptor. Margaret was a decade or so older. She was a retired investment banker with a tight gray perm and a wallet full of pictures of her grandchildren. The Captain was doing her best to dump Cedar Tree, but I kind of hoped that Margaret was a keeper. It was nice to find a Fort Sister resident who actually had a surname.

Tipper looked up as we entered the room. He motioned for us to come over and join them. The Captain was rubbing her forehead with her hand, and Kate had her arm around the Captain's shoulders. Neither of them moved. Sylvie and I sat on the floor in front of them. Soon, we each had a large hairy dog on our lap. I got Elvis and Sylvie got Priscilla.

"Tipper?" I said.

"We're past shock and horror," he said. "We've moved on to anger and disbelief."

The Captain looked up. "The only reason that man made Major is because he speaks Russian fluently. After the war, men were being turfed out of the military left and right. You know how it works in the Navy and the Marine Corps? They pass you over for promotion. If that happens twice, you're forced to retire. I can't believe he rose above Captain. He was not rah-rah enough for the Marines."

"He seemed pretty rah-rah to me," Tipper said.

"You've known him five minutes," she said.

"And you knew him for two weeks," Tipper replied.

"I'm sorry to interrupt," I said, pushing Elvis off my lap. "Sylvie and I aren't here to butt in."

"You're not butting in," the Captain said quickly. "You're family. Both of you," she added with a significant look at Sylvie.

My girlfriend looked at her mother, who took her arm off the Captain's shoulders and leaned forward. "What is it?" Kate asked.

"Go ahead, Bil," Sylvie said.

"I talked to Naomi," I said. "Idaho is a community property state. You need to hire an attorney, Captain."

"For the divorce?" she said. "You bet I do. If you want something done right, don't leave it to a man. I'll call Barbara Norris. She's handled my property for years and—"

"No," I said quickly. It was the first time I had ever interrupted the Captain, much less disagreed with her. "Barbara Norris is a very good attorney, Captain, but what you need is a shark. You need someone like my sister, Naomi, only it has to be someone who specializes in divorce and family law. I'm sorry to say this, but you need James Beam."

"You mean Jim Beam? The drunk? I wouldn't give him the time of day. He's an arrogant, sexist, Republican—"

This time Sylvie interrupted. "Idaho," she repeated, "is a community property state, Captain Schwartz. Mama," she turned to Kate, "think about what we're saying. Any property or wealth acquired after the marriage belongs to..."

"Both parties," Kate finished. "I see."

"I don't," said the Captain.

Tipper, who had been leaning back against the sofa with his eyes shut, was now sitting up and wide awake.

"Mother," he said sternly. "In the years since your marriage to Major Tom, you have acquired a one-hundred-acre ranch in Idaho and the money that grandma Mimi left you. Father has a military pension and a Winnebago. Do the math."

We sat in silence for what felt like eons. The Celtic music had stopped and I could no longer hear the clack of the knitting needles. Cedar Tree, wafting across the room in her purple gauze skirt, floated in front of the sofa.

"Sisters," she called. "It's time for a processing circle."

Kate looked frozen. The Captain stared off into space. Tipper rolled his eyes in disgust. A lighted stick of incense appeared in Cedar Tree's hand, and she flopped down next to me on the floor.

"No," Sylvie whispered desperately in my ear.

I stood up.

"We have to go," I said, pulling Sylvie to her feet. "We've got a puppy to walk."

"Traitor," Tipper mouthed.

"Goodbye," I mouthed back.

* * *

Sylvie and I stood on the front porch and looked around. Fort Sister had come a long way since the early days. Some of the older cabins still stood, attractive ruins from the 1930s, but the Captain had demolished the worst of them and built several new luxury cabins with en suite bathrooms and satellite TV. These were always rented. The house was completely remodeled, and the new conference room had video hookup and a steady stream of progressive clients from Spokane, Seattle, and Portland. I knew that Tipper had invested some of his Microsoft money in the place, and it was all beginning to pay off. Major Tom might not have given a fig for the place if he'd seen it a few years ago, but if he got a good look at it now and considered the potential, he might well decide that he wanted a percentage.

Fort Sister was still Fort Sister, however. The softball diamond, complete with dugouts and lights for evening games, dominated the front yard. At a ninety-degree angle to the diamond was the firing range. Spinning targets at thirty, fifty, and one hundred yards moved in the breeze.

"Is James Beam as good as all that?" Sylvie asked.

"Naomi says he could beat her in court."

"Oh."

I put my arm around her waist and pulled her close. The evening light gave her hair a golden cast, and her eyes were a dark sea green. "Come on, honey. Let's go home."

"Bil," she said, looking at me closely. "Thank you."

"For what?"

"For getting me out of that processing circle. I just wish there were some way to rescue my mother."

"Your mother," I said firmly, "is a big girl. If she wants to be rescued, she'll rescue herself."

I waited for Sylvie's reaction. Would she be pissed? Had I been disloyal?

"You're right," she said at last. "My mother can take care of herself."

"And we can go home and take care of the rest of that cheesecake."

Sylvie laughed. "I see that you've got your priorities straight."

She tossed me my helmet and started the bike.

"Hop on the back," she said, "and hold on tight. It's been a long day, and I feel like taking a few curves."

Chapter 23

When Suzy knocked on the door at nine-thirty, I assumed he was Tipper.

"Oh," I said morosely. "It's you."

"Yes, and it's you, too. Thanks for the enthusiasm."

Suzy had abandoned Donna Reed in favor of vintage Cher. He wore a long black wig, platform boots, and a dress that looked like three potholders tied together with shoelaces. He had a good figure, and the overall effect was surprisingly nice. It wasn't sexy, at least not to me, but it was homey in a trashy, bizarre, Halloween party sort of way.

"Sorry," I said. "Of course I'm glad to see you. It's just that I thought you were Tipper." I took his arm and looked him up and down. "Suzy, I know the bags of birdseed you've got tucked into the top of that get-up don't technically count as breast tissue, but I still think you might be in violation of the new ordinance."

"Flatterer," he said, reaching out to pinch my cheek.

"Would you like to come in?"

"Actually," he said. "I want you to come over to my place. Sylvie too. Yoo-hoo!" he called to her over my shoulder.

"Yoo-hoo, yourself," she called back. "Bil, invite Suzy in."

"I've tried. Looks like we're going to his place."

We followed Suzy across the hall and into the Den of Iniquity, where the Cher theme was receiving full play. "Gypsies, Tramps, and Thieves" blared from the stereo. Suzy had covered the tartan sofa with a purple chenille throw, draped the lampshades with gold lamé, and edged the coffee table, the piano, and an eight-by-ten photograph of Mrs. Smith, Donny's mother, with brown suede fringe.

"Very nice," I shouted over the music. "Will Donny play Sonny to your Cher?"

"It's your fault." Suzy slapped me lightly on the arm. "All that talk at choir practice the other night made him nostalgic. Of course,

172

he'd prefer to play Donny to my Marie, but I draw the line at incest." Suzy turned the stereo off. "It's all in the name of good, clean fun. Speaking of which, if you'll follow me into the bedroom, ladies, there's something I think you should read."

Suzy's computer was logged onto the Slip-Fifty listserv, and the message on the screen was from my mother who, for some reason, had adopted a new e-mail handle.

I looked at Suzy. "'The Sieve?' As in her mind is like a...?"

"No. Emma is signing herself 'The Sieve of Vanity,'" he explained. "It's a Biblical reference. Knox signs his posts 'Godzway.' He's also got that written on his license plate."

"I'm not worried about Knox," I said. "I'm worried about my mother. Christ, what an ego! Why not sign herself 'The Plagues of Egypt' or 'The 'Wrath of God'?"

"Don't be silly," Suzy said. "It's just a little joke. I've been calling myself 'A Joy of Wild Asses.' Now be quiet and read."

Dear Slippers,

Tired of driving all that way to the tribal casinos? Want to save yourself a visit to church? Here's an opportunity for a little one-stop shopping, some gambling mixed with religious fanaticism, courtesy of our local cult. The Sieve says like a ring of gold through a pig's nose is an illegal Christian casino, but not so others. Apparently, this operation is quite a hot little number. I happened across the following website run by a group of disgruntled ex-Vines. Click on the link below to learn all about the casino, the bar, the escort service and the sleazy roadhouse that young master Calvin Knox has been running in Elder Julius Radnor's barn. The scallywag! Then call the county prosecutor (as I have) and ask him why he's not pursueing this dreadful young leaf off the strange-but-true vine. Could it be because the prosecutor is a member of the church? Could it be because Mr. Knox is white? Does our prosecutor save all his zeal for prosecuting—nay persecuting—people like my late BLACK son? I'm not trying to suggest our prosecutor is a RACIST but if the sheet fits...

Suzy breathed over our shoulders while Sylvie and I digested this.

"Well," I said at length. "Three comma faults and she spelled pursuing wrong. Is The Church of the True Vine racist?"

"Yes," replied Suzy. "And no. Is the church all white? Yes. They're not crudely racist, like Aryan Nations, but The Root of Jesse Press publishes a lot of horseshit about reverse discrimination, the evils of multiculturalism, that sort of thing. Your mother also uncovered some links between George Knox and a nasty little southern heritage group down in Mississippi. Knox is originally from there. I can't remember what the group is called, but they're all about 'restoring America' and our Confederate Christian values."

"Like slavery?" Sylvie asked.

"No!" Suzy shrieked in mock horror. "That's the mistake you ignorant liberals always make. The Civil War wasn't about slavery; it was about states' rights. It was about trying to preserve our agrarian way of life. It was about truth and beauty and Scarlett and Rhett. You get my drift?"

"Yeah, we get it," I said. "Did you follow this link to the casino stuff?"

"Oh, yes." Suzy grinned. "And it was most interesting. A split has been brewing in the church for months. There's a fight over the line of succession. Old George has little Calvin, the fruit of his loins, but he also has two very ambitious sons-in-law. Rahab and Moira may look like Barbie dolls, but they're not idiots. There's a lot of power behind the husbandly thrones. Still, Calvin has been groomed since infancy to be King Solomon when David kicks the bucket. He is the heir. The sons-in-law are the spares."

"What you're saying is that Calvin is the Prince Charles of the Church of the True Vine?" Sylvie said.

"Exactly."

"The Reverend Calvin Knox." I scoffed. "I suppose that was Monty Python's holy hand grenade that he and my brother lobbed into the sewer main."

"It doesn't matter if he's the bad seed," Suzy said. "Don't you remember our little talk about the doctrine of election? Calvin is among the elect. This disgruntled lot that your mother found," he said, tapping the screen with his forefinger, "are fomenting a rebellion based on the doctrine of salvation by works. Heretics! Their leader is Julius Radnor."

"The guy with the casino in his barn?"

"The very one. He moved here from California in the hopes of working his way into the line of succession. He swung Knox around to his way of thinking on the subject of infant baptism—Radnor is for it—but they fell out over this works business."

"Can we skip the theology?" I asked. "I don't get it."

"Neither do I," Sylvie admitted. "I want to know more about Calvin's illegal casino. Why was it in Radnor's barn?"

"Good question," Suzy said. "Julius Radnor has a son named Zachary. He's younger than Calvin, only eighteen or nineteen. Daddy Radnor claims he didn't know what his son and Calvin were up to. Donny thinks Radnor knew full well and that he was one, getting a kickback, and two, waiting for the right political moment to bust Calvin. You can't actually see the barn from the Radnor house. It's up a dirt road about half a mile from the house. Elder Julius doesn't offer any explanation for why he didn't know what Zachary was doing, or why so much traffic whizzed by his house every Friday and Saturday night. Maybe he thought they were having a hayloft Bible study."

"Oh, right," I said. "Who's buying that?"

"Lots of people," Suzy said. "Calvin is not universally beloved. He is widely believed to be a corrupter of youth."

"How long ago was all of this?"

Suzy shrugged. "Six months, maybe. No one knows. It could have been more recent. The website, which is anonymous, just says that the Radnor Barn casino is now defunct. Donny is tracking down a rumor that Calvin has a new location and a new partner in crime."

"Does Donny know where and who?"

Suzy winked at me. "He does. Can you keep a secret?"

"What?" I asked. "Better than you?"

"Bite that sarcastic tongue or I shan't tell you," Suzy said. He paused with his lips primly pursed until I grabbed him by the arm and shook him. "Fine," he said, "I'll tell you. It's out at Forbidden City."

"Oh, go on," I said. "Everyone knows about Forbidden City. They've always had poker tables and blackjack in the back room. Every sheriff and prosecutor has turned a blind eye to that since the beginning of time."

"It's true," Sylvie agreed. "No one goes there for the chow mein and egg rolls. The restaurant is just a front. People drink in the bar and gamble in the back room."

"No," I objected. "Some people do eat there."

"Who?"

"People from out of town, alcoholics, and students who want a three-dollar lunch. If you don't mind rats and cockroaches, Forbidden Village is a bargain."

"Stop," Sylvie said, blanching. "Bil, please."

"It's the perfect place," Suzy insisted. "Don't you see? Calvin has found a new partner in crime. The owner of the Forbidden Village Chinese-American Restaurant."

"Who owns the place? It used to be Ray Chin, but he's been dead for years."

"Dick Kornmeyer," said Suzy.

"Fuck me with a feather!"

Sylvie and Suzy both stared at me.

"I'm sorry," I said. "Dick Kornmeyer is the bastard who sold my parents two hundred acres and a shack full of dead guy. He's the biggest crook in town."

"No kidding," Suzy said. "And now he's in business with young Calvin Knox."

"Why doesn't the sheriff's department shut them down?"

Suzy sighed heavily as if we were the biggest saps he'd ever known. "The county prosecutor is a member of Daddy Knox's church. Dick Kornmeyer is a county commissioner. Sid Castle would like to be the next sheriff. Donny hasn't exactly been told to avoid Forbidden Village, but he has no time or budget for an investigation. He's been instructed to help Sid investigate the Peterson murder and not go haring off on his own. It's killing him, it really is. You know what the Mormons are like. They believe in truth, justice, and the American way."

"Super Mormon! Able to leap tall drag queens in a single bound!"

"Oh, shut up, Bil."

"Okay," Sylvie brought the meeting back to order. "This Radnor fellow has had a falling out with George Knox, and some anonymous someone has set up a website detailing the operations of the original casino." She glanced at me. "Emma has picked up on this."

"And she's stirring the pot," I said.

"Yes. How did Radnor find out about Calvin's business, Suzy? I mean, what's his story?"

Suzy smiled and poked his tongue out. He really had his Cher impersonation down pat. It was downright eerie.

"Radnor's youngest son, Eliot, ran up a three-thousand-dollar tab. Eliot's only sixteen. His brother refused to help him, so he panicked and confessed to Daddy. The truth came up like a-bubblin' crude. Radnor demanded that Calvin be shunned. Knox wouldn't do it. This sort of thing happens all the time in Protestant churches.

Martin Luther had no idea what kind of trouble he was starting with his ninety-five theses."

"All fascinating," I said, "from a local gossip point of view. What I want to know is why my mother is all over this? I mean, apart from the fact that she thinks everything that happens in this town is her business, and she hates George Knox and Dick Kornmeyer."

"Civic-mindedness," Suzy replied. "It was True Vine that pushed through that breast ordinance, and True Vine is buying up property in Cowslip left and right. True Vine is taking over."

I rolled my eyes in exasperation. "Oh, they are not. How many people live in this town, twenty-five thousand? The Church of the True Vine claims to have six hundred members, and that's counting children. Let's say each family has a father, a mother, and two kids—and that's being stingy, since we know they don't believe in birth control—what's that amount to in actual voting adults? Three hundred. One percent of the population. True, they're punching above their weight these days—"

"And they're spending a lot of money," Sylvie interrupted. "I'm with Suzy on this. They now own three of the historic buildings downtown. Hopkins Pharmacy, Allen Brothers Department Store, Watkins Feed and Farm Supply..."

"That's a little scary," I admitted. "But still. How did Emma get onto this casino website? Does she just surf around looking for dirt on the True Vines?"

"Yes," Suzy said. "That's exactly what she does. The woman is a bloodhound. No, I take it back. She's a pit bull with a really good nose. She pokes around and follows their little web-rings. One of the students at the seminary had a link to an ex-student who had a link to the casino site. Amazing, isn't it?"

"What's amazing is that she doesn't work for the CIA. Any idea when this anti-Vine site went up?"

"I don't know," Suzy said. "The casino information is new. It was posted last Wednesday, though Calvin's apparently been at it for ages. According to the site, every juvenile delinquent in town has been hanging out in that barn, listening to the devil's music and drinking hard liquor. He was selling tax-free cigarettes he bought down on the Nez Perce reservation. He had a roulette wheel. He didn't miss a trick."

"Enterprising little monster." I turned to Sylvie. "Wasn't it Wednesday when we saw him up in Coeur d'Alene?"

She thought for a moment. "Yes, it was."

"What do you suppose he was doing up there? Running away?"

"Could be, I suppose. Kind of pathetic to get caught in a candy store."

"You've lost me," Suzy said.

I described our meeting with Calvin. "We assumed that he was up there for his dad's military reunion, but maybe not. You should have seen the look on his face when we spoke to him. My brother used to get that look. We called it the 'oh, fuck' face. Later, he and George were outside talking to Tipper's father, and—"

"What?" Suzy shrieked.

I gave him an abbreviated history of Major Tom.

"That's why Tipper's here?" Suzy asked.

"That's why Tipper's here."

"And this Major Tom knows George Knox?"

"Apparently."

"Maybe his father was taking him out of the line of fire," Sylvie said. "This website appears, exposing Calvin's misdeeds. It's a four-hour drive to Coeur d'Alene and back. A chance for father and son to strategize?"

"Or have a Come to Jesus talk?" Suzy said. "Could be. I want to know more about the connection between George Knox and Tipper's father. Bil, what do you know?"

"Next to nothing," I said, "but I have an idea."

I reread my mother's message, copied her e-mail address, and exited Suzy's account. I logged onto the web.

"What are you doing?" Sylvie asked.

"E-mailing the 'Sieve of Vanity.' She might not have all the answers at her fingertips, but no one's better at digging up dirt. Suzy, would you give me an Old Testament handle?"

"An Old Testament... why?"

"I'm creating a new account on the university server—don't look at me like that! It's a sub-account of my regular student account, but never mind anyway. I know how to hide my tracks. What I need is a pseudonym, something Biblical. I'm going to subscribe to Slip-Fifty and ask the Sieve a question. The idea is to get her doing some more research and to put the wind up George and Calvin. If you and Emma can play the shit-stirring game, so can I."

"Wonderful," Suzy said, hopping up eagerly. "Let me get my King James."

I spotted something small and silver beneath the edge of Suzy's mini-skirt.

"Hold on a minute, Cher! What's that tucked in the top of your garter? It looks suspiciously like a Derringer."

"Close," Suzy said. "It's a .22 magnum mini-pistol. Donny bought it for me."

"You're packing?"

"Sort of," Suzy winked. "Donny insists that I carry a gun. He does not want me walking the streets without protection."

"Suzy, your sheer presence is protection enough. You're terrifying."

He leaned down and gave me a lavish smack on the lips. "Darling, you're wonderful! I wish you would have a talk with Donny. He's making me go to the firing range to learn how to use this thing. Don't tell him, but I've got it loaded with a shell full of steel shot, painful but not lethal."

"I've never heard of such a thing," Sylvie said.

Suzy pulled the gun out of his garter and opened it. The pistol was so small that it fit easily in the palm of his hand without touching the bottoms of his fingers. He handed me the shell. It was also very small with a clear blue plastic tip. Inside the tip, I could see the shot, small steel balls of non-lethal pain. Suzy was right— you'd have to really try hard to kill someone with it. Maybe if you stuck the gun up their nose and fired it would be fatal. Still, that shot would be the very devil to pick out of your skin. I handed the shell back to him. Suzy reloaded the gun and tucked it back into his garter.

"Suzy," Sylvie said, "I'd prefer it if you weren't packing while we're here. Guns make me very nervous."

"No problem," he said. "I'll put it in my dresser. Sorry. I'm carrying now out of habit. I have a concealed weapons permit."

"Good God."

"Yes! Here and queer and packing a pistol. I am George Knox's worst nightmare." Suzy went into the bedroom and returned with a well-thumbed Bible. "Let's find you a Biblical moniker. Old Testament, you said?"

"Yeah. Something like 'A Joy of Wild Asses.' I like that."

Suzy hummed "I'll Fly Away" as he flipped through the Bible, rejecting this and that. "Let's see, 'A Gin and a Snare?' That's Isaiah 8:15. No, no! How about Jeremiah 25:15? 'The Wine Cup of my Fury.' That's you!"

"No, it isn't. Try again."

He flipped some more. "Okay, this is it. From the Book of Amos, Chapter 4, Verse 2. 'The Lord God hath sworn by his holiness that, lo, the day shall come upon you, that He will take you away with hooks, and your posterity with fish hooks.'"

"Fine." I created an account called "Posterity Fish Hook," logged on to the Slip-Fifty listserv, and wrote my message.

Dear Sieve of Vanity. Nice to see you're keeping busy. As long as you're researching the fell deeds of the True Vine, perhaps you'll tell us about George Knox's time in the Marine Corps. What was his rank and with whom did he serve?

Before I could sign this, Suzy shoved me aside and typed,

PS: A Joy of Wild Asses here. Woe to the bloody city! It is all full of lies and robbery; the prey departeth not.

"What the hell does that mean?" I asked.

"You said you saw George Knox talking to Tipper's father. How would they know one another unless they served together? Major Tom didn't strike you as the True Vine type, did he?"

"No," I agreed. "But what about that bloody city crap? What's that for?"

"It's a spur," Suzy replied. "She'll get right on this. I'd be surprised if you didn't have some sort of answer either later tonight or first thing tomorrow."

"Let's make it tomorrow." I cast a significant glance at Sylvie and feigned a yawn. Suzy laughed.

"Fine, you two," he said. "The heart melteth. Be off, fornicators, and have some fun for me. Donny won't be home until three o'clock in the morning, and this wig is starting to itch."

Chapter 24

I had long since given up on Tipper when, just after midnight, I heard a key turn in the front door lock. I remembered, belatedly, that he had my keys because he'd taken my truck, and I wished I'd bothered to put on my pajamas before walking from the bedroom to the kitchen to get a glass of water. In another second or two, Tipper was in the apartment and walking past the open kitchen door.

Desperation gave birth to twins: necessity and invention. I opened the refrigerator door and stood inside, my back wedged against the shelves, my front making intimate acquaintance with the butter tray.

"Hello," Tipper said, stopping to lean against the doorframe.

"Hello."

"You forgot I had your apartment key, didn't you?"

"Yes."

"And now you'd like me to close my eyes while you sneak back into the bedroom."

I nodded.

"Hmm," he said, eyes still wide open. "I'll bet you're getting chilly, standing there mooning the eggs and the milk."

"If they curdle, you won't get breakfast."

"Too bad. We've got a call in to Jim Beam."

"That's good, right?"

"If he calls back, yes. I'm trying to picture what my father might do with his half of Fort Sister. Park his Winnebago on the softball diamond, maybe. That way my mother can access her half of his Shih Tzu."

I delicately adjusted my position as parts of me were perilously close to the leftover cheesecake. "The processing circle didn't go well, then?"

He signed wearily. "Does it ever? Ms. Cedar Tree, it turns out, is a jailhouse lawyer. She was positively bursting with helpful advice. She thought there might be some way my mother could sue

181

Major Tom for screwing up the original divorce, and Leaf and Rain and Willow said aye-aye. Goddamn lesbian feminists and their consensus problem solving. Gay men believe in privacy."

"Except for sex," I said. "And naked friends trapped in refrigerators."

"Oh, who cares about that?" he asked. "I'm talking about serious things. I'm talking about marriage and money and real estate. Do you have a Diet Coke in there?"

It was with some difficulty that I pulled a can out of the door and tossed it to him. "Do you think the Major will want half of your mother's property?"

He popped the Coke open and downed half of it in a single swallow. Then he belched profusely. "I don't know. You were at the Café this morning. What did the man say? That he wanted me to break the bad news about the divorce to my mother. That was it. No explanations, just blah, blah, blah. For all I know, he's off to Reno tomorrow to file for a quickie, no-fault divorce, and he'll never darken our doorstep again."

I considered this possibility and dismissed it. "Or?"

"Or he's moving in. Or he'll force Mama to sell up. He'll take half the cash and use it to finance a jarhead tour of the world from Disneyland to Tijuana." He downed the rest of the soda and tossed the can into the trash. It bounced off the swiveling lid and rolled across the kitchen floor. From the bedroom, JC barked.

"I see that being rich and working at Microsoft has done nothing for your manners." Tipper stared off into space. I relented. "What's the plan?"

"So far," he said, "there is no plan. We wait for Jim Beam to call my mother back."

"In the meantime," I said, "you and I might get in touch with your father. We know he's parked at Traveler's Rest. Why don't we go over and see him tomorrow?"

Tipper shook himself out of his stupor. "No, that's okay. I'm sorry, Bil." He picked up the empty soda can and put it in the trashcan. "I've got the Major's cell phone number. I'll call him in the morning and try and get some sense out of him. Is there anything to eat? I forgot to have dinner. And lunch."

"There's cheesecake," Sylvie said, appearing behind him with my pajamas in her hand. "Raspberry."

I noted with some annoyance that she'd taken the time to don her own night attire before coming to my rescue.

"I see that you put your dignity ahead of mine," I said. "I'll remember that."

"When?" she asked. "The next time *I'm* standing naked in the refrigerator?" She handed me the pajamas and kindly held the door for me while I put the top on. "How's your mother?" she asked Tipper over her shoulder.

"Concerned," he said. "Angry. Frustrated. When I left, she'd turned the pitching machine on and was knocking balls out into center field."

"And my mother?" Sylvie asked. "How's she?"

"That's the funny thing," he said, frowning. "She's fine. Calm. Cool. Reasonable. Thank God she was there—she put an end to the processing circle. She said it was all very well and good to speculate and make doomsday predictions, but the thing to do was to call an attorney. She was the one who actually picked up the phone. Left to her own devices, my mother would be in jail for killing my father, and the rest of the women would be organizing a drumming circle or drawing down the moon. Except for Margaret. She knit the whole time. Finished a pair of baby booties."

"I'm sorry," Sylvie said.

"It's all right." He stood up straight and smiled. "Your mother asked me to pass along a message. If you have a chance, would you please stop by tomorrow? She'll be at home. Her home," he added significantly. "She left Fort Sister just after the processing circle broke up."

"Oh," Sylvie said. "Did she take the dogs?"

"She did."

I cleared my throat. "If you don't mind, Tipper, I can't put my pajama pants on without bending over, and if I bend over, you won't want any cheesecake."

He laughed, made a half-hearted attempt to stand on tiptoe and sneak a peek, and then he ambled off down the hallway. As soon as I heard the bathroom door close, I escaped from the refrigerator and finished getting dressed.

"Could have been worse, I suppose."

"What do you mean?" Sylvie asked.

"The Captain's bent out of shape. We expected that. Your mother, on the other hand, seems to be fine."

"Bil," she said softly. The look on her face was a perfect blend of condescension and pity. "You've got to quit measuring people on the Emma scale. My mother is not fine. She went home, and she took Elvis and Priscilla with her."

I tried to shrug this off. "You've never really experienced a Fort Sister processing circle. It's like a root canal only with lots of patchouli and a polyphonic running commentary."

"Tipper said that my mother was calm, cool, and reasonable. If you told me something unpleasant, something that upset me, like you were having an affair with Vivian Nguyen-DiRisio at Pho From Home..."

"I would never—"

"If you told me that," she pressed on, "and I was calm, cool, and reasonable, what would you do?"

I stopped rubbing the cold parts of my body and looked at her. "I'd run."

"You'd better run fast," she said.

Chapter 25

We arrived at Johnson Pawn the next morning just as the University clock tower chimed eight. Though we'd been up until three listening to Tipper's doomsday scenarios about the fate of Fort Sister and Captain Schwartz's finances, I'd insisted that Sylvie and I get up early and get to the pawnshop quickly lest anyone poach my jacket.

I needn't have worried. The jacket was still in the window, taunting me. I took a deep breath, girded my loins, and gave the door a mighty shove. It was locked. I tried again, pushing so hard this time that the glass shuddered. When it still didn't budge, I cursed energetically and looked around for a large rock.

Sylvie interrupted my vandalizing plans by putting one hand on my arm and pointing with the other at the large CLOSED sign in the lower right-hand corner of the front window. Beneath it were the hours: Monday through Saturday, ten to six.

"I think you're scaring the dog," she said.

JC was standing at the end of his leash, as far away from me as possible. I deflated like a popped balloon.

"Stupid son-of-a-bitch bastards. We could've slept in."

Sylvie very kindly refrained from pointing out that if I hadn't been so busy trying to kick the door down the day before, I might have noticed the sign with the store's hours.

"Never mind," she observed mildly. "So we've got some time to kill. Why don't I buy you breakfast?"

Embarrassment, lack of sleep, and the sight of my jacket, untouchable and less than a foot away made me sulky. "Where?"

"Wherever you like. Except," she lifted one eyebrow, "the House of Pancakes. I'm not up to dealing with that redheaded bimbo who's made a hobby out of trying to guess what you're going to order."

I refused to smile. "I'm flattered by your irrational jealousy, but you don't need to worry about it. Her name is Kim, and she doesn't work on Monday. Ouch. No hitting. Besides, I thought you were jealous of Vivian."

"I am. Stop provoking me. We'll go to the Cowslip Café. If we sit outside, JC can sit under the table, and you can keep an eye on the pawn shop."

"And what will you keep an eye on?" I asked.

"You."

She took my hand and we crossed the street. The Sunday hangover crowd had been replaced by the Monday indolent and under-employed. We found a table near the door and sat down to wait for one of the many interminably slow college boys who theoretically worked there. Sylvie's luminous presence cut the waiting time down to a fraction of what Tipper and I had endured the day before. I tried not to be aggravated when one of the Café's oaf-cum-waiters took my order without taking his eyes off of Sylvie. I waited until he'd delivered our meals and schlepped back inside before complaining to her bitterly.

"I'm sure it's your imagination," Sylvie said, polishing off the last of her orange juice.

"It is not my imagination that you ordered a small orange juice and he brought you a large. Your breakfast is perfect. My eggs are like rubber. I ordered the coffee and you got the free almond biscotti. I wonder why the boys don't fawn over me?"

"Perhaps it's because you're a great big honking dyke." When I opened my mouth to object, she said, "Look at your T-shirt."

I glanced down. Great Big Honking Dyke said the four-inch rainbow letters.

"Tell you what," I suggested, "let's trade clothes and see if it makes any difference. Quick, whip off that cleavage flashing number you've got on and hand it over."

"Idiot." Under cover of laughing, she reached out and stole my last piece of toast. "I suppose we should have called Tipper. He is our guest. It's rude to go out to breakfast without him."

I disagreed. "He ate half a cheesecake last night. If he ever eats again, I'll be stunned. Besides, if you'll recall, I tried to wake him up just before we left. He swore at me."

"You tried to wake him up by dropping a piece of ice down his shorts."

"Served him right for that trick he pulled last night. I'm afraid I got a little too close to that cheesecake. When I finished my shower this morning, I found a raspberry in the drain."

"You didn't!"

"No, I didn't. I'm lying." Sylvie laughed. I pushed away the remnants of my bouncing eggs. "Do you believe in prophetic dreams?"

"Why? Did you have one?"

"I don't know. Maybe it wasn't prophetic. Maybe it was just weird. I dreamed that Sam was standing at the foot of our bed, only it wasn't our bed, it was his bed. The big four-poster—you know, the one with the wooden knobs that unscrew?"

Sylvie finished chewing a bite of granola. She was the only person I knew who ordered cereal in restaurants. It was one of her many odd quirks that I found completely enchanting. I also liked her refusal to attend potlucks, the fact that she twirled her hair when she was nervous, and that she sometimes snored, very quietly, like a purring cat.

"I know," she said, swallowing. "You and your brother used to take the knobs off and play croquet with them."

"Right. We used an old baseball bat and horseshoe pegs for the wickets and..." I noticed she was crinkling her nose, another quirk. "Have I told you *all* of my stories?"

"Not all. Just this one. A couple of times. Now finish telling me about your dream. Sam was at the foot of the bed and...?"

"And he was laughing. It was that helium-filled pothead giggle he used to have when he was really stoned, all high-pitched and flutey. He said, 'Have you unscrewed the knobs yet?' I said no, and he laughed again and winked at me. That was it."

"That was it? Dream over?"

"Not exactly. Then I was naked in a big bathtub with Joan of Arc and Lisa Marie Presley, but I'm sure you don't want to hear about that."

She rolled her eyes. "No, I don't. Did you look?"

"Of course not," I lied. "I kept my eyes shut. Stop pinching! Oh, I see. You mean did I look inside the bed knobs? No, and it occurs to me that I haven't looked since he died. He used to hide stuff in there. If I had to venture a guess, I'd say that right now, they contain a couple of joints, a love note from his jailbait girlfriend, and anything small he didn't want my mother to find."

"She doesn't know about the bed knobs?"

"Ha! Of course she does. She knows all, sees all. If there was anything in there, I'm sure she found it when she cleaned out his clothes."

"But you're not sure."

I sipped my coffee and considered. "No. Sam had a lot of little hidey-holes, and if Emma forgot about the knobs... Sylvie, I know this is going to sound strange, but I got the feeling that this was more than a dream. More like, I don't know, a message from beyond the grave or something."

"Sam came back higher than a kite to giggle at you. That sounds about right." She reached under the table and squeezed my thigh. "Joan of Arc and Lisa Marie Presley, eh? You're demented. I suppose you want to go to Emma's this afternoon while I visit my mother?"

I put my hand on hers to stop it from traveling further up my leg. "Shows what you know. Let's do both together. First we visit your mother, then we go unscrew."

"When you put it that way," she said, her hand escaping my grasp, "it sounds absolutely illicit."

Her index finger trailed up the inside of my shorts. I exhaled slowly. "I see that you're in a sportive mood."

"Do you object?"

Though her tone was innocuous, I recognized the challenge. If Kate had broken up with Captain Schwartz, how did that affect us? Sylvie wasn't certain how she felt about the breakup. She might be happy. She might be angry. She might be both. She wanted to know how I felt. What if she was happy and I was sad? Would that put me off my game? Would I find her less attractive? Would I judge her?

The answers were no, never, and of course not. Sylvie's feelings were her own. What I felt under the circumstances didn't matter. The Captain was my friend, and Kate was Sylvie's mother. Whatever happened between the two of them was none of my business. My only concern was the teasing, serious, beautiful woman sitting next to me, and I would always side with her, no matter what.

"When have I ever objected to your making a pass at me?" I asked.

"Never," she said with a laugh. "But there's always a first time."

"And there's always a chance they'll need hockey skates in hell." I decided to up the ante. "If we're lucky, my mother won't be at home. We can sneak into my old bedroom and make out like desperate teenagers. The twin bed in there is narrow and lumpy, and I'll bet my mother hasn't changed the sheets since I moved out, but..."

Sylvie stopped her under-the-table predations. The bemused look on her face told me that she'd also stopped listening.

"Bil," she said. "Your mother just went into the pawn shop."

"What?" I looked across the street and then at my watch. "It doesn't open for another hour. Are you sure it was her?"

"I'm sure." I must have looked skeptical because Sylvie added, "She was wearing a red T-shirt, red sweatpants, and red tennis shoes—three different shades of red."

"That's her." I stood up and reached for my wallet.

"No," Sylvie said. "You go on. I'll pay for breakfast and meet you over there."

"Now look," I began.

"Don't argue," she said. "Not with me, anyway. I have a feeling you might need to marshal your resources."

*   *   *

Emma stood at the front counter in all of her sartorial splendor. I opened the door quietly, reaching above my head to grab the bell before it had a chance to ring. It was my plan to slip up behind my mother as quickly and quietly as I could. As soon as I was inside the shop, I realized I needn't have bothered. Emma's fingers were drumming on the counter top, and she had launched into a loud rant at someone who was invisible to me.

"Listen, you moron, I don't care if your brain is kippered with reefer smoke. Even a Mary Jane-addled twerp like you should be able to find the letter H in an alphabetical file. It comes after G and before I."

"Gee, eye," I declared in my best Foghorn Leghorn voice. "Gee-eye, boy, GI, get it? It's a joke, son. A yuk, a funny, a ha-ha."

"Good God," said my mother. "If it isn't Posterity Fish Hook. What the hell are you doing here?"

"I'm here to retrieve my jacket, Sieve of Vanity," I snapped. "It was pawned to these Mary Jane-addled twerps by your Mary Jane-addled twerp of a son."

"Oh, really?" My mother ignored the no-smoking sign on the counter and lit up. "Don't even start with me," she warned. "Take a whiff—no, not a deep breath, not unless you want to float home. Do you smell the pot fumes?"

I did. However, I didn't care. I pointed at the jacket in the window.

"That," I said firmly, "is mine. I loaned it to Sam the last time I saw him. Loaned it, Ma—not gave it. Sam pawned it." I stopped looming over my mother and turned my attention instead to the bleary-eyed clerk behind the counter. I recognized him immediately. It was Steve, the short freckled redhead I'd last seen climbing out from under the tarp in the back of my truck.

"You!" I was pleased when, after a thirty-second delay, he flinched. "Get my jacket out of your window! It's stolen property."

"I just work here," he said slowly. "I don't own this place."

"I'm sure you don't," I said. "Just as I'm sure that you rent your pot and quite possibly your fucking underwear, but I don't give a goddamn. You get my jacket out of that window and give it back to me, or you're going to get a visit from my friend, Lewis County Sheriff's Deputy Donny Smith."

I'd used my nastiest tone. I'd threatened him with the law. I was ten inches taller than he was, and yet he was staring blankly past me and at my short, round, gray-haired mother.

"The name is Hardy," she said. "Look between G and I and you'll find it."

He shuffled off into the back room. As he shifted the curtain in the doorway, I caught a glimpse of his partner in crime, Joe, the lanky, skanky blond with the dreadlocks. I could hear muffled screams coming from the television Joe watched—familiar screams. It didn't take me long to place the dialogue. Joe was watching *Evil Dead 2*, one of my favorite horror films.

Outside the doorway on a bench sat a stack of VHS tapes. *Night of the Living Dead, Dawn of the Dead, I Walked with a Zombie, Raiders of the Living Dead, Alien Dead*. Steve and Joe were having their own undead film festival. Between the screams, thuds, and creepy music, I strained to overhear the conversation.

"Where's the fucking card box, man?"

"What fucking card box?"

"The one with all the shit in it."

"What shit?"

"The pawn shit."

"Watch this, dude. This is how you do it. You've got to take their fucking heads off with a shovel."

"It doesn't have to be a shovel. You can use any tool. Is that the fucking card box?"

"I don't know."

"Yeah, it is. Get the fuck up. Sam's mother is out there and she's like, pissed and shit."

"Who?"

"Sam's mother. You know, Sam. Goddamn, you fucking stoner. He died. Move your fucking ass."

Steve came back out holding a dirty beige box. He placed it on the counter and opened it, revealing a batch of grubby three-by-five index cards. They were, as my mother had insisted, filed alphabetically. He started searching in the As. My mother reached across the counter and took the box away from him. She pulled out a card marked "Hardy, Emma," and handed it to him. He peered at it closely.

"That's thirty-five dollars," he said. "Plus a week's interest."

"I know," she said. "Here's $48.65. Now go get it."

"I need to write a receipt."

"Later," Emma snapped.

I did some quick math. "That's thirty-nine percent interest!"

"No shit," she hissed. "And if you miss a week's payment, they put your stuff up for sale. I learned that the hard way."

"Why are you pawning things? Are you broke?"

"No. Now shut up. I'll explain later."

Steve came back and put a leather jacket on the counter. My leather jacket. I stared at her. She ignored me.

"Steve, I'll take that receipt now. No—wait. Why don't I write it out for you, and you can just sign it? I don't want to die standing here waiting for you to remember the alphabet."

Emma handed me my jacket. "No harm, no foul."

"Mother," I began.

"Oh, just say it!" she snapped. "You know you want to."

"Fine. Motherfucker! What in God's name were you—"

I didn't get a chance to finish. The zombie screams were growing louder, and Joe was yelling from the back room to Steve, "Dude! This is how you do it! This is exactly how you make sure they stay completely dead."

"No belching and shit?" Steve called back.

"No! Totally dead-ass wasted."

I looked at Emma, who pulled out a cigarette and lit it calmly. "It's important to have a wide range of life skills," she said. "I wish they'd offered zombie killing back when I was in high school."

"Really?"

"Yeah. When have I ever used stenography?"

Chapter 26

"You pawned my jacket. For thirty-five dollars. It cost three hundred dollars. My name is written in indelible ink on the inside of the collar. Why did you do something so... so... so incredibly thoughtless and stupid?"

My mother leaned against the front window of Johnson Pawn, calmly smoking. Despite the heat that had already begun to rise from the sidewalk, I'd put the jacket on. I had no intention of taking it off again until I was back home and safely out of Emma's reach.

"It was an experiment," she said. "Do you know who owns that pawn shop?"

"Someone named Johnson," I replied. "It's Johnson Pawn."

"No," she said. "Ollie Johnson has been dead for forty years. That's just a name. Calvin Knox owns that pawnshop. I am looking into Calvin Knox, and his father, George, and that bastard, Dick Corn-holer. There's an unholy alliance of religion and politics and gambling casinos in this town, and I mean to expose it."

"And who are you?" I asked. "Woodward or Bernstein?"

"I'm Ida Tarbell," she said, blowing cigarette smoke in my face. I coughed.

"Who's Ida Tarbell?"

"She was before your time and before my time, too. She was a muckraking journalist back in the day. You should have learned about her in history class."

"The schools have gone to hell," I said. "We didn't learn shit about Ida Tarbell. Too busy with Al Capone, Bugsy Siegel, John Dillinger, and you—the really big crooks. Now why did you pawn my jacket? Why not pawn something that belonged to *you*?"

She shrugged and stubbed out the remains of her cigarette against the pawnshop window. "Your jacket was convenient. I don't have anything worth pawning, and I didn't dare take your father's binoculars. He'd notice. I didn't intend for your precious jacket to end up in the window. They weren't supposed to try and sell it."

"But you missed a payment."

"I missed a payment," she agreed. "Aren't you going to ask what I've learned?"

"No," I said. "I don't care."

While she'd been talking, I'd had my hands in the pockets of my jacket. I could feel a joint and a packet of rolling papers in the left pocket. In the right, I felt a small piece of thick paper, not quite as heavy as card stock but close. I pulled this out and looked at it. On the front was written, "S.H. Credit $1250, subtract $800 for payment in kind. Owed: $450. C.K." Blue ink on ivory paper. The back of the card was deep purple embossed with a pale green snake wrapped around a white dove.

"Fucking Nora," I said. "He's slicker than goose shit."

"Who?" asked my mother.

"Calvin Knox," I said. "Remember that deck of cards you found in Sam's room? The ones we used to decide whether or not I was going to deliver his eulogy? Calvin Knox isn't running an ordinary backroom casino. He's got his own playing cards and"—I handed her the piece of paper— "his own credit and debit chits."

"The little bastard! You know what this means, don't you?"

"No."

"He owes your late brother four hundred and fifty dollars."

"And you mean to collect?"

"What do you think?" she asked.

"I think if you get a dime of that money, you'd better give some to me."

She screwed up her face until she looked like a dried apple doll. "What for? Pain and suffering over that damned jacket?"

"No," I replied. "Jesus Christ was Sam's dog. He eats like a fucking horse. He needs shots. He's got 'tapworms.' Consider it posthumous child support."

"Can't argue with that," she said.

* * *

"What's this $800 credit?" my mother asked. We'd rejoined Sylvie, who'd been waiting for me at the Cowslip Café. My mother was dipping half of an already soggy doughnut into her coffee and talking with her mouth full.

"I think that's for Jesus Christ," I said. "Under this very table, we have a purebred $800 deity." I broke off a small piece of sausage to feed to JC.

"Wait!" said Sylvie. "Don't give him that."

"Why not?"

"He's going to the vet this afternoon." She leaned forward and whispered. "He's being neutered. I made the appointment days ago. Don't you remember?"

"Tutored?" asked my mother.

"Neutered," I corrected. "And no, I don't remember."

"Bil..." Sylvie began.

"Nazi dog," my mother interrupted. "Your brother was a sap."

"And what does that make me? The sap of a sap? Leave JC alone. He's an Alsatian, and he's actually quite a nice animal. He's a hell of a lot less trouble than his original owner. And speaking of the devil, we ought to be asking what Sam was doing for Calvin Knox that would earn him $1250. Sam was on disability. He couldn't earn anything legally without losing some part of that, so we know that Calvin was paying him under the table, and paying him generously. Sam never saw $1250 in his life."

"I'm sorry to suggest this," Sylvie said, "but do you think Sam might have been acting as a go-between? Jake Peterson was Sam's pot supplier. Could Sam have been selling the stuff on to Calvin Knox? That website you found, it said Radnor barn casino supplied its patrons with booze and pot."

Emma stole the last bite of my Genesee sausage. I complained bitterly, even though this was my second order of the day.

"Don't look at me like that," she said, chewing heartily. "You can feed that SS canine but not your mother? I don't see Sam as a go-between, Sylvie. Why wouldn't Calvin buy directly from Jake?"

"A degree of separation?" Sylvie suggested. "Maybe Calvin wasn't hooked up. I wouldn't know where to buy pot in this town. I don't smoke it." She gave me a significant look that was not lost on Emma.

"Bil," my mother said. "Is there something I should know?"

"No, there is nothing you should know. There's plenty you do know that you shouldn't know, but I'm not adding to your store of information."

"Hmm," said Emma. "Defensive. If I find out you've been smoking weed, Bil Hardy, you'll smoke at both ends."

"Oh, for God's sake, Emma. I'm twenty-four years old. And talk about a double standard. Sam toked up every day."

"Sam," she said, "was dying of cancer."

"Sam," I said, "was not dying of cancer when he started on the wacky weed. And dying of cancer has nothing to do with dealing dope. I can't see how else he could have gotten $1250 out of Calvin Knox."

My mother gave me a toothless, doughnut-and-sausage encrusted smile. "Can't you? What did you find in the pocket of that leather jacket of yours?"

"You mean the jacket you pawned?" I stared into the black gap between her top left incisor and first molar. "You know, Ma, your partial plate is for everyday use. You don't need to save your teeth for special occasions."

"You found a chit from Calvin's casino," she said, ignoring me. "Hasn't it occurred to you that your brother might have gotten lucky at the card table? How many nights did we spend in the hospital with him playing Hearts and Spades?"

I blinked at her. She was right. Sam wasn't lucky in life or lucky in love, but he was uncanny when it came to cards. The only one who could beat him was Sarah, who could take twenty dollars to the Blackjack tables in Las Vegas and come back with a few thousand in her purse. She was hell on wheels at poker, too.

Sylvie spoke quietly. "I apologize," she said. "I made an assumption about Sam that was unwarranted. I'm very sorry."

My mother reached out and took her hand. "No," she said kindly. "Don't apologize. I thought the same for just a moment, but I knew Sam much better than you did. When he had a bag of weed, he smoked it. He might have done a little light dealing here and there, buying for friends, but I'll be damned if he ever made a dime at it. Users are often dealers, but no one who was in the business seriously would have trusted Sam with a major stash. He was Mr. Generosity. He'd have shared it out with every juvenile delinquent in town and then been stunned when someone like Jake Peterson presented him with the bill."

Emma turned to me. "Bil, tell Sylvie about the knives in our kitchen."

"The knives?"

"Yes," she said. "You know, the table knives. Describe them for her."

I tried to follow my mother's peculiar train of thought, and then it came to me. I laughed. "The hot knives," I said. "Sure."

I turned to Sylvie. "For their twenty-fifth anniversary, Emma and Hugh went away for the weekend to the Oregon Coast. Sam, of course, had a party. Beer bottles all over the yard when they got back, and the table knives were all burned at the tips. Scorched black. Emma couldn't figure it out. She asked Sam, but he blew her off. It was Naomi who clued her in. When you've got no money for weed—you've just got a few bits of bud in the bottom of a bag—you can balance the tiny pieces between two table knives and hold it over the stove. You sniff the smoke as it rises. It's called hot knifing. You get maybe one or two huffs before it's all burned up."

"It's the act of a broke and desperate hophead," Emma said. "No one with access to a real stash would be reduced to hot knifing. I took cleanser and a scouring pad to those knives, but the scorching is permanent. We're still using them—a permanent tribute to Sam, the dope with the dope."

"Hugh was so pissed," I said.

"But you'll notice that he hasn't bought any new knives."

JC crept out from under the table and put his head in my mother's lap. She petted him absentmindedly. From German Shepherd to Alsatian in one smooth move. I decided that the next time I was out at the house, I'd take one of the knives to keep as a memento. Maybe I'd build a shadow box for it.

It was Sylvie who broke the silence. "I think," she said, "that we should find Calvin Knox."

"Why?" I asked.

"Because your mother is right. He owes your brother four hundred dollars. Let's present him with that chit and ask him to make good."

"But..." I began.

My mother smiled. "I like the way you think, Sylvie. Bil, you'd better marry this girl before she comes to her senses and gives you the heave-ho."

"That's nice," I said. "My own mother."

"Tonight," Sylvie suggested, "why don't we pay a visit to Forbidden Village?"

"Not tonight," said Emma, "but soon. We need to plan this carefully. I want to get a look at that casino, and you have to be a member to get in."

"How do you know these things?" I asked.

Emma tapped the side of her nose. "Research," she said. "Speaking of which, I have an answer for Posterity Fish Hook. George Knox in Echo Company, Second Battalion, Fifth Marines. Want to know something else? Jake Peterson served in the two-five as well, as did a Lieutenant Thomas P. Schwartz. They were all in Vietnam together."

"You're shitting me."

"No, I'm not," she said smugly. "George Knox is shitting the cops. That bastard has got a turd in every pocket."

"Have you told Donny this?"

"No."

"If you don't, I will," I said firmly.

"You rotten snitch."

"You jacket thief. Don't even start with me, Emma. Telling Donny is not like telling Sid Castle. Donny has some ideas about this case, and we would do well to remember that he's not the enemy. He's my friend."

Emma folded her arms over her chest and pouted for all she was worth. I let her stew for a good five minutes, quietly sipping my coffee and enjoying the sunshine.

"Let me know when you've finished your huff, would you?"

"You're just like your father," she observed. "He's a controlling fucker, too."

"Meaning he's got a mind of his own. I am telling Donny, Emma. If there's a connection between George Knox and Jake Peterson, there is no sense in keeping it to yourself. As much as you hate Knox and The Church of the True Vine, you ought to be delighted."

The change was instant and remarkable. My mother unfolded her arms, lit a cigarette, and smiled her toothless smile.

"You're not as dumb as you look," she said. "Okay. You go tattle to your little cop boyfriend. I assume you're in touch with Tom Schwartz?"

"How did you know that?"

"Please," she said, as if I'd just asked the Pope if he were Catholic. "You think someone like that can just roll into town without me hearing about it? Talk to Donny, talk to Major Schwartz, and let's see if we can't put the wind up George Knox. Let's drop that Fat Pharisee right in the middle of his own pile of shit."

Chapter 27

We brought Tipper an order of sausages, several biscuits, and a large cup of coffee. He was just beginning to stir when we walked in the front door.

"Oh God," he said. "That smells good. Jesus Christ, stop licking my face! Bil, do something about this unholy beast."

"Holy beast," I corrected. "JC, come here. Look at the smart puppy!"

I bent down and ruffled the dog's ears.

"I don't know about smart," Sylvie said. "You're still holding the bag of food. Sorry, Barbara Woodhouse."

Sylvie handed Tipper the coffee and the bag. I went into the kitchen and poured myself a glass of milk. On the way out, I noticed that Tipper had written a number on the pad next to the telephone. I picked it up.

"What's this?" I asked.

"My father's cell phone number," he said. "He called here last night after you two had gone to bed. You didn't hear the phone ringing, did you? No surprises there."

"We're heavy sleepers," I lied.

"You're heavy liars," Tipper replied. "Major Tom wanted me to leave this cozy abode and meet him somewhere, but I told him I was worn out. I said I'd call him this morning at reveille."

"Well, you've missed reveille. Would you like to go for taps?"

"Oh, shut up. When did you become such an early bird? You used to wake up every day at sunset."

"You must be thinking of someone else." I picked up his legs and made room for myself on the sofa. "Have you tried to call him? What's the plan for today?"

"I have tried to call him. I have not reached him. As far as I know, the plan for today is hari-kari. Major Tom and I are going together to meet with my mother."

"Good luck to you."

"No," he said. "Good luck to us. You're coming with me."

"Oh, no I'm not!"

"Oh, yes you are," he said. "You owe me."

"For what?"

"For not telling this lovely woman here," he pulled Sylvie down onto his lap, "all of your sordid secrets. Does she know what a Doña Juana you were in college?"

"She knows," I said.

"Every last detail?"

"Every last detail."

Sylvie nodded in agreement. "Sorry, Tipper. We have no secrets."

"Damn," he said. "That means I'll have to bring out the big guns. When mother and I moved here, Bil was my first friend. She was a good friend, tried and true. When my dear Southern mother decided to enroll me in cotillion across the border in Pullman, Washington..."

"No!" I shouted.

"It's a Southern thing," Tipper explained. "At cotillion, Sylvie, you learn how to behave properly, how to eat with the correct fork, and how to dance the waltz. My mother attended cotillion in North Carolina, and she was thrilled to find an expatriate Southerner running one out here. The only problem was that I needed a dance partner. Guess who sweetly obliged? We were all of thirteen, but I have here in my wallet a picture of the two of us at a gala ball. I'm wearing a tuxedo, and Bil is wearing..."

"I'll go," I said quickly. "No more arguments."

"Good," Tipper replied. "But you really were pretty in pink."

Sylvie was in hysterics, and even Jesus seemed to be laughing.

* * *

We tried Major Tom's cell phone several times. No answer.

"We know his RV is parked at Traveler's Rest," I said. "Why don't we just drive out there and look for him?"

"You two go," Sylvie said. "JC and I need a run."

Our eye contact was brief but I got the point.

"Five miles?" I asked lightly.

"Five miles," she said. "At least."

"Okay then." Two years and at last I was beginning to read the tea leaves. "Would you mind waiting in the hallway, Tipper? I'll be out in just a minute."

"What? Oh, of course."

As soon as the door had shut behind him, I pulled Sylvie into a close embrace and kissed her. "Try not to run the dog to death. Or yourself."

"I appreciate your concern. Now go." She tried to pull away but the effort was half-hearted. I pulled her back.

"Nope. Tipper can wait. If necessary, he can sit out there all afternoon. You are my first and greatest concern. Always."

She looked at me. Those beautiful green eyes with bright golden flecks around the irises—Sylvie was perfect in every way, but it was her eyes that got me. They stripped me bare, assessed me, and, right now, in this sun-filled moment, they did not find me wanting. They found me just fine.

"Have I told you lately that I love you?" she asked.

"You told me last night," I said, "but I like hearing it again in broad daylight."

"I love you, Bil."

"And I love you, Sylvie. More than I can say. If you keep encouraging my mother, though, I don't know what I'm going to do with you."

"Marry me?" she suggested.

"In a heartbeat." I looked into her eyes again. Something had changed—a flicker, barely discernible. "You mean it, don't you? You're really asking me to marry you?"

"Yes," she said. "I'm really asking you to marry me. Will you?"

Marriage. 'Til death do we part. A joint mortgage. A joint checking account. A lifelong commitment. Arguing like my parents in thirty years' time.

"Of course I'll marry you. I thought you'd never ask."

She kissed me, and then kissed me again. By the time I caught my breath several lifetimes had passed. I'd been to the moon and back, and I'd sung the first butch lesbian *Carmen* at the Sydney Opera House. It was flying time.

"The Unitarian Church?" I suggested. "When?"

"We can talk about the details when you get home," she said. "Go on. Tipper's waiting."

I could hear him tapping his foot outside the door. I said loudly, "If Tipper doesn't behave himself, I'll make Suzy my bridesmaid."

"God forbid," she said, laughing. "I do love you."

"I know," I mused. "And you're willing to announce it to a whole church full of people. You poor, deluded thing. What will everyone say?"

"They'll say I'm very lucky," she replied.

Chapter 28

Traveler's Rest was a gorgeous old-growth cedar forest on the northern edge of town. It was a popular make-out spot for horny teenagers but there were also a few campsites and RV spots. It wasn't hard to find Major Schwartz's rig. It was the only one there, and it was fucking enormous. According to the script painted along its football-field length, it was an Ocean Breeze Deluxe, a shiny tan monstrosity with purple and green swoops painted down the sides. A canopy extended over a large picture window, and outside the front door, the Major had set up lawn chairs and a cast-iron fire pit. It looked quite comfy-cozy.

I pulled in behind a bright red Ford Expedition, brand new by the looks of it. On the back door was the Marine Corps emblem, a large plastic fish with IXOYE written in it, and a bumper sticker that said "Abortion Stops a Beating Heart."

"Oh right," I said. "Abortion stops a beating heart and the Marine Corps doesn't?"

"If you're looking for consistency or rational thought," said Tipper, "you're looking in the wrong place."

"I wonder how many bedrooms that thing has."

"Or if the swimming pool's in the front or back." Tipper shook his head. "Good grief. It's worse than I thought. My father is the stereotypical military retiree. Officers all buy these things, you know—Marine Corps especially. It's all of that traveling they do. I don't think they know how to settle down."

"How can you say that?" I objected. "You've only just met your father."

Tipper snorted. "You think he's the only Marine I know? Any idea how many of these RV travelers I've met in Seattle's gay bars? These guys do their twenty years and retire at thirty-eight. They've got three-quarters of their salary, time on their hands, and a taste for living in a mobile Quonset hut. A big, flashy mobile Quonset hut."

"Okay," I said. "You've just connected your dad to your bar pickups. Am I obliged to think about that or can I just erase the last two minutes from my memory?"

"You big baby," he said. "Let's... hold on. Who's that coming out of Gilligan's Island? I do believe it's the Reverend George Knox."

I peered through the windshield. Unfortunately, it was less than clean. I turned on the wipers and squirted the window with cleaner. This just smeared the bugs and road grime even more. Through the haze I could see a fat man in a pale green suit climbing with some difficulty down the RV's steps. The hair, however, was unmistakable. Dark brown, piled high, and curled around George Knox's head like a sleeping cat. Behind him was a young woman of very slight build, shaking her head in a vigorous "no".

"Come on," I said to Tipper. "We can't hide, so let's be nosy."

Knox looked up when he heard the truck doors open. I believe he would have scuttled away if that had been possible, but my small truck was blocking his big, red, shiny SUV. I knew that it belonged to Knox because I could see the personalized license plate, Godzway. I suppressed the urge to barf up my breakfast.

Knox backed away as we approached. The young woman standing behind him smiled but said nothing. She was of Asian descent, Vietnamese unless I missed my guess. She was gorgeous and also no more than twenty-five, about the same age as Tipper and me. I smiled back at her.

"Hello," I said.

"Hello," she replied.

"I'm Bil Hardy."

"Hello," she said again.

Inside the RV a small dog was yapping.

"Is that Drudge?" I asked. Knox laughed. It wasn't a pleasant sound.

He said, "Don't bother. 'Hello' is the only word she knows."

George Knox was one of those fat, smug, pompous men who didn't think of themselves as obese and shiny but instead imagined that they were still the high school football star. He had a barrel chest and no neck. When he looked in the mirror, I was certain he saw a manly man—the big guy with the big plans.

When I looked at George Knox, on the other hand, I saw a bloated tick on a hound dog, gorged with blood and ready to pop. I decided that the best plan was to address him head on, as if we'd just met in the produce aisle at Foodway and I'd caught him fingering a melon.

"Funny meeting you here," I said. "How do you know Major Schwartz?"

"I'm sorry," Knox replied. "Do I know you?" His teeth were a dingy pipe-smoker's yellow.

"You might. I'm Bil Hardy. My mother is Emma Hardy, AKA the Sieve of Vanity. You've been exchanging words with her on the Slip-Fifty listserv."

Knox thought he could pull this one off by laughing. He gave us a hearty guffaw that never reached his beady eyes. "The Sieve of Vanity. So you must be Posterity Fish Hook? You might be surprised to learn that I enjoy your mother's posts. She is most entertaining."

"You enjoyed her post about your son's illegal casino?"

That wiped the smile from his face. "That was an internal church matter," he said. "Like any congregation, we are always concerned with sin and sinfulness, but we choose to address the sins of our church family in private. That a malicious person who bears us ill will would choose to take our personal trials and tribulations and make public hay of them is a cause for sorrow, Miss Hardy, not rejoicing."

"An illegal casino?" said Tipper. "Sounds to me like cause for a police investigation. Have you seen to that, Bil?"

"No," I said. "I'm afraid Mr. Knox here has friends in high places."

George Knox shook his head sadly—a mistake as his hair slipped to one side in the heat.

"I can see that this is not going to be a productive exchange," he said. "I'm sorry for that. The enemies of our ministry are many, and they are very vocal. However, it is right and good that we should suffer for the sake of our lord and savior. In the end, we will prevail. Now, if you'll move your *vehicle*, I'll be on my way."

I hadn't realized that it was possible to say the word vehicle with the kind of inflection usually reserved for freshly trodden dog shit.

"Are you comparing yourself to Jesus Christ?" Tipper asked with mock astonishment. "As I recall, *He* tossed the moneychangers from the temple. He didn't walk in and set up a Blackjack table and a roulette wheel."

The young woman had moved so that she was standing some distance behind Knox. I certainly didn't blame her. The suit he wore was sweat-stained under the armpits. Still, given his attitude, I was in no hurry to move my truck for him. I decided instead to try introducing myself to the young woman again.

Pointing at my chest I said, "I'm Bil Hardy. And that," I pointed at Tipper," is Tipper Schwartz. We are looking for Major Thomas Schwartz."

"Thomas Schwartz," she repeated. "No."

I tried again. "No, he's not here?"

She shook her head. "Tom Schwartz, no. No Tom Schwartz."

Knox was laughing again. "I told you. She doesn't speak English. Do you speak Vietnamese?"

"Absolutely." I pointed at Knox. "*Dien cai dau.*"

The young woman laughed.

"What did you say?" Knox asked suspiciously.

"I just ordered a bowl of *pho*. Tripe flavored."

The woman smiled at me. It was the same smile of relief I'd seen on the faces of Japanese tourists when I'd lived in Seattle after I had somehow—through a complex mix of my three words of Japanese, their equally challenged English, a bad but colorful map and an assortment of hand gestures—managed to direct them to the Space Needle.

"*Pho*," she said. "Yes, *pho*."

"How's your Vietnamese, Mr. Knox?" I asked. "I hear that you, the late Jake Peterson, and Major Tom all served together with the Second Battalion, Fifth Marines. You're old friends, aren't you?"

"Move your vehicle," Knox snapped.

I ignored him and turned back to the young woman. "*Này, này*," I said.

"What was that?" Tipper asked.

"I think it was hello. I might have pronounced it wrong."

"Yes, hello," said the young woman. "*Này, này.*"

"Please," said Knox. "I really do have somewhere else to be. Are you going to move your truck or not?"

"I don't know," said Tipper. "Are you going to tell us what you're doing here?"

"I don't see that it's any of your business."

"No," he agreed. "But I'm asking anyway."

Tipper took a step closer to Knox. The contrast couldn't have been greater. Tipper was very tall and very fit. Knox was very short and very fat.

"Why are you here, Pastor Knox? How do you know my father?"

"I answer under protest," Knox replied. "And under threat. Yes, Tom Schwartz and I served together in Vietnam. Jake Peterson, God rest his soul, also served with us. We were comrades in the two-five. I don't suppose you would know much about that. Don't ask, don't tell," he said.

"And don't pursue," Tipper added. "Your type never remembers that last part. You're quite wrong about what I know and what I don't. The Second Battalion, Fifth Marines is the most decorated battalion in the Marine Corps. Their motto? 'Retreat, Hell!' I know where my father served, George Knox. I know where my mother served, too. She completed two tours of duty. Captain Rebecca Schwartz, Army Nurse Corps. My mother finished her second tour while heavily pregnant with me. Now that's what I call guts. That's 'Retreat, Hell!' for you."

Knox frowned. "The greatest shame of our nation is that we allow our women to serve in uniform. A country so fallen is not worthy of God's grace."

"And a roly-poly motherfucker like you is not worth a swift kick up the ass, but you're sure as hell about to get one," Tipper said. "Unless you want my size eleven Gucci loafer wedged between your butt cheeks, you'll find some way to seesaw that oil tanker of yours out of here. Bil will not be moving her truck because she will not be doing one single solitary thing to accommodate you. I'd advise you to take care and not hit her *vehicle* as you practice your maneuvers. She may look sweet, but she has a nasty temper."

Knox turned his back on us and, with as much dignity as a sweaty fat man in a shiny nylon wig could muster, he huffed and puffed his way up the hill to his SUV.

"Nice one," I whispered when Knox was out of earshot. "Now what?"

"Now you talk to the nice young woman," he whispered back. "Use your Vietnamese."

"Tipper," I whispered back. "I don't know Vietnamese. I know how to order seven kinds of *pho*, and I can deliver the odd insult. That's it."

"What about the dinky-dow thing?" he asked.

"It means crazy."

"*Dien cai dau*," the young woman behind us said. She pointed at George Knox, who was delicately moving his truck back and forth, a few inches at a time. "*Dien cai dau*."

"Yes!" Tipper laughed. "George Knox is dinky-dow."

"Your pronunciation is awful," I observed.

"Shut up," Tipper said. "Tell her hello again."

I turned back to the young woman and smiled.

"*Này, này*," I said. "I am Bil Hardy. What is your name?"

No answer. I decided to guess. "Nguyen?"

"What are you doing?" Tipper asked.

"Nguyen is to the Vietnamese what Smith is to the English."

"No," the young woman shook her head. "Not Nguyen." She held up her left hand and showed us the shiny gold band on her ring finger. "Mrs. Schwartz," she said. "I am Tom's wife. You?"

Uh-oh. I avoided meeting Tipper's gaze. We'd have to sort this one out back at the bunk house. If there was one thing I'd learned in the final years of my brother's life, it was to tackle disasters one at a time.

"Mrs. Schwartz," I said politely, "this is Tipper Schwartz, Tom's son. I am his friend, Bil Hardy."

"Tipper and Bil..."

"Hardy," I repeated.

"Hardy. You mare Ed?"

Tipper looked at me. "Am I Mister Ed?"

"Mare ed," I repeated. "Mare ed. Married! She thinks we're married, Tipper."

"Good God! She must be *dien cai dau*."

"Shut up," I hissed. "Do you want to offend her?"

I smiled at the young woman and pulled out the best explanation I could manage under the circumstances. "No. We are not married. Tipper is *bay-day*. I am *ô-môi*."

Her eyes widened. She put out her hands, palms facing us as if she were stopping traffic, and backed up the RV's steps. She stumbled inside and shut the door in our faces. Firmly.

"What the hell did you say to her?" Tipper asked.

I sighed heavily. "I told her we were Jehovah's Witnesses."

Chapter 29

"*Cac to cha may.*"

"What?" said Tipper.

"That's the only other Vietnamese I know. It means something like 'fuck the ancestors of your father.' Somehow, I thought *ô-môi* and *bay-day* might be a better choice."

"Oh yeah? Well, I wish you'd stuck with the seven different kinds of *pho*. Where are we going?"

I turned the truck off Main Street and onto Third. There were no parking spaces in front of Pho From Home, so I circled the block.

"To get help," I said. "If that young woman is any older than you or me, I'll eat those seven kinds of *pho*, including the tripe. She could be your father's daughter, but she says she's his wife. You know what that means?"

"Yes. Major Tom is a cradle-robber."

"Not quite. Major Tom is a cradle-robbing bigamist."

I glanced at him. He was staring out the windshield but looking at nothing.

"Tipper! Wake up! Don't shut down on me now. I know you. You switch off when you're stressed. You go all Zen or whatever it is that you do. This is not the time for Zen. Think action. Think plan."

"You do know who you sound like, don't you?"

"Don't say it! It is possible to make a plan, you know, without becoming my mother."

I found a spot in the Cowslip Co-Op parking lot. There was a chance that they'd tow my truck. The Co-Op was getting fussy about non-shoppers taking up space in their lot. I decided to risk it, hoping that the "Visualize Whirled Peas" bumper sticker on the back of my Toyota would serve as proof of my Co-Oppiness. I switched off the engine and looked at Tipper. He'd stopped staring into space and begun instead to minutely examine his fingernails.

In some ways, Tipper reminded me of Sam. He was as tough as an old boot on the outside but inside, he was a complete marshmallow. His feelings were easily hurt, and it was possible to wound him without meaning to. For all of his bluster, his camp, and his mini-skirts, he had a very tender heart. He was the polar opposite of Suzy, who was as hard-bitten as they come. If Suzy swallowed a lump of coal, he'd shit a diamond.

I took Tipper's hand and forced him to look me in the eye.

"Listen to me, honey. Your father has got to sort out this divorce with your mother or he will be in deep shit. Don't you understand? This is a good thing. Major Tom can't touch the Captain's property—he can't take her to court without exposing himself to prosecution. I don't think he wants anything from her except her signature on some paperwork, and I'd bet money that he wants that quickly and with no questions asked. Your mother holds all the cards here, Tipper. What will happen to that young woman if your father gets caught? He's a bigamist! She'll be deported."

This seemed to rattle Tipper out of his stupor. He squeezed my hand.

"Will she? I don't want anything bad to happen to her. I don't even know her, poor soul. I just... I want my mother to be okay."

"She will be okay," I assured him.

"I'll tell you something else," Tipper said, reviving. "My father is risking a court martial."

"But he's retired."

"That doesn't matter," Tipper explained. He's only just retired. If he married that young woman before he left the service..." His face assumed a thoughtful look. "I'll have to check the Uniform Code of Military Justice about the statute of limitations on bigamy. My mother will have an old copy somewhere. If I could get my hands on a new one..."

"Easy," I said. "We'll ask Sarah, the queen of all reference librarians or, in a pinch, we'll ask Naomi. Right now I'm going to introduce you to my friend, Vivian Nguyen-DiRisio. If we can get her to leave her restaurant for half an hour, she can talk to that young woman who may or may not be your father's wife."

It was a short walk up the alley from the Co-Op to Pho From Home. Vivian, as usual, was behind the counter. The restaurant was nearly empty—just a couple of people eating lunch—one of whom was Vivian's young Joe Pesci-looking husband.

"Bil! Where have you been?" Vivian shrieked and ran around the counter to embrace me, the top of her head just barely touching the middle of my chest. She pulled back and gave Tipper the glad eye. "And who is this? Did you trade that mangy dog for a good-looking man? Look, Robert," she said to her husband. "That crazy preacher is right—you can turn straight. Just pray to Jesus, and the leopard change her stripes."

"Spots," Robert said automatically. "And that crazy preacher doesn't know his ass from a hole in the ground. How you doing?" He shook my hand. "So you're Bil. I've heard a lot about you. All good, of course."

"I doubt it." I made the introductions. As soon as Tipper said hello, Vivian shook her head in mock sadness.

"So much for Jesus," she said. "You're as gay as this one."

"Vivian!"

"Oh, shut up, Robert." Vivian slapped her husband on the arm. "You think I don't know gay? I am so much hipper than you, it's not funny. You need to get with the schedule."

"Program," said Robert.

"I need a favor," I interrupted. "Vivian—we need a translator. Urgently."

I explained about the young woman in Major Tom's RV. When I got to the part about *ô-môi* and *bay-day*, Vivian slapped her forehead and then she slapped me, much harder than she'd slapped Robert.

"Ouch!"

"You scared the seven shits out of her," she said. "Imagine. First the crazy preacher knocks on her door. He probably knows some Vietnamese, maybe some awful words he learned in the war. He was in the Army, right?"

"Marines," Tipper corrected.

"Okay, Marines. So he knows about boom boom and things like that."

"Boom boom as in bombs?" I asked.

This earned me another slap. Robert grimaced in sympathy and signaled for me to shut up. I shut up.

"Boom boom as in 'I'll fuck you for a dollar.' You should do some travel. It's widening."

"Broadening," said Robert.

"You," Vivian wheeled on him. "Don't you have office hours this afternoon?"

"Yes," he said.

"Cancel them. I need you to mind my restaurant. I'm going with this moron and her handsome friend. I'll be back soon."

"Vivian," Robert objected, "you know I don't cook."

"Robert," Vivian smiled. "I married you because you are so— what's the word? It means good at everything."

"Versatile?" I suggested.

"Accommodating?" Tipper offered.

"Pussy-whipped," said Robert.

Vivian laughed. "That will do. Stay here and mind my shop." She sealed her orders with a kiss and turned to Tipper and me. "Let's go."

"Don't be too long, baby," Robert said, tying on the apron she handed him. "If I run out of noodles, I'm putting up the closed sign."

"Just empty all the pots and send them to McDonald's," Vivian said. "You lazy man. Bil, you will owe me a fortune for this translating work."

"What's a fortune to you, Vivian? Three bowls of *pho*? Maybe four? You're far too generous. I don't know how you stay in business. You charge too little, you don't advertise, and no one around here knows what *pho* is. I keep having to tell people."

"Ha!" Vivian said. "Word of mouth sells the *pho*—the word of your mouth. You eat enough *pho* to pay my rent."

"Does she really?" Tipper asked. "That would explain the extra ten pounds."

"I wish you'd all shut up about my pounds. My girlfriend loves me, so what the fuck do you care? We'll have to bunch up together in my truck," I apologized to Vivian. "It'll be a tight squeeze. Sorry."

"Listen to this one," Vivian said to Tipper. "She's not worried about her ten pounds. She's worried about my fifty. I'm doing her a favor, and she's complaining about the size of my ass."

"That's the story of my life," Tipper observed solemnly.

Vivian laughed. "I like him!" she declared. "Robert, you better watch out. Gay or no gay, if you screw up my restaurant, I'll leave you for this cute blondie."

"Yeah, yeah," said Robert, who had already stepped behind the counter and begun counting the till. "I spent four years at Columbia for this?"

"No." Vivian twitched her round ass as we went out the door. "You spent four years at Columbia for this. Now come on, you two. You take my words, that woman is in the RV right now, looking for a gun. We better get there before she find it."

Chapter 30

Tipper and I sat in the lawn chairs outside the RV. Vivian had been inside for a good fifteen minutes. She'd had no trouble getting in. She knocked on the door, shouted a few words in Vietnamese, and the young woman threw the door open and threw herself into Vivian's arms. You'd have thought they were long-lost friends.

Tipper was fiddling with his cell phone. He'd tried calling his father on it several times. All he got was a message saying that the Major's phone was either switched off or out of service.

"Why don't you call your mother?" I suggested.

"And tell her what?"

"I don't know. The truth?"

"We won't know the truth until Vivian comes out of that RV. All we've got now is ripe speculation."

"No," I said firmly. "What we've got is a young woman with a wedding ring on her finger who says she's your father's wife."

Tipper gave me a piercing look.

"In Vietnam my mother nursed everyone, Bil, not just soldiers. She nursed Vietnamese civilians. Women and children, little old men, the Viet Cong, and the North Vietnamese Army. She is not what you'd call fluent, and it's been twenty-five years since she spoke Vietnamese, but I reckon she could summon up enough to talk to that young woman, and she could understand enough to get hold of the wrong end of the stick. Let's just wait, okay?"

I kicked at the dirt in front of my lawn chair. "I hate waiting."

"I noticed. You get more like Emma with every passing day."

"That was uncalled for, not to mention cruel. I'm getting really tired—"

I was interrupted by Vivian's return. She stood in the doorway of the camper and shook the young woman's hand. They both looked somber. Then Vivian said something in Vietnamese. The woman looked at me and laughed. She and Vivian shook hands again, the door closed, and Vivian made her way carefully down the rickety metal steps.

"Just now," I said, "what did you say to her?"

Vivian waved a hand dismissively. "It's hard to translate. Something about you being dumber than snake shit."

"Thank you, Vivian."

"You're welcome. Now, you want to know what's going on here?"

"Yes," said Tipper. "But first, tell me, was there some sort of chill in the air? I know she laughed at the snake shit thing, but you shook hands. When we got here, she fell on you like you were the last gin and tonic at closing time."

"That was desperation," Vivian said. "My people don't hug and kiss. *I* hug and kiss because I'm married to an Italian. Also, I have lived here for thirty years. I adapt. Your father's wife is very young and very traditional. When we came, she was scared. Now she's not, and so we shook hands. It's all good. Bil, I am old and tired. Get up. I want your chair."

I didn't argue. I got up and helped Vivian settle herself into my webbed chaise lounge. I sat down in the dirt.

She took a deep breath and continued. "Your father met Thuy in Saigon."

"Twee?" Tipper said.

"No," Vivian said. "Tuwee. That's her name."

"Tuwee," I repeated.

"Very good, Bil. You're learning. Now, if you just stop repeating everything I tell you, I won't have to explain to my people why you know all about lesbian fruit. She thought I was as dinky-dow as you are."

"*Dien cai dau*," I corrected. This earned me a swat.

"Shut up." Vivian leaned back. "Tipper, last year your father went to Vietnam with a group of old soldiers. It was a special trip for the government, a kind of peace mission. Heal old wounds, maybe open the rice market to American product, that sort of thing. Some of the men had been prisoners of war. They were very welcomed by the people. That made the soldiers happy, and it made my people happy. It was a good trip. Your father speaks Vietnamese. He's very good with languages. Did you know that?"

Tipper shook his head. "I don't know much of anything about him, Vivian. He was never part of my life."

"Okay," she said. "Thuy says he knows the language very well. Almost perfect. He studied at some military school."

"The Defense Language Institute," Tipper supplied. "It's part of the Presidio at Monterey. I don't know that my father went there. I'm just guessing."

"Your mother said he was fluent in Russian," I said.

"That's right," Tipper said, nodding. "She did."

Vivian continued. "Your father met Thuy and it was love at first sight. For both of them. She's an orphan. No aunts, no uncles. She had nothing to keep her in Vietnam, and so they married in Saigon and he brought her here. It took a special visa and some string-pulling. Your father is not just a retired Marine. He still works for the government." Vivian tapped her nose, which reminded me disconcertingly of my mother. "CIA, I think, or something like it. Thuy isn't sure. She's very confused, she's very traditional, and she is not as young as she looks. She's thirty."

"Twee," said Tipper, still mispronouncing the name. "My stepmother. She was six when I was born."

"A child bride," Vivian said. "And it's Tuwee. Listen to me."

He tried repeating it. Vivian shook her head.

"Never mind, Blondie. You come to the restaurant, I'll give you lessons. Thuy is a very common name, like Jane. Her last name is common, too. It's Tran. Bil made a good guess with Nguyen."

"Tran is like Jones," I explained to Tipper. "Not as common as Smith or Nguyen. I think half of Vietnam is named Nguyen."

Vivian leaned back in the chair and stroked her chin. "Close," she agreed. "Thuy is worried. She hasn't seen your father since last night. She tries to call his cell phone but he doesn't answer. He's never left her like this before. She doesn't know what to do. She's only been in this country for three months. She's learning to speak English by watching *Sesame Street*."

"You're joking."

"No, I don't joke," Vivian said. "That's how I learned, too. And I can speak some Spanish. *Sesame Street* teaches you enough to go out and get around. You learn how to count, you learn your letters. It's the *Children's Television Workshop*."

"Fine!" I held up my hands in surrender. "You don't have to sell me on *Sesame Street*. I know how to Count von Count."

"My father is gone," Tipper said, "and his wife doesn't know where he is. His old platoon mate, George Knox, is also looking for him. Where the hell is he? Vivian, is Thuy going to be okay?"

"I'm coming back here tonight," Vivian said. "I'll sit with her and wait. You," she said, pointing at Tipper, "are going to find that stupid man, Major Tom. Check the hospital. Check the whorehouse.

Look in the bars and the bowling alley. I knew Marines in Vietnam when they were on R and R. Maybe your father is a drunken idiot."

"Maybe," Tipper agreed. "It's good of you to help us out, and it's very good of you to help Thuy."

Vivian dismissed this with an airy wave. "Nonsense. It's good of Bil to run my restaurant."

I snapped to attention. "What?"

"I can't leave Robert in the store all night," Vivian pointed out. "What does he know about *pho*? Nothing! He can sell what's in the pot and that's it. You come and eat so much, you know how to make every dish except the tripe. When I come here, you go there. You make sure I don't go bankrupt while I do my charity work for your handsome *bay-day* friend. Now take me back. Time to rescue my poor restaurant from Robert."

"Now who's pussy-whipped?" Tipper asked.

Vivian laughed. "This one," she said, poking me in the chest with a hard finger. "But not by me. Three sisters, a mother, and a girlfriend. She's got the pussies whipping everywhere!"

Chapter 31

Thank God no one asked for the tripe. I made *pho* from three o'clock until nearly eleven when Vivian returned. She sat down at the counter and rested her head in her hands. I stifled a yawn.

"Did you eat up all my profits?"

"I had one bowl."

"You had two," she said, matter-of-factly.

"You're psychic."

"I am," she agreed. "And I was right about your friend's father. Stupid drunk Marine."

"Tipper found him in a bar?"

"No," she said. "Tipper found him in the hospital. He's got a concussion. He went out drinking and got knocked on the head. Someone took his wallet, his car, and his money. Left him all bloody in the tall grass. No one found him for hours. He's lucky he's not dead."

"How do they know he was drinking?"

"Blood alcohol," Vivian said. "Huge blood alcohol, enough to poison him. And he was hit on the head with a crow thing."

"A crowbar?"

She snapped her fingers. "That's the ticket. Take off that apron. It's time for me to work."

"It's time for you to rest," I said. "Why don't you close up for the night? The only person who ever comes in here this late is me, and I've already eaten three bowls."

"Two," Vivian said. "If it's three, I'll charge you. You're right. I think I'll go home to my young, handsome husband, the one who never gets drunk. You want some Vietnamese coffee?"

"You mean that awful crap with sweetened condensed milk? No, thanks."

"It will help you stay awake," she said. "You've got to go to the hospital. Your friend needs you. He said to tell you that everything has gone to the breasts."

"What?"

"No, that's wrong," she said. "The breasts are in the air?"

"You mean it's all gone tits up?"

"Yes. That's what he said."

"Did he explain why?"

She nodded. "He told me everything and I translated for Thuy. But I only told her what she needed to know. Her husband is injured, and she needs to be with him in the hospital."

"What was it that Thuy didn't need to know?"

Vivian raised her eyebrows. She climbed off the stool, took the apron from me, and tossed it through the curtain into the storage room. "She didn't need to know a lot of things. Major Schwartz is your friend's father. Is Captain Schwartz your friend's mother?"

"Yes."

"She's at the hospital with Thuy."

"Oh, shit."

"Yes, oh shit and the tits are up. Your mother is there with them."

"My mother? Why?"

"You know that tall grass where they found the Major, his big drunk head all bashed and bleeding? Your mother owns it. It's something called the Old Corn-holer's Place."

I didn't bother to correct her.

* * *

It was eight blocks from Vivian's restaurant to Cowslip Memorial. I ran all the way, skidding to a halt at the Emergency Room entrance. I paused to catch my breath, resting with my hands on my knees. The parking lot was nearly empty. My mother's car, the Queen Mary, was front and center. The Captain's truck, an elderly but well-maintained Ford, was at the far end of the lot. I breathed in the cooling night air and listened to the grain trucks rumbling past on their way down south to the port in Lewiston. It had been hot in Vivian's kitchen, and I really needed a shower, especially after my impromptu jog.

No time for that now. I straightened up and ran my fingers through my hair, then triggered the automatic doors and entered the hospital's waiting area. The tableau that greeted me looked like what might have happened if Salvador Dali had painted *The Last Supper*. In the middle was Thuy. She was crying. Captain Schwartz sat on Thuy's right, holding her hand. Behind the Captain stood

Kate, frowning, her hand resting on the Captain's shoulder. Behind Kate was Sylvie, arms folded across her chest. She looked so much like her mother, complete with matching frown, that it was unnerving.

On the other side of Thuy, huddled together like the three witches from *Macbeth*, sat Tipper, my mother, and Sarah. My mother had her back to Thuy, and she was holding forth in her usual fashion, gesturing wildly. A few paces away, hands behind their backs and awkward looks on their faces, stood Donny and Buck DeWitt. Buck waved at me and smiled, as if we'd just met one another at Wawawai. I ignored him.

In the role of Judas Iscariot was Nurse Suzy Parker-Smith. He had on the most ridiculous set of hospital scrubs I'd ever seen. They were the light green color of regular scrubs but hippos in bright pink tutus danced across the fabric. Combined with a purple stethoscope and an orange cap, Suzy's scrubs looked like a circus visiting a psychiatric ward. And yet, somehow, Suzy managed to convey the appropriate air of authority. He was clearly the person in charge, a no-bullshit ER nurse with the answers to all of my questions. I made a beeline for him.

"What in the hell is going on here, Suzy?"

He closed his eyes and shook his head. When he opened them again, he said, "I am exhausted. Sylvie," he called over my shoulder. "Would you mind? I want you and Bil to follow me. I'm going to take you into the forbidden zone."

Without a word to one another, Sylvie and I followed Suzy into the ER. No one except Donny and Buck acknowledged our passing. Suzy paused long enough to give Donny a peck on the cheek. Buck blushed.

The first curtained bay was empty. I tried not to think about how many times I'd sat beside that very ER bed with Sam. Dozens? More? Suzy waved to the nurses at the station desk, a young man named Bob and an older woman I knew as Jan the Man, wife of Stan the Man, Cowslip's Fire Chief. Sam had also called them Mr. and Mrs. Catfish because they both had thick black whiskers growing from their chins.

Suzy said, "Pull up a stool, Bil. Sylvie, you take the chair."

"What about you?" I asked. "You said you were exhausted."

"I am."

Suzy hooked a line of disposable plastic tubing to the oxygen feed on the wall. He turned the knob on the top, put the tube up his nose, and took four or five good hits.

"Okay," he said, switching the machine off and tossing the tube into the trash. "I'm good for another couple of hours. Don't look at me like that, Bil Hardy—it's common practice. I've been on duty for ten hours now, and I'll be on for another two. Nothing like a hit off the oxygen bong to help a girl get through her shift."

"You mean you don't snort cocaine?"

Suzy laughed. "Of course not. I'm a nurse, not a doctor. Now, you've got questions. I've got answers. Where would you like me to begin?"

I looked at Sylvie. Her gaze was clouded, her expression tense. I hadn't seen or spoken to her since Tipper and I had left that morning. This was my fiancée, the woman who'd asked me to marry her, my gorgeous, patient, long-suffering future wife. I'd stood in Vivian's restaurant and dished out *pho* for hours without calling Sylvie to tell her where I was, when I'd be home, or why I was gone.

"Suzy," I said. "Would you mind leaving us alone for a few minutes? Maybe you could go to the nurse's station and sniff the dry erase markers."

"Ah," said Suzy. "I see. Five minutes?"

"Yeah." As soon as he'd gone, I pulled the curtain closed behind him. "Honey," I said, "please come here. It's been such a long day."

Sylvie didn't hesitate. She wrapped her arms around my neck, and I put my hands firmly on her hips, pulling her to me. I rested my head on her shoulder. We stood that way for some time, not talking, just breathing. She smelled like citrus and amber, the blend of her perfume. I reeked of beef broth and garlic. She kissed me anyway.

"I should have called," I said. "I'm sorry."

"It's okay. Tipper called. I knew where you were."

"Are you sure you want to marry someone as thoughtless as I am? I really do try. It's just that I don't seem to get any better."

"You're not thoughtless." She pulled back and smiled at me. Her eyes were no longer clouded. They were again deep green, and the golden flecks in her irises shone brightly. "I am ticked off that you didn't call yourself, but one of the things I love most about you is that whatever you're doing, you do it completely, body and soul. You get caught up in the moment. It's not that I think you forget about me. I think you forget that I'm not psychic. I can't read your mind, Bil."

"I know that," I said. "For what it's worth, I can't seem to read my own mind, either. I never forget about you, though. Not for one moment."

"What I ought to do is have you micro-chipped. Like JC."

"You had JC micro-chipped?"

She looked at me with a mix of resignation and amusement. "JC had an appointment with the vet this afternoon. You forgot that, too, didn't you? He's no longer a real boy. I had him neutered. Do you remember that we agreed to that?"

I had no recollection whatsoever, but I pretended that I did. "I thank you, and the Humane Society thanks you. JC is probably not so grateful."

"No," she agreed. "I gave him a pain pill before I left my mother's house. He's had his shots, including his rabies vaccine, and I have some wormer to give him when he's feeling a bit better. We should probably go back fairly soon and check on him."

"My God," I said sincerely. "I don't know what I'd do without you."

"Wander the earth," she suggested, "one shoe on, one shoe lost, living on hamburgers, noodles, and junk food, and trying to remember where you parked the truck."

"I need a babysitter."

"You've got one," she said. "What the babysitter needs is a global positioning system. I can't think of any other way to keep track of you."

"A what?"

"A global positioning system." She laughed. "A GPS. It's high-tech stuff. You know that Ph.D. I'm getting in geography? We use GPS systems for mapping. Boring girls like me could also use them to keep track of harum-scarum types like you."

I stared at her in amazement. "You think you're boring?" When she nodded, I said, "Baby, there is no one on earth more exciting than you are. There is no one more intriguing, mysterious, dark, and deep. *You* are still waters. No." I put a finger to her lips. "Don't argue. Hear me out. Just when I think I know where I am with you, when I think I understand you and that I know what you want or how you feel, you throw me a curve ball. You keep me forever off balance."

"Do I?" she asked, clearly surprised. "Is that good or bad?"

"It's very, very good," I assured her. "You thrill me."

"Hold me, thrill me, kiss me?" she suggested.

"I thought you'd never ask."

Suzy made a production number out of pretending to knock on the curtain. I released Sylvie reluctantly. Without looking at Suzy, I said, "Sylvie and I are getting married."

"Mazel Tov," he replied. "And best wishes to you, Sylvie. May I ask which one of you is pregnant?"

"Neither, jackass. We don't need kids. We've got Jesus Christ."

"Oh good. I'm glad you two are spirit-filled. I feel like a sack of wet potatoes." Suzy flopped down in the chair Sylvie had been sitting in. I sat on the doctor's stool, and Sylvie stood behind me, pulling my hair through her fingers.

"Tell us everything you know," I said. "Beginning with Major Tom. What happened to him? Vivian told me he'd been whacked with a crowbar."

"News travels fast," Suzy said. "Yes, a crowbar seems to be what did the trick. I suppose it could have been a length of rebar— something long, hard, and metal. The Major is a lucky man. Someone hit him a glancing blow on the top of the head. He came in here with a huge laceration. It took thirty sutures to close, and let me tell you, it was hell to lavage."

"English, please," I requested.

"Lavage—wash. He's got a non-depressed skull fracture. It's clean, meaning there are no bits of bone in the brain, and there is very little intracranial swelling. The wound on the other hand, that was nasty. Donny found him. The Major was up at Jake Peterson's old shack, lying well hidden in that tall grass. If my big, sweet Barney Fife weren't a whole hell of a lot smarter than he looks, Tipper's father would still be up there, and he'd be deader than a doornail. As it was, he'd been there long enough for all sorts of bugs and flies to turn that wound into a combination buffet and larva nursery. We washed out dirt, grass and maggot eggs, but it looks like the mice may have..."

Sylvie stopped tugging at my hair.

"Suzy," I said quickly. "Sylvie and I are not nurses. Unless you want to lavage a big pool of vomit, please stop with the gory details."

"Sorry," Suzy said, looking suitably chastened. "Working in this place, you forget. Without being too gross, I'll just say that the only reason Donny found the Major was because of the magpies. There was so much blood from the head wound that the Major had attracted—what do you call them? A murder of magpies?"

"It's a murder of crows," Sylvie said. "A tiding of magpies, though they're also called a mischief. You're supposed to be able to tell the future based on their number. One for sorrow, two for joy, three for a girl, four for a boy."

"You're a walking encyclopedia!" Suzy exclaimed. "In this case, it was a tiding and a mischief. According to Donny, there was a baker's dozen fighting like mad over the Major, and one skulking coyote. Donny saw the birds from the road and walked up to investigate."

"What was Donny doing out there?"

"Snooping, of course. I told you, Bil—Sid Castle doesn't give a flying fuck about who shot some rotten old pot dealer in some rotten old shack. Donny does. My baby cares about everyone, bless his little Mormon heart, and he won't stop until he finds out what happened. Today is his day off. He didn't have his radio with him, and he didn't have his cell phone. If Emma hadn't come along, Donny would have had to leave the scene—leave Major Tom up there to the magpies and the coyote. No, don't interrupt, Bil. Your mother ought to be a cop. she's as nosy as my husband. In this case, that was a good thing. She was sitting on her front porch when Donny drove by. Emma being Emma, she got in her car and followed him. Luckily, she had her cell phone with her, and so she called the paramedics."

"Great," I said. "My mother's interference has now saved someone's life. Does she know this?"

"I'm afraid so," Suzy confirmed. "She's been soaking in adulation for most of the day. The only one who hasn't called to congratulate her is Bill Clinton, and I expect that's only a matter of time. The news went out on the scanner, so we've had every rubbernecker in town stopping in to have a look-see. Actually, I'm glad that your mother is here. She keeps them all out of my hair."

"Why don't you keep her?" I suggested.

"Not on your nelly," he replied. "Major Tom had a raging fever when the paramedics brought him in—104.2 degrees and he was badly dehydrated. We cleaned the wound, got an IV in him, and sent him for a CAT scan and an X-ray. His wallet was gone. No ID. Again, it was your mother who came to the rescue. She announced that he looked exactly like Tipper, and she called Captain Schwartz. Once we knew who he was and that he wasn't allergic to penicillin, we could get him started on Keflex."

"How did you come to be here?" I asked Sylvie.

"Tipper had the truck, so I'd asked my mother to drive me and JC to the vet. Then I went home with her to wait. We had lunch, we talked, we drank a lot of coffee. About four o'clock, the Captain called my mother and asked if she'd come with her to the hospital. She came to pick my mother up and they left. As soon as JC was ready, I went to get him in my mother's car. I took him back to her place, and then I joined the party here at the hospital. I didn't know the Captain spoke Vietnamese. I gather the young woman in there is Tom Schwartz's wife, Tuwee?"

"Very good," I said. "Your pronunciation is excellent. Vivian would be proud."

Sylvie smiled. "Vivian and the Captain gave us all lessons. I like Vivian, by the way. You should have introduced me."

"Not jealous anymore?"

"Oh, no. I'm jealous as hell. You didn't tell me how attractive she is."

"You have nothing to worry about. I'm only after her for the *pho*. About your mother and the Captain..."

Suzy was sitting very still, his ears on stalks, but I didn't care. Neither, apparently, did Sylvie.

"They're working things out," she said. "And before you ask, yes, I am okay with that. I told you that my mother and I talked this afternoon. We talked a lot. I told her that I'd asked you to marry me."

"You asked Bil?" Suzy interrupted. "Shouldn't that have been the other way around? Bil on bended knee, begging you to make an honest woman of her?"

"Oh, shut up," I said. "You're as bad as Tipper. What did your mother say?"

"She said it was about time, and she congratulated *me*, Suzy. She's saving her best wishes for Bil."

"She didn't have a problem with the Captain's divorce or Major Tom's bigamy or anything else to do with this whole mess?"

"Oh, no." Sylvie laughed. "She had plenty of problems with all of that. It's not the big issue, though. What my mother can't stand are the Fort Sister processing circles. She feels that there should only be two people in the relationship: herself and the Captain. Not my mother, the Captain, Cedar Tree, and anyone else who happens to be hanging around. Fort Sister is a commune, Bil. My mother doesn't want to live in a commune, and so she's given the Captain an ultimatum."

"Which is?"

"If Captain Schwartz wants to be with my mother, she'll have to move in with her. She'll have to pack up her stuff, leave Fort Sister, and take up full-time residence at my mom's place."

"But Sylvie, I don't think... that's not entirely fair. An ultimatum?"

Sylvie shrugged. "I know. We agree on this, Bil. I think my mother may have gone too far. Fort Sister is the Captain's home, and she loves it. These days, however, it's also a business. My mother wants the Captain to treat it like one. Somehow or another, the place makes money. The women pay rent, and the Captain is doing well with her conference bookings and retreats and such."

I hesitated before I spoke. Under the circumstances, what would my grief counselor, Sally Hernandez, say? I thought for a moment.

"How do you feel about this?"

"Unsettled," Sylvie admitted. "Invaded. Shoved aside. Put out. If the Captain agrees to this, I'll have a stepmother, and she'll be living in my childhood home. That'll take some getting used to. That said, it's my mother's life, and she's in love with the Captain. Very much, it would seem. I suppose it doesn't really matter how I feel."

"It matters to me."

"And that's why Sylvie is marrying you," Suzy said. "You can be thick as a plank, Bil, but you understand the important stuff."

"Meaning I'm stupid but trainable?"

"Something like that," he said.

"Finish telling your story, Suzy, before I slap that orange cap off your head. Any idea who whacked Major Tom? What do you know about the when and the why?"

"The when, according to your sister Ruth, would be around noon. I know nothing at all about the why. It looks as if the charming Major spent most of last night getting plastered. He stank of alcohol when he arrived. Your sister has ordered a full tox screen. How he wound up out at Jake Peterson's place, no one knows, but he acquired his head injury sometime in the early afternoon. Donny found him at about six-thirty. That's a long time to lie in the hot sun, bleeding."

"Is he going to live?"

Suzy nodded. "I should think so. He's been awake off and on for a grand total of maybe fifteen minutes. He's delirious. He doesn't know his name, he doesn't know his wife, and he seems to think your sister, Ruth, is a drug-dealing tank driver he knew in

Vietnam. If we can get his temperature down, he'll come out of this with a terrible headache and a lovely scar but no permanent damage. Now, are you two ready to go back out there and rejoin the freak show?"

"No," I said. "But let's go anyway."

Chapter 32

Before we left the sanctuary of the ER, Sylvie and I agreed on a divide and conquer strategy. She'd take her mother and the Captain and I'd deal with the three witches as well as Donny and Buck. My plan was to speak to Sarah first. Tipper looked shell-shocked, and my mother looked eager. I didn't expect to get any sense out of either of them. Sarah, on the other hand, was always ready with clear, concise information. God bless librarians.

Ignoring my mother's beady-eyed assessment, I walked past her without pausing or flinching when she made a vicious grab for my arm. I stopped in front of Sarah. My sister looked up at me with a bemused expression. It was the same face she used on particularly annoying patrons at the reference desk, the ones who asked her if the library had a life-sized map of the earth or how many licks it really took to get to the center of a Tootsie Roll Pop.

I said, "Suzy has filled us in on the pertinent details. What I'm wondering is why you and Buck are here."

"Buck is here," she said, "because he has a police scanner that he listens to for fun. He heard Emma's name and came down to investigate. I am here because where Emma is, you are, or you soon will be. I've been looking for both of you for the past two days. Emma, you wanted me to gather some information about Jake Peterson's time in the military. I've got it."

"Let me guess," my mother interrupted. "Jake Peterson was—"

"Please," I said. "You're not a contestant on *Jeopardy*. Just let Sarah tell us. She's sitting right here. Besides, if you get any more attention, you'll get the delirium tremens."

Buck laughed and then quickly covered his mouth. Too late, I thought. It's no use trying to appease a woman who's going to stomp your dead body into the ground once she finds out you've been tag-teaming two of her daughters.

Sarah said, "I suppose you know that Jake Peterson served with George Knox in Vietnam?"

I nodded. "Echo Company, Second Battalion, Fifth Marines."

"Very good," she said. "Both men served under a Captain Lester 'Dutch' Hamilton. Everyone in the Marine Corps seems to have a nickname like Dutch or Spike or Gunner. It makes reading the microfiche very entertaining."

"If you say so."

"The company XO—that's the executive officer—was First Lieutenant Thomas P. Schwartz. From what Tipper and the Captain tell me, the XO is the company's chief administrative officer. He handles all of the paperwork, administrative functions, supply, and intelligence, and he assists in operational planning. Some XOs have a lot of interaction with the troops. Some have none. It depends on the company commander. Lieutenant Schwartz had a lot of interaction. Jake Peterson was court-martialed for dealing heroin. Captain Hamilton filed the report, noting that it was Schwartz who caught Peterson."

"So what happened?"

"You've heard the rumors," Sarah said. "We all have. Turns out they're true. Jake the Snake did six years at Fort Leavenworth. Lieutenant Schwartz, now Major Schwartz, is the man who put him there."

"Any more?" I asked.

"Only the minutiae. You're probably not interested in that."

Sarah rubbed her hands together, so I knew it was good. I waited politely for a moment or two, and then I grabbed her arm and shook it.

"Out with it!"

"Well, if you insist," she said. "Here's what happened. Echo Company was up in the hills somewhere in Vietnam. Peterson was getting his drugs and his contraband from someone back in supply. Someone else was ferrying it to and fro, someone who made a lot of trips to the rear."

I pulled up a chair and sat down. Donny and Buck moved closer.

"Here, Donny," I said. "You're the cop here. You sit down, too."

"I'm off duty," Donny said.

"You and I both know there's no such thing." I was pleased when Donny smiled. The more I got to know him, the better I liked him. I turned back to Sarah. "You didn't get all of this from microfiche. You couldn't have."

"No," she admitted. "I didn't. I've been putting two and two together with the Captain, Tipper, and Mother Busybody."

"What would you do if I weren't a busybody?" Emma asked defensively. "Where would any of you be if I didn't ask questions?"

"I expect we'd struggle through," I said.

"Sweet Fanny Adams," my mother snapped. "That's what you'd know."

"Sarah?" I begged. "Please?"

My sister inclined her head. "Captain Hamilton wrote that he suspected a tank driver was ferrying the goods to Peterson, but he didn't name any names, and, when it came down to the investigation, Peterson wouldn't cooperate. Schwartz caught him with a balloon of heroin, but Peterson swallowed it. Right down the old gullet. Schwartz ordered him evacuated to a hospital and had him held in protective custody. The military police watched Peterson day and night. He refused food and water. No bowel movement for four days."

"But in time, all things must pass?" I said.

"You guessed it. The balloon came out, it was taken into evidence, and Jake Peterson went down. His court martial was quite the case. Peterson's JAG attorney argued that Schwartz had no right to put Peterson in protective custody."

"But he did have the right," Tipper said.

"Absolutely. It actually set a precedent. That made the case very easy to find. I handed the names over to Barbara Chisholm, the government documents librarian. I gave her the time frame, and she had it up in no time."

Sarah smiled pleasantly. The woman loved being a librarian. She loved her reference materials, her maps, her data, and her musty old books. She was a beautiful woman, tall, dark, and sleek. She was model gorgeous, and yet she had chosen to devote her life to the *Encyclopedia Britannica*. Though I was often grateful for this, I was also puzzled. If I'd had the good fortune to look like Sarah, I'd have run amok. I'd have danced naked on tables, streaked through the streets in my birthday suit, been photographed basking on a bearskin rug for the cover of *Vanity Fair*.

"Bil? Bil?"

"I'm sorry," I said. "I was just picturing you posing naked for the cover of the *Periodicals Citation Index*."

"Thank you," she said. "I can't decide if I'm grossed out or flattered. I suppose it doesn't matter as the *Periodicals Citation*

Index doesn't have pictures on the covers. The volumes are all in a plain red binding."

"Don't be so literal-minded," I chided her.

Buck spoke up for the first time. "So where does this leave us with the Peterson murder?"

"I don't know," I said. "Do we even know what killed him?"

"Yes," said a voice behind me. "A bullet to the head, twenty-two caliber."

I turned around to find Ruth standing there, yawning. She covered her mouth with her hand. "Don't worry, Donny. I'm not giving away state secrets. It'll be in the *Cowslip Herald-Examiner* tomorrow. Your boss, Sid, has been leaking information to the press. Jake Peterson was killed by a single bullet. It entered here," she tapped a forefinger in the space between her eyebrows, "and exited here."

The way she casually cupped the back of her skull was nearly as unnerving as all of Suzy's talks about flies laying eggs and nibbling mice.

"And the shotgun blast?" Emma asked.

"Obliterated his face and the top of his skull," Ruth said. "But I was able to trace the bullet's path. Not a brilliant job on my part. The thing was embedded in a piece of his occipital bone. The angle of entry suggests that the shooter was either a good deal taller than Peterson, or that he was standing and Peterson was sitting."

"It's the latter," Donny admitted. "That's what I think anyway."

"And what does Sid Castle think?" my mother asked.

"I don't know."

"Don't know or won't say?"

"Knock it off, Emma," I warned her. "You've got no business giving Donny the third degree."

My mother gave me her "Which Side Are You On, Boys" face. I knew which side I was on—the side that wanted to knock her into next week. Before we had time to launch a battle royal, Tipper asked Ruth a question.

"How is my father?"

"That's actually why I came out here," she said. "He's awake. I don't know for how long. His fever is still high, and he's slipping in and out of consciousness. He's not making much sense. He is, however, asking for his wife."

"What do we do?" Tipper said.

"We take her in to see him," said the Captain. She stood up, spoke a few words of Vietnamese to Thuy, and helped the young woman to her feet. "If you'll update me on his condition, Ruth, I'll relate it to Thuy as best I can."

Ruth and the Captain conferred about fevers, shallow respirations, and blood pressure. What I gathered, along with all of the other eavesdroppers, was that the Major was no longer in critical condition. He was not, however, out of the woods. He was likely to drift in and out for the next couple of days, and he'd need a lot of sleep. Sid Castle had been in a couple of times trying to ask him questions. Ruth had thrown Castle out, the last time with the aid of hospital security.

"Wish I'd seen that," muttered Donny.

"Me, too," said Emma.

"Sweetheart," Kate spoke to the Captain. "Of course Thuy will need you here tonight. Vivian said she'd come back first thing in the morning. Will you be okay until then? Do you need me to stay to keep you company? I'm happy to wait down here."

I expected Captain Schwartz to say no, to tell Kate to go home and get a good night's rest, but a look passed between them.

The Captain said, "I do need you here, Kate. I don't want you to be uncomfortable, though."

Ruth yawned again. "I can take care of that," she said. "We've got three recliners in the ICU. I've only got three patients tonight. Unless there's a massive wreck or an epidemic, I don't expect to fill the other beds. We'll bend the rules. You can all three come up."

"Thank you," said Captain Schwartz.

"No problem," Ruth said. "Who's going to tattle on me?"

"Suzy?" I suggested.

Ruth laughed. "Have you seen those goddamned scrubs he's wearing? I don't know where he ordered them, but someone ought to burn the catalog."

"I'll do that," Donny said.

"I hear you've been mistaken for a drug-dealing tank driver," I said. "Just how delirious is the Major?"

"I don't know," Ruth said. She put her hands on her head and wiggled her scalp back and forth like a wig. "Do I look like George Knox to you?"

Chapter 33

"Since when do you eat granola?" my mother asked.

"Since now," I muttered. Sylvie was sitting directly across the table. I could feel her watching me. "I like granola."

"You hate granola," my mother insisted. "What you wanted was what the waitress suggested—a tall stack of huckleberry pancakes with a double side of bacon. I saw your face. You were drooling. Are you on a diet? Are you worried about that extra ten pounds?"

"For the last time, I have not gained ten pounds!"

"Nine?" my mother prodded.

"If you keep poking," I said, "you will wake the sleeping bear."

Emma rolled her eyes and heaved an exaggerated sigh. "I hope you're listening to this, Donny. If you find me in the tall grass with my head bashed in, you'll know who did it. Do you want one of my sausages?" she continued. "Smoked Genesee pork, the best in the world. You cannot possibly be happy with those sticks and twigs."

"Bil," Sylvie said, a hint of malice in her tone. "I could do with a warm-up on my coffee. I've been trying to signal our waitress but she seems to be ignoring me. Perhaps you could attract her attention?"

I looked at my girlfriend. Green-eyed jealousy. If I hadn't been so tired, I'd have been flattered.

"Sure," I said. "In fact, I'll just go and have a word with her. Anyone else want anything? I'm sure Kim—that's her name—will be happy to oblige. She's usually very accommodating."

This earned me a swift kick under the table. I smothered a laugh, snatched one of my mother's Genesee sausages, and limped off to have a word with our pretty, redheaded waitress. Kim was the only server working, and she was running herself ragged dealing with the drunks, the college students, and the chronic insomniacs who always filled the House of Pancakes in the wee hours of the morning.

I was one of those insomniacs. Before Vivian had opened Pho From Home, I'd regularly haunted the House of Pancakes. Kim and I knew one another by name. As far as I was concerned, the relationship was entirely platonic. I could see, however, why Sylvie might be suspicious. Kim had guessed my order correctly, and it had been painful to have to contradict her. My mother was right. I hated granola. If I had to eat cereal, I preferred Frosted Flakes or Fruity Pebbles. Only love of the purest and most self-sacrificing kind could have compelled me to order a bowl of sawmill sweepings when I was offered silver-dollar buckwheat pancakes loaded with fresh huckleberries.

I caught up with Kim at the cash register, and I waited while she rang up a pair of aging hippies, clearly stoned out of their minds. As soon as they got their change sorted, fought about whether to tip ten or fifteen percent, and finally got out of my way, Kim smiled up at me. And then I saw it. The same flirty, come-hither, speculative look I'd seen on the college boy waiters who served Sylvie at the Cowslip Café. Oh, holy hell. Sylvie was right, and I was wrong. Again.

"Bil," Kim said breathily. The hand that reached out to stroke my arm as I leaned on the counter was thankfully hidden from Sylvie's relentless gaze.

"Kim," I answered firmly, pulling away. "I know you're very busy, but would you mind bringing some fresh coffee to our table when you get the chance? It looks like we're going to be here a while."

"Is that your family?" she asked.

I turned to gaze at the motley assemblage in the large booth by the window.

"Yes," I said. "My family and friends. The tall black woman is my older sister, Sarah. The skinny cowboy with the walrus mustache is Sarah's boyfriend, Buck, and next to him is Lewis County Sheriff's Deputy Donny Smith. The short, fat, toothless old biddy who's picking food off other people's plates is—actually, I have no idea who she is. As for the beautiful blonde giving us the evil eye, that's my partner, Sylvie Wood."

I waved at Sylvie. She put her thumb to the end of her nose and wiggled her fingers.

"Your partner?" Kim asked.

"Yes," I said. "Life partner. Girlfriend, significant other, source of my domestic bliss. She's also my fiancée. We're going to be married in the Unitarian Church."

"Congratulations," said Kim, her tone noticeably cooler.

"Thank you. About that coffee..."

"I'll have to brew a fresh pot."

"I hope that's not too much trouble," I said, knowing from her sullen tone and sour look that a fresh glass of air would be too much trouble. I pressed ahead anyway. "You know, you were quite right—that granola is not exactly hitting the spot. Could I get the huckleberry pancakes after all?"

"You'll have to make do with blueberry," Kim said dismissively. "The huckleberry batter is all gone."

* * *

"I hope you're happy," I whispered in Sylvie's ear. "Kim will never guess my order again."

"I am happy," she said. "And it won't kill you to eat blueberries."

"What are you two whispering about?" demanded my mother. "If it's anything to do with the Peterson case..."

"You probably already know it," Sarah said. "You always seem to be a mysterious few steps ahead. I expect, however, that Donny knows more than the rest of us put together. Is there anything you can tell us without breaking police confidence or compromising your investigation?"

Sarah turned the full force of her considerable charm on Donny, staring at him intently and, unless I was very much mistaken, batting her eyelashes. Donny blushed, Sarah smiled, and that was it. I shuddered to think what would happen if Suzy ever learned of Sarah's power over women, men (gay and straight), babies, the elderly, and the birds in the trees. When it came to jealousy, Sylvie was a bantam-weight amateur. Suzy was the undisputed world heavyweight champion.

"Sid's been talking his head off all over town," Donny said. "I suppose I can tell you what he's seen fit to share with Commissioner Kornmeyer."

"This town," my mother bellowed, "is turning into *The Dukes of Hazzard*, and Dick Corn-holer is our very own Boss Hogg."

"Would you shut up about the corn-holing?" I begged her. "Do you even know what that means?"

"Of course I do." She made a circle with her index finger and thumb and poked a sausage through it. "I didn't just fall off the turnip truck."

"No," said Sarah. "You just fell off the roll-in-the-hay wagon. Now do shut up and let Donny finish. Honestly, sometimes I despair."

Donny cleared his throat. "The envelope Emma gave us, the one Jake Peterson used to mail his rent check to Corn-hole—Kornmeyer—had a small brown stain on the back flap. I thought it might be blood, so I sent it to the lab to be tested. It was blood. Type O Negative, same as Jake Peterson's."

"Are you going to get the envelope DNA tested?" Buck asked.

Donny shook his head. "We don't have the resources, and even if we did, Sid would never approve the expenditure. The type match is enough for him. He believes Peterson was killed during a drug deal gone wrong. He's looking at the local meth boys. We've raided a few labs, interviewed some known dealers. Nothing. No weapons have turned up—no twenty-two and no twenty-gauge shotgun."

"You think he's barking up the wrong tree," I said.

"Yes, I do. We had to trace the canceled check from Kornmeyer's bank to Jake Peterson's. By then, at least twenty people had handled it. If Kornmeyer weren't such a cheap old bast—person—we might have been able to do something with it. We don't even know if the writing is really Peterson's. I've had a look at the bank's paperwork from when Peterson opened the account, but I'm no handwriting expert. It's all chicken scratch as far as I can tell."

"You." I poked my mother in the shoulder. "When did you give Donny that envelope? Did you give him the letter, too?"

"Of course," she answered smugly. "You shock me, Bil. I would never withhold evidence."

Before I could tell the House of Pancakes that Emma Hardy was a lying sack of shit, Sylvie asked, "Any large deposits going in and out of Peterson's account?"

"No," Donny said. "He worked nights as a custodian at Cowslip University. He was paid by direct deposit. That was the only money going in. He seems to have lived frugally and mostly used cash. Kornmeyer's one of the few people he paid by check. He even paid his cell phone bill in cash. Came in once a month on the day it was due, handed them the exact amount, and asked for a receipt. He was kind of odd. One interesting thing..."

We all leaned forward. My mother put her arms on the table, dipping her elbow into the maple syrup on Sarah's plate.

"Damn it, Emma!" Sarah said with irritation.

"Shh," said my mother. "I'm trying to listen."

"I believe that the coyote and Peterson might have been killed with the same gun."

"What coyote?" Buck asked.

"The one Bil and her mother found nailed to Peterson's door. I took it to a friend of mine, a taxidermist. It was shot with a twenty-two. I can't prove it was the same gun, I just think—well, it's a gut instinct. My friend reckoned the coyote had been dead for about twelve hours. Sid didn't see the point. Sometimes he can be..."

"Thick as a brick?" my mother suggested.

"Stubborn," said Donny. "The point is that Peterson didn't shoot the animal, and he didn't nail it to the door. Someone else did. I don't know why, and that bothers me. Maybe it was nosing around up there. Maybe it smelled the body, came in the house, and started pawing around. Did that bother someone? If so, why? Who was up there? I've got a lot of questions and no good answers."

Kim arrived with our coffee and my pancakes. I noticed that they were not the perfect silver dollars I was accustomed to. Instead, they looked as if they'd been poured from a great height onto an uneven and very dirty griddle. Small black bits of God knew what dotted the edges. Sylvie laughed out loud.

"Anything else?" Kim asked, looking at her watch.

"No, thank you," I said.

Kim tore the ticket from her order pad and put on the table. Next to my plate.

"I guess you're buying," Sylvie said. "Your usual twenty percent tip?"

I looked at my mangy pancakes, lifting the edge of one with a fork. The underside was even less appetizing than the top.

"Fifteen," I said. "Or maybe ten."

Sylvie reached across the table and rested her hand lightly on my arm.

"Never mind. My mother's got huckleberries in the freezer. I'll make you a batch of real pancakes when we pick up JC."

"Why don't we just spend the night out there?" I suggested.

We'd stopped by Kate's house before meeting the others at the House of Pancakes. JC had been groggy but happy to see us. We'd given him another pain pill, refilled his water bowl, and left him to the tender mercies of Elvis and Priscilla. Priscilla, like all Samoyeds, had smiled at us. Elvis had contrived to look somber and sympathetic. Both were getting old and lazy and were inclined to cuddle up to JC for warmth.

Tipper we'd left at the hospital in Suzy's tender care.

"Good idea," Sylvie said. "We can sleep in my mother's room. I don't expect that she and the Captain will be making an appearance until late in the morning."

I wiggled my eyebrows at her. "Your mother's room, eh? Fun."

This earned me a cuff on the ear from Emma. "Do you mind?" she said. "Too much information."

"This from the corn-hole queen?"

Buck DeWitt laughed like a braying donkey. For some reason—it might have been the bad pancakes, the late night, or Buck's hideous dead cat of a mustache—I felt a surge of unreasonable annoyance. What was he doing there? And where was Naomi? Was she sitting up right now, waiting for him to call? Had she left messages on his answering machine or his cell phone? Just how long did he intend to keep playing his double-dating game with the Hardy sisters?

"You," I said, pointing at him. "How long have you known Sarah?"

"Bil." My sister spoke in a low warning tone.

"A month? Maybe two?"

"I'm not sure," he said equably. "We met at the university library. I saw her standing behind the reference desk and decided to introduce myself. Any man would. Begging your pardon, Donny," he added.

So Buck wasn't homophobic. Big deal. He was still a two-timing scumbag.

"You've met most of the members of my family," I said. "Have you met my father yet?"

"I haven't had the pleasure," said Buck. And then he offered it up on a silver platter—a great big bald-faced lie. "I haven't met the other Hardy sister yet, either. The gal who lives with Ruth."

"Naomi," I said. "That's her name. Anyone ever told you that you talk like that guy on the radio, the cowboy poet Baxter Black?"

"Nope," he said. "I'm from Montana. I believe Mr. Black is from New Mexico. Very different accents."

"Do you have any family?"

"One brother," he said.

"Older or younger?"

"Funny you should ask," Buck began.

"Bil!"

I snapped to attention. Sarah didn't get angry often, so when she did, it was time to pay attention. "It's getting on for three a.m. I have to work tomorrow, and so does Buck. Let's schedule a date and time for the third degree. You'll need a bright light and a polygraph."

"I was only..."

"You were only acting just like our mother. Believe me, one of her is quite enough."

"Oh, ha," Emma said. "I don't think it's unreasonable for Bil to—"

"Donny," Sarah interrupted loudly. "What do you make of what Ruth told us? George Knox was a drug-dealing tank driver in Vietnam. He may have been Peterson's supplier over there. Peterson did six years in prison while Knox walked off scot-free. Reason for murder?"

"I don't know," Donny said. "Why after all this time?"

"Blackmail?" Sarah suggested. "George Knox is doing well, and Peterson lived in a shack. Maybe he thought he could get some money by threatening to tarnish the preacher's image."

"Maybe," Donny agreed. "I'll have to look into it."

"Oh, for Christ's sake," Emma said. "Do you have any leads at all? Why would anyone other than George Knox want Jake Peterson dead?"

"I'm sorry," Sarah apologized. "In light of Emma's tirade, I take back what I just said. Jake the Snake was a dope dealer. He was our late brother's pot supplier. Low quality, low prices. Exactly what Sam could afford. The meth lab was a surprise. I wouldn't have thought Jake would have bothered. He wasn't a clever man. Still, he must have had quite a few enemies."

Sarah finished by glaring at my mother. However, it was Buck who flinched. Emma was oblivious.

"That's the thing," Donny mused. "I don't think Jake *was* cooking the meth. I think he'd acquired a couple of business partners, some young guys."

"You have suspects," I said. It wasn't a guess. Over the past two years, I'd learned to read Donny's open, honest face nearly as well as Suzy could.

"Let me guess. A couple of skanks, both known associates of Jake Peterson's, and they have just enough brainpower to make meth without blowing themselves to bits, but not enough to completely cover their tracks."

Donny said nothing.

"I knew most of your brother's friends," Emma said. She began listing them. "The slut, Francie Stokes. Lee Kreager, Jim Lander, Amy Kwan, Jeremy Bessemer."

"Those are Sam's *old* friends," I said. "We're looking for the new friends. Just before he died, Sam was hanging out with Calvin Knox. Calvin, we know, was and maybe still is running an illegal casino. He also owns Johnson Pawn. He's young enough, he's got the right connections, and he's smart. You'll never find his fingerprints on anything."

I watched Donny sip his glass of milk. No coffee for our favorite Mormon.

"Steve Iverson and Joe Edwards," I declared. "Those are your suspects. Am I right?"

Donny spat milk across the table, giving Emma the brunt of it.

"Fuck!" he said. "How did you know that?"

Chapter 34

Outside in the parking lot, Donny abased himself for the thirty-sixth time.

"I am so sorry, Mrs. Hardy. Ask Bil, ask Sylvie—I never curse like that."

"Donny," Emma said and grabbed him by the shoulder and gave him a shake. "If you can do your job without cursing, you need to ask yourself, are you *really* doing your job? Think about it. Goddamn, motherfucker, son-of-a-bitch—these are the tools of your trade. You have to cowboy up, son. How do you live with Suzy Parker-Smith?"

"Suzy never curses in front of me," Donny said. "He knows how I feel about the F-word. It was never uttered in my house when I was growing up. My father never swore."

"And he never smoked or drank coffee or enjoyed the occasional beer," Emma guessed. "Was your father ever just a little bit tense?"

"All the time," Donny admitted. "My mother, too. I'm one of eleven kids."

"God help your mother," Emma said heartily. "I had five, gave birth to two. Our house was like a train wreck."

My mother patted Donny on the back. The night had turned cold, and I was anxious to be home. Emma, however, was in a chatty mood.

Sylvie and I leaned against the side of my truck. Buck had insisted on playing "Hey, Big Spender" and paying the check for the whole table. After Sylvie had stomped on my left instep, and Sarah on my right, I'd stopped arguing and thanked him. Nicely.

Once the bill was paid—Buck tipping Kim a ridiculous twenty-five percent—we all said our goodnights. Slim Pickens and Sarah headed off with their arms wrapped around one another's waists. It was only a few blocks from the House of Pancakes to Sarah's apartment, and the shortest route took them right past Naomi and

Ruth's front window. If Naomi were awake and happened to look out... but Naomi was not awake. She was in bed every night at ten and up every morning by five. She was a disgustingly disciplined person.

And that was only one of the reasons it was so hard to picture her with a *bon vivant* like Buck DeWitt. The man liked a good time. If I were being honest, I'd have to admit that he looked more like Sam Elliott than Baxter Black. He was good-looking in his cowboy way. Sarah had said that Buck was an equine veterinarian. Maybe he specialized in racehorses. Maybe he was richer than God. Maybe he could afford two wives. Maybe he was a fundamentalist Mormon.

"Donny," I said. "I've got something in my pocket that you ought to see."

My mother raised her eyebrows and Sylvie giggled.

"Don't be silly, you two," I said. I pulled out the chit from Calvin Knox. Donny examined it carefully and then read it aloud.

"S.H. Credit $1250, subtract $800 for payment in kind. Owed: $450. C.K. Interesting," he said. "Your brother was working for Calvin Knox?"

Emma said nothing. She lit a cigarette and blew out a thin plume of smoke.

"I don't think so," I said carefully. "But we can't rule out the possibility. Sam might have won the money at Calvin's casino. The eight hundred dollars is exactly what JC cost."

"I see," Donny said. "I don't understand the snake and the dove. Is there some kind of symbolism there? I'm not good at symbolism."

And you're a Mormon? I thought. I could see the edges of Donny's temple garment poking out past the sleeves of his T-shirt. Suzy told me that Donny had been endowed or whatever it was after he came back from his mission to Germany. I couldn't remember all of the symbols on a Mormon temple garment or where they were located—not that I'd ever seen the real thing. I'd seen drawings of garments in scurrilous books claiming to reveal the secrets of the Latter-day Saints. Most featured an embroidered compass over the heart and a collection of other neo-Masonic drawings and devices.

Donny was a member of Affirmation, a gay Mormon support group, and though Suzy refused to convert, he was certainly supportive. Suzy was the son of a Pentecostal Holiness preacher, after all.

"My father succeeded in coming between me and God," Suzy had said. "If I can do anything to ensure that never happens to Donny, I'll die happy."

I said to Donny, "Thanks to your husband, I know what the snake and dove thing means. It's a quotation from Matthew. 'I send you forth as sheep in the midst of wolves: be therefore wise as serpents, and harmless as doves.'"

"Matthew 10:16," Donny said. "I should have recognized it. I'm getting rusty."

"I doubt that," Sylvie said. "No one is as good with a Bible as Suzy."

Donny beamed. "That's true. He's brilliant. He knows it front to back."

Sylvie squeezed my hand, and I knew we were thinking the same thing—what a strange, happy, and incongruously well-matched couple Suzy and Donny were. Each thought the other was as fine as frog's hair.

"We need to get into that casino," said Emma. "Any ideas?"

Donny considered this. "Sid would have to approve a raid," he said. "And he'll never do that, not as long as Kornmeyer owns Forbidden Village. We all work for the county commissioners. I think we have an obligation to do justice, no matter who's in charge, but Sid—"

"Is out for what he can get," finished my mother. "He's a snake. They're all snakes. Forget the dove."

"Let's think about this," I said. "You need a membership or something to get into the casino, right? Forbidden Village is a restaurant and bar with a supposedly secret back room that everyone knows about. Who's gambling in there, young or old?"

"Both," Donny said. "I saw Major Schwartz's jeep out there night before last."

My mother, Sylvie and I all stared at him, agog. Emma was the first to speak.

"You what?"

Donny shrugged. "I told you. I've been watching the place, taking note of who comes and goes. Major Schwartz was there for less than forty-five minutes. That's not long enough to gamble, so I assumed he was getting something to eat."

"What do you mean that's not long enough to gamble?" I asked.

"Bil," Donny said, in a tone that suggested he was disappointed in me, "I might be naïve about some things. When Suzy mixes up that nasty concoction he calls 'a cup of astonishment,' I know it's really vodka and orange juice. I also know it's called a screwdriver. The gamblers at Forbidden Village stay for hours. No one sits down at a card table, plays one hand, and then leaves. No one I've been watching, anyway."

"Have you ever eaten at Forbidden Village?" I asked.

"No."

"That's because no one in their right mind does. It's cockroach heaven. Only ignorant out-of-towners or locals with a death wish would touch anything cooked in that kitchen. Major Schwartz has a young Vietnamese wife. I expect he gets plenty of real Asian food at home. Why would he go out for a greasy egg roll with condensed Kool-Aid sauce at a dump like that?"

"Okay," Donny agreed reluctantly. "Say you're right. Why was he there?"

"Meeting someone?" Sylvie suggested.

"Or spying out the landscape," I said. "What was he doing up at Jake Peterson's place last night, the day after this trip to Forbidden Village? Who hit him and why? He was whacked on top of the head. The Major is pretty tall. Does that mean he was hit by someone even taller? Someone standing on a box? Or was the Major kneeling down? That seems most likely, in which case, was he hiding in the tall grass or looking for something?"

"Maybe he dropped his watch," said my mother.

"Belt up, Ma. Let's think about what we know. Major Tom, George Knox, and Jake Peterson all served together in Vietnam. Major Tom sent Jake the Snake to Fort Leavenworth. Jake is now dead. Somehow, all of this must add up. We've got the edges of the puzzle."

"But we don't have the pieces in the middle," Sylvie said.

"No," I said. "We have one piece. Major Tom is delirious. He thinks Ruth is a drug-dealing tank driver he knew in Vietnam. Who was the real tank driver? George Knox. Let's add two and two here. Who was the guy Jake refused to rat out when he was sent to Leavenworth? Who was his partner in crime?"

Donny looked skeptical. "I don't know. You're making a lot of leaps here, Bil."

"I don't think so," Sylvie said. "I think Bil is right. Sarah has done the background research. The first part of the story is at least partially confirmed. George Knox drove a tank, and he knew both the Major and Jake Peterson. We might ask ourselves some other questions, like why Knox brought his Green Tree Ministries to

Cowslip in the first place. Was it purely coincidence that he should move to Jake's hometown?"

"This is an out-of-the-way place," I said. "It's a rare thing for someone to throw a dart at a map and just move here."

"That's what the Captain did," Donny objected.

"No, she didn't," I said. "The Captain had a thing for Vardis Fisher's novels. She'd had romantic fantasies about Idaho forever. When she decided that she wanted to move out to the middle of nowhere, this was the only nowhere she considered."

Emma said, "I'll find out what I can about Green Tree's decision to locate here. I'll also ask Sarah to look more closely into Knox's military record. Maybe there's something in Jake's court-martial, something Sarah missed. In the meantime, we have got to get into that gambling den."

"I have an idea," I said. "Why don't Sylvie and I pay a visit tomorrow to Johnson Pawn?"

Emma squinted at me. "Why?"

"Because I have something they might want."

"Money?" Donny asked.

"Of course not."

"Then what?" asked Emma.

"Sam's last stash. His terminal Mary Jane. The final bag of bud."

"I didn't hear that," Donny said.

"Neither did I," added my mother.

Sylvie kissed me on the cheek.

"Hooray," she whispered in my ear. "I'm glad I didn't flush it down the toilet."

* * *

Tipper was awake when we came home the next morning. He'd made a pot of coffee and a coffee cake. He looked fresh and energetic. I looked like I'd been dragged through a hedge backwards. Sylvie said a quick good morning to him and bagged the first shower. Had Tipper not been there, I'd have gotten in with her. Instead, I sat down at the kitchen table and begged him for a cup of coffee.

"You must have slept better than I did," I observed.

"I slept alone," he replied. "In your bed. Sometime in the middle of the night, I woke up with a crick in my neck from your wretched sofa, realized that you two had not returned, and decided to snag some comfort time on your mattress."

"Sorry we didn't put on fresh sheets." I covered a yawn.

"Please," Tipper said, plunking a cup of coffee down in front of me. "Do you think I was raised by wolves? I changed the sheets before I climbed into your bed. How much coffee cake would you like? Big, bigger, or biggest?"

"Does it have nuts?"

"Yes. Pecans, brown sugar, cinnamon, and just a hint of cardamom."

"In that case, biggest. Thank you. Any word from the hospital?"

"My mother called at seven," he said. "My father had a troubled night. Woke up quite a few times delirious and yelling. Scared the living hell out of his poor wife. He was screaming in English and Russian. My mother did her best to translate, but what's the Vietnamese word for zombie?"

I finished chewing rather than risk a lecture on my manners. As soon as I'd swallowed and washed everything down with a gulp of coffee, I spoke. "Zombie?"

Tipper pulled up a chair and sat down at the table. Without my asking, he pushed the coffee cake across to me.

"This is what my father said last night, or what he said that was intelligible. 'Goddamn tanker. Who's always going to the rear? You are, you son of a bitch.' He also talked about a fragging. Like my mother, Major Tom did two tours of duty in Vietnam. He volunteered for the second. My mother..."

"Hold on." I stopped in the middle of cutting myself an obscenely large slice of coffee cake. "What's a fragging?"

"It's a nasty business," Tipper said. "It was more common in the Army than the Marine Corps. If the troops get a commander they don't like, say a shit-ignorant lieutenant fresh out of Officer Candidate School, they roll a grenade into his tent or his foxhole and blow him to bits."

"You're joking."

"You're naïve," he said. "Friendly fire. Missing in action. All of these are polite euphemisms for what happens in war. Sometimes you're shot by your own side. Most of the time that's an accident but sometimes, it's not. And missing in action? How often is someone really missing? The military uses that one when they can't find enough pieces of you to box up and send home."

I changed my mind about that second piece of coffee cake. I pushed the plate away.

Tipper continued. "Vietnam was an unpopular war and, toward the end, it was fought by increasingly reluctant and unhappy troops. In 1971 and '72, when my father was there, it was all going to hell in a handbasket. The troops knew that the daily reports coming out of headquarters were pure fiction. We were not winning. We were losing. Men were dying for no reason. Fragging incidents increased."

"Who fragged whom? Did Major Tom say?"

"Not last night," Tipper said. "But my mother already knew the story. It's the reason my parents met. The Major was sent on R and R because he went a little nuts in the field. The man who was fragged was a good friend of his, a guy named Baseman Moody. They were at OCS together. The Marines recorded the death as an accident. My father knew better. The guilty party was an enlisted man. He and my father had a bare-knuckle fight out in the jungle. My father stripped off his shirt and all signs of his rank and nearly beat the man to death."

"My God."

"I know," Tipper said. "Hard to picture jovial Major Tom with his stupid little dog trying to kill anyone with his bare hands. But he did."

"Who?"

"I have no idea," said Tipper. "And neither does my mother. Major Tom talked a lot about his friend, Baseman Moody, but he never mentioned his killer's name."

I opened my mouth to speak but Tipper put his hand to his forehead, palm facing out, and closed his eyes.

"Wait," he said. "The all-seeing third eye anticipates your next question. How did my father manage to remain in the Marine Corps after this? How did he rise so high and do so well? Easy. The entire company knew that Moody had been fragged. They knew who did it, but they couldn't do a damned thing about it. No concrete evidence. Our killer used a Chinese grenade. My father administered battlefield justice. He didn't kill the man—he settled the score in the most macho way possible. Then, he was sent on R and R to recover his equilibrium, and that's where he met my mother. He told her what he'd done, and she understood. She told him her deep, dark secret, and he married her. They did one another a profound service, they conceived me, and then they parted company."

"You learned all of this last night?"

"Most of it, yes," he said.

"Was there anything else?"

Tipper thought for a moment.

"Nothing of great importance. Major Tom mistook my mother for the actress, Bea Arthur. Kate fared better. He thought she was Cybill Shepherd. He recognizes his new wife, which is good, but he can't remember any Vietnamese, which is bad. He said that stuff about the tanker. He muttered in Russian about God knows what. He said something about Baseman Moody and he talked in his sleep about the fragging. He told Nurse Suzy that he was really looking forward to buying new underwear at the PX, and, finally, he woke up screaming, 'I am not a fucking zombie.' He was all over the place, but Kate did a good job of keeping track and writing it down."

"Kate wrote it down? Why?"

"Because Donny asked her to keep track of anything my father said. It could be complete nonsense, or it could be significant. Who knows?"

Sylvie joined us, her hair wet from the shower. She cut a modest slice of coffee cake for herself and set the pan on the counter, out of my convenient reach.

"How's married life?" Tipper asked, winking.

"Funny you should ask," I said. "We're going to make it official. Want to be my bridesmaid?"

He held his hands over his heart. "Can I wear pale blue tulle?"

Sylvie joined us at the table. "No. I intend to have a dignified wedding, complete with engraved invitations, a sit-down dinner, and a champagne toast."

This was news to me. "Really?" I asked.

"Really," she said. "I want you and me looking our very best. I want to invite all of our friends, all of our family, all of our colleagues, and I want them to see that we take this marriage very seriously. More seriously than a couple of drunken straight people who meet in a bar and get married in Vegas."

"By an Elvis impersonator," Tipper said.

"Exactly."

"So," I speculated. "No kegger?"

"No."

"Can I have a bachelor party?"

Sylvie pondered this for a moment. "How about a bachelorette party?" she suggested.

"Meaning I can go out with Tipper and Suzy, who will be dressed in drag. We'll drink Piña Coladas and Bahama Mamas and they'll embarrass me to death."

"And we'll beat the girls off with a stick," Tipper added.

"Exactly," Sylvie confirmed. "Beginning with the redheads."

Chapter 35

Sylvie and I stood at the counter of Johnson Pawn. Steve Iverson and Joe Edwards were behind the curtain, enjoying another scream-fest. I rapped on the counter with my knuckles.

"Hey! Evil dead! Jason and Freddie! Phantom of the Opera and The Thing!"

"Stop that," Sylvie told me. "Steve and Joe! Are you back there?"

That did the trick. Joe poked his skanky blond head through the curtain. "What the hell... uh, hi."

"What is it about you?" I muttered.

"It's my wit and charm," she said. "You're Steve?"

"No, I'm Joe. Can I help you with something?"

Sylvie leaned across the counter. "I'm looking for some action," she said, her voice low and suggestive. I glared at her for a moment. Then I realized what she was doing. She'd taken a leaf out of Sarah's book of tricks. Very clever.

Joe shot me a look that contrived to be simultaneously triumphant, smug, lascivious, and confused. I looked at his dirty T-shirt, his peach fuzz mustache, and the pimples dotting his forehead, and I forgave him for dreaming.

"Oh, yeah? What kind of action?"

"A little card action," she said.

"Can't help you with that," Joe said. "This is a pawn shop."

"I know." She smiled. "But I heard through the grapevine that you and Steve did a little moonlighting for Mr. Knox."

Joe shook his head. "Not *Mister* Knox..."

"You fucking idiot," Steve shouted through the curtain.

Sylvie laughed and leaned even further across the counter. I promised myself that when we got home, I was hiding every tight, low-cut, sexy black T-shirt she owned. I didn't want her pulling this trick when I wasn't around to supervise.

"I meant Calvin Knox," she said. "It's okay. I wouldn't be here if I didn't already know. I like Blackjack. I'm looking for a good game. Something with real people, real cards, and high stakes. I understood that you might be able to help me."

Steve pushed his way through the curtain, intent on putting a stop to the conversation. Then he, too, caught sight of my girlfriend's cleavage. I might as well have been JC or a garden gnome or the *Encyclopedia Britannica*. Steve cast a quick glance over me and turned his attention back to Sylvie.

"We'd like to help you," he said. "But we can't."

"Are you sure?" She turned to me without smiling. I knew it was part of the game, and yet I bitterly resented it. "Bil?"

I reached into the cargo pocket of my shorts and pulled out the brown paper bag.

"What's that?" Steve snorted. "Your peanut butter and jelly sandwich?"

"Yeah," I said. "With a carton of milk and a nice healthy banana. Why don't you open the bag and take a look?"

Steve opened the bag and reached in.

"Don't do that," Sylvie advised. "You don't want to pull that out in here. Just put the bag to your nose and breathe deeply."

"Like you're hyperventilating," I added.

Steve did as he was told. "How much is in there?"

"Why don't you weigh it and find out?" I said.

Steve bounced the bag up and down in his hand.

"What's the quality?"

"Hell if I know," I said. "It belonged to my brother, Sam. You tell me—you probably sold it to him."

Steve's eyes narrowed. Once again, it was Sylvie to the rescue.

"I can attest," she said, "that the quality is just fine." She cast a sideways glance at me. "It seems to have the desired effect, anyway."

"So what's the deal?" Joe cut in. "You want us to buy this back?"

Sylvie shook her head. "No," she said. "I want to trade you this nice bag of Maui Wowie for entrance into your friend Calvin's casino. Can you do that for me?"

Their eyes nearly crossed with the effort of thinking. Steve spoke first.

"We're on the door Saturday night. Come by around ten, and we'll let you in."

"I have a couple of friends," Sylvie said.

"I don't know..."

Sylvie picked up the bag.

"How many friends?" Joe asked quickly. I could see that he was twitching. Typical junkie pot-smoking meth-head. I hated to think of Sam spending his last free days on earth with such a loser. I hoped—no, prayed—that Sam actually had won that $1250 at Calvin Knox's casino. I didn't want him to have worked for that little bastard. I wanted him to be a winner, any kind of winner, not a colleague of Steve and Joe.

"Two friends," Sylvie said. "Big players."

"Her?" Steve jerked his thumb at me.

"No," Sylvie said. I tried to stop my eyes from bugging out of my head. This had not been part of the plan. The seconds ticked by and my breath grew shallow. Sylvie and I had entered uncharted territory. I knew that I had to trust her. I had to trust that she knew what she was doing and trust her to deal with these jackasses in the best and smartest way.

But she didn't have my experience with Sam and his friends. She was an only child. She didn't know Maui Wowie from the low-grade, backwoods, cheap, Idaho grow-lamp bud that was in the bag she'd offered Steve and Joe. Fortunately, what she lacked in dope knowledge, she more than made up for in fast-thinking and good looks, a lethal combination.

"Who are your friends?" asked Steve.

"A cowboy and a librarian," she said.

The boys wrinkled their noses and Joe giggled.

"Okay," Steve said. "But no one else."

"Fine," Sylvie said. "See you Saturday night."

"Wait!" I said. Sylvie gave me a warning look. I ignored her. "I want to look at something in this case. Do you mind?"

"No," Steve said, huffing the word out like I was a complete idiot. "This is a pawn shop."

"Yes, it is," I said pleasantly. "What I'd like to see is that leather wallet."

He unlocked the case and pulled out a gorgeous piece of leatherwork. It was calfskin, light brown, and almost new. The only marking on it was an eagle, globe and anchor and, underneath, the words "Retreat Hell."

"How much?" I asked.

Steve didn't look at the wallet. Instead, he appraised me.

"Thirty-five," he said.

"Bullshit. I'll give you fifteen."

"Twenty."

"Done." It was then that I remembered that I had no money. "Um," I said to Sylvie.

"Happy birthday," she said, pulling two tens out of her wallet.

"Plus one dollar for tax." Steve and Joe grinned like a couple of monkeys.

Sylvie handed them the dollar.

"We want a receipt," I said.

"A what?"

"A receipt," I repeated slowly. "Get out your receipt book, write down the stock number of this item, the price—twenty-one dollars inclusive of tax—and the date. Is there any problem with this request?"

"No," Steve answered sullenly.

"Good."

I collected the wallet, the receipt, and my girlfriend, and we left the shop.

Once outside, I pulled Sylvie into a close embrace and kissed her thoroughly. People on the street stopped and gawked. People in passing cars slowed down to rubberneck. Someone across the street at the Cowslip Café yelled "Get a room!" And, through the grimy pawn shop window, I hoped that Steve and Joe got a damned good eyeful.

I was pleased to leave Sylvie breathless, her chest heaving and her eyes glazed.

"Not that I didn't enjoy that," she said, "but what in the world?"

"You are mine," I said firmly. "And I am yours. Completely."

"True. But Bil?"

"Yes, darling?"

"Why did I just buy you that tacky wallet?"

"Because it's evidence."

"Of what?"

I pulled her close again and whispered in her ear. "I think it belongs to Major Tom. That's the Marine Corps emblem on the front, and 'Retreat Hell' is the motto of the Second Battalion."

"Oh my God! Are they that stupid?"

"Yes. I think it was Steve and Joe who knocked Major Tom on the head, and I think they took his wallet. Because the wallet was shiny and new, they decided to sell it rather than toss it. In addition to being stupid, they're also greedy. You know what else? I think they were the ones who fired a shotgun into Jake Peterson's dead body and, what's more, I think I know why."

"Are you going to share?" she asked.

"Because they believe in zombies."

Chapter 36

We all read Jake Peterson's autopsy report. The *Cowslip Herald-Examiner* printed the highlights and Donny supplied the rest. Thanks to Ruth, we already knew that Peterson had been killed somewhere other than the Kornmeyer shack, that his body had been moved, and that the corpse had lain on its side for several hours in a small, hot enclosed space—a storage shed, perhaps, or the trunk of a car. This sped the decomposition process considerably.

The livor mortis, or bruising of death, was extensive on Peterson's right hip and shoulder, and, by the time Donny found it, the corpse was puffed up like a balloon in the Macy's Thanksgiving Day parade. Ruth kept describing Peterson as a bloater. She talked about the buildup of gases in his gut and the possibility that, in another few hours, he might have popped wide open like an overstuffed sausage.

Sylvie left our kitchen table several times during this discussion, always coming back smelling of toothpaste. It couldn't be helped. We had to get the details sorted out. It all fit. I explained my zombie theory.

"When Emma and I broke into Jake's place, it stank of death and decay," I said. "The dead coyote was to blame for that. It was also bloated. It twitched and popped and hissed out gas from either end. Scared the living hell out of me. If Jake Peterson was in a similar condition, and Steve and Joe moved the body from, say, the trunk of a car into the living room..."

"That's a big if," Donny said.

"Hush," said Suzy. "Stop being such a cop. Go on, Bil."

"Thank you. Steve and Joe moved the body from some hot place. I say the trunk of a car."

"Why a car?" Donny interrupted.

"Because it's where all the best criminals put their dead bodies," Suzy said.

"A car is convenient," I explained. "It's a coffin on wheels. They could have driven it down to Lewiston and tossed the body into the Clearwater."

"But they didn't," Donny said.

"No," I agreed. "Something came up. Someone had a better idea. Maybe they couldn't afford gas money. Who knows? We're not talking about Hannibal Lecter here. Most criminals are not geniuses. Sam taught me that."

"And look around your jail cells," Suzy added. "How many of your repeat offenders are in there working on their GEDs?"

"All of them," Donny conceded. "But I don't think it's fair to hold that against them, Suzy. People can be rehabilitated. Some of our prisoners read and take classes. They try to break the bad patterns of the past and—"

"Sweetie," Suzy interrupted. "No one here is questioning the innate goodness of the occasional jailbird, or the potentially redemptive power of time spent contemplating three concrete walls and a set of steel bars. That said, you have told me yourself that most crimes are committed by the drunk, the high, and the terminally stupid."

"Well, yes, but..."

"What happens next, Bil?" Suzy asked.

"They move the body out of the car," I said. "And they put it on the sofa in Peterson's shack. The body is hard to shift and it smells horrible. Once they've got it in place, it twitches. It moves, it belches, and it makes horrible hissing noises. It looks like hell. Peterson is purple and blue and clearly dead as a doornail, but those two idiots panic. They know nothing about decomposition. They know a lot about horror movies. Every time I've been in that pawn shop, Steve and Joe have been in the back watching *Night of the Living Dead* or some other zombie flick. What do they think when a dead body moves? They think it's the living dead, come back for vengeance."

"I'm not saying Steve and Joe killed him," I added quickly, "just that they moved him. Do you know if the body was moved during the day or at night, Donny?"

"At night," he said.

I nodded. "You've been to the Kornmeyer place. It's creepy in broad daylight. I can't imagine going up there after dark."

"You couldn't get a car up that steep driveway," Donny said. "If—and this is a big if—it happened like you say, then Steve and Joe had to carry that stinky body all the way up the hill."

"I'll take it from here" Suzy said. "They sit Peterson on his living room sofa. Maybe they prop him up with a few pillows. He begins to move. Joe screams 'Zombie!' and Steve blasts him in the head with a shotgun."

"That's how you kill zombies," I agreed. "You take their heads off."

"How many of these movies have you watched, Bil?" Sylvie asked.

"Peterson weighed 178 pounds," Donny said. "That's quite a load. Who carried the shotgun?"

I had to admit that I didn't know. Tipper, however, came to my rescue.

"The shotgun was in the car," he said. "The body twitched or belched or whatever it is that bloaters do. Our morons ran back down to the car, got the gun, and went on a zombie hunt."

"Good!" Suzy clapped.

"Dubious," said Donny. "You want to talk about stupid criminals? What about complete chickens? Once those two started running, there's no way they'd come back."

"He's got us there," Suzy said.

"What if the shotgun was already in the shack?" Sylvie suggested. "Jake Peterson was a dope dealer. Wouldn't he have a few firearms lying around the place in case someone broke in or refused to pay?"

"He did time in Leavenworth on a serious felony," Donny said. "He couldn't have legally owned a firearm."

"Honey," Suzy shook his head sadly. "Peterson couldn't legally deal drugs. I think we can assume that if the man had a gun, it wasn't something he bought at the local sporting goods store."

Donny rested his head in his hands. Sylvie thoughtfully poured him a fresh glass of milk. The rest of us refilled our coffee cups.

"Jake had at least one gun," I said. "A Swedish sniper rifle—according to Sam, anyway. You didn't find any firearms in the shack?"

"No," said Donny. "We didn't."

"You might try looking at Johnson Pawn," Suzy observed archly. "How common are Swedish sniper rifles?"

"Not very," Donny said. He looked up. "What you say makes sense, Bil, but it's all speculation. I can't do anything with this. I can't search the trunk of Steve Iverson's car because I can't get a warrant. Your mother gave us a partial plate number on the car she saw in the Ag Chemical lot. It doesn't match Iverson's car."

"Does it match anyone's car?" Sylvie asked. "I mean locally."

"A few dozen," Donny hedged.

"Any names?" Sylvie continued.

"No," Donny said firmly. "I can only tell you that we're working on it. We still don't have an answer to the most important questions: who killed Peterson and why?"

"George Knox," Tipper said. "In the American who-done-it, fundamentalist preachers are like English butlers. Guilty as sin."

I disagreed. "No, it was Calvin Knox. He had a business relationship with Jake Peterson. He's not just into casinos and pawn shops. He's running his own little drug ring. He got tired of paying the middleman."

"You can't prove any of this," Donny despaired. "And this is not how we do things in the sheriff's department."

"Of course not," Suzy said. "Cops never sit around the doughnut box and gossip like old women. Honey, you know that it was Steve and Joe. Possession is nine-tenths of the law. They had the body in the trunk. They killed him, they stuffed him in there, they waited for dark, and then they took him home. It all happened just like Bil says."

I ignored the desperate look on Donny's honest face. "I'll tell you something else. It was Steve and Joe who whacked Major Tom over the head with a crowbar. We have the Major's wallet," I waved my pawnshop find in the air. "Proof!"

"That would explain why my father woke up screaming 'I am not a fucking zombie,'" Tipper said.

"Oh, come on. Why would Steve and Joe attack the Major?" Donny insisted.

"Why was the Major up at Jake Peterson's?" I countered.

"What was he looking for?" Tipper asked.

Suzy broke into song. "Why do birds sing so gay? And lovers await the break of day? Why do they fall in love?"

Tipper joined him. "Why does the rain fall from up above? Why do fools fall in love? Why do they fall in love?"

"We get the point," I said loudly. "Too many whys."

"Sing it," demanded Suzy. "Next verse, please, Bil. The concert is Friday. Are you in good voice?"

I was in good voice. I knew Suzy wouldn't let me alone, however, until I'd demonstrated it.

* * *

Steve Iverson owned a 1977 Oldsmobile Cutlass Supreme. Donny wanted a good look at the trunk of that car. He also wanted probable cause.

I gave the wallet and the receipt to Donny. Though Tipper thought it likely that it belonged to his father, he couldn't swear to it. Major Tom had paid for our breakfast at the Cowslip Café, but Tipper hadn't noticed his wallet. Did I remember it? I reminded Tipper that I'd had more important things on my mind, like the sight of my leather jacket in the Johnson Pawn window.

Donny showed the wallet to Thuy, who said yes, it definitely belonged to her husband. Then she said no, it didn't. She finally settled on maybe. Vivian, acting as interpreter, told Donny to go away and come back when the Major had recovered his senses. Suzy agreed and hustled Donny out of the ICU posthaste. Thuy was scared, confused, and exhausted, and Donny had made the mistake of questioning her while in uniform. One look at his badge and his gun and she'd come close to fainting.

Major Tom was at last sleeping soundly. His cracked skull was slowly knitting itself back together, and his recovery was no longer a question of if, but when. Donny decided that it was best to wait.

Unfortunately, there was nothing he could do to stop Sid Castle from talking to the *Cowslip Herald-Examiner*. Sid, the self-aggrandizing moron, told the reporter that the Major was expected to make a full recovery. Donny began to worry about what might happen if the Major's attackers believed that he would be able to identify them. I reminded Donny that Steve and Joe were unlikely to read anything more complicated than the menu at McDonald's, and Donny reminded me that we couldn't be certain that Steve and Joe were responsible. He took it upon himself to guard the Major when he could, and to unofficially deputize Captain Schwartz to take his place when he couldn't.

We were at an impasse and that annoyed the hell out of me. I asked Donny what more he wanted—a signed confession? Sylvie politely observed that Donny was a cop and I was not. He was bound by the rules of evidence while I was free to speculate. I knew she was right, and I knew he was right. I also knew that I was acting like Emma.

What could Donny do? Take Steve and Joe into custody and question them about zombies? We were dealing with complete idiots. Until the Major regained his senses it was better, as Donny said, to wait and to watch.

On the whole, I was surprised to find that I preferred Emma's investigative methods—breaking and entering, flouting the law, getting things done. This, in turn, forced me to consider the very real possibility that I might be turning into my mother. Sylvie tried to comfort me, but it was no use. When this revelation struck, I had to go lie down with a cold washcloth on my forehead.

I felt better when Donny objected to Sylvie's casino plan. I objected to it myself. If she was going into Forbidden Village, I wanted to go with her. It was not enough for me that Sarah was enthusiastic and Buck DeWitt was positively thrilled. When Suzy announced that he was going, too, Donny and I both pitched a fit. It did no good to remind Suzy that he wasn't expected, and he wasn't invited.

"Since when has that stopped me?" he asked.

Donny reminded him that someone had murdered Jake Peterson. "You don't know what you'll be walking into," Donny said. "Suzy, I won't have it."

"Donny Smith." Suzy fumed. "You will have it! I may dress like your mother, but I am not she. And you are not your father. This isn't the Mormon patriarchy. Besides, I've got a concealed weapons permit. I'll be packing."

"Packing what?" I asked. "That miniature twenty-two, no bigger than the palm of your hand? The one you've got loaded with tiny shot shells so you don't hurt anyone? You might be able to stop a determined parakeet with that thing, Suzy. Not Steve and Joe—not if they've got their crowbar."

"You'd be surprised what that gun will do," Suzy said sagely. "It's all in where you aim."

And that was the end of that. Donny and I would wait in the parking lot of Forbidden Village, twiddling our thumbs, while our spouses and my sister and Wild Bill Hickok went inside and had all the excitement. Saturday seemed a long way off and yet not quite long enough.

I paid my weekly visit to Sally Hernandez, who listened politely to my theories of murder and mayhem for a grand total of fifteen minutes. Then, she insisted that we talk about my feelings. I hated her for that, but I complied.

"How do you feel about today's session?" she asked at the end.

"Annoyed," I replied. "With you."

"That's a good sign," she said. "Same time next week?" she'd asked. I'd said yes.

The JUGS rally at the Unitarian Church was nearly upon us. We had a final choir practice Thursday night at the Captain's house. I had to admit that we sounded pretty good. We had several choices for an encore. Suzy wanted me to sing "Over the Rainbow" but I refused.

"No Judy Garland," I said.

"Liza?"

"Definitely not."

"Lesbian."

"Fruit loop."

"Thank you!" he said. "You're so sweet."

Chapter 37

Three o'clock Friday came much too soon. The JUGS rally began with speeches. A wonderful old woman named Florence Detwiler spoke of having marched as a child with her mother for Women's Suffrage. Sarah spoke, and so did Sylvie. Both were very polished speakers. I felt quite proud.

"That's my sister," I whispered to Suzy.

"She's terrific," he agreed.

"And that's my fiancée," I whispered, as the crowd cheered for Sylvie.

"Stop bragging," he said.

A few more speakers—some rabble-rousers, others painfully dull—and then it was showtime. A civil rights attorney from Boise named Mary Mileske read the language of the breast ordinance aloud while Sarah, Sylvie, and five other women paraded across the stage in various states of undress that technically met the legal requirements. Displays of cleavage, nipples, and the sides of the breast were prohibited. This left a lot of wiggle and jiggle room. Sylvie wore a bikini top made of duct tape. It covered what had to be covered but left the bottoms of her breasts exposed.

Sarah displayed an appalling amount of lower frontal nudity. When she appeared on stage, Buck DeWitt put his thumb and his forefinger in his mouth and whistled like an air horn.

Best of all was Suzy who, because the breast ordinance was gender-specific and Suzy was at least technically male, appeared dressed as a plumber, complete with a fully loaded tool belt and three inches of butt cleavage. Backstage, Donny cued a tape of "The Stripper", and Suzy worked the crowd like Gypsy Rose Lee. Off came the blue work shirt, the tool belt, and finally the Carhartt brown duck trousers. Suzy finished his dance in his tighty-whiteys.

It was in the middle of Suzy's dance that I noticed the women who had filed into the back of the room. There were ten of them, four of whom I recognized: Mary Sue Knox and her daughters,

Rahab, Moira and Fiona. I could see from where I stood backstage with Donny, Granny, and Captain Schwartz that they'd brought a large banner with them.

Mary Mileske stepped to the microphone again. She thanked Suzy, who bowed and blew kisses shamelessly, and delivered her closing remarks. Suzy slipped backstage and dressed quickly. With the exception of Granny, the Mighty Queer Gospel Quartet wore matching white linen suits. I hadn't known about that until Thursday evening, when Suzy unveiled them at choir practice.

"You like?" he asked.

The Captain fingered the fine linen. "How much?"

"My treat," he said.

"Oh, no," the Captain objected. "Suzy, we can't let you..."

"This serves a dual purpose," Suzy said. "Bil has to have something decent to wear to her wedding. I've seen her assortment of fine dress T-shirts, and they will not do."

"Bil!" Granny screeched. "Are you getting married? Who to?" She cast a hopeful glance at Donny.

"I'm marrying Sylvie," I said. "You know, my girlfriend? The woman I've lived with for the past two years?"

"But how?"

"In the Unitarian Church," I replied. "Granny, I'm a lesbian!"

"Hush," she said. "I know that. But don't you have to marry a man?"

"No."

"How funny," she said with a laugh. "Oh my stars and garters, I just can't keep up with the times!"

Granny followed this pronouncement with one of her patented Southern twitters, the kind of high-pitched, feminine, squeal of a laugh that might have driven Rhett Butler mad with lust. Or perhaps just mad.

For the JUGS rally, Granny had chosen her outfit carefully. She wore a pink floral print dress and a wide-brimmed straw hat. She looked every inch the church lady and, I had to admit, it was likely to be effective. No one expected anyone who looked like Wilhelmina Aldershot to come down on the side of breasts and cleavage.

Mary Mileske finished her speech and Sarah stepped up to introduce us. Suzy was bent over tying his shoelaces.

"Hurry up," Donny hissed.

"Are we ready?" Granny asked.

"As ready as I'll ever be," I said. "But look in the back. Do you see what I see?"

Granny squinted at the banner George Knox's female posse had unfurled. "Who's Timothy?"

"He was a friend of Paul's," Donny explained.

Granny laughed merrily. "Is that like a Friend of Dorothy's? You people and your slang."

"It's a Bible verse," said the Captain. "Timothy 2:9. That's the one about women being silent in church, isn't it?"

"Close." Suzy stood up and recited. "'In like manner also, that women adorn themselves in modest apparel, with shamefacedness and sobriety; not with braided hair, or gold, or pearls, or costly array.' The bit about women being silent is in verses eleven and twelve. 'Let the woman learn in silence with all subjection. But I suffer not a woman to teach, nor to usurp authority over the man, but to be in silence.'"

"There's going to be a riot," Donny said.

"Not unless these Unitarians know their Bible as well as Suzy," I replied.

* * *

We sang our songs and, even if I do say so myself, we sounded damned good. We began with "Blessed Assurance" and "Bringing in the Sheaves." There had been some eleventh hour changes, and so instead of "In the Sweet By and By," we sang a Baptist favorite of the Captain's, "The Old Rugged Cross." We finished with "Will the Circle Be Unbroken?" In the last verse of the last song, I noticed a short fat woman in the front row flipping through a large black Bible. It was my mother.

I knew from the whoop of outrage that Emma had found Timothy 2:9. Donny was right. There was going to be a riot. I tried to signal Sarah, who was standing on one side of Emma. Buck DeWitt was standing on the other. We finished the song, and I waved frantically. Sarah was staring off into space, dreaming about the old card catalog or a world in which everyone paid his or her overdue fines. I caught Buck's eye, pointed at my mother, and made a slashing motion with my finger across my throat. He seemed to understand. He took Emma's arm and whispered in her ear. She paused.

Granny, coming around from behind the piano, seized the microphone in front of Donny. "An encore?" she suggested. "I think we could probably—"

I snatched the mic from her hand.

"We could definitely," I said. "If you wouldn't mind a capella?"

The clapping suggested that that would be just fine. I turned around and mouthed the words "I'm sorry" at Donny. He looked puzzled.

"I'd like to dedicate this song to Daniel Smith, the brother of my friend, Donny, and to my own brother, Samuel Hardy."

That caught Emma's attention. She stopped struggling with Buck DeWitt. Sarah stopped staring into space. Granny quit preening. The crowd, including Mary Sue, Rahab, Moira and Fiona, lowered their banner so that I could see their faces. I didn't sing to them. I sang at them. I sang "Danny Boy," and I sang it even better than I had that night on the Captain's front porch. It was pitch-perfect, and with each soaring note, I held the audience in a kind of suspended animation. For those few minutes they were enraptured, and they were mine.

I finished. If I'd been hoping for the peace which passeth understanding, I would have been disappointed. What I got was the peace which passeth very quickly. Emma looked stunned, as did Sarah. Behind me, Donny was bawling. Loudly. Rahab and Moira looked uncertain, but Mary Sue and Fiona Knox were made of sterner stuff. They raised their banner again and, as they were standing on either side of the church's big double doors, they blocked the entrance.

But not for long. A small, angry woman punched straight through the paper banner and marched down the aisle, looking wildly from side to side.

It was my sister, Naomi, and she was madder than hops. She saw what, or rather who, she was looking for in the front row. She sped up. Buck DeWitt let go of my mother and turned to face her, a stupid smile plastered on his face.

"You son of a bitch!" Naomi yelled. "Vasectomy, my ass. I'm pregnant!"

And with that, she slapped the living hell out of him. The sound rang through the church. Naomi turned on her heel and walked back the way she'd come, the crowd parting before her like the Red Sea.

Buck covered his cheek with his hand and stared after her.

Everyone began talking at once—my mother, Sarah, and the Mighty Queer Gospel Quartet. A scuffle broke out in the back of the church between the JUGS people and the women from Church of the True Vine. Granny pulled me down to her height and asked, in my ear, "What just happened?"

"Buck DeWitt's chickens have come home to roost," I said.

"Is he the cowboy?"

"Yes."

"Then who is that?" she asked, pointing at the side entrance behind my mother and Sarah.

"That's Buck DeWitt," I said. "Oh, wait..."

Buck DeWitt number two, complete with walrus mustache, made his way down the front row and greeted his brother, Buck DeWitt number one. White linen suit be damned, I sat on my backside and slid off the stage. With some effort, I fought my way over to the squabbling group.

"Pregnant?" my mother said, dumbfounded. "She's pregnant?"

"Oh, come on, Emma. It's not beyond the realm of reason. She's got the same equipment you and I have," Sarah snapped.

"Sorry I'm late," said Buck number two. "Did I miss the fashion show?"

"You missed more than that," said Buck number one.

"What?"

"This." Buck dropped his right hand from his swollen red cheek, balled his fingers into a fist, and knocked his brother flat to the floor. He stood over the prone figure and said, "That's from this woman's sister, Naomi. Goddamn it, Chuck. Looks like you were poking fun, but she took it serious."

Chapter 38

"Chuck and Buck," said my mother. "Sweet Jesus, only in Montana. Did you know that you were dating a twin?"

"Of course," said Sarah. "Buck and I talk about our families all the time."

"Fine. Did you know that your boyfriend's twin was banging your sister?"

"Emma," I said. "Enough. You are a foulmouthed old woman. The real question here is what are we going to do? Naomi is pregnant, and Chuck DeWitt is a bum. This is big trouble. How are we going to help her?"

"A shotgun," my father suggested. "I'll shoot the bastard."

"I knew this was a mistake," I said to Sylvie. "If I wanted to make peace in this family, I'd have to call Jimmy Carter."

"He has a better shot at making peace in the Middle East," Sarah said. "Listen to me. Buck is out looking for Chuck. Ruth will talk to Naomi. When it comes right down to it, none of this is any of our business."

"What?" Emma, Hugh, and I spoke in outraged unison.

"Think about it," Sarah continued. "Is anyone in this room pregnant? Is anyone here involved with a moron named Chuck? Naomi is thirty years old. She's a seasoned trial attorney. We can be supportive of whatever decision she makes, but that's as far as it goes. Perhaps she and Chuck will want to get married..."

"You're damned right," my father said.

"Or," Sarah went on, "Naomi might decide she doesn't want a baby. She's never shown any wild desire to be a parent. In fact, she hates kids. She never babysat any of us. Ruth did that."

"Well, of course," said my mother. "Naomi had other priorities. She was always in her bedroom doing her homework, and Sam and Bil were such a handful..."

"Ruth managed them, and when she left for college, I managed," Sarah said. "Naomi was never there."

"Oh, no," I corrected her. "Naomi babysat us a couple of times. I've got the scars to prove it. She was quick on the draw with the wooden spoon."

"I'm sure you exaggerate," my mother said.

"And I'm sure Naomi was guilty of child abuse."

"If Naomi has the baby," Sarah said, "and, mind you, that's a big if, you two will be grandparents. Have you thought about that?"

"No." My father chewed on his pipe. "A grandfather? Me?" He smiled.

"Don't get your hopes up," I advised.

"Well, why not?" he said. "I'm an optimist, Bil. Let's look on the bright side. I might get to be a grandfather without acquiring a worthless son-in-law. You're right. There are two separate issues here. What do you think of this Chuck, Sarah?"

"Not much," she admitted. "He and Buck are like night and day. Buck is an equine veterinarian. Chuck—he's working on an undergraduate degree in cowboying."

"Is there such a thing?" Sylvie asked.

"Oh, yes," Sarah assured her. "It's not called that. It's called Range Science. Chuck was a bull rider on the professional rodeo circuit before that. He never won much money because he was a stinking cheat. Kept coming out of the chute with his spur in the rope."

"I don't know what the hell you're talking about," I said.

"I do," Emma chimed in. "I've been to a rodeo. Tell me—was he in it for the buckle bunnies?"

"You got it," Sarah said.

"Then Naomi is not marrying him. I won't have it."

"You sound remarkably like Donny Smith," I observed. "Are you by any chance a Mormon man?"

"Shut up, Bil."

"Sylvie," I said, standing up. "We're going home. Bang the gavel, Ma. This session of the United Nations has come to a close."

"Amen," said Sarah.

"We haven't resolved a single thing," my mother objected.

"It's not for us to resolve," Sylvie said quietly. "This is Naomi's call. All we can do is be there when she needs us."

I held my breath. Sylvie had never been an active participant in Hardy Family Feud. She'd been an observer. She'd listened patiently and offered the occasional innocuous suggestion, but mostly, she quietly bided her time in a kind of in-law limbo.

My parents were both gazing at her thoughtfully.

"You're quite right," my father said at last. "This is a case of wait and see."

"And love and support," Sylvie added.

"I can do support," I said.

"You can do love, too," Sylvie replied. "Stop pretending to be such a hard-ass, Bil. You're a complete marshmallow."

My mother and Sarah hooted with laughter. My father stood up and embraced Sylvie in a tight hug.

He said, "Rumor has it that you two are going to tie the knot. Perhaps this is presumptuous of me—it might even be sexist—but I'd very much like to walk you down the aisle."

Sylvie kissed him on the cheek. He blushed.

"I'd like that very much," she said. "And now," she took my hand, "I have to take Bil home before she bursts into tears."

* * *

"I was not going to cry."

"Well," said Tipper, blowing his nose loudly, "you're a better woman than I am. That's the sweetest thing I've ever heard."

"We need to set the date," I said in a vain attempt to change the subject. "How much time do we need to plan?"

"At least a year," Tipper said. "If you're going the Martha Stewart route."

I stared at him and then at Sylvie. "Are we?" I asked.

"Not quite," she said. "I thought next spring, if that suited you. Perhaps spring break. I should finish my dissertation by Christmas, and you'll have one master's thesis down and one to go. Your teaching load will be lighter in the spring, won't it?"

I nodded. "Will we have a honeymoon?"

"What do you think?" Sylvie asked with a look that could have melted steel.

"Oh, God." Tipper sighed. "If you two are going to get all lustful and gooey, I'm not helping you plan a thing."

"I'm sorry," Sylvie said, laughing.

"I'm not," I said. "Get off my sofa and go stay with your mother."

"Bil!"

Tipper laughed. "No, I think I'll stay. You two want a white wedding, don't you? Better start with the celibacy now. Rejuvenate that virginity. Anyhow, I am happy to whip this," he said, and slapped me on the arm with the back of his hand, "into some kind of shape. We'll have that beautiful linen suit dry-cleaned and buy her some decent shoes. Tell me again how you got filthy black ass marks on your pants?"

"Climbing off the stage to rescue Buck DeWitt."

"The next time you put on that suit," he said, "I want you to remember that you're a lover, not a fighter. If that dirt won't come out, that's three hundred dollars' worth of ruined duds. It was Jones of New York, wasn't it?"

"How the hell should I know? It could have been Smith of Butt Fuck, Egypt." I stopped, processing the other piece of what Tipper had just said. "Three hundred dollars? Suzy did not pay three hundred dollars for my suit!"

"Ahem." Tipper cleared his throat.

Sylvie, I noticed, was staring at the ceiling.

"You," I said to her. "You paid for my suit, didn't you? Tipper and Donny bought their suits. The Captain bought hers. You paid for mine. You are the only person who knows my measurements."

"Bil..."

"I will not be kept like a... a... harlot."

"Is that what you think?" Sylvie's eyes glittered a dangerous dark green. "I have a lot of useless money. You are my partner, soon to be my spouse. We should pool our resources."

"Pool?" I asked. "Pool? You could fill a pool with your resources. Me? I could barely fill the bathroom sink."

Tipper slid his chair back from the kitchen table and stood up.

"Where are you going?"

"I thought I might pop out for a stroll."

"At midnight?"

"The moon is very bright."

"Sit back down," I said firmly. "This fight is very over. I will pay for my own wedding attire. As soon as I've had that suit dry cleaned, it goes back to whatever outrageously expensive department store it came from. I don't want it."

"You were just fine when you thought Suzy had paid for it," Sylvie said.

"Yes, I was. Suzy does most of his shopping at the Cowslip Thrift."

"Bil, you're being unreasonable."

"Am I? How would you feel if the shoe were on the other foot?"

"One of your old sneakers in place of her Kenneth Coles?"

"Shut up, Tipper," I said. "You have no idea—"

I was interrupted in mid-tirade by the phone ringing. At midnight, I knew it was either bad news or my mother, or, rather, bad news and my mother. I was right on both counts.

"Naomi is over here," Emma said. "She's in tears. Chuck DeWitt has done a runner."

"A what?"

"He's fucked off home to Montana. Buck is fit to be tied. He says he's going after him as soon as it's daylight and he's going to drag him back by his heels."

I sighed heavily. "Would it help if I came over?"

"Believe it or not," said my mother. "I think it would. Naomi wants your advice."

"About what?"

"About what kind of parent you think she'd be."

Chapter 39

I have never lied so much in my life. I made up stories wholesale about Naomi's terrific babysitting skills, about how much Sam and I had looked forward to being left alone with her, about how she'd been firm but fun, a strict disciplinarian but always fair. And then, with her head resting on my shoulder and her tears and snot drenching the front of my shirt, I told her that I loved her, that I'd always be there for her, and that she wouldn't have to go through this pregnancy alone.

"Thank you." She sniffed. "Bil, I'm really scared."

"I know. Believe me, it'll be okay."

"I'll be a single parent."

"You'll be terrific. Who's better organized than you are, Naomi? No one."

"You really think so?"

"I know so. You keep all of your shoes in their original boxes. You stack them on the shelves in your closet with typed labels on the ends describing the shoes and when you bought them: 1995, black pumps, two-inch heel. You have the caseload from hell, and yet you've never been unprepared or late for a court date. You've never let a client down. You are an amazing woman, Sis. You can do anything. You can be a single parent. And that's single in name only, right? You'll keep on living with Ruth, won't you? You know she'll help. She loves kids."

Naomi burst into tears again. "Ruth," she wailed. "We've only got a two-bedroom apartment."

"You can get a bigger one," I said.

"Or you could move out here," Emma suggested.

Naomi howled. My mother pulled a cigarette out of her pack and tucked it between her lips.

"You don't want to move out here," I said. "No pregnant woman should have to live with Puff Daddy."

"I could quit," my mother suggested.

She put the cigarette back in the pack and stood there fidgeting with the box. I knew that Emma had smoked through both of her pregnancies. Ruth pointed out that that's why she'd been born weighing six pounds and Naomi only five and a half. My mother rejected this analysis. She was the last woman in North America who believed that the joy of cigarettes far outweighed the health risks. Having spent time with her the few times she'd tried to quit, I had to agree. My mother coming off nicotine was like Keith Richards coming off heroin.

Naomi laughed. "Puff Daddy," she said. "Old Smokey Joe."

"That's our Ma," I said. "Listen. You and Ruth will get a bigger apartment. There are three-bedroom units in your building. Sylvie and I will only be a few blocks away, and Sarah lives just up the street."

"With Buck," Naomi cried. "The man I slapped this afternoon. I'm sure they both hate me."

"I'm sure they don't," I said. "Buck is taking your side in this. I promise you, everything will be all right. Buck's not a bad guy. I thought he was, but I was wrong."

"No." Naomi made a horrible snorting sound. "Buck's not a bad guy. I picked the bad guy. Sarah got the good one. Why?"

It was very late, and I was very tired.

"Luck of the draw?" I suggested.

The tears started again.

"Big mouth," said my mother. She pulled the cigarette back out of the pack and stepped out onto the front porch, closing the door behind her. The old traitor.

*   *   *

It was a relief to climb into bed with Sylvie, even if she did have her back to me and was pretending to be asleep. I ignored the get-away-from-me vibes she was emitting and pressed myself against her, wrapping my arm around her waist.

"It's no use," I said. "I know you're awake. I'm sorry I got angry, Sylvie. You don't know how much."

"As sorry as I am?" she said, turning to face me. "I'm so thoughtless about money. I've got too much of it. I know you hate it when I just buy you things."

"I do hate it," I said, "but not for the reasons you think. I love the things you buy me. They're beautiful and fine and very thoughtful. I hate that I can't reciprocate in kind. The things you buy me are far better than anything I could ever dream of buying for you."

"I don't need anything," she said.

"Exactly. Do you see how that might make me feel really bad?"

"Yes."

"Oh, no," I said. "Please don't cry."

"I'm trying not to," she said, sniffling. "How is Naomi?"

"Crying. She cried when I got there, she cried while I stayed, and she was crying when I left. She's a complete mess."

"What did you tell her?"

"I said she'd be the best parent in the history of the world, a cross between Dr. Spock and Mr. Rogers, with a little Mary Poppins thrown in for good measure."

"I can't picture Naomi with a baby," Sylvie said.

"I can and it terrifies me. She'll raise it in a Skinner box."

"Bil," Sylvie said. "Please tell me you're not angry with me."

"I'm not angry with you, baby. Are you angry with me?"

"No. Bil?"

"Hmm?"

"It's four o'clock in the morning. How tired are you?"

"I'm never too tired for this," I assured her.

Chapter 40

We slept until noon. Tipper banged on the bedroom door at seven and offered to buy us breakfast at the House of Pancakes. Sylvie politely declined. I told him what he could do with his huckleberry flapjacks and with that damned redhead Kim, should she happen to be working. He suggested I needed an aspirin and a high colonic and went off on his merry way. I fell back asleep almost immediately.

I didn't rest easily. I dreamt that Sylvie and I were walking down the aisle at the Unitarian Church. Naomi was heavily pregnant and dressed in black from head to toe. Sarah and Buck DeWitt wore Dale Evans and Roy Rogers cowboy garb, my mother wore one of her disreputable sweatshirts, and my father had on a black tuxedo with white socks. Sam was there, too, smiling at me, his arm around Francie Stokes.

"Bed knobs," he said.

I woke to find that I was alone in the bed. I could hear Sylvie moving around in the kitchen. JC was sitting on the floor next to the bed, waiting courteously for me to show signs of life.

"Come on," I said, patting the blankets. "You've been washed, neutered, and de-wormed. I think you're fit for a cuddle."

He climbed up on the bed and stared at me soulfully with his brown dog eyes.

"Mrs. Olafsson is charging us two hundred bucks for the pleasure of your company," I told him. "I hope you don't let us down. No peeing on the floor. No unnecessary barking. No chewing holes in the antique doors. Not that they're really antiques. Suzy says they sell them at Home Depot. As these apartments were built at the turn of the century, you have to wonder what happened to the original doors. Door thieves? The Rootin' Tootin' Defenestration Gang?"

"Defenestration means throwing someone or something out of a window," Sylvie said. She came in and sat down on the end of the bed. "What are you doing up on the clean sheets, JC?"

"I know what defenestration means," I said. "But JC doesn't. I thought I could slip that one past him. And he's on the bed because he was invited. You weren't here, and I was lonely."

"Nice try," she said. "Are you ready for some breakfast?"

I sat up. So did JC.

"That dog understands the word breakfast," I observed. To prove my point, he twitched his ears.

"Or," Sylvie suggested, "it could be that his sense of smell is about a hundred thousand times more sensitive than your own."

"So what's he smelling that I'm not?"

"Huckleberry pancakes, cooked to perfection."

"Clever dog!"

* * *

We ate breakfast, spent the day watching black-and-white movies on television, and then joined Tipper at Pho From Home for a late supper. Against my better judgment, I had the tripe. It was okay but not delicious. Vivian kissed me on the lips, called me some unpronounceable name that at first she claimed meant "brave Yankee who tries something new" but, when pressed, admitted meant "sucker." She sat with us off and on and helped Tipper explain what was happening at Cowslip Memorial.

"The big news is that my father is conscious. He's not thinking clearly due to the aftereffects of the concussion. Information is trickling out, though. He hates George Knox with a purple passion. We have our tanker and, I think, our fragger. Knox is the man my father beat the hell out of in Vietnam."

"Really? God, Emma must be dancing."

"Emma doesn't know," Tipper said. "And I don't want you to tell her. Not yet. Do you swear?"

"I swear."

"Fine," Tipper said. "Major Tom saw Knox on Fox News. Remember that interview Knox gave about the breast ordinance? My father saw that. He knew this was Peterson's hometown, and he knew my mother lived here. He's confused on a few points. He thinks my mother knew all about Knox and the fragging, and that she moved here to make Knox's life hell. There's no point in explaining that my mother has been here since 1978, ten years longer than Knox, or that she never knew the name of the man my father attacked."

"The day we went out to the Major's RV, he'd read about Peterson's murder in the *Herald-Examiner*, and he'd gone up to the shack for the same reason your mother did."

"What's that?"

"He's nosy," Tipper said.

"He's beyond nosy," Vivian cut in. "He's a damn fool. I'd have called the cops."

"Would you?" Sylvie asked.

"That's why I pay so much taxes," Vivian replied. "Let the cops do their work."

"Donny Smith would love you," I said. "We'll have to introduce him to the joys of *pho*—just not this tripe *pho*. Beef, I think."

Vivian gave me a shove that knocked me off my chair. As soon as I sat back down, Tipper continued.

"We already knew that Knox was a tanker in Echo Company. Like all tankers, he made a lot of trips back to the rear. My father suspected that Knox was Peterson's source for drugs, pot, and other contraband. Baseman Moody thought so, too. My father and Moody talked it over and agreed that it was best to watch and wait, but something happened and Moody jumped the gun. He confronted Knox. He couldn't pin anything on the slippery bastard, and we know what happened to Moody. My father came unglued."

"And Knox?"

"Nothing. Peterson took the fall for him."

"I don't understand that," I said. "Why didn't Peterson rat him out?"

Tipper shrugged. "I don't know, Bil. Did your brother ever rat out any of his friends to save his own skin?"

"Never."

"Why not?"

"An insane sense of loyalty. Sam once spent three months in the North Idaho Correctional Institute because he wouldn't roll on a couple of worthless losers who left him holding the bag. Literally."

"Well," said Tipper, "maybe Peterson was insanely loyal to Knox."

"Or," Sylvie suggested, "maybe Knox had something on Peterson, something worse than dealing drugs. We've established that George Knox is a despicable character. He collects dirt on people, he saves it up, and he reveals it when it's to his advantage.

That church of his is nothing but a cult. People who try to leave find that information they thought was confidential—medical records, things they've revealed in pastoral counseling, divorce details—is leaked to the broader church community and from there it makes its way out into Cowslip at large."

"How do you know this?" I asked. "Suzy?"

"And your mother," Sylvie said. "They've done their homework, and most of this information is on the Slip-Fifty listserv. Your mother has spoken with several ex-church members. If Knox can ruin them financially or personally, he will. He's a bitter, vindictive man. And, according to my mother, he's also grossly overextended. Her banker tells her confidentially that Knox has double-mortgaged the concrete octopus. He has to keep growing the church, bringing in more members and more tithes to keep it all afloat. My mother's banker doesn't know how much longer Knox can keep going."

"Your mother's banker?" I said. "Is this the smallest town on earth? Is it run entirely by rumor and gossip and the Old Boys Network?"

"Yes," said Tipper, Sylvie and Vivian.

"Poor Naomi," Tipper added. "I hear Chuck DeWitt has done a runner."

"He has," I said. "But I think that may be for the best. Naomi is going to have a baby to take care of. She doesn't need a worthless cowboy as well."

"When is little Chucky due?"

"She's seven weeks along, so I guess sometime in March."

"Good time to have baby," Vivian said. "That means it learns to walk in the summer. No shoes. Much better for baby's feet. Make them strong."

"Do you have any kids, Vivian?" I'd never thought to ask before. I knew that she and Robert didn't have any together, but Robert was the last in a long line of husbands.

"Two," she said. "A boy and a girl. The boy is your age. The girl is two years older. Brian and Cheryl. He's at the University of Washington. She's studying to be a doctor at Johns Hopkins."

"You must be very proud of them," Sylvie said.

Vivian nodded. "Yes, but I don't brag."

"American names?" I asked.

Vivian shrugged. "American husband. Kids born in America. You think I want them having to spend their lives trying to teach you how to say Thuy?"

"What about your name?"

"It's Vivian," she said. "Stop being nosy or someone will knock you on the head with a crowbar. You want some more *pho*?"

"Yes," I said. "But not tripe."

"You are chicken."

"I tried it, Vivian. I also tried that fruit that smells like dog shit."

"Durian," she laughed. "Yes, you ate that. I take it back. You are not chicken. You are much braver than Robert. If I let him, that man would live on ravioli in the can. One beef coming up. You two?" she asked Tipper and Sylvie.

"I'll have another beef," Tipper said. "Though it's going to play hell with my girlish figure."

"I'd like a coffee," Sylvie said. "Can I help you with anything, Vivian?"

"No," said Vivian. "I've got it all in control. And it's Trac," she added.

"What's track?" I asked.

"Not track. Trac. That's the name my mother gave me. It's for Trung Trac, the great Vietnamese heroine. She and her sister, Trung Nhi, fought the Chinese two thousand years ago. Trung Trac named herself Queen of Vietnam. My mother had high hopes for me. And look! I am the Queen of *Pho*!" At this, Vivian laughed until she had to wipe tears from her eyes with the edge of her apron.

"I think you're pretty remarkable," I said.

She made a disgusted sound. "Ass-kisser," she said. "No need. *Pho* is on the house."

"No," I insisted. "The *pho* is not on the house. You can't keep on this way, Trac. You must charge me. I want this restaurant to be here for a good long time."

"Fine. I'll charge you double. And it's Vivian!"

"Vivian," I said. "Give me the bill!"

"No! You," she said to Tipper. "Did you know your father was a spook?"

"What?"

"Ha!" said Vivian. "I thought not. He's retired from the Marines, yes, but he is working now for the CIA. Thuy told me. They travel all over the place. They're going back to Southeast Asia as soon as he fixes some big mess here."

"George Knox?" Sylvie asked.

"No," Vivian said. "Some other big mess. Something very hush-hush."

I elbowed Sylvie and motioned for her to do the same to Tipper. If Thuy didn't know, then Vivian didn't know, and vice versa. It was time for Captain Schwartz to sign those divorce papers.

Chapter 41

I let Steve and Joe see that I'd arrived with Sylvie, Sarah, and Buck. I let them have the pleasure of watching me kiss Sylvie, wish her good luck, and then climb back into Buck's truck to wait. Steve grinned like a monkey. The best I could do was glare malevolently and wish I knew how to cast the evil eye.

Buck's truck was a large, shiny, F-350 crew cab with dual rear wheels and something called a gooseneck for towing huge horse trailers. Maybe he was rich. Too bad Chuck wasn't more like Buck. According to his brother, Chuck let money burn a hole in his pocket. Naomi could sue him for child support, but good luck collecting it.

Buck had finally managed to track Chuck down. He was lying low in Billings with an old buckle bunny girlfriend named Tiffany Amber Clack. This was so self-evidently trashy that Naomi fell into a fit of weeping all over again.

The official casino plan was for Suzy to arrive in his own car. Sylvie would hang around just inside the front door and wait for him. Donny, who was on duty until midnight, would walk from the sheriff's office to his and Suzy's apartment, change into plain clothes, and then walk the rest of the way to Forbidden Village. We'd parked Buck's truck so that Steve and Joe could only see the passenger's side doors. If Donny was careful—and if I remembered to disable the overhead light when he knocked on the driver's window—we could wait for the gamblers to emerge in relative comfort.

As I say, this was the official plan. It was Sylvie's plan, and she was proud of it. I had a plan of my own. When Suzy came roaring up in his ridiculous vintage Cadillac convertible, we were going to trade places. I was going to slide out of Buck's truck, into Suzy's car, and then into Suzy's clothes. Suzy didn't like my plan. I told him that was too damned bad.

"Let me get this right," said Suzy. "You'll be a woman pretending to be a man pretending to be a woman. That hasn't worked since *Victor/Victoria*. You cannot walk in heels, Bil. You will never fool Calvin."

"Don't give me any of your lip," I said. "I don't need to fool Calvin. I need to fool those idiots on the front door, Steve and Joe. With any luck, they'll be high. They've got a nice bag of weed, courtesy of Sylvie, and they're not all that swift on the uptake even when they're sober."

"It will not work," Suzy insisted.

"It will," I said firmly. "It has to. You and I are the same height and roughly the same build. I want your Cher outfit."

"No!" he shrieked.

"It's bell-bottom pants," I said. "It's platform boots—not heels—and it's a long black wig. I can't do Donna Reed, but I can do that."

"You'll rip it. You'll stain it. You'll fall and break your neck."

"You will pull up next to the truck," I said, "on the driver's side. I will slip out of the truck and into your car. You will have the clothes waiting for me on the back seat. I'll wriggle into them or whatever it is that you do, and then you can help me with the wig and make-up."

"Lord have mercy," Suzy said. "It's a travesty."

"It's a travesty of a travesty," I said. "Just do it."

Suzy's Cadillac was black with a red leather interior. It got about nine miles to the gallon, but he loved it. He put the top down in the spring and left it down until he absolutely, positively had to put it up. Until the first snowflakes fell, a ride with Suzy was like a trip to the North Pole.

As soon as he pulled up, I slid out of the driver's seat and into the Cadillac. JC whined but I shushed him. Suzy sat in stony-faced silence. Perhaps in protest of what I was about to do, he was dressed in terrible straight drag. He wore a blue polyester suit and a pair of shiny white slip-ons. He also wore a wig—one that looked like it came from the George Knox collection. Fair enough. If Suzy wanted to look like a used car salesmen from Elko, Nevada, that was his business.

I struggled into Cher's hip-hugger jeans, her low-cut purple blouse, and her suede vest. Suzy didn't speak to me until I reached across the front seat for the wig.

"Stop," he ordered. "You've got fringe in your cleavage."

He adjusted the fringe and my breasts, pointing out that I didn't want to look "too real." Then he sat the wig on my head, yanking it around with what I suspected was an unnecessary amount of violence. He flipped on the overhead light and examined my face. I wasn't worried that Steve or Joe might see us. Buck's truck was large enough to block out the sun.

"Eye shadow, eyeliner, a metric ton of mascara, and enough lipstick to sink a battleship. It's the best I can do," he said.

"It will be enough," I assured him. "Think Steve and Joe. Think moron."

"I'm thinking blind," he said.

I didn't argue. I just sat in the back seat and let Suzy slip in beside me and work his magic. When he was done, he broke down and smiled.

"I'm a genius," he said. "Check yourself out in the rearview mirror."

"Wow," I said.

I didn't look like Cher. I looked like a drag queen playing Cher. I had achieved my goal. Suzy had highlighted my cheekbones and given my lips a dangerous coat of lipstick that tasted like fish oil. It perfectly matched the purple of my blouse. Thanks to the mascara, eyeliner, and shadow, my eyes were no longer blue but a smoky violet.

He turned off the overhead light and opened the car door.

"Fly, my Eliza Doolittle," he called after me. "But for God's sake, stop walking like John Wayne. Remember—swish, swish!"

"Shut up," I snapped.

I was in luck. Steve and Joe's pupils were so dilated I could hardly see their irises. They were higher than kites.

"And you are?" Steve asked, swaying slightly in the breeze.

"Suzy Parker-Smith," I whispered in a husky tone. "But tonight you can call me Cher."

"Why would I want to do that?" Steve asked. Joe snickered.

"Never mind," I said. "I'm here for a game of cards."

"Dumb place to come," said Joe. "This is a Chinese-American restaurant."

"Ha ha." I laughed. "And I'm Mother Teresa."

"Who?"

I gave up trying to talk my way in. I flashed them Suzy's gold money clip, an awful thing shaped like a dollar sign. They didn't inspect it too closely—which was fortunate as it held two twenties wrapped around a wad of ones. I peeled off the top twenty and tucked it into Steve's front pocket.

"Push it all the way down," he ordered.

I closed my eyes and thought of the empire. Steve did not have a hole in his pocket and, thanks to the marijuana, he didn't have a canoe in there, either. Saved by hophead's droop.

"There's a twenty in your pocket," I said, "but you're just not happy to see me. May I go in now?"

"Sure," he said, shrugging. "Be my guest."

The door opened, I walked in, and the door closed. Sylvie, who had been loitering next to the front counter took one look at me and said, "Holy guacamole! How did you get Suzy to agree to this?"

"Be quiet," I said, "and come with me to the bathroom."

Once inside, I checked all the stalls to make sure they were empty and asked Sylvie to lean against the door to the outside.

"Don't let anyone in or out."

"Why?" she asked.

"Because I have got to get out of this wig and make-up. Everything's itching."

"Bil..."

"I did this to get past those two junkies at the door," I explained. "I am not worried about Calvin. Once you're in a place like this, you're in. He could throw me out, I suppose, but he'd have to throw you out, too, and that wouldn't be a bad thing."

"Bil," she said, her voice now dangerously low. "You can trust me to take care of myself."

"No," I said. "I don't. I love you, and I trust me to take care of you."

Sylvie shook her head. "That's sweet," she said, "if not very flattering."

"I can't leave you in here by yourself. I can't just sit out in Buck's truck and wait. I can't stand it. Why the hell isn't this mascara coming off?"

"Because it's waterproof?" Sylvie suggested. "Stop scrubbing your face with that antiseptic soap. You're going to rub the skin right off."

"If only."

I looked at myself in the mirror. The lipstick was gone, and I'd tossed the wig into the trashcan. I'd buy Suzy another. My eyes were hopeless. The mascara was still there, but the shadow and eyeliner had smeared. I looked like a raccoon—a raccoon that moonlighted as a rest stop hooker.

"It's too bad I have to wear these clothes," I said, "but needs must when the devil drives. Let's go."

"Those platform boots are something else," Sylvie whispered as we left the bathroom. "You look like you're on stilts."

"That's how I feel, too. Have you ever tried walking in these things?"

"Honey," she said. "I walk in heels all the time."

"I forgot," I said. "Why do you do it?"

"Because you say they make my calves look sexy."

That shut me up. I followed her awkwardly through the restaurant. It was decorated in vintage Chinese American diner. On the walls hung bad copies of bad watercolors, each mounted in a cheap gilt frame. Every picture was crooked, as if it had been tossed from a distance at the nail. A scratchy recording of someone plucking indifferently at a Chinese guitar played over a single loudspeaker hanging above the bar.

There were one or two diners hunched over plates of chow mein, and a white-haired old woman stood behind the counter, staring at us. I nodded at her. She glared at me.

"Who is that?" I whispered to Sylvie.

"The original owner," she said. "Mrs. Gunderson. She still runs the restaurant side."

"Mrs. Gunderson? The woman who put the Swedish in Chinese American food?"

"That's her."

"She must be one hundred and three."

"Older," Sylvie said. "Now be quiet. The casino is through here."

The door to the back room was hidden behind, of all things, a beaded curtain. If the rest of the casino followed suit, I'd be right at home in my Cher costume. It was noisy inside—I could hear it through the door. The Forbidden Village parking lot was nearly empty but the casino was hopping. I looked at Sylvie.

"The house is packed," she said. "You know that parking lot two blocks up, between the antique store and the Toot and Tell It? Ever wondered what that was for?"

We went through the door and I wondered no more. Sitting around poker and Blackjack tables were gamblers of all ages: old, middle-aged, college students, and quite a few who were clearly in need of carding. I recognized Kim from the House of Pancakes. She took one look at my outfit and started laughing.

Buck and Sarah were sitting at a large table with five other people. Judging from the grins plastered on their faces, they were having the time of their lives. The dealer, who was wearing a green vest with the snake and dove logo, looked familiar. After a moment or two, I placed him. He was a waiter at the Cowslip Café.

"What are they playing?" I whispered to Sylvie.

"Texas Hold-'em," she said.

"Are they winning?"

"Who knows? That grin is Buck's poker face. Win or lose, he just keeps smiling."

"Sarah must have decided to follow suit. What do we do now?"

"You mean you don't have a plan?" Sylvie said.

"My plan was to get in here. I didn't think beyond that."

"Come with me," she said quietly. "I fancy a game of Blackjack."

I followed her to a table in the back corner where Calvin Knox stood in a tuxedo, looking for all the world like the poor man's James Bond. He turned to smile at us, but catching sight of me, his lips curled down. Anger? Fear? I couldn't read his expression. He was smiling again in a matter of seconds.

"Bil," he said. "And Sylvie. Welcome."

"Your establishment?" I said.

"Mine?" He smiled even wider and shook his head. "Not really."

"Then why the penguin suit?"

"This?" Calvin stroked his lapels. "I thought it might be fun. A touch of class."

"Goes nicely with the cockroach," I said, pointing at a large specimen crawling up the wall behind him.

"Are you sure you didn't bring it with you?" Calvin asked, casting a critical gaze over my outfit.

I felt Sylvie's hand on my arm, and so, instead of decking Calvin, I smiled. "A touch of class meets a touch of crass," I said easily.

Calvin laughed. "Might I interest you in a friendly game of cards?"

"Blackjack," Sylvie said. "If you have room at one of your tables."

"They're not my tables," he insisted. "But I think I can find you a spot."

As soon as Sylvie was seated between an insurance agent I recognized as Dan Bosco and Chip Ferguson from Foodway, Calvin was off, slithering through the crowd like a cobra.

Chip winked at me. "Fancy meeting you here," he said. "And the lovely Sylvie. I didn't know you liked a flutter."

"I like a lot of things," Sylvie said.

Chip squealed with laughter and made rude innuendoes until I thought I'd have to brain him with a bar stool. Sylvie ignored him and gambled an impressive amount. She seemed to be breaking even, but when I realized that she'd bet five hundred dollars' worth of chips, I felt nauseated.

I whispered in her ear, "I'm going to check on Sarah and Buck."

"That's fine," she said. "Win or lose, this is my last hand."

Thank God for that. I wove my way unsteadily among the tables, ignoring Kim's amused stare. Damned platform boots. The heel on the left one seemed to be loose. It wiggled as I walked, killing my ankle. If it broke off, I was doomed. Suzy would kill me.

With some care, I made it safely to the Texas Hold-'em game. Buck was still grinning like a fool. Sarah, on the other hand, had assumed a look of studious concentration. There seemed to be an inordinate number of chips on the table.

"Hey Bil!" Buck called. "That's quite an outfit you've got on there. Did you mug Charo in the parking lot?"

"Cher," I said. "But thanks for noticing."

Either my sister's boyfriend had been sitting for too long or he'd had a few shots too many. His gaze was unsteady, and the hand he was waving nearly knocked the hat off the man sitting next to him.

"Watch it, cowpoke," said the man.

"Easy, fella," Buck replied. "I didn't mean to invade your space."

Sarah looked up at me and rolled her eyes. I leaned down so she could whisper in my ear, "He's not drunk. He's winning. Big."

"And so?"

"And so he'll get away with it if they think he's three sheets to the wind. Otherwise, there's likely to be a fight."

I stood back to watch. I knew how to play five-card stud. I knew nothing about Texas Hold-'em. When someone called and Buck threw his cards down, I only knew he'd won because he raked in an enormous pile of chips.

I looked around the room and spotted Calvin. He was watching the table carefully, and I wasn't surprised when the dealer signaled for him.

Calvin came over and beamed at everyone. "That's it for the night, I'm afraid. Game's over."

"Come on, now," said Buck, slurring his words. "Be fair. I'd like another drink and another hand."

The dealer whispered something in Calvin's ear.

"You've had a very good night Mr. DeWitt," Calvin said. "Why not quit while you're ahead?"

"Quit?" Buck hollered. "Hell, boy! Double or nothing, that's what I say."

Sarah laid her hand on his arm. "No, Buck. Don't do it."

The other tables had grown quiet. Sylvie slipped up behind me and tucked her fingers in the back of my waistband.

"What's happening?" she whispered.

"I have no idea," I said.

"Double or nothing?" Calvin asked. "You've made fifteen thousand dollars tonight. That's quite a lot of money, Mr. DeWitt."

"Call me Buck."

"Very well, Buck. How do I know you can cover a larger bet? We don't take checks or credit cards," Calvin laughed. "This is strictly a cash game."

"Sarah, honey, give me my truck keys."

"No," my sister said again. "Please, Buck, don't do this!"

"My keys, woman," Buck demanded. "Are you trying to spoil my good time?"

My sister handed him his keys and buried her face in her hands. Something was definitely up. The Sarah I knew would have decked the man—any man—who dared to speak to her like that.

"These," Buck continued, "are the keys to a brand new Ford F-350 with dualies and a gooseneck hitch. It's got less than 10,000 miles on it. I reckon it's worth at least $30,000."

Calvin sucked air through his teeth. "Maybe."

"I've got the pink slip," Buck said. "That truck is bought and paid for."

He leaned forward and slammed his hands down on the table. "You got enough bank here to cover that, boy?"

Calvin's eyes narrowed, and I wondered if Buck had gone too far.

"I've got enough," Calvin said.

"Let's see it." Buck dangled his truck keys in Calvin's face. "I've shown you mine. Now you show me yours."

Calvin said something to the dealer who scuttled off. He turned back to Buck.

"You'll have to wait a bit," he said. "I don't keep that kind of bank here in the house."

"I've got all the time in the world," Buck announced. "How about another drink? In fact, how about a drink for everyone in the house? On me!"

Next to him, Sarah's shoulders began to shake and I heard what sounded like a muffled sob.

Buck had two drinks while we waited. Sylvie and I had one each.

"How did you do?" I asked.

"I finished up by seventy-five dollars," she said. "Then I decided to quit while I was ahead. I don't really like gambling."

"Smart you. Now this poor jackass..." I gestured at Buck, who was telling a long joke about a poor boy, a rich boy, and someone who had shit his pants.

"Just watch," Sylvie advised. "I think your sister might be laughing."

Sarah sat up. Tears were streaming down her face. She didn't look as if she were laughing.

"Buck DeWitt," she said. "If you do this, we're through!"

"Oh, now." Buck grinned. "I'm a gambling man, sweetie. You knew that when you met me."

"Are you?" Sarah demanded. "Are you a real gambling man? Then let's see just how far you're willing to go. Let me play this hand."

Buck stared at her. Sarah's eyes glittered darkly and her face was inscrutable.

"You mean that?" he asked.

"I mean that," she said. "Consider it a double-dog dare."

"Aw, honey," Buck said as he smiled. "You know I can't resist a double-dog dare. Calvin, would you mind if my girlfriend here plays my hand?"

Calvin looked as if he'd just won the lottery.

"Not at all," he said as the dealer came back into the room. "Here comes the bank."

The dealer carried a locked cash box. Calvin took a large key ring from his pocket and opened it. Stacks of one hundred dollar bills filled the box, neatly banded with brown paper markers.

"Thirty thousand dollars," Calvin said. "Against your fifteen thousand in chips and quite possibly your truck. Are you sure you're up for a high stakes game?"

Buck looked at Sarah and nodded.

"I'm sure," he said. He gave my sister a quick kiss and said, "It's all yours, honey. Do me proud."

The game began. To my surprise, Calvin sat down to play.

"Doesn't that double his chances?" I asked Sylvie.

"No," she said. "You can't play Texas Hold-'em against the bank. You need at least two players and a dealer."

We waited for the dealer to get out a new pack of cards, sealed in cellophane. He passed it first to Buck and Sarah for inspection and then to Calvin. They all nodded their approval. The dealer opened the deck, put the cards into an automated shuffler, and dealt Sarah and Calvin two cards each. Calvin lifted the edge of his cards, as did Sarah.

Calvin bet ten thousand. Sarah matched him and raised him another ten. Calvin matched that and raised her another five. Sarah matched him again and knocked twice on the table.

"Time for the flop," Sylvie whispered.

"The what?"

"Just watch," Sylvie said.

The dealer laid out three cards: a ten of clubs, a four of clubs, and a jack of diamonds. Calvin checked his cards again and a faint smile tugged at the corner of his lips. Sarah glanced at her cards but her face remained expressionless.

"Time for the turn card," Sylvie said.

The dealer dealt a seven of diamonds.

Calvin knocked on the table. Sarah looked at him.

"All in, you son of a bitch," she said.

"River card," Sylvie whispered.

The dealer turned over an ace of diamonds.

Calvin leapt up, knocking his chair over backwards. He whooped with joy.

"Three tens," he shouted. "Read 'em and weep!"

My sister cracked the faintest of smiles and turned over her own cards—the two and the ten of diamonds.

"Stop all that hopping about," Sarah said. "I've got a flush, sunshine."

Calvin stopped hopping. He also stopped breathing. Just as he was beginning to turn from red to blue, he gasped. Sarah stood up and reached for the cash box.

"I believe that's mine," she said. "Buck, here are your truck keys."

"Wait!" Calvin said.

"No," Sarah replied. "You got to know when to hold 'em, and know when to fold 'em. Me and my money are going home. You can keep your cash box. Just deposit the money in here."

She held out her big Guatemalan bag. In a daze, Calvin transferred the bills from the cash box into my sister's purse.

"And the cash for the chips," she reminded him.

Silently, I finished singing the song Sarah had quoted. Was it time to walk away or time to run? I looked around; in this place, it was always time to run.

"Move," I whispered to Sylvie. "Quickly!"

Sylvie, Sarah, Buck and I threaded our way through the card tables. We went out the casino door, through the beaded curtain, past Mrs. Gunderson's dreadful stare, and, finally, we burst out the front door. Steve and Joe were still on guard outside, but they were slow-witted. Buck knocked them aside easily and, in a matter of seconds, we were halfway to the truck.

Buck said quietly, "I wish Donny were here. I have a feeling we're going to need him."

"You don't think Calvin's going to let us go?" Sylvie asked.

"Once he gets over the shock, no," Buck said.

"That was a hell of a game, wasn't it?" I said.

"Yes," agreed Buck. "I was sweating bullets, but I know your sister, and she knows her cards. I'm not really much of a betting man. I set a limit, and I stick to it. Not so that preacher's son, and not Sarah. Those two would play to the death."

*　*　*

It was déjà vu when the boom sounded in town. I had to remind myself that Sam was dead—that he wasn't tossing blasting caps down manholes anymore. Poor JC. He hated loud noises. Inside the Cadillac, he was probably crawling all over Suzy.

"What the hell was that?" Buck asked.

"Who cares?" Sarah laughed. She opened her pocketbook, stuck her nose inside and sniffed. "I love the smell of money! Buck, honey—I broke the fucking house!"

"Would you keep your voice down?" he pleaded.

I followed his line of sight. Behind Sarah, standing in the doorway, was Calvin Knox. He was talking on a cell phone. Steve and Joe stood next to him, looking confused.

Suzy stepped out of his Cadillac, JC quivering at his heels.

"Poor dog," I whispered. "Come here."

Just then, a siren wailed in the distance, and a piercing whistle came from the front door of Forbidden Village. Before I could stop him, JC had dodged past me and run straight to Calvin Knox. Calvin picked up the dog and smiled.

"Steve," he said. "Your pistol, please."

"No!" Sylvie and I yelled.

Calvin put the gun to the dog's head. "I need that money back," he said.

"You'd shoot a dog?" Buck asked in a tone that suggested that this prospect amazed him more than the spectacle of human greed and indignity he'd just spent the past three hours watching.

"Yes," Calvin said. "My money, please."

"I think you mean my money," Sarah said. "What the hell kind of casino is this?"

"An illegal one," Calvin said. The "duh" was implied.

"Give him the money," I said.

"What?"

"Give it to him, Sarah. I love that dog."

"Do you know how much is in this bag?"

"I don't care!" I shouted. "Have you lost your mind? He's going to shoot JC!"

"I am," Calvin confirmed.

I turned around. "If you hurt that animal, I'll kill you with my bare hands." I walked toward Calvin, forgetting in my rage that in platform shoes, I needed to swish. The left heel gave way, and I tumbled to the ground.

My face had no sooner made contact with the ground than a red Ford Expedition came roaring up and stopped in front of me. George Knox jumped out, not even bothering to switch off the engine. In the glare of the headlights, his face was a picture. Dark purple blotches covered his cheeks, his forehead was bright red, and his wig was askew.

"Not so fast," he said.

Suzy stepped forward. "Is there a problem, Pastor Knox?"

Until that moment, I'd forgotten that Suzy had chosen to dress like a televangelist. The picture would have been funny if Calvin hadn't been holding a gun to my dog's head. With Sylvie's help, I stood up—lopsidedly.

"My son," Knox spat, "has been gambling."

"But you knew that," Suzy said.

"No," Knox shook his head. "I knew of his past sins. Calvin asked God for forgiveness, and he made restitution. I did not know about... this."

"Then why are you here?"

Knox ignored Suzy's question and went straight to the point. "It is my understanding that my son borrowed from church funds this evening in order to make bank. I will have to ask you to return those funds."

"Ask away," Buck said with a laugh. "But ye shall not receive."

"Don't make this difficult," Knox warned.

"Or what?" Suzy said, stepping closer. "You'll frag us? No, don't bother to look shocked. We know all about you. In 1971, you fragged a troublesome lieutenant named Baseman Moody. He caught you red-handed delivering a few balloons of heroin to Jake Peterson, and so you rolled a grenade into his tent and killed him. You're a very bad man, Pastor Knox. Oh, and if you didn't know about your son's illicit gambling operation, then I'll be Ben Doon and you can be Phil McCavity."

Suzy and George Knox stood face to face. I heard the click before I saw the gun. Knox had pulled a pistol out of his pocket. Like father, like son.

Knox looked at Sarah. "I'll take that bag, young woman. No arguments. And then," he turned to glare again at Suzy. "My boy can shoot that poor dog. He was sired by champions. He wasn't bred to live with a pair of disgusting perverts."

In less than a second, I weighed all of the possibilities. On our side were two out lesbians, a cowboy, and a black woman with a bag full of church money. On the other we had a minister and his son, both armed, a gambling parlor that no one in authority except Suzy's gay lover would admit existed, and my dog, who was dead no matter what we did. There was only one thing for it—I was going to jump George Knox and choke him to death with his own wig. I planned my attack, but I didn't move.

I was shocked into action by the sound of a gunshot. Unfortunately, that action was to close my eyes and scream like a baby. When I opened them again, Suzy was standing in front of me with his mini-pistol in his hand. George Knox was bent double, grabbing his crotch and screaming bloody murder, and JC, miraculously, was at my feet. The sirens still wailed, louder now, and a huge figure was limping toward us. It tried and failed to run.

"Suzy," it yelled. "Suzy, are you okay?"

The closer it came, the worse it looked. Its clothes were torn, its face was caked in sludge, and it stank to high heaven.

"It's another fucking zombie!" Steve yelled.

"Donny," I screamed. "Drop to the ground!"

A shot rang out, shattering the windshield of George Knox's truck. I picked up the pistol Knox had dropped and fired it into the air three times.

"Put down that rifle, you asshole," I yelled. "And you can drop that pistol, Calvin Knox. That is not a zombie. That is Lewis County Sheriff's Deputy Donny Smith."

Chapter 42

"Will Suzy go to prison for shooting George Knox in the dick?"

"I very much doubt it," Tipper assured me. "They were only little pellets. No harm, no foul. Besides, where Knox is going, a functional penis is not a boon. If he's very, very lucky, erectile dysfunction will be his new best friend."

We sat outside the interview rooms in the sheriff's department. Thanks to Sam and his short but very full life of crime, I was familiar with the hard benches and the bad coffee. Sylvie, Sarah, and Buck had given their statements and were being processed for release. Sadly for Sarah, her big bag of money would be held as material evidence. Suzy was still being interviewed. Donny had assured us that everything would be fine. Suzy had a concealed weapons permit. George Knox had threatened us with a gun. The wound Suzy had inflicted was in self-defense and far from fatal.

If I hadn't been quite so nerve-wracked, I might have been laughing with Tipper. George Knox had certainly been a picture, writhing on the ground and crying about his wee-wee.

"What grown man calls his dick a wee-wee?" Tipper asked. "Are you sure you heard him correctly?"

I said, "Do you think that's something I could make up? He said wee-wee. He said his wee-wee was broken. He also said he was dying. He hollered all the way into the ambulance. The paramedics were nearly hysterical with laughing."

"And so would I be," Tipper said. "Good news, by the way. My mother has signed the divorce papers. Thuy is safe, Fort Sister is safe, and everyone is happy."

"Did you know that your father was a CIA spook?"

"Yes and no," Tipper said. "My mother had her suspicions. It's not easy to get an immigration visa on short notice, especially not from a communist country with which we have only just normalized relations. My father got a visa for Thuy in less than two weeks."

"Tipper, after Calvin dropped his pistol, Steve held on to his rifle. He was taking aim at Donny. He would have fired another shot, I'm sure of it, if Calvin hadn't taken the gun away from him. Calvin punched Steve right in the face. He took the rifle, unloaded it, and tossed it away. The man who threatened to shoot my dog..."

Tipper squeezed my knee. "Don't think about it, honey. You're all safe and sound. No extra holes in any of you and JC is just fine."

Tipper smothered a laugh. "George Knox, on the other hand... they might have to make him a prosthetic penis. A woody woodpecker."

* * *

Donny came out of a back office looking like nothing on earth. He'd rubbed his face and made a few clean spots, but his clothes were still a wreck and he smelled like a cesspool.

"Bil," he said. "Thank you." He stepped toward me.

"No hugs," I said. "Please. What in the hell happened to you?"

"It's a long story," he said. "I'll have to tell you later. In the meantime, I've got to get cleaned up and go with Sid Castle to make an arrest."

"What's your hurry?" I asked. "It's not as if George Knox can run away."

"We're not arresting Knox," he said. "At least not yet. We're arresting Dick Kornmeyer."

"Dick Kornmeyer? Why?"

"He's being charged with the murder of Jake Peterson."

* * *

I hated being wrong, and there was small comfort in being half right. I was, of course, one hundred percent correct on the zombie thing. I had learned a thing or two in the two decades I'd spent with my superstitious, horror movie-loving brother. Sam believed in zombies. He believed in witches, ghosts, and vampires. If I wanted to scare him, all I had to do was stick my hand in the freezer for a few minutes, hide under his bed, and grab his ankle. It worked every time.

In addition to his many other business concerns, Dick Kornmeyer was the county meth king. He supplied Jake with the goods, and Jake did the cooking. Jake, however, was greedy. He wanted a bigger cut, and so he approached his old friend, George

Knox, who was strapped for cash. Calvin's illegal casino was an ideal distribution point, and what could Kornmeyer do about it? He owned the casino, and he'd still get some of the meth money—just not as much as before.

It all made sense to Jake the Snake, but not to Dick Kornmeyer. Jake stopped by to pay the overdue rent. He was putting the envelope into the mailbox when Kornmeyer shot him. The envelope was addressed but not stamped. Kornmeyer mailed the thing to himself, creating a nice alibi.

As for Steve Iverson and Joe Edwards, they worked for Kornmeyer and Calvin Knox. They were flunkies for hire. They had moved Peterson's body, and when it twitched, they'd shot it. I was wrong about the car—they drove Kornmeyer's. The shotgun belonged to Kornmeyer, too. It was a sawn-off. Sid and Donny found it in the front closet when they raided his house.

Steve and Joe's testimony made for grimly hilarious reading.

"The body was all stiff and shit from being in the trunk of Kornmeyer's car. It stank. It was really heavy. We tried to use Jake's wheelbarrow, but the fucking wheel fell off. We threw it into the woods and dragged the body the rest of the way up. We put the body on the sofa and propped him up with some pillows and we left it there. But we forgot. Kornmeyer said to get the cooker and shit. We had to go back to Jake's. When we got there, we knew he wasn't really dead. He kind of gurgled and belched and reached for us. We shot the fucker in the head before he could eat us."

Steve and Joe disgusted me. I was sorry I'd ever given them a ride that day in the back of my truck. I was sorry they hadn't fallen out and been run over by a grain truck.

Dick Kornmeyer was worse. Farmer, county commissioner, and drug dealer by proxy. He owned a remote farm and workshop down near Kendrick, and he'd begun working directly with Steve and Joe. He didn't need Peterson, especially as Peterson used nearly as much product as he sold. Steve and Joe could do the cooking, and Kornmeyer could rake in all the profits. No middleman.

Calvin Knox paid Kornmeyer a hefty cut from the gambling operation at Forbidden Village. Even so, Calvin made enough to help subsidize his father's ministry. The problem was that as fast as Calvin pulled it in, George Knox spent it. Calvin wasn't talking. He was playing the loyal son. It wouldn't help him much. Donny and Sid Castle had learned enough from Steve and Joe to send Calvin to Cottonwood.

* * *

Over breakfast the next morning, Naomi told me that George
Knox would not be joining his son in the North Idaho Correctional
Institute. In fact, it was likely that he'd get no more than a slap on
the wrist.

"No way!"

"Yes way," she replied, back to her usual crabby self. "Calvin
says his father knew nothing about Forbidden Village."

"Oh, come on. If he didn't know about it, then what was he
doing down there trying to get back his church funds?"

"Calvin called him on his cell phone. He confessed to
borrowing the church money, and he asked his father for help.
That's their story, and they're sticking to it. Knox claims that he
thought his son's donations to the Church of the True Vine came
from Calvin's part-ownership of the pawn shop."

"The pawn shop? Where they sell three hundred dollar leather
jackets for thirty-five bucks? Not to mention wallets stolen from
brain-damaged Marines?"

"Now there's a question," Naomi said. "What was Major
Schwartz doing at Jake Peterson's place?"

"Snooping around," I said. "He knew Peterson and Knox in
Vietnam. He thought it was likely that Knox had killed Peterson.
George Knox has killed before, you know. He fragged a young
lieutenant in Vietnam."

"Unless you can prove that," Naomi said, "you had better not
repeat it. You want to be sued for libel?"

"Yes," I said. "What would Knox get? My dog? Fat chance!
My old truck? It's not worth anything."

"How about a portion of your wages for the next fifteen or
twenty years? Stop arguing, Bil. I want you to know that thanks to
you and the rest of our criminally inclined, busybody family, I have
had to recuse myself from this case. I will not be defending Steve
Iverson or Joe Edwards. We'll have to farm this one out to the
public defender down in Lewiston."

"I'm sorry."

"You should be." She patted her stomach. "In my condition, I
need all the billable hours I can get. Do you know what it costs to
put a kid through college?"

"I've got a good idea about that," I replied. It didn't seem the
time to remind her that I'd spent the past six years in and out of
institutions of higher learning.

"I have a question," I said. "Why did Kornmeyer have Steve and Joe return the body to the shack? Wasn't that kind of a stupid move?"

"Not really," Naomi said. "Our parents own the place. Having Peterson's body found there didn't put Kornmeyer in the frame any more than having had Jake the Snake as a past renter did. Besides, Kornmeyer didn't actually tell Steve and Joe to put the body there."

"Sure he did. He killed him, loaded him in the trunk of his car, and..."

"And told the boys to get rid of him," Naomi finished. "No further instructions, at least not with regard to the body. He did tell them to clean out the meth lab, collect some ammonia, and get Jake's cooking equipment."

"So why did they drop him off in the shack?"

My sister laughed. "Convenience! Kornmeyer was too cheap to give them gas money. They had just enough to drive to the shack and back. Not enough to drive down to the river."

"Score one for my understanding of the moron mind," I said. "I suppose you've had to recuse yourself on Kornmeyer as well."

"Please," said Naomi. "He may be cheap, but he's not a fool. He's giving the public defender's office a body swerve. He's hired James Beam to defend him. Best attorney in town."

"Jim Beam? Fuck."

"I know," she said. "If anyone can get Kornmeyer off, it's the Beamer. Goddamn it!" She pushed away her bowl of Frosted Flakes. "I think the pregnancy hormones are kicking in. I feel miserable, and I'm already throwing up. Forget Kornmeyer and Beam. Goddamn that Chuck DeWitt."

"Goddamn them all," I agreed. In sympathy, I pushed my bowl away as well. As it was my second, I could afford to be generous.

"Where's Sylvie?" Naomi asked.

"She's taking Jesus Christ for a run. He was scared to death last night, and there was no peace when we finally got home. The bathroom was flooded and the toilet was shooting up a geyser."

"Ah, yes," she said. "The sewer main bomber. Was Donny hurt?"

"A few minor cuts and bruises. He was less than a block from the main blast. He got winged by a flying manhole cover. His clothes were destroyed, and he was covered in shit."

Naomi smiled, a surprising sight. "Can you keep a secret?"

"Probably not. Tell me anyway."

"Last night, while you were playing casino vigilante, guess who was tossing blasting caps into the sewers of Cowslip? Francie Stokes."

"No!"

"Yes! Sadly, I'll have to recuse myself on that case, too."

"Because she was Sam's girlfriend?"

Naomi laughed. "Because she was using caps that Sam stole. It seems he had a whole stash of them. Just before he died, he wrote a little booklet for his friends. You or I might have called it *The Fine Art of Making Mischief.*"

"You or I might call it that. What did Sam call it?"

"*Fucking with People.*" She pulled her cereal bowl back and lifted a spoonful to her mouth. "If you're nice to me," she said, "I'll sneak you a photocopy. It's destined to be a petty criminal classic."

Chapter 43

Tipper met with his father one last time before Major Tom and Thuy left to continue their RV tour of the western United States. He insisted I come with him, and he wouldn't take no for an answer.

"He's a nice enough man, Bil, but I like things the way they are—me and Mama and now my stepmother, Kate. I'll exchange holiday cards with him if he insists. Otherwise, I want to be left alone."

"I don't think I understand."

"I'm sure you don't," Tipper said. "You love your father. He's always been a part of your life. Try to imagine if one of your biological parents suddenly showed up, wanting to join in. How would you feel about that? Have you ever thought of looking for them?"

"No," I said. "I haven't. I've got a family."

"So have I," he said. "And my family, like your family, is quite enough to be getting on with. I don't want anyone else. I don't need anyone else."

"I get it," I said.

"I thought you would."

* * *

Tipper, Major Tom, Thuy and I sat in the lawn chairs in front of the RV and talked. The Major translated for Thuy from time to time but not very often. She seemed content to sit and watch and sip a cup of hot tea.

I asked the Major about Peterson, Knox, and the fragging.

"I was assigned to that unit," said the Major, "because headquarters knew there was a drug problem. I'd known Baseman Moody for a couple of years. We were in OCS together—Officer Candidate School. He was a brave man. He'd received a field promotion within two weeks of arriving in country and, before his death, he was the most highly decorated Marine in the Battalion."

He turned to me. "That means something, Bil. Tipper will tell you and so will Becky—the Army in Vietnam handed out medals like candy. Not the Marine Corps."

"Becky?" I said.

"I'm sorry," the Major laughed. "You call her the Captain, don't you? It suits her. I don't mean to cast aspersions on the WACs or the Army Nurse Corps. Becky's got more medals than you can shake a stick at and she earned every one of them. She volunteered for two tours of duty. You know that, don't you? If she hadn't been pregnant with you, son, she'd have fought like hell for a third. I've never known a tougher woman."

"There is no one I admire more," I said firmly.

"I admire her, too," the Major assured me. "It was admiration that led me to marry her."

"Did you love her?" Tipper asked quietly.

"Yes," the Major said. "Not like a man should love his wife— not in the same way that I love Thuy. I loved who she was. My mother was a strong woman, a widow. She raised me on her own. Your mother was in some trouble with the brass. Because of my position, I knew what kind of trouble. I made a few phone calls, asked a few questions, and then I offered to marry her."

"That was pretty selfless of you," Tipper said.

"Nonsense. Don't make me out to be something I'm not. Son, I knew a lot of good Marines who were gay. Lieutenant Moody was gay. No one will ever convince me that that didn't have something to do with his murder. Bastards like George Knox, they call themselves Marines, but they see war as an opportunity to profiteer. I will always be sorry that I wasn't able to prove that Knox killed Moody. Jake Peterson was a patsy and a stooge. It didn't surprise me to find that he and Knox were living in the same town. Some men are born followers. I'm just sorry I couldn't pin Peterson's murder on George Knox. There would have been some kind of poetic justice in that."

He stared into his coffee cup.

"Your mother was a good soldier, Tipper," he said. "She was dedicated body and soul to the United States Army. She was going to be drummed out on suspicion of being a lesbian. I married her so that wouldn't happen. For a couple of weeks, we tried to give it a real go.

"That was your mother's idea, Tipper. I didn't force myself on her. I want you to know that. It wasn't meant to be. You can't change who you are. Becky got pregnant. When she said that she didn't want me in her life, I understood. I'm sorry to say this, but I wasn't prepared to be a father. I had a career I loved. I traveled constantly, moved every eighteen months, and I could volunteer for the kinds of assignments men with wives and children didn't want and shouldn't take. Your mother did a fine job of raising you, as I knew she would. I've been very selfish, son. I admit that. I'm a selfish man, and I'm a single-minded man. I hope you don't think I'm a monster."

After a long silence, Tipper said, "On the contrary. I hope we'll keep in touch. Birthdays, Thanksgiving, that sort of thing."

"I'd like that," the Major said. "Thank you."

Thuy spoke a few words. Major Tom smiled at her.

He said, "My wife wants me to invite you both to stay for lunch. She's made *pho* with tripe. Your friend Vivian said it was Bil's favorite."

Epilogue

Sylvie and I rested, naked, in Sam's old four-poster bed. We were happily basking in a post-Freudian glow. My parents were spending Labor Day weekend camping on the Lochsa River. Sylvie and I had spent two days helping the Captain move her furniture, her clothing, and a drawer full of Army medals over to Kate's house.

On Monday, the sky was clear, the weather was cool, and I'd been taken with an overwhelming urge to go out to my parents' place. Sam visited me often in my dreams. He laughed, he smiled, and somehow I knew that he was up to something.

"Bed knobs," he said.

Sylvie and I had unscrewed one bed knob. Inside we found a half-smoked joint, squished flatter than a pancake. It was clear that Sam had shoved it in the bed knob in one hell of a hurry. The wood inside was charred. It was a wonder he hadn't set the bed—and the house—on fire. The joint, the charred wood, and memories of my brother made Sylvie and I laugh until we had tears in our eyes, and then we fell on the bed. The rest came naturally.

I knew what I was doing. I knew about the stages of bereavement. I'd been numb, sad, angry, agitated, and guilty. I'd been a pot-smoking insomniac who snuck out after midnight to eat bowls of *pho*. In the three weeks since the Major had moved on, Tipper had gone back to Seattle, school had started again, and I'd been jogging every morning with Sylvie and JC. I'd lost five of those ten denial pounds.

"What are you feeling?" Sylvie asked.

"Satisfied. And, maybe, just a little perverse."

She laughed. "I feel satisfied and very perverse."

"He's always with me, you know. Even now."

"I know that," she said. "And I'm glad. He should be with you."

"Not that I think he's watching or anything." I reached up and pulled her to me. She laughed until I kissed her, and then we both grew very serious, so serious that we didn't hear the door opening until it was too late. Two giggling figures fell into the room. Sylvie yanked the sheets up over her head, leaving me exposed from the waist up. I folded my arms across my chest.

"Sarah! Buck!"

"Bil!" Sarah said. "I sincerely hope that's Sylvie under there. If not, I'm going to beat the living shit out of you."

"It's me," said Sylvie, her voice muffled.

"Do you mind?" I asked. "What the hell are you two doing here?"

"I'd ask you the same," Sarah said, "but what you're doing is self-evident."

"Would you get the hell out? Buck, cover your eyes."

"Sorry," Buck said, turning his back to me.

Sarah didn't bother. She watched as I reached down to the foot of the bed and retrieved my shirt.

"Nice tattoo," she said. "What are you going to do if you move?"

"Shut up," I said. I grabbed my jeans off the floor and put them on. "Here," I said, collecting Sylvie's clothes and shoving them under the sheets. "I'll take these two out into the living room. You're free to stay in here if you like and retain what's left of your dignity, but if you expect me to marry you, you'll come out as soon as you're dressed."

"Oh, that's nice," Sylvie muttered. "An ultimatum."

"It's the only one I'll ever issue, I promise." I turned to Sarah and Buck. "Now get out, you two."

They were still giggling like a pair of morons when Sylvie came out of the bedroom and sat on the arm of the recliner. I rested my hand on the small of her back.

"Let me ask again," I said. "What are you doing here?"

"This is going to sound odd," Sarah managed, "but I had a dream about Sam and bed knobs. It was bizarre. I talked Buck into coming out here to have a look."

"That's funny," Sylvie said. "Bil's been having the same dream."

"Hidden treasure?" Sarah suggested.

I shook my head. "Nope. A half-smoked joint and a lot of burned wood."

"Did you check all of the bed knobs?"

Sylvie and I looked at one another. There was no help for it.

"No," I said. "Just the one."

"Got distracted?" Sarah didn't wait for an answer. She and Buck fell over one another laughing.

"Why don't Sylvie and I check them all now?" I said. "You two can stay out here and pee your pants."

"Oh no," Sarah objected. "I'm coming with you. It's my dream, too."

We unscrewed first one bed knob and then another. Empty. With the third, however, we hit pay dirt. A small wad of paper was shoved up inside it.

"I can't get this thing out," I said. "Not without a pair of needle-nosed pliers. It's in there too tight."

"I can help with that." Buck pulled a multi-tool out of a leather case on his belt.

"Thanks." I tried the pliers, but they were too wide. The screwdriver was a better fit. I worked at the wad of paper until, at last, I could pull it out with my fingers.

It was a sheet of yellow legal paper with a note written on it. Inside, wrapped tightly, were four one hundred dollar bills and a single fifty. We stood looking at them as if they might burst into flames.

"Read the note," Sylvie suggested.

I handed the money to Sarah and read:

Emma,
If you read this you are nosy. Stop minding my business. I won this money fare and square so put it back.
Sam

"He wasn't working for Calvin Knox," Sylvie said. "Bil, he won the money."

I was amazed at how relieved I felt. I hadn't wanted to believe that Sam was in the same league as true morons like Steve and Joe, and yet I couldn't be sure. Not until now.

"Emma was right," I said. "Sam was unlucky in life, but he was always lucky at cards."

"What should we do with the money?" Sarah asked.

"Put it back. Let Emma find it."

"Bil," Sylvie said. "Flip the letter over. There's more writing on the other side."

Bil,
Told you so.
Your mother

It was dated August 17, the day Emma and I had recovered my pawned jacket.

"That old biddie," I said. "Did she find this before or after she declared flat out that Sam had not been working for Calvin Knox? Sometimes, I hate that woman. She loves to pretend she's omniscient."

Sarah laughed. "And that means that it's no use asking her. We'll never know. Can you live with that, Bil?"

Sylvie slipped her arm around my waist and the world fell back into place. "Yes," I said. "I can live with that."

Author Joan Opyr   Photo Credit: Nicole Opyr

About the Author

Joan Opyr is still alive. This may surprise some people, as Opyr is the Ukrainian word for vampire. *C'est la vie*.

Ms. Opyr is a graduate of North Carolina State University, where she earned a BA and an MA in English. She has exactly one half of a Ph.D. from the Ohio State University, where she studied Beowulf and other light classics. She reads Viking sagas for fun, is a huge fan of Tolkien, and often wishes she were a forensic archaeologist because she has an insane fascination with Iron Age bog bodies.

In a vain effort to mitigate the geek factor, she listens to old punk bands, only wears button-fly jeans, and is training for an Iron Man Triathlon. Her wife says it's working. Her kids just laugh.